Santa's Christmas Year

by
Michelle Grenville

"I thought the heart of Christmas was spending it with family and loved ones." ~ **Pip Russell**.

1

"Happy New Year, Mrs C!" I pulled my wife towards me as the repetitive blast of fireworks exploded from the television. I pressed my lips firmly to hers before I playfully brushed my chin up and down her cheek.

"Hey!" She pushed me away giggling. "That's not fair! You know my soft, delicate skin is no match for your whiskers." She then pressed her hand on my belly. "Hang on, what's this?"

"Oh… are you talking about my jumper?" I looked down proudly at my navy jumper and admired the brightly coloured sequins sewn onto it to represent fireworks. "I thought I would get into the New Year spirit."

"No, not your jumper. I'm talking about what's behind it. Did you eat every mince pie that was left out for you on Christmas Eve?"

"Err, I may have done," I said, cautiously.

Several days had gone by and she'd never mentioned it, so I was optimistic that she had forgotten the order she'd given me before I left on Christmas Eve.

She gave me a disapproving look. "You promised me you'd take it easy this year."

"Hey, I'm doing a public service by eating them. It makes the children happy."

"A public service? You were supposed to put them in the bag I gave you, so we could take them to the food banks and homeless shelters."

"Ah yes, now I remember," I said, looking away sheepishly. "Well, I promise I will do that next year."

She raised an eyebrow, and I knew that look anywhere. She did not believe me, not one bit.

"You know," I said, changing the subject. "I wanted to thank you for all your help this year, and for putting up with my grumpiness when we couldn't get that toy horse to gallop the way it should. It's not been the easiest of years, but I couldn't have done it without you." I knew exactly what to say to bring out that cute little smile of hers that I loved... and there it was.

"Oh you," she said, wafting me away with a pleased smile. "Go sit back down and enjoy the show. I'll fix you another tipple before bed."

"Perfect." I flopped into my comfortable tartan armchair I liked to call my throne. I placed my feet on the footstool, warming them in front of the fire, and looked at my large squishy reindeer slippers with protruding antlers that bounced up and down when I moved them. They were a present from Mrs C, and I loved them.

"Here you go, sherry and tonic," Mrs C said.

I looked at the glass she was handing me and then glanced up at her with a questioning eyebrow. She'd popped a candy cane into the glass, which was hanging over the rim.

"We've got hundreds, so expect one in every drink for the next year." She grinned as she curled up in her own armchair.

"Yeah, we did go overboard this Christmas, didn't we?" I then popped it into my mouth to suck.

I chuckled happily and stretched out my toes, feeling relaxed. I raised my glass to Mrs C. "Now, here's to a new year, where we can ease back into everything over the next few months, whilst everyone else winds down and forgets about me and my little antics," but as I spoke, my smile slipped slightly at the bittersweet reality.

The next morning, I pulled on my dressing gown and boots, and made my way across the floodlit snowy grounds to the shed, where I eagerly pulled back the large wooden door.

"Where's my lad?" I muttered, peering into the crowd of reindeer which were huddled together in their pen.

Within moments, a large red, shiny nose edged out of the herd and Rudolph raced across to see me. "There you are, boy." I gave him a good scratch behind his antler. He then tilted his head so I would focus my attention on the spot he loved. "How about some yummy breakfast for you?" I said enticingly, and Rudolph stamped his hoof to tell me how excited he was.

I smiled and went over to the workbench in the corner of the shed, tipped some reindeer feed into a small slop bucket and grabbed the special ingredient that Mrs C didn't approve of. I twisted the cap off a bottle of beer, poured it into the bucket and mixed it up, good and proper. "Here we go lad."

Rudolph instantly stuck his head inside the bucket and started lapping up the food with hungry vigour.

"Donner, I'll get to you soon," I said, as she edged forward to sniff the bucket, but she quickly backed off, leaving me and Rudolph to it.

"We did well this year, didn't we, lad? It's one to be proud of. Much better than last year when we accidentally skipped past Luxembourg and had to double back on ourselves," I chuckled. "There were a few hiccoughs, but this year's flying conditions were glorious, and the moon was magnificent, wasn't it?" I smiled, recalling how it had appeared so luminous and full whilst nestled between a blanket of thousands of stars.

I continued to chat to Rudolph, reminiscing about the events that had happened only just over a week ago. Then, as I stroked his head, a sombre silence fell while I watched him lap up the last dregs of the bucket. "Yeah, I know how you feel, lad. It always feels strange when it's over, doesn't it?" I said, as a familiar hollow feeling took hold of my gut.

Rudolph didn't respond. He just gave the bucket one last lick and pulled his food covered head out to look at me.

Vixen instantly began licking Rudolph's face and bright red nose, which was now covered with brown mush.

I gave a tight smile and sighed before I filled up the large trough with more reindeer feed for the rest of them and, as I turned to leave, I decided to add a bottle of beer for them to share.

"Enjoy everyone," I called, before sliding the shed door shut.

I returned to the house to find Mrs C now up and clattering around in the kitchen, listening to some sort of music that sounded unfamiliar to me. "Hi, darling," I called, half smiling and half frowning as I watched her wiggling her hips as she hummed whilst flipping over some pancakes. "What's this music?"

"It's a new tune from the boy band who won that singing contest. It's quite catchy, don't you think?"

"I don't like it," I muttered as I sat down at the kitchen table.

"You just don't like it because it isn't about you anymore. You get like this every year when the hype and adrenalin dies down, but the feeling will pass."

She placed the plate of pancakes stacked with crispy bacon in front of me and kissed the top of my head. The sight of the food cheered me up and I reached for the maple syrup and smothered my pancakes in it.

"Were you out with the reindeer this morning?" Mrs C asked.

"Yeah, I gave them their breakfast."

"I hope it was just breakfast you gave them," she said, raising an accusatory eyebrow.

"Of course!" I declared, wondering if Mrs C had eyes everywhere.

"You know, you really should treat them all equally. They all work hard and do a great job for you, not just Rudolph."

My mouth opened as I stared at her. "I treat them all the same."

Mrs C scoffed and shook her head in despair.

"But it's not that straightforward. Rudolph and I are mates. He's my boy. Don't get me wrong, I appreciate them all, but you can't beat the connection Rudolph and I have."

"Yes, everyone can see the connection you two share, but sometimes the others fall short of your appreciation. Perhaps this year your New Year's resolution should be that you treat them all more fairly and not show so much favouritism. That, along with watching what you eat." She looked down sternly at my syrup covered feast.

6

"Sure," I muttered, barely paying attention.

"Great," she said, sipping her coffee. "I plan to lay off the biscuits this year." She gave a decisive nod and I wasn't sure whether she was telling me or herself.

I nodded half-heartedly as I finished shovelling the food into my mouth and stood up. "Will you put me on the line today?" I asked, having been distracted thinking about the idea.

Mrs C looked up. "Sorry, what do you mean?"

"I want to go on the line, to do some research," I said, unable to get rid of the niggling desire to find out how our year had gone this time.

"I don't get you at times. You can manipulate time, reduce the size of billions of presents to fit into your sleigh, and change your size to fit down any chimney, but you still can't grasp that you go online."

"I don't need to understand technology like that. I have you and a billion other things to occupy this mind."

Mrs C rolled her eyes. She booted up the computer in the small cosy study in the next room, entered a password and clicked a few buttons. "Here," she said, standing up.

"Thanks darling." I sat down in front of the colourful Google logo. "Now then," I muttered, as I stared intently at the keyboard and searched for the letters I needed, before I thumped each key with my index finger. '*Moco, the galloping horse,*' I typed and began reading the reviews. "Yes," I cried out, delighted. "Five stars. They love it."

Mrs C wandered into the room. "Oh wonderful. What are they saying?"

I leant closer to the screen. "My daughter absolutely loved Moco. It kept her extremely entertained, watching Moco race around the room and jump over the fences that came with it, giving us adults plenty of time to enjoy the festivities and the alcohol."

"That's good news. All that worrying and you smashed it." Mrs C squeezed my shoulder before she returned to the kitchen.

"Here's another one," I called, and read it aloud. "My two kids got a Moco each. We all had a great laugh, placing bets on which of our kids' Moco would win. It brought about a healthy bit of competition between them. Absolutely delighted with the product." I leant back in my chair to take a moment to revel in our success. "Yes," I whispered, smiling. "You go Moco."

I then thumped the keys to enter another toy. '*Space Cadet Collins and Space Craft*,' before I did a double take. "Huh? That can't be right." I stared at the screen in confusion. There in front of me was the perfect profile image of the toy we had created, a man with a moustache, in an astronaut outfit and a rocket which opened up to reveal its control mechanisms. "One star!" I cried, as I read the rating next to it from hundreds of reviews.

I clicked on a thumbnail photo on a review and it extended to reveal an image of the space cadet with his arm unattached and placed next to it. The review next to it read. "Absolutely gutted about Space Cadet Collins. My son was so excited after watching the adverts on TV before Christmas, and he was in tears when he received the toy and its arm came off within minutes of opening the box. Not good at all!"

Another image of the toy showed a close-up of his face, which was smudged and melted slightly with a message that read. "Terrible, Terrible, Terrible. Its face looked like my own child had painted it on, and the moustache gave a very unfortunate representation of a slug."

I stared at the screen in disbelief. I couldn't understand how this had happened, as I was certain Alabaster had quality checked everything before it had left the workshop. It surely had to be the only toy that hadn't received good reviews, so I continued my search. Soon I became completely absorbed in what people had told the world about their presents, but the more I read the more disheartened I became.

"This surely can't be right! I have never seen so much disdain for what we have done."

"What have you found?" Mrs C asked, coming back into the room whilst drying a plate with her dishcloth.

"Only thousands of people who hate what I have provided them over Christmas. Look," I grumbled before showing her some of the reviews I had seen.

She leant over me to read them and a small frown of confusion came across her face. She then stood up. "It is strange, but I think you're being melodramatic. You seem to forget that times have changed. People simply expect more and when they don't get it, they moan about it."

I shook my head. "I don't understand it. Is it always like this? Does this happen every year?" I was completely baffled. I had never investigated feedback before and I wouldn't have done so today, if it hadn't been for that persistent strange feeling in my stomach I had struggled to ignore.

"I don't know, sweetheart," she said. "Now, come on, you silly sausage. Don't let this spoil things. You were so happy yesterday."

"That was when I thought I had brought smiles to all those faces. If it wasn't for Moco, I wouldn't have had any success stories this year."

"Don't read anymore," she urged. "You are the most gracious and giving person in the world. Ignore these silly reviews. Most people who are happy don't write reviews. They just get on with it. It's the people that like to complain who do."

"I don't want anyone to complain."

"Well, that's the world we live in nowadays," she said softly. She kissed my forehead and disappeared to return the dish to the kitchen, whilst I continued to look at the comments.

I knew there were some really lovely ones, but I could only see the bad. We hadn't delivered a perfect Christmas, and I was wondering if we ever had. The reality was a tough pill to take, as I always wanted Christmas to be wonderful.

I fumbled around with the printer, another piece of technology I usually left with Mrs C, and finally managed to print the comments off. Sheet after sheet of paper fed through the machine as I tried to capture everything that had been reported. It took me hours and Mrs C kept coming back and tutting at me, telling me I should let it be, but she also kept bringing me mugs of hot chocolate with a sprinkling of five marshmallows on top.

"There we go," I said finally and shoved the papers into a folder. "I think it's time we got to the bottom of this."

2

I traipsed across the snow, walking past the snowman Mrs C and I had built years ago, which was now a permanent fixture. Mrs C often dressed him in new hats and scarves that she'd made, and today he was wearing a white and blue striped hat and matching scarf. "Hello Mr Frosty." I nodded curtly at it as I marched past.

I reached the workshop door, which was red and had green foliage arched around it, decorated with baubles and bows. The sign on it read, '*Busy, Hectic Elves at Work, Enter at Own Festive Risk*', which now needed to be removed after the Christmas rush.

I opened the door and was greeted with chaos. The workshop was in complete disarray. There were ribbons and discarded bits of wrapping paper all over the place. Defective toys were piled high in the corner, and the elves weren't cleaning up. Instead, they were adding to the mess.

Pepper was running all over the place, frantically looking for something. She had bits of glittery string in her hair as she peered under workbenches and in cupboards. "I will find you, Sugarplum," she called in her high-pitched voice.

She ran straight past Shinny, who was sitting on top of a workbench with his head and back against the wall, and his eyes tightly shut. He was clutching a ball of ribbon to his stomach and was snoring loudly, completely oblivious to the surrounding noise.

Meanwhile Alabaster, my head elf, and Wunorse, were throwing a ball of wrapping paper to each other across the room. They were both extremely quick at diving for it and managed to catch it every time. It looked like quite a serious competition, and Alabaster wore a very determined expression as he threw it back at Wunorse with as much force as possible.

It was rare for me to check in so early in the New Year, so I stood by the door watching them for a while, wondering if this was how they usually behaved at the very start of the year.

After a minute, not one elf noticed my arrival, so I interrupted them. "What is going on around here?" I shouted. This caused Shinny to give out a loud snore, Pepper to trip over her own feet as she attempted to turn at the same time as run, and a cupboard door to spring open and Sugarplum to poke her head out. Then the ball of wrapping paper landed at my feet as Alabaster and Wunorse gave up their game and looked at me, startled.

Alabaster turned his wide eyes to me. His green and red striped hat sat askew on his head, and he had smudges of dirt across his face. He looked sheepish and his voice sounded even more high-pitched and uncomfortable. "We didn't think you would be coming here now, sir."

"Clearly not. So, is this how you behave when I'm not around?" I asked sternly.

The elves exchanged looks with each other, wondering whether or not to confess.

"Yes," Sugarplum said, widening her eyes in guilt and honesty at the same time Wunorse shook his head.

Alabaster straightened his hat and glanced over to Shinny, who was still snoring peacefully. "We are sorry, sir. We'll get this workshop tidied as soon as possible," he said, bowing slightly.

Suddenly, a door at the side of the room burst open, and Bushy ran inside. "Guys! How about a game of Flaming Christmas Pudding?" She was carrying a dish which was on fire and didn't notice me at first, but stopped short at the shake of Alabaster's head and pointed look. She then slowly twisted around to look at me and nearly dropped the flaming dish. "Oh my," she gasped.

"Put that out," I ordered.

Bushy attempted to blow on the pudding but didn't get anywhere close to extinguishing the flame. She continued to take big, loud gasps of air, to blow it out, until I sighed.

"Just put it down, Bushy. It will burn out on its own."

She nodded and nervously placed it on the bench, causing it to tilt and clatter onto the surface, which finally woke Shinny from his slumber. The dish rocked back and forth before it settled in one place, and fortunately, the flames stayed in the dish.

Shinny glanced around bewildered, and then settled back down, shut his eyes and was snoring again within seconds.

"Sorry, sir," Alabaster said, looking rather alarmed. "We'll get to work straight away."

"Leave it for now," I huffed. Normally, I would have found the elves' antics rather amusing, but today I felt exacerbated. "Everyone, meet me at the planning board. We have things to discuss."

Sugarplum flinched and then gave Shinny a big shake whilst pointing at me then towards the opposite side of the workshop.

He instantly leapt up from the tabletop, shocked to see me, and followed the elves obligingly with a confused expression.

The planning board was at the far side of the room. It contained all the details, designs and plans of our toys, and it was so large that it spanned the full width and height of the workshop. The elves hadn't wiped it clean yet so it was still covered in the toy designs for the previous Christmas, which I was mildly pleased about.

As the elves gathered round, I glared at them. "I'm not happy!" I snapped. "I have just found a lot of negative and upsetting feedback about our toys this year. Please feel free to read them yourselves."

I handed Alabaster the stack of papers I had printed off, and true to elf form, he began examining them. His fingers leafed through, and his eyes scanned them so quickly, I could barely keep up before he passed them onto Sugarplum, who flicked through them just as fast. It was no surprise, as they used their elf skills of devouring children's Christmas lists along with their nimble fingers for wrapping presents.

"Eek!" Sugarplum's eyes widened before she passed them along the line.

"I don't understand how Space Cadet Collins has so many issues," Bushy gasped, glancing questioningly at Alabaster.

"Precisely. Me either," I said, scanning the planning board for his design, and locating it in the middle. "Look, his face should not be drooping like it is in this picture."

"It's awful," Bushy whimpered, covering her eyes with her little hands.

"But it's not just the Space Cadet. What about the Talking Train Set? Here it says that they couldn't make out what the train was saying because its words were jumbled." I folded my arms to stare accusingly at the elves.

"Oh no! Some of these are from my station," Shinny cried, as he reread the reviews. "I tried really hard to get everything right, but… but it was so frantic. I thought Alabaster was checking them and I would have remade them had I known, I promise." Shinny looked baffled and close to tears.

Pepper looked at Alabaster as he shuffled on the spot. His cheeks grew rosier as he fiercely kept his eyes on the floor. "Yes. There are mistakes with mine too, and I also thought Alabaster had checked them all," Pepper said, giving Shinny a small reassuring smile. "It also appears that the intricate toys are where most of the issues are and that is Alabaster's workstation, too."

I nodded, feeling disheartened, and turned to Alabaster. "I thought they did. Alabaster, you are my head elf, my star worker. Do you know what has happened here?"

He lifted his head and stared at me for a moment as if contemplating what to say, his eyes harder than I was used to seeing.

"Yes," he said. He took a deep breath. "It was chaotic. We spent too much time getting Moco perfect and then had to rush ticking the children off the list." His voice was assertive and cold. "Some children got missed, so I had to double back on myself, and towards the end we just needed to get things made, wrapped, and into the sleigh, no matter what state they were in."

Sugarplum's mouth dropped open as she stared at Alabaster while my anger bubbled.

"So, you knew we were sending faulty presents out this door?" I asked incredulously.

"Yes sir. Otherwise, the job wouldn't get done and some of those children wouldn't get a present at all." His expression was less shameful and more confrontational.

Wunorse looked genuinely ashamed.

"Were you part of this?" I asked him.

"Not all of it," he said, glancing at Alabaster. "I... I saw it and we had an argument over it, but I didn't say anything. Sorry, sir."

"I can't believe you knew about this and allowed it to happen. Please tell me this is the first and only year we have had these mistakes and shortcuts?"

Wunorse gazed at Alabaster with a panicked expression.

Alabaster sighed. "No. I would say that for the last five years we have been struggling, and there have been…. issues."

"Five years! Why on earth didn't you tell me?" I cried, completely flabbergasted. "I've been going around thinking everything was all hunky-dory and it clearly hasn't been."

"It's never been as bad as this, but we have been struggling more and more every year to keep up with the increasing demand and to get the job done in time. Toys are becoming more advanced and trickier to make, whilst the children are just insisting on larger quantities of presents," Alabaster declared.

Sugarplum glared at him. "It's not a job. I hate it when you call it that."

Alabaster glared back at her and stated. "It is a job. I have to manage all of you, fix your mistakes, and ensure all these children are satisfied."

"Well, perhaps we would make fewer mistakes if you didn't bark at us all the time, and create such a grinchy atmosphere," Sugarplum argued. Shinny gasped in shock at Sugarplum's coarse words, and Bushy nodded vigorously in agreement.

"I doubt it," shouted Alabaster. "If I didn't tell you what to do, you'd be off in dreamland. I'm constantly picking up after you all and having to sacrifice my work to do so. I'd be better off doing the job on my own."

"That's not true! And stop calling it a job. It's what we are born to do, and it should be an act of joy and passion. You really aren't behaving like an elf anymore," Sugarplum retorted.

14

Alabaster opened his mouth in retort, but I cut him off. "Stop squabbling, you two. I don't know what to do about all this. I really don't. Why haven't you come to me about this before?"

Alabaster shrugged. "I didn't want to disappoint you. You always want Christmas to be perfect, and it's just unachievable these days."

I stared in shock at his flippant attitude. He didn't even seem remorseful. This was not the Alabaster I knew and I couldn't believe I hadn't seen it before. Usually when I went into the workshop, he was too busy working for me to speak to, so I just assumed everything was going according to plan.

"So many of the children's Christmas days were ruined because of this. Some children couldn't even physically play with their gifts because of the rubbish we have allowed to leave this workshop," I said as Alabaster stared back at me with hard eyes.

The other elves stared at me in silence and I was now shaking as the horrific reality sunk in.

"It is my reputation that is on the line here, and the sanctity of Christmas is being ruined. It is not acceptable, Alabaster. This cannot happen again."

Alabaster continued to stare at me. His silence shocked me even more. There wasn't a nod of agreement, or regret, and no desire to change the future.

"I need to get out of here and speak to Mrs C because I truly don't know what to do about this."

The elves remained by the planning board, and as I yanked the door to the workshop open, I could hear them shouting at each other.

3

I stomped into the house and slammed the door behind me.

"What is going on with you?" Mrs C looked at the floor with disapproval as I traipsed snow through the house into the kitchen.

"Alabaster and those elves have made a mockery of me."

"How so?" Mrs C frowned as she sneakily tucked a pack of biscuits into her apron pocket.

"They knew they were sending out rubbish to those children. It's all down to them!"

"That seems peculiar," she said a lot more calmly than I felt. "What's happened?"

Mrs C listened and nodded as I continued to rant on.

"Five years it's been going on. Five whole years! What am I going to do? It seems that none of the elves have been performing up to standard. And what can I say about Alabaster? He's lied to me all this time, and he's acting like I need to accept it." I slumped into the seat at the kitchen table and placed my head in my hands. "I might need to cancel Christmas forever at this rate."

Mrs C pulled out the chair opposite me and sat down. "Sweetheart, I think you're overreacting. You are upset, of course, and that is because you care. Christmas means the world to you and right now you are feeling disappointed and betrayed by Alabaster, but perhaps you need to see things from his point of view."

"What do you mean?" I felt shocked she hadn't jumped on board with my rage.

"I've seen the demands the children send in to you these days. I see it every year, and that list keeps growing. The children want everything and you continue to insist on catering to them and simply push Alabaster and those elves to the max. I can never fathom how the elves pull off what they do, but they do, and they do it for you, just as much as they do it for the children. So, what I'm saying is, whatever the issues are, don't doubt that Alabaster and the elves want exactly what you want."

"I'm not so sure. You should have seen Alabaster. It's like he doesn't care anymore."

Mrs C leant over and placed a hand on my arm. "I find that very difficult to believe. Alabaster has been with you from the very beginning. He's done more for you than anyone else. If it wasn't for him, there wouldn't be a Christmas. So, whatever is affecting him isn't because he doesn't care. Not deep down."

"Then why send out such terrible toys?"

"Well, it sounds like Alabaster was more focused on getting the quantity out than focusing on quality. Someone who didn't care wouldn't have been so desperate to get presents out to every child, no matter what."

I frowned. "I just don't get it, though. Even with the increase in demands, I was certain the elves could cope. They can do anything, particularly Alabaster."

Mrs C nodded in agreement. "Alabaster is an incredible elf, but there could be a multiple of reasons things aren't going well. It could be that he is burnt out and needs a break, or a reset." She looked down at the table briefly. "Sometimes we all need something new in our lives, or a change." A fleeting look of sadness crossed her face.

I shook my head. "No, I don't think it's as simple as that."

Mrs C took a deep breath and looked up at me. "Perhaps not, but maybe you need to work out what's going on with him and come up with a plan to help him."

"What should I do?" I pleaded for her to give me the answers.

"I don't know, dear. I'm afraid that you and the elves are going to have to figure that out." She patted my arm and stood up. "But now I'm going to clean up after your paddy. The corridor is a complete mess."

I kicked off my boots, plodded into the sitting room, and sat on my throne, deep in thought.

Thoughts swirled through my mind, ranging from cancelling Christmas, promoting Wunorse to head elf, forcing Alabaster to lie down on a therapy couch and tell me his problems, give him an ultimatum to improve or else, inserting cameras to spy on them, and simply hoping things would naturally improve this coming year and do nothing.

I sat there for hours, right into the night.

The next morning, I sluggishly joined Mrs C at the breakfast table, having only had about two hours' sleep. Not only had it left me feeling groggy, I still hadn't come up with a definitive plan to tackle the problem.

Mrs C poured herself a large cup of coffee. "So, are you still feeling angry with Alabaster and the elves?"

"Yes," I grumbled, staring down at my coffee. "But you know, if you happened to be planning to rustle up more of those cinnamon and cranberry cookies, I guess I could take them round to the workshop later." I flicked my eyes at her, trying my best to be nonchalant.

Mrs C's expression changed to recognition, and she smiled knowingly. "Yes, absolutely. You're quite right. I was planning on making some more this morning, and it would save me the bother if you deliver them for me."

I nodded curtly, and looked away, still in a huff as Mrs C jumped to her feet and got to work.

Later, I left the house with a plate piled high with delicious smelling cookies.

I entered the workshop to find it was a complete contrast to the day before. All the wrapping papers and bits of ribbon were now tidied away. The leftover toys had been packaged up, ready to be taken to some children's charities later. The workbenches sparkled in a way that only the elves could achieve, and the floor gleamed with polish.

Sugarplum and Bushy were huddled together, fiddling with something on a workbench. "Do you think we should add more glitter?" Bushy whispered.

"Just a touch," Sugarplum replied. "And make that ribbon curlier."

The rest of the elves were at their work stations producing some stock toys for the year ahead.

"Morning, everyone," I said, my tone on the cusp of being rough.

Sugarplum and Bushy gasped as they turned and stepped towards each other to block my view of what they had been fussing over.

"Can you gather round?" I called.

The elves all approached me with caution. Shinny slid slowly across to me, as if he feared making any unnecessary sound. Sugarplum and Bushy stuck together like Siamese twins joined at the hip as they walked over to me. Clearly, whatever they were hiding was now behind Sugarplum's back.

The others gathered around me and swapped silent expressions of concern. They didn't know what mood I was going to be in, and at that moment, neither did I.

Wunorse sniffed the air as his eyes lingered on the plate of cookies in my hand.

Alabaster looked much better than the day before. His hat was now perched on the top of his head and the smudges that had been on his face were gone, but there was still something missing from behind his eyes.

We stood silently for a moment as I weighed up my anger levels.

I took a deep breath and then sighed. "Look, I know yesterday was difficult for all of us. I learnt some things I wish weren't true." I gazed sternly at Alabaster, who turned his face away from me. "But I want to put it all behind us and start again. It is a new year, so I want to draw a line in the snow and find a way for us all to work together to make this year better and easier than the last." I looked around at the elves and tried to put my anger to one side.

Pepper let out a breath of relief. She had been standing so rigidly, she must have thought I was going to lay into them again. "That's what we want too," she agreed, glancing at Alabaster.

I smiled at her. "Good. I brought cookies for everyone, so we can all start again."

Wunorse looked delighted. "Does this mean Mrs C isn't angry with us?"

I chuckled. "No, Mrs C isn't angry with you."

Wunorse visibly relaxed and grinned even wider. "Phew," he whispered, grabbing several cookies at once from the offered plate.

"We've got something for you too," Sugarplum said, revealing the gift she had behind her back.

"Oh," I exclaimed, only mildly surprised following their conspicuous secretive behaviour.

I accepted the gift from Sugarplum and handed her the plate of cookies in exchange. As I unwrapped the gift, my heart skipped a beat.

It was a red and white striped photo frame and inside was a photo that Mrs C had taken of me standing proudly with the elves in the workshop at the beginning of November, just before the mad rush started. Everyone was fresh faced, excited and raring to go, and the energy was palpable from the picture.

I chuckled at the comical expressions Shinny, Pepper, Bushy and Sugarplum were pulling with their cocked heads, raised eyebrows, huge grins, and their tongues sticking out in various directions. Wunorse was the most well behaved. He was beaming directly at the camera with bright, glowing eyes, his hands clutched behind his back, and he had puffed his chest out proudly, probably because it was Mrs C taking the photo. It was only Alabaster who didn't seem to wear a natural smile. His smile seemed forced, and there was a faint sign of a frown across his large eyes that I hadn't noticed. It was now clear that even then, Alabaster was concerned about what was coming.

As I continued to study the photo, something switched inside of me and my body slumped. Mrs C was right. The picture was a perfect reminder of their loyalty and charm, and that what they all wanted above everything was to work hard to provide a successful Christmas, just like they did every year.

I glanced up at the elves, who were all staring at me, watching my reaction, and my heart swelled for them. Even Alabaster, who I could see more than ever, needed help.

"It's brilliant." A lump formed in my throat as all my anger drained away, causing Sugarplum and Bushy to exchange relieved grins.

I cleared my throat, finding it impossible to still be angry. "Everyone, help yourself to cookies, then meet me at the planning board for a chat."

By the time I arrived at the planning board, the elves were already there, with cookies in each hand.

Alabaster's expression was hard set as he stared at the board, waiting for me to begin.

4

"Right!" I studied the wall of the new designs we had made last year. There were thousands, all of which were completely different in specification and design. It was overwhelming looking at it, and it still amazed me how the elves achieved millions upon millions of presents ready and packaged every year. My eyes then drifted to Space Cadet Collins, and I felt a pang of sadness. "We all know there were major issues with some products and we couldn't keep up. Alabaster, do you have any ideas on how we can get around all the issues? What do you need?"

Alabaster shrugged and shook his head in anger to himself. "Well, Christmas is what it is. We can't change the fact that children keep asking for more complex toys. Long are the days when children were happy with a whip and top. We all just need to work harder and make fewer mistakes."

I blinked at the harshness in his tone, and I exchanged a look with Pepper, who looked concerned.

"Work harder?" Sugarplum snapped. "It's impossible to work any harder."

Alabaster shot her a filthy look. "Maybe if you stopped dancing around and singing, we'd all be able to concentrate better and there would be fewer mistakes."

"Well, maybe if you weren't such a Grinch and joined in the singing, we'd all make fewer mistakes," she bickered.

Shinny winced as if in pain. Elves just didn't use that word.

Alabaster stared at Sugarplum. "I don't have time to sing when I'm too busy fixing your mess."

"My mess? We all know the serious issues have come from your bench," Sugarplum argued, putting her hands on her hip.

I glanced at Pepper, who had closed her eyes as if she was praying. "Please stop arguing and blaming each other," I said. "It won't get us anywhere. Now, let's start from the beginning. What trouble did we have with Moco?"

The elves looked at Alabaster. He was in charge of the complex toys and usually he could turn them out like magic, but not Moco. I should have seen the signs back then, when Alabaster was getting irritated and overreacting when the horse wasn't galloping the way he wanted it to.

Alabaster shrugged. "It needed to be perfect. As usual, we got the idea from a child's dream. The child had pictured the horse in such specific detail, from the colouring, to the name and to the way it moved. We wanted it to match, but it was just impossible to get it to work the way she had envisioned."

"I suppose that makes sense," I muttered, trying to understand what had happened. I knew that a lot of our toy ideas came from children's thoughts. I just hadn't realised that Alabaster would be so rigid in copying the idea.

Alabaster gave a firm nod. "I guess there is such a thing as being too complicated. Even for me," he grumbled.

"Well, this is great." I said overly brightly. "Recognising the problem is a good thing. This year we need simpler toys, nothing too awkward to make." Job done, I thought, despite feeling confused why Alabaster had struggled so much.

Alabaster shrugged when Pepper piped up. "Sir, I don't think that the complexities with Moco were the sole cause of the issues."

"What else?"

"I think…" Her eyes strayed to Alabaster. She then blinked and looked at me. "I think we have too much variety…" she muttered, as though she had changed her mind about what to say.

I glanced up at the huge board again. It was completely full of designs ranging from large templates to miniature drawings, and I recalled the days when we had only filled a fraction of the board with new ideas and everyone seemed happy.

"But if we remove ideas, then not all the children will get what they want," Bushy said.

"Unless they all want the same thing," Pepper suggested. "Do you remember that year with the Blabbing Blob toy?"

"That weird alien blob thing which you had to teach how to speak before it died from lack of nurture?" I asked.

"Yes," Pepper said. "Practically all the children requested it. It wasn't just popular like Moco, it was a mad craze."

"I remember that," Wunorse recalled. "At one point I thought there was an error because every child on the list wanted one. But it certainly made things easier."

"Yes, so it would be great if we could create something that really takes off," Pepper said.

Alabaster sighed. "Great, so one person's station gets all the work, which would most likely be me."

"Not necessarily," Pepper replied, looking straight at me as if she knew something I didn't.

"The problem is we can't predict what is going to take off. We design these toys, and then it's out of our control," Wunorse said. "That Blabbing Blob year was an anomaly."

Pepper sighed and looked deflated. "I guess so. But all I'm saying is that it helps when all the children like the same thing."

"Are there any other examples of crazes we've had that we can learn from?" I asked.

Sugarplum thought for a second. "Wunorse is right. You just can't predict them. The strangest things have turned out to be alarmingly popular. Like there was that other good year when most people asked for those foam caterpillar toys that the children could stretch out and bend into different shapes and patterns. I only came up with that as a joke, but everyone wanted one. It was mad."

Shinny stepped forward. "There's also those witchcraft and wizardry toys that everyone is into. They like those flying golf balls and broomsticks,

24

don't they?"

"Eugh, don't get me started on that," I huffed. "I've made it known that I've been flying and doing magic for centuries, but now it's all exciting for them. It's downright rude if you ask me."

Shinny squirmed, knowing he had touched a nerve.

I shook my head. "Well, it looks like we can't consciously force a craze to happen, but fingers crossed, we do. Now, is there anything else we can do to improve this year?"

Alabaster sighed and looked itchy to get back to his bench. "We just need to crack on with fewer interruptions and everyone needs to pull their weight."

I shook my head, feeling deflated. "Very well. I will leave you to get back to work."

Back at the house, Mrs C instantly greeted me by shuffling towards me in her padded snowman slippers, which were a gift from me.

"I'm glad you're back because I need to speak to you," she smiled. "I've been looking at places to go on holiday this year, and as we did Barbados last year, Germany the year before and America before that, guess where I thought would be a good place to visit this year?"

"The South Pole?" I asked, chuckling and finding myself hilarious, considering it wasn't a patch on the North Pole.

"No, you, silly sausage. I thought, England. It's not too warm, the accent is very charming, and they have your favourite type of tea. What do you think?"

"Sure. Anything you wish, dear." I knew full well that she didn't have to ask me. Holidays were always her decision, and I would go along with whatever she chose.

"Great," she exclaimed, looking delighted. "I'll get something booked in."

That evening, Mrs C approached me with some sheets of paper. "Right, I've done it!" She sat down in her armchair. "I've booked us in for a few nights in a hotel in London. We can have some nice food, do some window shopping and I've bought tickets for a show. We leave early next week."

"Wonderful," I muttered. I wanted to be enthusiastic for her, as I could see how excited she was, but I felt apprehensive about leaving.

Mrs C looked at me and frowned. "I think it will be good for you to get away for a bit, have a change of scenery and reset the batteries… I think we all need it."

I looked at Mrs C and I noticed that odd look I sometimes spotted on her face, as if she was reflective. It made me wonder if Mrs C was struggling a little with her routine and needed a holiday more than I realised.

I forced a more natural smile. "It will be great. I just need to make sure the elves behave whilst we're away."

The following morning, the atmosphere in the workshop was worse than before. Alabaster and Sugarplum were glaring at each other as Sugarplum purposefully slammed the dolls she was making down on the counter.

Pepper was leaning over her workbench, fumbling through some pieces of paper she was holding and reading them intently. She looked distant and distracted. Whilst the others were trying their hardest to keep their heads down and work silently.

"I see the mood hasn't improved," I remarked.

Pepper jumped at my voice and shoved the papers into her pocket.

"I've come to tell you that Mrs C has booked our annual trip," I said, causing Sugarplum to gasp and rush over to me.

"Where are you going?" she asked, now looking excited.

"London," I said, causing Sugarplum to place her hands across her heart.

"That's wonderful," she gushed. "England looks so pretty."

Pepper nodded in agreement as she slowly approached, looking slightly distracted.

"Mrs C must be looking forward to it," Wunorse said. "She deserves a break."

"Well, it means that I won't be here to oversee things, so I hope whilst I'm away you will continue to work on coming up with some new toy ideas. Particularly ones that could be the next craze."

Sugarplum smiled. "You have nothing to worry about. You and Mrs C just need to enjoy your holiday and have a wonderful time." Then her smile widened. "Will you bring me back a piece of England?"

"This again?" I chuckled. Every time Mrs C and I went away, Sugarplum would ask for something extra special as a holiday gift. "What do you want this time?"

Sugarplum pondered for a moment. "Let me think. I want it to scream England, and something I can treasure."

Pepper looked at Sugarplum, and then a thought seemed to strike her. "What about a postbox? Only a few days ago, you were telling me how much you liked them."

Sugarplum's eyes widened. "Of course. A postbox would be perfect."

"Why would you want a postbox?" I asked, frowning.

Sugarplum's grin widened even further, and her eyes sparkled. "They look so pretty and red is my favourite colour. Plus, so many children in England would have walked up to one of those red boxes with their Christmas letter to us in their hands, and watched it disappear inside, hoping that the next person who would read it would be us in the North Pole," she beamed as she glanced around at everyone. She looked so excited. "A real-life postbox will be wonderful, as it would connect me to all those children."

I chuckled. "Well, I'll see what I can do, and if Mrs C will let me."

"I'm sure she will," Sugarplum said, her beaming smile turning to satisfaction.

Over the next few days, I popped into the workshop to check on progress, but by the time I came to say goodbye, I had little confidence in the elves finding the next craze.

"Right, Mrs C and I are leaving soon." I glanced around at everyone, as they barely paid attention to me. I cleared my throat roughly to make them all look up. "When I get back, I want to go through what's on the planning board in depth. Also, you must promise me you'll look after my boy and the other reindeer whilst I'm gone." I stared at Alabaster and then around at the other elves.

"Yes, sir," they all said, as Alabaster gave another firm nod.

Pepper hurried over to me, clasping her hands behind her back and looking anxious. "I wanted to wish you good luck on your travels." She then held out her palm, which contained a handful of elf dust, took a deep breath and blew the dust along with her spittle, as hard as she could all over me.

"What was that for?" I spluttered, wafting my face.

"It's err… guidance dust," she said, her eyes darting towards Alabaster to make sure he wasn't in earshot. "I wanted to ensure you have a smooth journey with no mishaps."

"Thanks, but I've been to England several times before. I know where I'm going."

Pepper's cheeks turned pink. "Oh, well, never mind then, sorry."

I smiled at her as I looked down at her flushed face. "It's a nice gesture though, thank you. Now, will you give me all the gossip when I return? I want to know everything," I whispered.

She nodded; her expression concerned as she looked around the workshop. I patted her on the head, hitched up my trousers, and made my way to the exit.

"Oh!" I called as I stopped at the door. "Don't forget, the reindeer like a little treat now and then."

The elves all looked up at me and waved me off. "Bye Santa, have a glorious holiday," they all called, except Alabaster, who gave a curt wave.

"Please don't forget my postbox," Sugarplum called, looking giddy with excitement at the idea as I shut the door.

5

"Hey. Love!" Mrs C called as soon as I returned to the house. "Can you come upstairs, please?"

I sighed and slowly stomped up the stairs, attempting to prolong the inevitable, and entered our bedroom to find stacks of clothes on the bed next to a small, open case.

"Do these trousers fit you at the moment?" She was holding up a pair of my usual green and red chequered trousers.

"Erm," I muttered, looking around the room, and not wanting to answer.

"I take it, that's a no." She then put them back in the cupboard.

"I'd say they are my July trousers, for when I've lost my Christmas weight." I gave my round belly a gentle pat.

"Yes, and before it creeps back on again." She gave me that stern look again. "Right, I think this will be all we need." Ms C glanced around satisfied at the mountains of items on the bed and most of the floor. "I'll leave you to finish." She leant up to kiss my nose before leaving the room.

"Great," I muttered. It looked like we were taking more clothes than we were leaving behind and we were only going for a few days. I started picking the piles up and shoving them into the case. I grumbled every year about packing, but I knew how excited Mrs C was, so I only grumbled when she couldn't hear. After a couple of minutes, I threw the last item in; a shoehorn, and snapped the case shut. I picked it up, smoothed the black leather out, and admired how sublime my skills were. I made my way downstairs, whilst swinging the little case by my knee, and placed it near the front door. "Right. Are we ready?" I asked.

"I think so. It looks like we have everything," she said as her eyes darted around the house.

"Great, let's go," I said, holding the door open for her.

She stepped out the front door, and I locked it behind us. We made our way past the reindeer pen and onto the building next to it, where I pulled back the gate to the hangar and took a moment to absorb the sleigh in all her glory.

I then frowned as I spotted a few scuffs and wondered where they came from, but despite that, I couldn't help but admire her magnificence, even after all these centuries.

Mrs C cleared her throat. "Are you going to stand there drooling over your sleigh all night?"

"Err, one second love." I raced over to grab the cover for her. "I've not put her to bed yet." I dragged the cover over her shining body and then gave her a pat. "There we go," I whispered, already looking forward to giving her the attention she deserves and getting her looking her best again.

Next to the sleigh was the two-man plane. "Here we are." I held my hand out to Mrs C to help her climb into the passenger seat, where she located her goggles and snapped them on her face. I skipped around to the driver's side, shoved the case across to Mrs C for her to hold on her lap, and heaved myself into position. It was a tight squeeze, tighter than perhaps it should be, and I had to breathe in to stop my belly from interfering with the controls. I pulled my goggles on and soon the propeller was whirring, letting off a loud hum as I drove it out of the hangar, and over the snowy ground, before we took off into the air.

"Do you know how to get there?" Mrs C asked, and I gave her a look as if the answer was obvious.

She smiled, shuffled in her seat to get comfortable and gazed out the window. "There's a beautiful display tonight," she called over the noise.

She was right. The lights of the aurora borealis were exceptionally vibrant and bright green tonight. They were dancing and shimmering across the sky as if they were waving us goodbye. It was truly glorious.

"Are you ready, love?" I yelled across to her as we flew closer to the target.

Mrs C nodded and grabbed hold of the door of the plane.

"Here we go," I shouted and manoeuvred the plane so it flew over the top of the actual North Pole. As the plane made contact with the magnetic field and the energy from the pole, a crackle of electricity surrounded the plane, flickering around the edges of it, as if it was attacking us. The power was concentrating into the plane, giving me the ability to create vortexes between my intended destinations.

Then we shot off as the plane sped up at warp-speed, directly into a vortex which had opened up in front of us. Green, blue and red, spiralled around us and in no time the plane re-emerged, where I continued to fly over sea and land.

I lowered the plane onto an open field and looked around at Mrs C. "Ta-dah! We're here, in good old England. I don't 'alf fancy a cup of Rosy Lee," I chuckled to myself as I drove the plane to a leisurely stop.

"Rosy Lee? What are you on about?" Mrs C exchanged her goggles for reading glasses so she could study her agenda.

I shook my head in disbelief. "It's cockney rhyming slang for tea. Love, you still have lots to learn, but don't worry, I'm a pro traveller, so you're in expert hands."

Mrs C's mouth popped open slightly as she gazed out at the view and she slowly lowered her reading glasses.

"Erm, honeybun? Seeing as you're such a pro and everything, would you mind telling me what that is?"

I followed the line of her finger and swallowed hard, then tugged my coat away from my neck. "Oh," I exclaimed, starting up the plane's engine. "Yes, that would be the Eiffel Tower." I instantly twirled the plane around so it faced the opposite direction.

"How curious," she said. "I didn't know they'd moved it to England."

I side-eyed her as I picked up speed and lifted the plane back into the air.

She chuckled. "What is it with men and accepting directions?"

"Hey, it's not my fault. Everything blurs into one country when you go all over the world in one night, but I definitely don't need directions."

Mrs C rolled her eyes and refrained from commenting.

Seconds later, I bumped the plane down in a similar-looking field.

"Well done, love." Mrs C said. "That certainly beats going through airport security checks."

"Definitely! Can you imagine how many stamps would be in my passport if I were to collect one for each country?"

"Yes, and I don't think they would believe your passport was real when they saw your name, address, and especially your actual age," she chuckled.

"Cheeky. I've got a good few decades left in me yet."

I pulled the plane up to the edge of the abandoned field. "Now what?" I asked.

Mrs C folded up her documents and lifted her reading glasses onto her head. "Now we find the train station, which is a five-minute walk in that direction," she pointed.

I helped Mrs C out of the plane, took the case, and we trekked across the frosty, crisp field, covered in a light dusting of snow, to a train station on the outskirts of London.

Mrs C then navigated us onto a train and when we reached Kings Cross station, everyone poured out of it. We fought through the thick crowds of people and stopped outside some shops so Mrs C could get her bearings. Beside us was a long line of people waiting to have their picture taken next to a trolley sticking out of a wall.

I shook my head. "Look at them. They get all excited about a magical story where they can manipulate brickwork and walk through it. Yet, I've been going down chimneys and controlling brickwork for centuries."

"Yes, and no one ever makes a fuss about you," Mrs C muttered sarcastically. "The hotel isn't far. We just need to turn left at the exit."

6

Mrs C guided us through the busy streets until we found the hotel she had booked. It was a grand-looking hotel, with a variety of flags sprouting from around the blue awning above the revolving door. The receptionist smiled politely as we approached.

"We're here to check in," Mrs C declared.

"Can I take your names?" she asked.

"Mr and Mrs Claus," Mrs C replied. Then she shook her head. "Sorry, I meant Claude. Mr and Mrs Claude."

The receptionist frowned and gave us a suspicious look before she typed the name into the computer. "Ah, yes. One superior double room. That's room 1225, on the twelfth floor." She then glanced behind me with a subtle nod.

"May I take your luggage, sir?" the concierge asked, appearing beside me and making me jump.

"Oh, err, yes. Thank you," I said and handed him the case.

He held it out in front of him, using just his index finger and thumb, and looked down at it in confusion. "Is this all?" he asked.

"Yes, it is." I grinned widely and puffed out my chest, knowing I was the best packer he'd ever met.

The young man hesitated. "Very well, follow me." He exchanged a raised eyebrow with the receptionist as she handed him our key card.

He escorted us up the lift and to our room. Then, just before he opened the door to reveal where we would spend the next few days, I spotted Mrs C's excited expression.

"Here we are," the concierge said, placing the case on the bed and handing me the plastic card. "I hope you both have a lovely stay."

Mrs C grinned widely. "Wow, this is a stunning room."

"It certainly is," I muttered, distracted, "but right now, I need the loo." I headed to the only door in the room, but when I opened it, it was pitch black inside. I ran my hand around the inside wall, fumbling for the light switch, but couldn't find one. "What's going on?" I cried, getting increasingly frustrated as I scanned the outside wall as well.

Mrs C hurried over. "It's all computerised now. You use this electronic pad to turn the lights on, open the curtains, set the alarm and tell the hotel staff to make up the room." She tapped the control pad on the wall. "Here we go, bathroom light, on."

I shook my head. "That's a lot of complicated hoo-ha for going to the loo."

Moments later I emerged from the bathroom, having also dabbled in trying out the hotel hand lotion and found Mrs C rummaging around in the case.

"I like how you've just thrown everything in! It's very Jackson Pollock-esk, but I can't find my tartan dress." She pulled out a stack of clothes from the case and then handed me my red velvet jacket to go with my red and green chequered trousers. "We're booked in for a meal at the Voydon restaurant up the road, so you need to wear your smart jacket. Now if only I can find mine… Ah, here we are, right underneath your shoe polish." She then disappeared into the bathroom to get changed.

I slipped my jacket on and waited. I sat on the edge of the bed; it was firm. I hung a few items up in the cupboard, then paced up and down the room, and finally stopped at the electronic pad on the wall. "Let's 'ave a go with this then," I muttered.

'Menu,' a button read, so I pressed it. Then a screen with several icons came up, but no instructions, so I started jabbing my finger onto the pad. Some did nothing. Then the curtains whirred at the side of me and opened. I continued to click around when I heard a clatter and Mrs C shouted from inside the bathroom. "Hey. You've turned the light off."

"Sorry!" I called, frantically fumbling with the pad. The curtains closed again, then I saw the strip of light appear from underneath the bathroom door. I stepped away from the device, holding my hands up in surrender, and thought it best to let Mrs C be in control.

Eventually, Mrs C stepped out of the bathroom, wearing the same tartan dress I had seen her in many times before. "You look absolutely lovely, dear, and extremely radiant." I wondered if she'd done something with her hair. This time I was pretty sure she had makeup on, but what I was most certain about was how important it was for me to compliment her at this moment.

"Oh, you," she gushed, waving her hand to dismiss me, but she was smiling to herself.

Phew, I thought. I'd said the right thing, even though she looked beautiful to me every day.

She picked up her matching clutch bag and coat and we headed out to the restaurant.

It was one of those fancy restaurants, where I instantly straightened my back and raised my chin when I entered.

The maître d' also looked us up and down with a slight raise of an eyebrow as he checked our fake names off the list. I couldn't tell if he suspected who I was, or if he was admiring my ensemble.

"Welcome Mr and Mrs Claude. Would you like a drink at the bar before going to your table?" he asked.

"Yes please," Mrs C said, and the man escorted us to a seat at the bar next to a middle-aged couple.

"What can I get you?" the bartender asked.

"Two glasses of champagne, please," Mrs C said with a polite smile.

The bartender nodded and turned his back on us as we both climbed up onto the extremely high bar stools, where Mrs C wobbled precariously at one point. The bartender then laid two frilly paper coasters in front of us and placed the champagne glasses on top, before he turned around to wipe the counter.

Mrs C sat up straighter and raised her glass in the air. "I'd like to propose a toast. To another wonderful year spent together and to many more successful years to come."

My smile flickered, as concern about Alabaster and the elves reared itself again. I hoped more than anything, that the forthcoming year wouldn't be a repeat of the difficulties, strife and disasters just gone by.

"To success," I toasted, forcing my smile and clinking my glass onto hers, which caused the man next to us to turn round and look at us.

"Celebrating, are you chap?" the man asked. "I must say my ears pricked up at the word 'success'." He picked up his whisky glass and led his partner, who was carrying a Cosmopolitan cocktail, over to stand in front of us. "I'm a sucker for a success story myself, so I'd love to hear about your cause for celebration."

No sooner had he stood in front of me, his eyes quickly moved over me and he gave a raucous laugh. "Wow, fantastic outfit!" he said, suddenly distracted by my attire. "I can always spot a man who exudes confidence, and you must have bundles."

The man inflated himself, perhaps wanting us to note his maroon-coloured tailored suit, black shirt and silver tie, which overtly told us he was confident, too.

I shrugged, as I exchanged a glance with Mrs C, not sure how to respond to the tornado that had just approached us.

The man smiled as he took a sip of his whisky, so that his cuff shifted to reveal a gold Rolex watch. He didn't seem to care that Mrs C and I hadn't responded to his nosey request.

"So, what do you do, old chum, or what did you used to do?" he asked, looking me up and down, and taking in my post-retirement age.

I side-eyed Mrs C. "I currently work in logistics and supply chain," I said.

"Ah, very good. I know a thing or two about getting products out the door, and it's great that a man of your age is still working away. And what about your wife? Let me guess. She doesn't need to work, like my wife. She likes to just keep the house in order while stretching the old purse strings. Am I right?" he asked, placing his arm around his wife's slim waist.

The woman smiled, but it didn't reach her eyes. I wasn't sure if that was because her botoxed face didn't allow any form of expression across her features, or her heavy makeup was weighing her eyes down. But the extremely expensive jewellery, designer outfit and her neatly coiffed blonde bouffant of hair certainly reiterated her lack of needing to work.

"No, I'm not a housewife," Mrs C asserted, her defiance taking me by surprise. "I'm a guidance counsellor."

I quickly hid my surprise and chuckled. "And a very good one at that," I said, winking at Mrs C.

The man raised his eyebrows. "How intriguing! So, what does that involve?"

"I give bespoke tailored advice to some of the most important, renowned people in the world. My aim is to keep them calm and productive during highly pressurised and intense work projects," Mrs C claimed.

The man's face lit up with intrigue. "Fascinating. I've worked with a few high-ranking tycoons myself. Which clients do you work with?"

"I'm afraid that's confidential." Her hand slipped across to my knee as she took a sip of her drink.

The man's face dropped slightly, disappointed he couldn't get the juicy information he clearly wanted. "So, is it business that brings you to London?"

"No, just pleasure," I said.

"Shopping spree for the Mrs?" he asked, winking at Mrs C, before he faced me again. "Whatever the wife wants, the wife gets, aye?"

"I think it will be just… browsing." I darted a questioning look at Mrs C because, in all honesty, I wasn't sure what our plans were for London. Mrs C was in charge of that.

The man chuckled. "Good luck with that. My wife never browses, do you, love?" he asked, glancing at his wife.

The lady shook her head, took a sip of her cocktail, then glanced around the restaurant, clearly bored with the conversation. The man, however, seemed intent on continuing. "She has to buy all the latest fashion items. Comes back with bags full of stuff. Me, on the other hand, I'm much more of a one item man, particularly a good watch, or piece of art."

He took a sip of his whisky and let out a breath of alcoholic air. "My name is Seamus, by the way. Seamus Conway. I'm an investor and businessman, hence being a sucker for success. Success may as well be my middle name." He reached into his jacket pocket to extract a shiny business card. "Therefore, if you're looking at elevating your supply chain or counselling businesses, or know someone else in need, call me. I'm excellent at taking businesses to their next level."

He handed the card to me, and I slid it into my pocket without looking at it. I was pretty certain I didn't need anyone else's help with my business antics.

"That's very interesting, thank you," Mrs C replied. "We'll be sure to do that."

"Anyway, it's been great meeting you." He placed his hand on his wife's back as a server beckoned them over to the dining area. "Enjoy your meal. The tuna's really good.".

Mrs C and I exchanged dazed expressions. I then blinked, as if trying to remove the dust the tornado had swept at us. "He was an interesting character, and he thought I was the confident one," I muttered.

Mrs C stared after Seamus, looking thoughtful, before she twisted back to me. "Interesting is one way to describe him. Now, come on, let's get back to celebrating," and she sipped her glass of champagne.

7

Moments later, the server guided us to our table which was draped in a white tablecloth and had two black silky velvet armchairs tucked under it. The server pulled the chair out for Mrs C, whilst I wrestled with mine, as it was surprisingly heavy.

"Can we get a bottle of the house white wine and half a dozen oysters to start with?" Mrs C asked, smiling at the server and adjusting herself in her seat.

"Fabulous choice, ma'am," the server said, bowing slightly to her.

"Oysters?" I exclaimed in surprise. "Are you trying to mess with me?"

Mrs C smirked. "Now, why would I do that? I thought it would be a delightful treat on our holiday."

The server returned and placed a tray with six oysters down in between us. He poured two glasses of wine and left the bottle beside us in an ice bucket.

"Lovely, thank you," Mrs C smiled.

I looked at the slimy dollop in the shell and swallowed hard, but I could see the grin on Mrs C's face. I picked up my oyster and scowled at her. She looked far too pleased with herself as she picked up her own.

"On the count of three," she grinned whilst studying my expression. "One, two..."

"Three," I called at the same time and quickly tipped the shell's contents into my mouth, keen to get it over with quickly. I screwed up my nose as the salty, slimy oyster slid down my throat, and then I smacked my lips together. I'd had plenty of oysters in my time, but still couldn't work out whether I liked or disliked them.

"Now, that wasn't so bad, was it?" Mrs C grinned.

"I guess so." I was unconvinced, so I wiped my mouth on the napkin and picked up my wine.

"You know," I said conversationally, "it's nice stepping away from the workshop for a little while. It's just a shame the elves can't be here with us."

"Yes, it is a shame. Like I said before, I really can't help but think a respite from their routine might be good for all of them, and not just Alabaster. Something to take their minds off their work. Something new and fresh to reset them and break up the pressure that is constantly on them." Mrs C reached for her second oyster and gestured for me to do the same. I copied her, not entirely convinced I was ready for round two.

I pondered for a moment. "Well, Sugarplum and Bushy nearly managed to escape from their routine one year. Do you remember?"

Mrs C chuckled. "The time they snuck into the back of your sleigh on Christmas Eve?"

"Yes, and they would have got away with it, had they not been giggling so hard."

"That's right. They were so disappointed you found them just before you hit the vortex." She tipped the shell to her lips and swallowed.

"Those elves do make me laugh sometimes." I tipped the second oyster into my mouth and grimaced again, causing Mrs C to look amused.

I glared at her amusement, and my lips curled into a cunning smile. "Speaking of amusing stories. Do you remember that time Wunorse was daydreaming and instead of painting the Cluedo characters onto cards, he accidentally made them all look like different versions of you?"

Mrs C nodded. "Yes, I remember that."

"I think the peacock blue with the posh earrings was a good look for you, but not as good as the mustard yellow with a moustache," I snorted.

"Oh, ha, ha," Mrs C laughed. "I happen to think I looked best as 'MISS' Scarlet," emphasising the Miss, and had we not been at a fancy restaurant, I was certain she would have stuck her tongue out at me. "Now let's go for round three," she said.

She reached for her last oyster, and so did I, but as I geared myself up for my final challenge, I couldn't help but feel strange as my laughter receded. Perhaps there was something to Mrs C's comments about the elves needing something to happen to revitalise them.

I shook away the feeling and lifted the oyster up, when suddenly the woman next to me screamed. "Of course, I'll marry you!" at the same time there was a loud pop of a cork which made me jump.

My heart was pounding from the fright, but it quickly settled and I returned my attention to the shell clasped in my fingers but the oyster had disappeared.

"What the…" I exclaimed, looking around the table.

Mrs C finished swallowing her oyster. "What is it?"

"It's gone," I gasped. "It's scarpered."

Mrs C looked at me with suspicion. I was certain she thought I'd lobbed it somewhere instead of eating it, but after a second of searching the area, Mrs C started to laugh.

I frowned as her laughter escalated, and tears formed in her eyes. She then took a moment to hide behind her napkin as she tried to control herself and take a deep breath before she lowered it to face me. "Honey, it's in your beard."

I held my beard up for inspection and found the oyster nestled in my bristles. I could feel my cheeks turn red as I attempted to wrestle the slippery blob out of it. All the while, Mrs C returned to intermittently covering her face with her napkin and then watching me, whilst finding the entire ordeal hilarious. Once I'd cleared myself up, I glared at Mrs C. "You can stop giggling now."

"Of course," she muttered, fanning her face, then she dabbed her eyes with her napkin. "Shall we get another plate of them?"

"No thank you," I retorted quickly, which only caused her to giggle some more.

We then ordered our main meals, steak for me and tuna for Mrs C, which we ate while we continued retelling amusing stories and reminiscing about old memories. We drank our wine, and I noticed the pink blush across her cheeks that she always got when she drank alcohol.

After a delicious lemon dessert, and a second bottle of wine, we headed back to the hotel, her arm linked through mine, her steps not always moving in a straight line.

"I had a lovely evening," she said, as we stopped at our room door.

I inserted the card into the hole underneath the handle and yanked it out quickly, but the green light didn't come on. "Pesky thing," I muttered as I tried again, yanking it faster to trick it into registering, but it didn't work. "We're locked out," I cried.

Mrs C shook her head and took the card off me. "I've never quite understood how you do it." She inserted the card into the hole and gently slid it out, so that the little light turned green. "You can do so many amazing things, but now it's a hotel room door that defeats you."

"Well, I didn't realise how sensitive it was. It seems temperamental to me."

Mrs C shook her head in dismay. "Right, we best get ready for bed. We have a busy day tomorrow."

8

The following day, after a buffet breakfast where Mrs C barely ate anything and made me take ten rashes of bacon back off my plate, we headed out to explore London. We clambered onto an overcrowded tube carriage where everyone squeezed in, like sticky candy canes overflowing from a jar, and we shot off.

I could tell Mrs C was tired today. She was quieter than usual, and her excitement had waned. It didn't take much for her to get a mild hangover, so I suspected it would pass soon.

We hopped off at Tower Bridge and saw crowds of people. "Well, hello there," I called, waving at some children I recognised. I grinned broadly at them, but their parents quickly pulled them away from me and hurried along.

"Calm down, dear," Mrs C whispered, pressing a couple of fingers to her temple as if she had a headache. "Please don't start asking the children if they liked their presents like you did last year."

"But I want to know. I enjoy seeing them smile."

"Yes, but we don't want anyone to call the police on you again. It will put a dampener on our holiday."

"Oh police, smeesh!"

Mrs C gave me a stern look. "I'm putting my foot down. If the police ask to see your ID, they won't believe you like last time, and then they ask questions about where we live, and how we got here without coming through border control. You know all this, so calm down, act British, and blend in."

I sighed, knowing Mrs C was right. So when I next saw some children I recognised, and my hand itched to wave at them, I consciously kept it by my side. It was a difficult challenge, but soon something else captured my attention as we walked past a bright red postbox.

I stopped dead and retreated to have a closer look. I had seen them before when I'd visited England in the past, but I'd never looked at them the same way. Sugarplum had somehow opened my eyes to their attraction.

Mrs C had carried on walking for a moment before she realised I wasn't next to her. "What's wrong?" she asked, hurrying over to me. She looked at me, then at the postbox, and then back again.

"Exquisite, isn't it?" I stood back to have a better look at it.

Mrs C frowned. "Yes, very. Come on, people are staring."

I patted the top of it, and stroked its coarse, crumbling red paintwork. "Sugarplum asked me to bring one back for her."

Mrs C's eyes widened. "Oh, no!" she exclaimed, slapping her forehead and dragging her hand down her face. "Not again!"

I gave her a guilty smile. "I promised to bring her a gift back from England, and this is what she wanted."

"Seriously, wouldn't a fridge magnet do?" She then placed a hand over her neck, which was turning red, and glanced around herself at the people still passing us by with curious expressions. "A postbox is not a simple request. Honestly, that elf really knows how to set you a challenge."

"Well, whatever makes her happy. I'm used to challenges. I like them and I know you do, too."

She sighed and feigned a look of irritation, but I could see the thrill dancing behind her eyes and I knew that the redness creeping up her neck was from excitement. There was no denying it. Mrs C loved Sugarplum's challenges, just as much as I did.

We laughed hysterically when we took a lamppost from the Champs-Élysées in Paris, although that wasn't half as much fun as a yellow cab from New York.

"I don't know where she puts them all," Mrs C said. "Anyway, let's get moving. We can tackle this later. There are plenty to choose from." I nodded and allowed her to drag me away.

We joined a tour going around the Tower of London and walked past statues, artefacts and paintings; through old rustic doors, and along castle walls, whilst the tour guide spoke to us about its history. It brought back so many memories of less demanding times when I would visit London in an era of men in ruffs and women in long dresses and corsets. One thing was for sure, London certainly didn't smell as bad as it did then.

We arrived at the Crown Jewels section, where the tour guide continued to speak about the multiple stones within the crown. As we stared into one of the glass cases displaying a crown, I pulled Mrs C closer to me. "It's a good job Sugarplum didn't ask me to bring this back. That would be a challenge and a half."

Mrs C chuckled, her eyes glued to the sparkling, regal crown. "It's beautiful, isn't it?"

"You know," I whispered. "You're the queen of the North Pole. Let's say I get you one of these."

She grinned at me and lightly slapped my belly. "Don't be daft. I don't need things like that. I'm more than happy with my snowman slippers."

"Well, either way, you'll always be a queen to me."

Once the tour had finished, Mrs C smiled happily. "That was a blast from the past. Come on, let's go to Liberty and do some browsing. I've not been in ages."

We hopped back onto the tube, then darted across to another one just as the doors were about to close, and finally stepped off at Oxford Circus. We made our way to the iconic Tudor styled, black and white building and I smiled as I recalled visiting it just after it had opened.

The place buzzed with adults and children, and the January sales sections were especially crowded. Mrs C was lingering over a hat and scarf set as I stepped through an archway into another section, which caused me to gasp loudly.

"What is it?" Mrs C asked, as she stepped through to see what I was looking at, before she smiled and sighed.

There in front of us were snow domes, artificial wreaths, ornaments and baubles, all on a discounted offer, and my face was everywhere. "This is so exciting!" I grinned, taking an ornament and holding it up. It was me carrying a sack of presents, about to climb down a chimney. I loved comparing the likeness of my features to the merchandise. Sometimes they were spot on, other times they were a bit amiss, which I always found amusing.

I then picked up another ornament. It was me in my sleigh, with just Rudolph and his bright red nose, guiding the way. "Miss you, lad," I whispered.

Mrs C came to stand behind me. "That's a charming ornament, but I think it's a shame the other reindeer aren't represented. They work just as hard."

I placed it back down, not wanting to get into another reindeer debate with Mrs C and ran my hand along the shelf, and stopped at a doll. "These elves look nothing like Alabaster and the others." I picked one up and waved it around. "These excuses for elves are far too gangly." A lump suddenly formed in my throat as it sank in how much I was missing everyone.

Mrs C sighed, spotting my demeanour. "You always do this to yourself. We'll be home before you know it."

I then sensed someone watching me, and I looked around to find a little boy staring at me. He looked in shock and he slowly lifted his hand to tug on his mother's coat sleeve. "What is it, Danny?" she asked, with her back to me.

"It's Santa," he whispered, pointing at me in amazement.

I quickly put the elf back on the shelf and attempted to dart out of view, but I was too late.

"Oh!" Danny's mother said, as our eyes met. "I do apologise." She pushed Danny's hand down as he had frozen in his point pose. "He thinks you look like Santa." Her eyes trailed from my head to toe and back again. "You must get it a lot."

I laughed. "Don't you worry. It happens, but I hope you had a lovely Christmas and Danny enjoyed his racing car." I winked at Danny, but Mrs C quickly jerked me away as Danny's eyes widened and his mother's mouth fell open in surprise.

46

"You're drawing attention to us," she hissed.

"I remember Danny. He's a good kid, always helping his friends whenever they need him."

"That's great, but I've told you time and time again to pretend you don't know any of the children."

Mrs C guided me across the shop floor, and we left the iconic shop to merge into the crowds on the street. It wasn't long before a row of red flags caught my eye as we approached another flagship London store. I tugged on Mrs C's arm. "Can we go in here?"

Mrs C glanced at her watch. "Go on then. Quickly, though, we have a lot to do today."

I grinned as we stepped through the entranceway to Hamleys. Instantly, I was greeted with the chaos of children and staff playing with toys. There was everything you could dream of. Teddies, dolls, Lego of every building and display imaginable, board games, toy guns, ball games, weird confusing toys, remote control cars and so much more. I breathed in the children's energy and absorbed the atmosphere as if it was an intoxicating drug. There was a buzz in this shop that was impossible to find anywhere else, as children were allowed to let themselves loose and play.

I smiled dreamily. "This is it." I glanced around at everyone. "This is perfect."

Mrs C nodded. "It's a wonderful store."

"It's stores like this that feed children with ideas and desires. It's what makes them dream of possibilities." I continued to roam the shop, spotting several ideas that my elves had come up with, and hundreds more that we had copied and delivered to millions of children across the world. "Look, there's Moco!" I pointed at a stand of boxed toys on a table. "And there's Space Cadet! Fortunately, without any quality issues."

Mrs C allowed me to roam around a while longer until she checked the time again. "Come on, I've booked to have lunch at a Japanese restaurant."

We reached her chosen restaurant, which was a small quaint place, and we ordered some sushi. Once it arrived, Mrs C and I had a great time, using our chopsticks to dip our sushi into the soy sauce, but once again, I found Mrs

C laughing at me, when I added far too much wasabi to one of my pieces and ended up doing some frighteningly loud sneezes as well as causing my eyes to tear up from the ticklish, painful heat.

"I think you need to get some fresh air," Mrs C grinned. "And it just so happens I have the perfect activity for us this afternoon. Come on, we're going ice skating."

I stared at her. "Oh no, these hips don't move like they used to. I'm still creaking from Christmas Eve."

"Then a bit of exercise will do you good."

9

Mrs C wrapped her scarf tighter around her neck, and led the way to an enchanting ice rink, which was lit up with strings of warm lights, that were even more emphasised by the darkness cascading down on us in the mid-afternoon. A beautifully decorated Christmas tree stood in the centre of the rink, now with scaffolding creeping around it ready to bring the tree down as the season wrapped up. There was always a strange foreboding feeling when the Christmas season ended, but I was delighted to at least be able to catch the tail end of it all.

"This is so wonderful!" Mrs C beamed as she absorbed the scene.

We queued to pay and the chirpy rink steward handed me a pair of blue plastic ice skates that felt damp and still warm inside. Compliments of their last user.

I grimaced as I slid my foot into the hard shell of the boot, which pinched all my toes together. I waddled over to the ice, bouncing awkwardly on the blade on top of the rubbery mat, conscious not to go over on my ankle. Mrs C followed much more fluidly behind me.

I stepped out onto the ice, and my foot slipped from under me. I regained control and staggered over to the hand railing around the perimeter whilst I got my bearings.

"Are you alright?" Mrs C asked as she smoothly slid up next to me.

"Yeah, it's just been a while since I was on a blade."

Mrs C smiled. "It will come back to you."

We started to move around the rink together in synchronicity. Slow and steady at first, but with each stride my confidence returned, and we picked up pace. It was a lovely atmosphere as we chatted effortlessly. "We should get the elves one of those." I pointed to a penguin shaped object that one child was using to learn how to skate.

"Oo, good idea. They always said they wanted to visit the South Pole. We could take that to them instead." Mrs C winked at me, before we both burst out laughing.

Suddenly Mrs C veered out the way of three boys in a pack speeding towards us going the wrong way. As I spun round, a little girl got swept up in the chaos. Her toe-pick caught on the ice, and as if in slow motion she flung her arms out in front of her, did several mini stumbles, then landed on the ground with a thud. We both gasped and rushed towards her.

Mrs C crouched down in front of the girl, who looked close to tears. "Would you like some help to get up?"

The girl nodded, still looking in shock as we helped her get to her feet, but as I held her arm, she glanced at me and stared. Her mouth dropped open.

"That was a big bump." Mrs C smiled kindly as she crouched down next to her to check she was okay. "Are you going to be alright, soldier?"

The girl half smiled and nodded, but her eyes darted back to me again.

Her mother quickly appeared and wrapped her arms around her. "Are you alright, sweetheart?" she asked, before turning to us. "Thank you for your help." She whisked the girl away, but as they made their way through the crowd, the girl kept looking back at me.

I glanced across at Mrs C. We both knew the girl could sense who I was. "Cute, aren't they?"

"Very," Mrs C whispered. "Come on, let's show these young ones how to really skate."

She then grabbed my hand and twirled under it before we continued to skate seamlessly, as though we were one with the ice, weaving around people effortlessly.

"Did you used to be professionals?" a woman asked, when we finally came to a stop.

"No, we just live somewhere with a lot of ice," I chuckled, causing the woman to look curiously confused.

After a few more laps, Mrs C and I made our way off the ice, where I flopped down onto a bench. "Ice skating is exhausting," I said, fanning myself.

I leant down over my protruding belly to untie my shoelaces, then used one skate to anchor down the other to yank my foot out, but it wouldn't budge. I leant over again, feeling like I was trying to be a contortionist as I attempted to grab hold of my skate and wrestle it off, but I could barely reach it. "It's not coming off!" I cried.

Mrs C stared at me in wonder as she stood in front of me in her socks, with her skates hanging from her hand.

"Now I've gone and pulled something in my leg," I moaned.

"Oh, come here, before you end up in hospital." She inspected the skate and sighed. "You know, it might help to loosen your laces all the way down." She fumbled with the laces and tried to pinch them with her nails, but she was unsuccessful at loosening them. "Erm, I could do with a hook of some kind to help." She glanced around in search of something to use.

"Ah, something like this?" I hesitantly pulled a candy cane out from behind my ear.

"Yes, something like that." Mrs C rolled her eyes and shook her head in amusement. "How convenient!" She hooked the candy cane into the lace and pulled it upwards, so the lace loosened.

Eventually, I felt my foot being released, placed it onto solid ground and wriggled my toes, whilst Mrs C got to work on the other skate.

Moments later, Mrs C and I swapped our skates for shoes as it was time to move on.

10

After we went for a wander around more shops, including the M&M chocolate shop, where Mrs C took a photo of me posing exuberantly next to a yellow M&M statue, we made our way to Covent Garden.

"So, what's this show you've booked us in for this evening?" I asked as I squeezed through the crowded streets and struggled to keep next to Mrs C.

"It's a surprise," Mrs C said as we stopped at a kiosk and Mrs C ordered two hot chocolates.

"A surprise?" I muttered, wondering why she wouldn't tell me, but as I sipped my creamy drink and took in the atmosphere created by buskers and street entertainers, I couldn't help but feel excited.

After a while, Mrs C checked her watch. "Right, well, there's just enough time to grab a quick bite to eat and then it's theatre time."

We stopped at a burger bar, before Mrs C led the way. We passed several theatres with recognisable plays being performed, making me very intrigued by what she had in store for us. Finally, she stopped at a grand old theatre.

"Here we are." She pointed to the sign above it and instantly a huge grin spread across my face.

"You really are the best wife in the world," I gushed as I beamed in delight.

She grinned back at me. "Well, I know how much you love a pantomime, and this one is still playing. Ready?"

"Oh, I'm ready." I loved a pantomime as it always puts people in a good mood for Christmas.

We headed from the bustling lobby into the compact but ornate auditorium and located our seats in the centre of the stalls, where a gigantic, majestic chandelier hung precariously above us. The theatre wasn't full but there were enough adults and children to create the atmosphere it deserved.

"It's a good job the elves don't know about this," I whispered to Mrs C.

"Why's that?"

"Oh, you know how they get about anything to do with fairies. They wouldn't be impressed if they knew we were watching something based on a fairy tale."

Mrs C chuckled. "Yes, they do get irrational at times. We best not mention it."

I sank back into my narrow chair and adjusted myself. My arms were touching Mrs C and the woman next to me, making me squash my body together uncomfortably. It was going to be a long couple of hours; I thought.

The lights went down, and the stage lit up. Then the Dame of the show, in all their glamour, stepped onto the stage, dressed in a voluptuous, flamboyant, colourful gown, with voluminous hair. Their eyeshadow and lipstick were so vivid and deep in colour they looked like they were painted on with oil paints. The Dame welcomed us to the show whilst making a comical joke about us turning up late for the real panto before Christmas, which caused me to chuckle.

"I was too busy," I muttered, as the audience laughed.

Soon, the panto was in full swing. The villain and the Dame were at war and interacting hilariously. The prince and princess were kept needlessly apart, and the fairy was casting her chirpy spell on everyone. And suddenly I became consumed by it all. I joined in with the boos and the hisses. I shouted back as loud as I could, "Oh no, it isn't," when the prince on stage insisted. "Oh yes, it is." Then when it came to the slapstick run around of the Dame naively telling us that there wasn't possibly a rat in the princess' bedroom, I eagerly joined in with the crowd, shouting. "It's behind you," as the rat popped up behind the Dame's shoulder.

It was then that the comical timing and the daftness of the scene caused me to lean forward and out came my great, big, booming laugh. Another stint on stage made me slap my thigh and howl again. A few people in the rows in front of us craned their necks to look around at me.

"Oh," the Dame cried, interrupting the show and scanning the crowd. "It sounds like we have our own Santa in the house. What happened? Did you get lost on the London underground and not find your way home?"

The audience laughed before the Dame continued as normal.

I felt my cheeks turn red as Mrs C placed her hand on my leg. "How does he know it's me?" I whispered.

"It's the laugh," she whispered in reply.

"Ah," I placed my hand onto my mouth, and for the rest of the act, I tried my hardest not to laugh too euphorically.

At the interval, Mrs C and I exited to the lobby to get an ice cream. We were standing enjoying our small pots of soft-serve when I felt a hand on my shoulder.

"I don't believe it. It's Mr Success, isn't it?" I turned around to find Seamus Conway standing behind me. "We met in the Voydon restaurant."

"Ah, hello," I winced. "This is a coincidence."

Seamus grinned. "If I didn't know better, I would have thought I had a stalker." He laughed loudly. "By the way, was that you I heard in the audience? You've got a big pair of pipes on you. Confident outfit and a confident laugh. I've got to admire that. Come to think of it, perhaps you should apply for one of those Santa roles for next season. I'm sure I could hook you up if you ever need help, as I know some people in the industry. Just call me if you ever decide to. Anyway, I must dash. The old ball and chain is beckoning."

I turned to face Mrs C, who was chuckling silently. "Err. I should apply to represent myself..." I said in numb amazement. "Is my laugh really that noticeable?"

Mrs C composed herself. "Yes. You know it is. It's loud and unique, and everyone associates a laugh like yours with.... well... you. So, I guess Seamus was right. You would make a mighty fine Santa."

A loud bell suddenly interrupted us, signalling the end of the interval.

"Looks like we best get back to our seats, and I'll try to rein my laugh in,"

I grumbled.

"Don't be daft. I love your laugh, so embrace it. Now let's go and enjoy the second half."

We returned to our seats for the rest of the show, and I heeded Mrs C's instructions. I laughed loudly, not caring about the looks I was getting, and soon everyone else stopped caring too.

After the play, Mrs C and I headed back to our hotel, where I allowed her to take control of the key card. "I've had a lovely day today." She smiled as she slid the card in.

"Me too," but as she opened the door, both our smiles slipped from our faces.

The duvet remained crumpled up on the bed. The towels still lay on the floor in the bathroom and no one had refilled the tea and coffee sachets.

"Oh!" Mrs C frowned. "This isn't very good service. The hotel is supposed to make our room up every day."

She sighed as she dropped her bag on the floor and started to make the bed. "I was really looking forward to being waited on."

"This is not on!" I hated seeing her deflated. "You deserve better than this. You're on holiday and shouldn't be doing housework. I'm going to complain." I marched to the phone, picked it up and pressed the button for the receptionist.

"Reception. How may I help?" the male voice asked.

"Err, yes. Well, we've just returned to our room, 1225, and discovered that it hasn't been made up. As you can imagine, we're quite upset by it." I watched Mrs C plump the pillows, then wipe the coffee ring off my bedside table.

"1225, let me just check for you."

I could hear a couple of taps as the receptionist keyed something into his computer. "Yes, we have a record that you requested not to have your room made up."

"No, we did not! Why would we have done that?"

"It looks like you put the request through last night."

"That's a disgrace. We were out for a meal last night, so that's impossible. We didn't even go anywhere near reception."

"Sir, the request was made around 6pm via the app in your room." The receptionist sounded as though he was trying his best to keep his patience.

"App?" I said, confused, and shook my head. Then, as my eyes fell on the electronic pad on the wall, I stopped shaking my head. "Oh, I see. Right. That makes sense," and after the receptionist advised where we could collect more sachets of tea and coffee, I was quick to get off the phone.

Mrs C had her head slightly tilted to one side. "What did you do?"

"I, well... apparently, I turned off the 'make up room' sign last night."

She sighed. "We really need to get you up to speed with tech. You can make the stuff, but you always struggle to use it yourself."

"Things should have two buttons. Stop and start. Everything else is mind-boggling, but I am getting better. Anyway, I'm very sorry. I won't touch anything I don't understand ever again." I held my hands up in surrender.

Mrs C laughed. "I wouldn't go that far, but next time, just be more mindful. Now, let's go to sleep. It's been a long day."

I yawned loudly. "Yes, I'm beat."

11

The following day, Mrs C dug around in our case and threw me my pair of swimming trunks, which were red and green chequered, just like most things in my wardrobe.

"Let's go for a morning swim. I think we could both do with a leisurely day today."

We grabbed the white dressing gowns the hotel provided and headed to the lift, where I pressed the button to the basement for the spa. The spa receptionist made us sign in and provided us with towels before Mrs C and I went our separate ways to get changed.

I gave a stiff nod at the men in the changing room as I shuffled to a vacant area to swap my clothes for swimming trunks. Once I'd done a sort of jig to get into my trunks, and mastered the challenging code lock on the lockers, I went out to the pool area.

The basement ceiling was lit with hundreds of warm, small lights that looked like stars that reflected in the bright blue water in the pool. It wasn't exactly the aurora borealis, but it was beautiful. Surrounding the pool were some comfortable-looking loungers and to the side of the pool was a Jacuzzi bubbling away.

Mrs C hadn't emerged from the changing room yet, so I went over to one lounger and put my towel and dressing gown on it. Next to the pool was a table which had a dispenser for cucumber infused water, so I poured a glass and sipped it whilst I waited.

"Excuse me!" a woman's voice snarled. I could tell by the tone I was in trouble. "You're meant to turn the tap off when you've finished pouring yourself a drink, you know, so other people can have some."

I looked at the increasing puddle of water under the dispenser and saw that the water in the large glass jar had almost disappeared. The woman was glaring at me so intently that I peered at my glass, then at the dispenser, and contemplated whether I could get away with denying it was me. I gulped down the water I had in my mouth. "I apologise ma'am, I forgot to turn the tap off."

"You just forgot," she announced rather loudly in the tranquil setting. "Well, don't you worry. I'll make do without."

She then stomped off through the water on the floor and her foot skidded out from under her. She jerked her body to stop herself from falling, but the evil look she shot towards me told me I was also to blame for her slipping. I watched her, feeling intrigued by her reaction, and I couldn't help but think she was a deeply unhappy woman. I turned round to see Mrs C emerging from the changing room.

She smiled at me, and then frowned as she saw my expression. "You look a little flustered, are you alright?"

"I just had a run in with that angry lady," I said, pointing at her as the woman stood beside a lounger and yanked her dressing gown on. I then explained what had happened.

"That's a strange thing to get so worked up about," Mrs C said, gazing at her. "Like I always say, there's no point crying over spilt milk, or cucumber water in this case."

I chuckled. "Very true, and in my defence, I'm so used to all these public taps turning themselves off automatically. I didn't even think I had to switch it off."

"These things happen, so don't dwell on it. Now, come on, let's go for a swim."

I still felt distracted by the lady's outburst, as we walked over to the steps that led down to the pool.

Mrs C placed her feet into the water and a lazy smile came across her face as she quickened her step to get in. "It's a lovely temperature," and she plunged her body into the water.

I followed, and she was right; it wasn't too warm, or too cold. It was perfect.

"I'll race you," Mrs C whispered into my ear.

I chuckled. "You're on."

Mrs C and I then waited for a second as we met each other's eyes, before Mrs C shot off, swimming as fast as she could to the other side of the pool.

"Oh, no you don't!" I sprang into action and caused the surrounding water to sway vigorously, creating a wave. I chased after her as fast as I could, but Mrs C always beat me at this game, and I just managed to grab her foot as her fingers touched the edge of the pool.

"Looks like I won," she boasted.

I smiled back at her, but when I looked up, several people were watching us from their loungers in distaste. I subtly gestured to point them out to Mrs C, who shrugged and moved to stand with her shoulders underneath a waterfall.

"People just don't seem to know how to have fun." She closed her eyes to enjoy the massaging effects of the water on her shoulders.

I moved closer to her. "Except at Christmas," I whispered.

She laughed. "Everything's Christmas with you." She then pushed me under the waterfall, so the water splashed onto my face.

By the time I emerged from the waterfall, Mrs C was several feet away. "Cheat," I called as I chased after her, loudly slapping the water in my keenness to catch up, but this time I didn't get in reaching distance before she touched the side of the pool.

Suddenly, Mrs C's eyes lit up as two people climbed out the Jacuzzi. "Quick, let's go. The hot tub is free." She rushed over to the steps, climbed out and went over to the Jacuzzi, before she stepped into the steaming, bubbling water. "Ahhh," she settled down and closed her eyes.

I clambered in after her, slipping and struggling a little as I stepped down the enormous drop from the seat to the ground. "This is hot!" I joined Mrs C in closing my eyes and feeling the bubbles pound my skin in a satisfying way. I felt instantly relaxed and sat there enjoying the tranquillity and peacefulness for a while.

Eventually, Mrs C sighed, blissfully. "I wish we had one of these at home."

I smiled, appreciating the sight of Mrs C looking happy. "Well, the one way we would get our tub to bubble is to…" but I was interrupted when a man climbed into the Jacuzzi to join us. He settled into position, sprawling his arms out around the sides of the hot tub and closing his eyes. The atmosphere instantly changed, and I no longer felt as relaxed now the man's knee was pressing up against mine.

I nudged Mrs C, who opened her hazy eyes. I stared at her, my eyes wide, and gave a silent gesture towards the man, then towards the exit of the Jacuzzi.

Mrs C sighed. "Shall we go to the steam room?"

I nodded eagerly and got up, causing a gush of water to slosh back into the Jacuzzi.

We padded along towards the steam room, with my feet slapping loudly on the floor. Mrs C opened the door and a wall of heat hit me. I squinted into the darkness, but all I could see was the steam, which fogged my view. I blindly waded my way through and stumbled over to a place on the bench next to Mrs C, but as soon as I sat down, an unfortunate loud squelch sounded from beneath me, which made her giggle.

I narrowed my eyes, but knew she couldn't see me. "I'm not sure how long I'm going to cope in here. It's stifling. It's like going to Australia on Christmas Eve in a thick red suit," I muttered.

"Oh, is your suit still having optimal ambient temperature issues?"

"Only a touch, mainly in the hotter climates, but I can cope. I'll just moan about it when I get back."

"Well, I'm used to that. Christmas wouldn't be Christmas without some festive complaining."

Suddenly, the sound of someone clearing their throat came from the opposite corner of the steam room, taking me by surprise.

"Hello," Mrs C called out into the mist, and I could tell she was trying her hardest to stifle more giggles.

"Er, hello," a female voice said, sounding unsure how to respond.

"Sorry, we didn't realise someone else was in here," Mrs C replied.

There was then a prolonged silence, and I shifted on the seat, feeling slightly awkward, but once again, there was another loud, embarrassing squelch.

The woman cleared her throat again and then I heard her get up, open the door and leave.

I cringed. "That was close. I nearly started rambling about my Christmas Eve antics."

Mrs C burst out laughing. "I think we scared her."

"Do you think we said too much?"

"No, but even if we did, she can't do anything with that information. She'll just assume we're joking, or she misheard."

"That's true," I muttered. I let out a long, steady breath. I was hot, sweat was pouring out of me, and I kept getting big drips of hot water landing on my head.

"Is anyone else in the roooom?" Mrs C suddenly called out, as if summoning a supernatural being, but there was no answer. "It looks like we are, in fact, alone," she whispered. "So, tell me, what's your plan for the Sugarplum mission?"

I sat up, having nearly forgotten about it. "I don't really have a plan."

"Oh dear, so it's going to be a repeat of New York then."

"No, no. I think we learnt from that experience, so we won't make the same mistakes. But I don't know what the actual plan is."

"Well, we don't have long left to squeeze it in, so we best get cracking." She stood up and led the way to the door, with me eagerly shuffling behind her to get out of the stifling heat.

We made our way across to the changing rooms when my foot suddenly caught on something on the ground, and I lurched forward into Mrs C, who stopped me from falling any further.

"Watch it!" she cried, but when I looked at the floor, there was now a collapsed *'caution wet floor'* sign, right next to the cucumber water dispenser which someone had refilled.

"Come on. Let's get out of here," I grumbled. "Who needs a wet floor sign next to a swimming pool? The whole room is wet."

Mrs C and I went to get changed and headed back to our room to freshen up properly for the day.

12

"Right! Are you ready for this?" Mrs C was looking eager as she pulled her bag over her shoulder.

"Oh, I'm ready." A fizz of excitement went through me. I loved it when Mrs C was in one of her determined moods.

"Good because Sugarplum won't want just any old postbox. She will want one that is a purely iconic piece of London, so if we're going to do this, we may as well do it right."

I skipped after her as we left our hotel room. "True, but there are just so many to choose from."

"Yes. We need to go to where there is a lot of hustle and bustle. One that has the connection that Sugarplum craves."

I followed Mrs C to the tube station, and we packed ourselves into a compartment like a heaped platter of mince pies. We moved from tube line to tube line and eventually got off at Piccadilly Circus to join the swarms of people milling around.

"Come on!" Mrs C headed to a crowd of people gathered over a set of steps surrounding a statue of a winged man standing on one leg and aiming a bow towards the crowd below him.

I frowned in confusion. "What are we doing here?" I asked.

"Well, I always found that the statue of Eros reminds me of Cupid. The original Cupid," she said, noticing my delight at the mention of one of my reindeer. "So, I thought, what better place than to get something special for Sugarplum. Something she can love and treasure, as if it's been hit by Cupid's arrow."

"Sounds wonderful," I smiled, appreciating the gesture.

"Plus, this place is the pinnacle of London, and whatever postbox we choose will be a very busy, active one, which Sugarplum will love."

We set off scanning the area for a postbox until we found one, standing there, gleaming in its bright red paint.

"This one will be perfect," Mrs C said, giving it a pat.

"This one?" I asked, looking up and down the crowded street.

She nodded with a crafty glint in her eye.

"Aren't we conspicuous here?" I asked, my lips twitching into a smile.

"Yes, but that's part of the fun. Who knows who will catch us."

I laughed, before turning to inspect the postbox. I ran my hand over the top of it, still baffled as to why Sugarplum wanted it. "Sugarplum had better be grateful," I muttered. "I'm breaking a Christmas law for this."

"Yes, one that you have broken many times before when it suits you."

"I only use it when I deem it truly necessary."

"Well, an elf making a strange holiday gift request always falls into that category," she laughed.

I smiled as I took a deep breath and rubbed my hands together to create some friction.

On Christmas Eve, the charge from the North Pole gave me enough power to put time-warps in place over the entire world. It was a special night with heightened energy, but after Christmas Eve, I had some residual power left in me to distort the space-time continuum in small doses, allowing me to have a little dabble in it now and then. I held my hands out to my sides and felt the energy force come out of me. Everyone in the vicinity paused, as the time-warp expanded around them, creating what looked like an enormous bubble, enveloping everyone and creating a warbling shimmer. Seconds later, once the time-warp was in place, everyone started up again and continued acting as normal by entering shops and having conversations.

Mrs C leant over the postbox as if she was having a conversation with me, trying to look casual and inconspicuous. "You've got this," she encouraged, as two ladies turned their heads around to look at us.

I dug my hand into my pocket and extracted a little sachet of elf dust that

Sugarplum had given to me. Then, whilst glancing to see if anyone was watching, I sprinkled it around the base of the postbox. Suddenly, the cement securing the postbox in place bubbled and began to disintegrate. Steam and froth surfaced out of it, creating a scene that was impossible to hide.

One man took one glance at it, grabbed his partner, and yanked her to run away. "I think a sinkhole is forming," he yelled.

Amusingly, another man blamed it on the council making cost cuttings, who were now using alkaline soap-based products instead of cement. Most other people shot us a disgusted look, whilst swerving the area as far as possible.

"Oh no," Mrs C suddenly called, looking ahead.

"What?" I muttered, my senses already on high alert.

"I don't believe this. It's that woman."

I turned round to see the same lady from the spa, walking towards us, her face already sour as she trawled a small suitcase behind her.

"Yikes, this is bad timing." The surface continued to melt as the woman's steps grew closer.

Mrs C appeared to brace herself, just as the postbox fell to the side, directly in the woman's path.

"What the hell!" she cried. She jerked her angry face towards me, and it changed to recognition. "It's you!!"

I gave her a feeble smile, unsure how to respond. "It is me," I nodded.

She glared at the postbox at her feet, then at our guilty expressions. "So first you try to kill me by making me slip over because of your incompetence and now you're responsible for a postbox nearly falling on me."

"Err, it's not quite like that." I wondered if this woman exaggerated everything in her life for the worse.

Her eyes moved to the postbox, then back at me. "Are you stealing this?" she shouted in a shrill voice.

I shook my head vigorously, whilst surprisingly Mrs C said, "Yes." I could never work out what tactic she would use when we did these missions. "We're stealing this to take back to our elf in the North Pole."

I flinched, then turned back to the woman, waiting for her response.

"I know you're trying to be clever just because he looks a bit like Santa Claus, but it's pretty childish, and you aren't doing yourself any favours reminding me of that hideous time of year," she snarled, her lip curling in disgust as she looked at me.

I stared at her open-mouthed, ready to protest, and unable to fathom why she could hate Christmas and perhaps why she had taken such a deep aversion to me when she cut over me. "I'm going to report you to the police right now."

"Please go ahead." Mrs C smiled politely.

The woman yanked her suitcase away from us, which had caught on an uneven bit of pavement, and pulled out her phone from her bag and dialled a number. "Yes, police." She turned her back on us, so we couldn't quite hear what she was saying. "My name's Carol, and I have just found a man and a woman…"

Mrs C shook her head, as she quickly helped me pick the postbox up and insert it into the special case that we had brought for it, with the postbox shrinking as it went inside.

Carol then turned round, whilst shoving her phone back into her bag. "They are on their way," she announced, before she scanned the area. "Wait. What have you done with it? Where is it?"

Mrs C stared at Carol and I could tell she was feeling the same as me, that there was something intriguing about her. Mrs C then stepped towards her and smiled kindly. "Carol, isn't it?" she asked, as the woman nodded. "Can I ask you… are you alright?"

"Me?" Carol placed her hand on her chest. "I'm fine. I'm more than fine."

"Really? Because you don't seem fine." Mrs C inspected her angry, flushed face. "I definitely think something else is troubling you, something more than us taking a postbox."

Carol shoved her bag in frustration. "What, apart from the number of horrible things that have happened to me today?"

"What happened today?" Mrs C asked.

Carol glared at her. "Well, to start with, I had to wait about half an hour for a lift this morning just to get down from my hotel room. Then I dropped toast, butter side down, onto my blouse. I also had the misfortune of meeting you two, and I found out that my train back home has been cancelled."

I grimaced as if in pain. "I've had that happen to me before. It's awful! Butter doesn't come out easily."

Suddenly, out of the corner of my eye, I saw a blue flashing light. Carol also spotted it and stomped past us towards the police car that was pulling up to the curb a few metres away.

"Looks like our time is up," I frowned. "Let's finish off and get out of here."

I extracted a miniature replica of a postbox that Sugarplum had given to me from my pocket and bent down to position it into the gaping hole in the street. The postbox suddenly expanded, and the surrounding cement reformed under a layer of froth and bubbles.

Carol was now pointing at us to the police officer, looking baffled and horrified by the new postbox. I inspected it one last time, cocking my head to look at it and wondering if it was slightly crooked. I then shrugged before I closed and expanded my hands again, contracting time.

The surrounding bubble warbled before the shimmering light disappeared as if the bubble had burst. Within a blink of an eye, the woman was now back down the street, approaching us. The police car was nowhere in sight and the people we had scared off were walking past us, and carrying on as normal.

What had happened was now a fraction of a second in reality, and would only leave behind a fabric of a memory in people's minds, which could present itself in a dream, or give a sense of Déjà vu. Only Mrs C and I would have a complete memory of everything.

Mrs C breathed out. "That was a strange encounter."

I nodded, watching the woman walk past us, yanking at her suitcase and huffing at anyone who remotely got in her way. "It really was," I muttered, as a strange tingling sensation came over me. "I wonder what's wrong with her."

"Me too," Mrs C frowned.

"Anyway, I hope Sugarplum is pleased with our choice. At least this time, we weren't chased."

"Yeah, even with that woman, the British are certainly less fiery and loud than those New Yorkers. They really had a lot to say when we took that taxi," Mrs C recalled.

"Yes, and enticing the taxi driver out of it for a few minutes was an interesting feat."

Mrs C laughed. "Overall, I think this went rather smoothly."

I grinned. "Me too. Now, what's next on the agenda?"

13

Mrs C looked at her watch. "Well, seeing as it's our last day in London, I've planned the perfect way to say goodbye to the city."

"Does it involve food?" I asked, giving my belly a pat. "It's nearly lunchtime."

Mrs C sighed. "Don't worry, we'll make sure you're well fed. We can pick something up from a food truck nearby."

"Excellent. Lead the way. I'm intrigued."

We then pushed through more crowds and squeezed onto more tubes like an overstuffed turkey, and got off at Waterloo.

She linked her arm through mine, and we eventually stopped to look up at the enormous circular structure towering above us.

"The all-seeing London Eye," Mrs C whispered. "I couldn't think of anything more perfect than to overlook the city before we leave."

I studied her as she stared up at it, before she grabbed my hand. "Come on, let's go join the queue."

Eventually, it was our turn, and we entered one of the London Eye's capsules with a group of other people. The wheel cranked upwards, and Mrs C grinned and stood close to the glass to look out.

"We're moving," a girl shrieked, stating the obvious.

"How fast do you think this bad boy can go?" another man said to his group of male friends.

"I don't know, but I hope it speeds up," his mate replied, sounding bored.

As we got higher, Mrs C appeared more absorbed, and her smile dropped as the whole of London came into view.

"Look, there's that vegetable building," the same girl shouted.

"It's called the gherkin," her friend replied.

"Oo, can we go get a cheeseburger after this?" I asked, my stomach giving a low growl.

Mrs C didn't reply. "Wonderful, isn't it?" she muttered, as her eyes roamed across Big Ben, the Tower Bridge, Buckingham Palace, the Houses of Parliament, and Westminster Abbey. "You must always get to see such wonderful scenes on your travels." And there it was, the once in a decade where Mrs C became a little sad that she never joined me on Christmas Eve. Now and then, she would become melancholy and dwell on how much of an adventure I would go on every year when she always stayed at home.

"It's not really something I have time to notice, because I'm way too busy to enjoy it," I lied, hoping to cheer her up slightly.

She smiled sadly. "You should always try to enjoy scenery like this. It's a remarkable gift."

The wheel moved further upwards, so that we were right at the top, and as I stared straight down, it suddenly made me feel guilty that Mrs C couldn't ever share with me what I shared with Rudolph and the other reindeer on Christmas Eve.

Mrs C then pushed back her hair from her face and stood straighter. "Our holiday is nearly over," she sighed.

I nodded and wrapped my arm around her as the wheel slowly turned and we made our way back down to the ground.

As we stepped off the London Eye, Mrs C glanced back at it and forced a smile. "Well, the next time I see this will be when we watch London's New Year firework display on television." She then sighed. "I guess we should head back to the hotel to collect our belongings before we go to the train station. But first, we need to get the elves some holiday gifts."

"Well, we have Sugarplum's." I patted my coat pocket where the postbox was.

After a quick bite to eat, we wandered through the streets, past several shops displaying merchandise with the union jack on it, and 'I heart London'.

"This shop looks interesting," I said, as I scanned a shop window. There were teddy bears in cute little t-shirts with different slogans on, packs of cards with London landmarks, pens, notepads, keyrings, and biscuit tins in the shape of red phone boxes. "Maybe we could have just got Sugarplum this." I picked up a piggy bank in the shape of a postbox.

"That would be funny. I can imagine her little face, forcing a beaming smile to cover up her disappointment," Mrs C chuckled.

I was half tempted to get it for her as a joke, but there was enough anguish and heightened emotions in that workshop that I didn't think I should cause any more. We continued to explore and found the perfect gifts for the elves.

"I think they will love them," Mrs C said, as the cashier handed our items in a little paper bag.

"I guess that's everything, then."

"Yes, that's everything," Mrs C sighed.

We made our way back to the hotel to collect our case before we headed to the train station. We climbed onto the train, which was relatively quiet, and I squished myself opposite Mrs C at a table.

I watched her deflated expression and leant across the table to squeeze her hand. "I've had a lovely time."

Mrs C turned to me and smiled. "Me too. I don't really want it to end. But at least we have the memories. Particularly another Sugarplum operation to add to the collection…" She then suddenly sat bolt upright in her chair and slapped her hand to her mouth. "Oh no, I didn't even think!"

"Think about what?" I asked, frowning.

"We didn't check if there was any post in the postbox. We can't steal people's post. It's against the law."

"But stealing the actual postbox isn't?" I chuckled.

"There's no harm done with that because we replaced it, but who knows what's in that postbox," she whispered, so that other people on the train couldn't hear us.

"Sugarplum would be even more delighted if there were genuine letters inside it."

Mrs C glared at me and cocked her head to the side, causing my smile to drop.

"Yes, yes, I agree," I confirmed quickly. "We can't take those letters back to the North Pole. Despite how happy it would make the elves."

"So, what are we going to do?" She tapped her lip with her finger as she thought. "We could put the letters in another postbox somewhere."

Then an idea floated into my head, and as I studied Mrs C and her underlying sadness about our holiday ending, my idea spiralled into excitement.

"I have an idea!" I said, whilst wondering if it was perhaps too unorthodox.

"What is it?" she whispered.

I then glanced around me and spotted that the man at the next table to us was unnaturally still and had lowered his newspaper slightly, as if he was concentrating on listening to our conversation. I realised how much we'd disclosed, having mentioned the North Pole, the elves and us being a postbox thief.

I gave a subtle nod at the man. Mrs C clocked on and started talking about more mundane topics, like the new fabric softener she was trying out, which I pretended to be enthusiastic about. Soon the man grew bored, lifted his newspaper again and carried on reading.

A short time later, the train came to a stop, and we disembarked. We made our way across the deserted, crisp grassy field and returned to our plane, which was just as we left it.

"Right, let's check out what the damage is," I muttered, as I fished out the postbox, placed it on the ground and waited for it to expand to its regular size. I wrestled with it to tip the post out, and after a few moments of grunting and heaving, several envelopes and a thin parcel fell out. I then shook it around to get the very last item out, which was a gold, sparkly envelope.

I let out a low whistle at the number of letters.

"This is a busy box," Mrs C exclaimed. "So, what is this intriguing idea of yours?"

I hesitated. Then I felt peculiarly compelled to explain my idea. "Well, you know how you always wanted a taste of my antics on Christmas Eve." I shoved the postbox back into the bag and gathered up the envelopes and parcel. "How about you and I deliver these ourselves? It will be like a mini-Christmas Eve adventure."

I could see her eyes were alight with excitement. "I'm not sure about that, won't people see us?"

"I'll make sure no one remembers, and then you'll get to experience what it's like darting around the place and dropping by people's houses. Plus, we'll get these letters to the correct destination before the postal worker can deliver them. It will be a delightful surprise."

"Won't we be playing with the time-warp too much? You've already used it on this holiday, which isn't allowed, and breaks the Christmas Law."

"It's fine. It's more of a directive, which means I can bend the rules to suit me. Plus, I can strangely still feel a lot of residual energy inside of me from Christmas Eve."

Mrs C hesitated as her eyes flicked to the plane, to the envelopes, then rested on me. "Let's do it," she grinned. "I'll put the envelopes in geographical order."

"Ah yes, good idea." I packed the case into the plane and settled into the pilot seat.

Mrs C soon climbed in after me. "Right, fortunately they are all going somewhere in the UK, with the last place in Scotland, so we can make our way north."

Mrs C showed me an address in the London area, so I drove along the field, hoping the owner wouldn't notice the two wheel tracks we were leaving behind and we set off into the air.

Mid-flight I glanced across at Mrs C in her goggles, which clung to her face and slightly squashed it adorably, to find a small smile was playing on her lips as she clutched the letters tightly. It only confirmed that I'd had a great idea.

As we arrived at our first destination, I rubbed my hands together, then expanded my hands out again. I felt the energy from the North Pole coming out of me, and the wobbly shine of the time-warp appeared. I zipped the plane down onto a residential road and drove along to find the right house number. People stared out their windows, doors opened and people stepped out to investigate what they were seeing, but I didn't care. They wouldn't remember any of it in a few seconds.

"Here we go. Our first stop, number 25," I said.

Mrs C grinned, grabbed the first letter and raced out of the plane. She hurried across to the door, slipped the letter through the letterbox before she spun on her heel and raced back to the plane. We flew off, and the time-warp contracted back into place, making everyone unable to remember. We continued on our mission, and each time we landed, Mrs C would race down the drive to post the letter before skipping and frolicking back. She wasn't fast enough to help me on Christmas Eve, but today she was a great Mrs Santa.

"This is so much fun," Mrs C called, as she darted past a man who was staring at her, and shouting, "You can't fly a plane onto this street. Who do you think you are?"

We chuckled as we flew off again and her glowing face certainly put me in the Christmas mood. So, when she hurried across to each house, I couldn't help but happily sit and twiddle my thumbs whilst whistling the tune to 'We Wish You a Merry Christmas,' before moving onto 'Jingle Bells'.

Before we knew it, we had flown to Oxford, Birmingham, Nottingham, Manchester, Liverpool and Newcastle.

"Why haven't we done this before?" Mrs C gushed as we flew over the scenic countryside of England. "It's so beautiful and so green compared to where we live. The only green we see is on the elves' costumes and our Christmas tree."

We headed to Edinburgh, and I returned to singing again, but when we arrived at our destination I cut off as I noticed the time-warp wobble more than normal. "Oh no, that's not good."

"What isn't?" Mrs C muttered as she gazed down at the last couple of letters on her lap.

"The time-warp is wearing out. I guess I don't have enough energy from the North Pole to get us through the entire trip."

Mrs C raced out to post the letter. "At least we only have one more letter to deliver."

"That's a good thing, as we might need to do this one without the time-warp." We took off into the air. "So, where are we going?" I asked, as we continued to aim north.

14

Mrs C read out the address of a village in Scotland, when something caught my eye. There was a slight shimmer on the envelope.

"Can I look at that?" I snatched the letter off her and ran my thumb over the envelope. Frowning, I tilted it one way, then the other, and noticed a familiar elf charm shine reflecting off it. I instantly suspected Pepper had something to do with it, but I wasn't sure why she would have tampered with it and what it meant. "Hmm, that's odd, but I guess it looks like we're off to Plockton to deliver a letter to David Russell," I murmured, handing it back to Mrs C, who was watching me.

"Why do you look so startled by a letter?" Mrs C asked.

"We'll have to find out. But we no longer have the protection of the time-warp," I said, as the shimmering warble completely disappeared.

We arrived above Plockton, where we flew over a mountain range and landed on a grassy bank beside the loch, where tiny boats dotted the water. Fortunately, landing a two-seater plane in the area didn't seem too far-fetched for the people who saw us, and so they continued walking past us.

Mrs C scanned the area whilst breathing in the fresh Scottish air. "Wow, this place is so stunning and peaceful." She marvelled at the scenery, as we set off toward David's house. "I really enjoyed today, having a whistle-stop tour of all those places. It's been a fun adventure."

"I'm glad you enjoyed it. You'd make a mighty fine assistant on Christmas Eve, if ever I was to have one."

Mrs C smiled. "Thank you. I've certainly had a wonderful taste of it. Now, here we are, our very last house." We stopped at a small wooden gate in front of a whitewashed quaint little building. "Oh, this house looks idyllic," she gushed.

"Yes, it does." I inspected the place. It was familiar, just like all houses were, but there was something niggling me about it, as if there was some distant special memory related to it.

Neither Mrs C nor I felt inclined to race across to the door, shove the letter into the letter box and race away, unseen. Instead, a calming sensation came over me. Mrs C linked her arm through mine as we walked down the cobbled path to the front door.

Then, before Mrs C reached the letter box, the door burst open and my eyes lowered onto a young girl. Her hair was curled in blonde ringlets, her eyes were wide, and her face glowed as she stared at me.

"Santa!" she cried. "You came!"

My mind immediately fumbled into denial mode, but I couldn't speak.

"Pip, I told you not to open the door by yourself. Who are you talking to?" a man's voice asked.

"It's Santa!" She looked like she was in shock.

"What do you mean?" The man pulled the door open and raised his eyebrows in surprise. "Oh, you certainly do share a resemblance. How can we help you?"

His eyes were sad and tired, and his rugged stubble was unkempt and overgrown. As I studied his withdrawn expression, words stuck in my throat whilst a swell of emotion rose inside of me that I couldn't quite account for.

Mrs C cleared her throat. "We're sorry to disturb you, but we came to deliver a letter to a David Russell. I assume that must be you."

David frowned. He was wearing a thick, oversized woolly cardigan over a t-shirt, which he wrapped tighter around himself. "Oh, so do you work for the postal service then?" he asked, his eyes roaming over us, no doubt wondering why we weren't in the correct uniform.

I couldn't keep my eyes off Pip, who was staring at me with a strange piercing look, as if she was expecting something from me. I tried to rack my brains for information on her, but by the time I get to Scotland, my memories become blurry from all the whisky and sherry I drink.

"Yes, we do," Mrs C confirmed. "There was a slight mix-up, so we wanted to make sure the letter landed with you directly."

David smiled tightly at Mrs C, then inspected the envelope and peeked inside. His face instantly went pale. "Another rejection," he muttered to himself, and it was as if the contents of that envelope had instantly aged him more. "Well, thank you for going out of your way to deliver the letter. Have a good day." He stepped back to close the door, but Pip didn't move. "Pip, come on," he said.

Pip shook her head. "But Daddy, it's Santa. Have you come to deliver my Christmas wish?"

David sighed. "Sweetheart, it's not Santa. It's just a postal worker."

"No Daddy, it is him. I just know it is."

She then burst out of the house and ran onto the cobbled path. "Is Rudolph here?" she asked, standing on her tiptoes and craning her neck to look up at the roof.

"No, Rudolph is back in the North Pole." My stomach yearned at the mention of his name, but then I slammed my hand to my lips and cleared my throat. "I mean, I imagine that's where he is, as I'm sure he'll be resting up after a long Christmas Eve."

Pip grinned, as if I had confirmed all her suspicions. "Do you want to come inside? I have so many questions for you."

"Pip, stop it, and stop bothering these…. postal workers," David snapped, exasperated. "It's just a man who looks similar to Santa. Come back inside now, it's too cold to go racing out the house."

"Yes, well, we need to get going as well," I said, feeling uncomfortable.

"No, don't go. You haven't helped me with my Christmas wish."

I scratched my head. There was something about this house that was affecting me deeply.

David shook his head. "Pip," he warned, before he looked at us. "Err, thank you for delivering my letter and sorry about all this. Now, say goodbye, Pip."

Pip looked deflated. "Bye Santa," she mumbled. Then she gasped, and her face brightened. "I'll see you soon, though. My Dad promised we would go spend a few days with you in the North Pole this year." Her grin was spreading across her face.

David sighed and ran a hand through his hair. "Pip, I didn't exactly say that. I said we might go to Lapland, but please don't get your hopes up." He looked tired and fraught as he folded his envelope in half.

"But Daddy, you said, after what happened this Christmas, we would go."

David glanced at us in embarrassment, and I suddenly felt like we were intruding. "Let's talk about this inside. Goodbye!" He gave us a curt nod as he closed the door.

I glanced at Mrs C, who raised an eyebrow. "Well, that was a strange interaction," she said as we made our way back to the plane. "Do you know what Pip was talking about? Was there something you missed off her Christmas list?"

I shook my head. "The elves always ensure I have all the right toys that the children ask for. Of course, we don't always give them everything they want, but it seems like I missed something important for the girl and I can't remember what it could be." I drummed my thumbs against the control wheel and frowned. "I remember coming to the house, and delivering a karaoke machine, some colourful hair extensions, and other presents, but I don't think Pepper had given me instructions to give her any form of a special gift. I also remember a stale mince pie, drinking some whisky and picking up a thank-you letter…." Then suddenly something struck me. Pieces began slotting together, and it suddenly occurred to me just what Pepper had done.

Mrs C was staring at me. "Is everything alright?" she asked.

"Huh?" I muttered, distracted. "Yeah, everything is fine. I think Pepper might have meddled with us, and I think I know why."

Mrs C studied me in confusion before I shook myself.

"Right. Let's head home. It feels like we've been away for ages." I smiled as I grew excited about seeing my pal again.

"Indeed." Mrs C turned her head to stare out the window at the scenery as we took off into the air.

15

We arrived back at the North Pole in seconds, having shot through a vortex, where I guided the plane to the hangar and pulled it up next to my sleigh, now content and tucked up. We crossed the snow, carrying the tiny case we took with us, entered the house and stomped off the snow from our boots.

Mrs C paused and looked around. "It feels extremely quiet, doesn't it?"

"Compared to London, definitely." I walked into the kitchen, where I found a packet of ginger biscuits and shoved some into my mouth. When I turned round, Mrs C was watching me. Her eyes rested on my hand holding the packet and she waited, giving me a pressing look. "Sorry. Did you want one?" I asked, holding the packet out to her.

She glared at me. "You've been back two seconds and you're already back into old habits."

I could see she was emotional and bothered about something, and I knew it wasn't about the biscuits. I stepped closer to her. "What is it?" I asked, holding out the packet to her.

She then sighed, her shoulders dropped, and she shoved her hand into the packet to pull out a biscuit for herself. "It's nothing. I'm just a little sad that our holiday is over and I'm back to the same old routine. Don't get me wrong, I love my routine. I love being home. It just suddenly feels emptier and lonelier than before."

"I understand how you feel, so how about I run you a bath and you can pretend you're back at the hotel in the hot tub?"

She smiled as she knocked crumbs off my belly. "That would be lovely."

I gave her a kiss at the temple and went upstairs where I twisted the hot tap on the bath, and then searched through Mrs C's bottles of shampoos, conditioners, and body lotions until I found a bottle of bubble bath. I poured a splash in, and the lovely smell of orange and cinnamon wafted up to me as a disappointing handful of bubbles lathered up.

"That can't be right," I grumbled as I poured in another glug and waited expectantly, but I remained dissatisfied with the pathetic volume of bubbles, so after a moment's thought, I tipped the entire bottle in. "It's done," I shouted out the bathroom door. "Your spa awaits."

Mrs C opened the door as I grinned at her and presented her bath, which now had bubbles dripping over the edge.

"Oh, my goodness!" she exclaimed, her eyes widening in surprise.

"Do you like it? I wanted it to be lovely for you," I said, feeling chuffed.

"How much bubble bath did you put in?" she asked, approaching the tub.

"The whole bottle, which reminds me, you might need to get more."

She smiled and beckoned me over to the bath. "Let me show you where the bubbles normally come up to."

My smile dropped as I stepped closer.

"I would say for a normal bubble bath, the foam comes to about…" but before she finished, she wafted a load of bubbles at me as she laughed. The bubbles smothered me, and I spluttered and wiped my face before I focused on Mrs C's innocent expression and coy smile.

"Oh right. I guess I better remove half of them then." Determined for revenge, I wafted twice as much right back at her.

She laughed even louder. She then inspected her reflection in the mirror.

"I think this look suits me." She turned back to face me to reveal the white foam stuck to her chin and around her mouth. "I could pass as you this coming Christmas, and I bet I could do a better job."

I stepped closer to her. "I'm afraid you won't stand a chance of doing that."

Mrs C placed her fist on her hip. "And why's that?"

"Because you're far too cute to pass as me." I wiped some of the foam from her fake beard onto her nose and she giggled. "Now, have your bath before the water goes cold. I'm going to check in on everyone."

She nodded and grinned. "Enjoy yourself." She lit a candle to put on the shelf next to the bath. "And take your time. I need to do some serious relaxing and unwinding for as long as possible."

I headed out to the shed and pulled the door to one side. Instantly I heard a chaotic clatter of hooves and a big red shiny nose came racing towards me.

"Aye up pal. Have you missed me?" I asked. The other reindeer stayed behind Rudolph. They all knew we needed a moment.

Rudolph stomped his foot and knocked his antlers against the wooden pen in eagerness.

"I know lad, I've missed you too." I gave him a scratch on his head beside his antler. "Have the elves been looking after you alright?"

Rudolph lifted his head, and I noticed his eyes were bloodshot. I frowned in concern and stepped closer to give him a more thorough inspection when my foot connected with something, which made a clink. "What the…" I rummaged through the straw to find an empty bottle of Rudolph's favourite beer. "I take it the elves have been giving you your treat," I muttered, taking it over to the bin in the corner only to find more empty beer bottles. Way more than there should be. I allowed Rudolph one bottle a week if I was feeling generous, which was practically all the time. I went back to the pen and studied the other reindeer. Some of their tongues were hanging out, and they appeared to be swaying as they walked. "Are you all drunk?" I asked, staring at them in horror.

Blitzen then shouldered Donner, as he stumbled to the side to move past her, and Vixen let out a snort, followed by the noise of a raspberry.

I grabbed the hosepipe at the side and refilled their water trough. "All of you, drink up, now!" I then marched from the pen and stomped my way over to the workshop.

16

I slammed the door open to find the elves hard at work. Piles of new teddies, dolls, board games and other standard toys now cluttered the floor beside each workstation, ready to be stored away.

Sugarplum wasn't in the room, but the others were all in deep concentration, and my anger dissipated slightly as I watched their hands move faster than my eyes could keep up with.

Bushy then glanced across at me, and her eyes widened. "Yay, you're home," she cried, throwing a doll and its head onto her workbench and skipping over to me.

Pepper gasped when she saw me, her eyes wide, before she shuffled over to me, biting her lip.

I glanced at her suspiciously before recalling exactly why I had stormed into the workshop.

"Santa, I'm so pleased you're back." Shinny grinned as he raced across to me, but his steps slowed, and with each step, his smile morphed into confusion and horror as he saw my serious expression.

"Everyone, gather round," I snapped, causing Alabaster to sigh and place his electronic toy robot on the bench.

I stared at them as Shinny stepped closer to Pepper, so that his little arm pressed against hers.

"I'm very disappointed," I announced.

Alabaster sighed. "Is there another issue with the toys?"

"No, I've just been to see Rudolph and the others, and they are all absolutely intoxicated!"

"What? How?" Wunorse exclaimed, looking around at the other elves, who looked equally shocked.

"Well, I was hoping you could tell me." I folded my arms and glared at them.

The elves started looking around at each other when Bushy slowly raised her hand. "It's my fault," she admitted, her ears bright red.

"I went to visit the reindeer and found them all looking very sad. They were all missing you so much that I thought I'd cheer them up. I only gave them a couple. I didn't know they would get intoxicated by them."

"Well, they definitely had more than a couple," I snapped, causing Shinny to give out a little whimper.

"Oh no," he said, placing his little hands over his face. "I did the same. I... I had heard they like it, so when I visited them, they were all looking at me and licking their lips, so I just gave it to them." His eyes were shining through his open fingers. "I thought it was what I was supposed to do." He looked at Bushy, then Pepper, for reassurance.

"They were probably just dehydrated from the previous lot," I huffed.

"You two were not supposed to look after the reindeer," Alabaster said, shaking his head. "That job was left solely in the hands of..."

"Me," Wunorse declared at the same time as Alabaster.

They turned to stare at each other. "What? I'm in charge, so of course they are my responsibility," Alabaster claimed.

"You're in charge of running the workshop, which means second in charge looks after the reindeer." Wunorse jabbed a finger at his own chest.

I placed my fists on my hips. "So, you're telling me, both of you gave them their allowance, on top of Bushy and Shinny. How did you not realise?"

"I don't know, sir," Alabaster answered. "I was in a hurry, as I was too busy trying to work out how to fix things around here and get ahead."

"Me too and I had to rush before Alabaster shouted at me," Wunorse chimed in, causing Alabaster to shoot him a glare.

Wunorse adjusted his hat. "Er, are you going to tell Mrs C what's happened?" he asked, his cheeks going bright red at the thought.

I was about to answer when Sugarplum burst through a side door. "Santa, you're back," she cried, clapping her hands together. Her face was glowing at the sight of me.

"Hello Sugarplum," I greeted. "Well, at least you didn't contribute to this reindeer shambles."

"What shambles?" she asked.

"Apparently, everyone has been doing the same job of looking after them, so at least you haven't added fuel to the fire."

Sugarplum glanced around at the others, looking baffled. "I'm not sure what you mean, but I assure you I have taken excellent care of Rudolph and the others whilst you have been away. Sadly, they were crying over you leaving them, which was really difficult to witness, so I hope you don't mind; I gave them a bit extra of their treat to cheer them up." She looked so innocent and proud of herself that the rage I was feeling was suddenly mixed with a flutter of hilarity.

My stomach gave a wobbly judder as I began to laugh. "Reindeer don't cry."

"They do," she insisted. "Their eyes were all bloodshot. They must have been crying."

"No, they don't, but in all seriousness, what is going on with you all? You've all been living with each other and working together for centuries, and now it's like you've forgotten the basics of simple communication." I shook my head in despair.

"What's going on?" Sugarplum asked, frowning as she looked around at the others, who looked ashamed. After explaining the situation, Sugarplum gasped and placed her little hands over her mouth. "Oh, my goodness. Are they alright?"

"They might have sore heads tomorrow, but I'm sure they will be fine," I sighed. "But next time, sort yourselves out."

"Yes, next time I will sort it out." Alabaster scowled at the others as everyone gave a small feeble nod, except Pepper, who seemed to be silently analysing everyone.

"Now, let's put this behind us, and move on," I said.

"How was your trip?" Sugarplum asked, clutching her hands together in front of her and rocking back and forth on the balls of her feet. She was clearly nervous and eager to find out if I had delivered on my promise, but I wasn't going to let her know that easily.

"It was excellent. London is a marvellous city. We had amazing food, did some sightseeing, watched a show and I brought you all a present." I reached into my pocket, pulled out the paper bag, and handed a gift to each elf.

Shinny accepted his gift with his mouth hanging open in awe and his expression full of delight. "Wow," he grinned. "It's wonderful. I love my London fridge magnet so much." He held it out in front of him and ran his fingers over the raised contours.

"Me too." Bushy held hers up next to Shinny's to compare.

"Wow, that's that London eyeball, and a red bus," Shinny said, pointing at Bushy's magnet.

"It's actually the London Eye, not eyeball," I corrected.

"I'm not sure what mine is." Shinny was rotating it, looking puzzled.

"Yours is Westminster Abbey and the London Bridge," Bushy said, causing Shinny to grin even wider.

"It looks like a wonderful place." Shinny clutched his magnet to his chest and beamed at me. "Thank you."

"You're very welcome." I felt chuffed by their eager reactions. All the elves seemed to love them and even Alabaster, who had placed his on the workbench next to him, kept glancing at it and running his fingers over it.

Sugarplum stepped forward, biting her lip and rocked forward on the balls of her feet. "Sir, did you err... bring anything else back?"

"Like what?" I asked innocently.

"Like a... Like a... postbox?" I could see she had her fingers crossed on both hands in hope.

"Oh yes, you mean this?" I opened the bag, dipped my hand in and pulled out the postbox between my two fingers and held it in the palm of my hand towards her.

Sugarplum suddenly jumped up and down and let out an excited squeal.

"Thank you, thank you, thank you," she gushed.

I then placed it on the floor as it expanded back to its usual size, causing Sugarplum's mouth to fall open. "It's beautiful! So many children have walked up to one of these, clutching their letters to us, before they part with them. This is so magical." She rubbed her cheek onto the side, making me hope it was clean enough. "Did you have any issues getting it?" she asked.

I darted a look at Pepper, who seemed overly fixated on her fridge magnet so she didn't have to look at me. "Nothing we couldn't handle."

"That's good," Sugarplum muttered, completely distracted by inspecting each millimetre of the postbox.

Alabaster shook his head. "I really don't understand why you want that."

Sugarplum stood straighter. "It makes me feel connected to the children."

Alabaster scoffed. "So, you want a scuffed-up lump of red metal from a faraway country to feel connected to the children? Maybe you should try connecting with your job instead and we'd be further along right now."

Sugarplum's ears and face went bright red. "Well, I think we all need to connect with them more, to help us recognise why we do what we do every year, especially you." She heaved the large postbox across her shoulder, and despite it being three times her height, she stomped off out the door, carrying it easily.

Alabaster rolled his eyes. "We all just need to get on with our jobs and stop wasting time on stupid irrelevant items."

The tension was clear. I turned to Pepper as the other elves returned to their workbenches. "I see things haven't improved between all of you since I left."

She shook her head. "No. Alabaster has been incredibly snappy, and he seems to be getting worse. It's like he's lost all his Christmas spirit and can only think about the number of toys we have created, which isn't a good thing because we're behind."

"How behind?" I asked.

"We're tracking ten percent less per day than we should be. Everyone is tired and tense."

"Well, this can't go on for much longer." I shuddered as I glanced up at our large countdown calendar which was projected onto the ceiling in gold glowing numbers. Every day that number was decreasing as we got closer to Christmas Eve.

17

Pepper took a deep breath and faced me. "I'm glad you had a pleasant holiday, though. Did my guidance dust keep you on the correct path?"

"It's funny you should say that, because we accidentally landed in France, not England, so that dust must be defective."

Pepper's eyes widened in alarm. "Oh my, so you actually did need navigation to England," then she placed her hand to her lips. "I mean, how strange. I'll have to look into that."

"Other than that, we had a very well-orchestrated holiday." I narrowed my eyes at her in suspicion.

"Orchestrated?" she asked, as innocently as possible.

"Yes, well, it's funny now I come to think of it. That postbox sent us on an intriguing adventure. After we stole it, we then had to deliver all the letters around the UK, which gave Mrs C a much-needed adventure."

Pepper smiled meekly. "Excellent, I'm so pleased Mrs C had some fun. Wunorse is always saying she deserves to have the world. Did you stop off anywhere nice?"

"Yes, as it happens. The last envelope, which seemed to have a very peculiar sparkle to it, sent us all the way to Plockton in Scotland, where we delivered it to a man called David and coincidentally also met his daughter, Pip." I studied her reaction as she wrung her hands together.

"Oh, how interesting," she responded, her eyes curious, but she was trying her hardest not to show it.

"Yes, it was a rather interesting encounter. The girl was particularly excited to see me, but there was also a lot of sadness underlying them both."

Pepper's eyes suddenly glistened, and she turned her face away from me.

"Oh, I wonder why?" she said, as she rubbed her eyes.

"Do you?" I asked. "Or do you know exactly why?"

Pepper faced me, her eyes now brimming with unshed tears, and she twisted her body so the other elves wouldn't see her. "I… I don't know what you mean."

My resolve softened, and I sighed. "It took me a while to figure out what was niggling me about them, and that house, but then it clicked. It was all to do with Pip's mother, David's wife."

"Holly," Pepper confirmed.

I nodded. "Yes, Holly. She used to write thank-you letters, didn't she?"

Pepper swallowed and slowly nodded, her little hand reaching to press against the pocket of her jacket. "The most beautiful letters I've ever read," she whispered. "She would always remember, every year, to write to us, thanking you, the reindeer and us elves, for a fabulous Christmas. She always referred to it as a magical time that she treasured and she wrote about how much she loved spending it with her wonderful daughter and husband."

Pepper took a deep, steadying breath and sniffed so loud it gurgled and made me jump.

"I've never read anything that was so full of love and when she got sick, she would reassert her gratitude to us," Pepper sniffed between gulps of disbelief, whilst pointing at herself. "That we had made her loved ones happy and how she hoped we always would, and that the lights of Christmas would never fade, even when she was gone."

My stomach jolted at the story, and it bothered me seeing Pepper's emotional, distressed face. Normally she was so happy, and now she was blubbering in front of me. I felt inclined to tap her on the head.

"It's a shame, as I can only vaguely remember these letters now, but I remember them standing out and packing a punch. Do you still have them?" I asked, wanting to understand what had got her so hooked on Holly and her family.

Pepper shot her head up and placed her hand protectively against her pocket again.

"Can I read them?" I asked.

"Erm… Okay…" Pepper dabbed her eyes and pulled out a fistful of envelopes from her pocket.

"Wow, these look like they've been read a thousand times." I carefully unfolded the delicate paper.

Pepper suddenly began calculating on her fingers. "My favourite one I've read six thousand, two hundred times, and I could read it another million more."

I raised an eyebrow in surprise, not knowing that someone could captivate my elves so intently. I scanned my eyes over each letter, which were all so lovely and kind about everything we do. A gigantic lump then formed in my throat as the last few were so heartfelt and emotional as Holly made her wishes known. She wanted nothing more than for her family to continue the festive joy and to keep living a happy, fulfilling life when she was gone.

"It's always sad when a family loses a close relative, particularly so young," I said, struggling to swallow. "But why did you guide me and Mrs C there?" I asked, folding the letters back up.

Pepper shrugged and slurped back her snotty nose. "Well, a couple of months ago, I wanted to check on Holly's family, to see how they were doing, so I started monitoring Pip's thoughts over the Christmas period. She was so sad and lost. But that brave girl did everything she could to ignore the sadness, and focus on what made her happy, which was Christmas because she associated it with her mother." Pepper then burst out blubbering, failing to hold back her emotions any longer. "She desperately wanted to experience a Christmas the way her mum used to make them, which was full of light, love, fun, and joy, so she could remember her and the time of year she loved the most. Only her dad isn't coping very well without Holly, and he doesn't know how to measure up or handle the situation."

I shoved the letters into my pocket as I rummaged around for a handkerchief for her. Eventually, I found one underneath a fistful of sweet wrappers and handed it to her. She gratefully took it and blew her nose loudly into it.

"That's a sad story," I said, before I looked at her suspiciously. "You know, I was trying so hard to recall that girl's special Christmas wish and it never quite came to me, which is odd considering I can remember everyone."

Pepper laughed awkwardly. "Well Santa, you know what you get like by the time you get to Scotland."

"Hey, I'm not that bad. My brain becomes a bit blurry, but I don't forget kids' Christmas wishes, as long as someone gives me the correct information."

Pepper looked at me. "Well, her Christmas wish was to meet Santa in the North Pole, so she could ask you lots of questions and confirm the stories her mother told her. Plus, she wants her dad to be happy again because he used to make her giggle so much." The tears started flowing again, and this time, when she blew her nose, it sounded like a trumpet.

I nodded thoughtfully, "I see. So, let me get this straight. You kept this from me because you wanted me to meet her accidentally. You then used that so-called guidance dust of yours to set it up so that my trip to London would lead me to her. Is that correct?"

Pepper bit her fingers, before she nodded sheepishly. "Yes, I wanted you to give her the gift of your presence. Children can feel it when they truly meet you." She wrapped her arms around herself.

"I see. Well, that's very crafty, and I'm pretty certain she knew who I was. She's a very intriguing girl, but unfortunately, she wasn't able to ask me questions, nor visit me in the North Pole." I gave Pepper a curious glare as David's sad expression came back to haunt me.

"Well, that can't happen because it would break the Christmas Law, wouldn't it?" Pepper asked, raising her eyebrows with a hopeful expression.

"Yes, it would! Plenty of children request personal Christmas wishes, but we can't let ourselves get too emotionally attached. It is what it is."

Pepper nodded and looked down at her feet as she shuffled from left and right. She looked up at me. "I guess it will never happen then," she whispered.

I opened my mouth to reply, when suddenly Sugarplum shouted at

Alabaster. "Stop glaring at me. If I'm not doing it right, do it yourself."

"Maybe I should," Alabaster grumbled. "If I need anything done right, I always have to do it myself." He then glanced across at us, clearly annoyed that Pepper had spent so long talking to me instead of working.

Pepper looked deflated. "I best get back to work before steam comes out of Alabaster's ears or Sugarplum throws paint at him." She wandered off looking tired and mentally exhausted, and all I could think about was that something needed to change.

"Hang on," I called to everyone, causing Pepper to spin around in hope. "I think we all need a catch up at the planning board to see what new toy ideas you have come up with since I was gone," I said, as Pepper's shoulders slumped again.

Moments later, the elves and I formed a group around the planning board, where I eagerly awaited an update. "So, what's new?" I asked.

Alabaster cleared his throat. "Well, sir, I'll be honest. We've been focusing on the basic toys for now, as we often find that creativity at this time of year takes a complete nosedive. Children are too busy playing with their new toys that they don't think about anything else, so getting ideas from their thoughts hasn't been very successful."

"Okay, so how are you getting on with the basic toys? I thought you were running behind."

Alabaster looked suddenly stunned before he shot Pepper an accusatory look. "Well, yes, just a little."

"That's not great, and in all the time I was away, you also didn't come up with anything new."

Wunorse fidgeted. "We did. It's just nothing that seems to be mind blowing,"

"Well, why don't you fill me in? What's that idea?" I asked, spotting a small diagram on the board that hadn't been there before.

"It's...It's..." Wunorse pulled on his green collar. "It's a remote-controlled doll that can rotate its head all the way around at the touch of a button."

"What? Is it an evil doll?"

"No, it's a normal doll," Wunorse said, darting an uncomfortable look at Shinny.

"Then why would we make a doll that does that?"

Wunorse shrugged. "Errm… so it can look at anyone and anything in the room."

"And that's not creepy?" I asked, a shiver going through me at the thought.

"Well, it was something one child really liked the idea of."

"Hmm, I'm not sure about that. What's that idea?" I asked, pointing at the wall.

"Oh, that's a device that you speak into and when you replay it, you can make it sound however you want." Wunorse looked happy about the idea.

"In what way?" I asked.

"Well, you could sound male or female. You can have any accent you choose across the world, and you can sound like any celebrity you want," Wunorse confirmed.

"Even Elvis?" I asked, wiggling my hips from side-to-side, attempting to do his signature move, but I halted when I noticed the elves staring at me.

"Are you alright?" Wunorse asked.

"Yes, carry on," I muttered, miffed that my moves weren't a glaringly obvious impression.

"Okay." Wunorse looked somewhat concerned for me. "I believe it will do Elvis as well, although I am unsure many children these days would ask to replicate Elvis."

"And what a sad thought that is. But I must admit, this sounds like a good gadget. Well done."

Wunorse let out a sigh of relief.

"Anything else?" I asked.

Wunorse continued to work through the handful of toy ideas they had, which included a rather questionable pregnant mermaid, a toy vet practice that was half a cafe selling chips and chocolate sauce that could also double up as medicine for the animals, and a tree that transformed into a pumpkin.

"Hmm, children come up with crazy stuff, don't they? I guess some of these look semi-decent, which we could potentially use as filler presents. Others I'm not sure about. Either way, it's clear we don't have anything that's going to take the world by storm. We need to come up with something incredible. Something that's new and fresh, and nothing to do with this witchcraft and wizardry that the world has gone crazy over."

"Nothing we have put out recently has been as popular as that," Bushy said.

I looked away and felt a determination come over me. We needed to do something to make this the best year possible and right now we were further away from it than I had seen in a long time.

I glanced at Pepper, who met my eye as if she was watching me intently.

"Well, keep me updated on any progress," I murmured, feeling the weight of the countdown calendar above me, before I made my way to the exit.

I needed some space and time to think about what we could do to make sure Christmas was just as magical as it ever was.

18

That night I lay there in the dark wondering what to do about the elves, before my thoughts moved back onto Pip and her father. They were playing on my mind and in no time; it felt like I had Pepper, Pip, David, Alabaster, and everything related to Christmas swirling around in my head like the North Pole vortex. I woke up the next day extremely tired and unable to shake a strange feeling I had.

After breakfast and three cups of coffee, I made my way to the reindeer hut. I pulled open the shed door, half expecting Rudolph to burst out of the herd to come and see me, but there was no sign of him. Instead, all the reindeer were lolling around, barely able to keep their eyes open, and in the middle was Rudolph. He was lying on the floor, his legs tucked under his body and his head was drooping to the floor.

"Hey lad, how are you feeling today?"

Rudolph slowly opened one bleary eye to stare at me, and it looked like he was struggling to focus.

I sighed, hating to see my mate hungover. "Not good, aye? I think you need a good hearty breakfast to sort you out. How about I whip up your usual?" I began pouring his feed into a bucket, and opened up a bottle of stout for him. "I'm sure a bit of hair of the dog will do you a world of good."

I held the bucket up for him and he slowly stood up and edged over to me. He delicately stuck his head in the bucket and nibbled the food, tentatively at first, but he soon found his appetite and began wolfing it down. "There you go lad, is that making you feel better?"

Rudolph opened his eyes to look at me as if to say yes, without taking his nose out of the bucket.

"Good, now eat it all up." I watched with affection as Rudolph licked around the sides of the bucket. I then sighed as the weight of everything came over me. "What am I going to do about this mess, lad?"

Rudolph pulled his head out and looked at me, then licked his chin and around his mouth.

"I honestly think drastic action needs to be taken, something we've never done before." I pulled up a stool so I could face Rudolph and ran my hands over my face. "Seriously, I can't get them out of my head. I don't know what Pepper has done to me, but I swear she's made me feel things I shouldn't be feeling." I took a deep breath and stared at Rudolph for some time as I kept deliberating what to do. "Should I do it, lad?" I asked.

Rudolph looked at me. He didn't have a clue what I was talking about, but he nodded helplessly.

"I think so too. It's risky, and it breaks the Christmas Law, but I think it will be worth it." I stood up, feeling my stomach flutter with excitement and anticipation. "Thanks lad. I best go break the news to Mrs C."

I filled the food trough up with feed for the other reindeer and mixed in a couple of bottles of stout for them to share and then topped up their water. The other reindeer slowly made their way across to it. I gave Rudolph a heartfelt look before I closed the door behind me.

I entered the house to the sound of the vacuum cleaner whirring loudly. "Hun," I called out to Mrs C's back. "Honey," I called louder, but she carried on, unable to hear me. "Oi," I shouted, just as Mrs C hit the off button on the vacuum. My voice pierced the air and Mrs C spun around, alarmed.

"Excuse me," she responded. "Oi to yourself."

"I need to speak to you. It's important."

Mrs C raised an eyebrow, wiped her hands on her apron and followed me into the kitchen to sit opposite me at the table. "What is it?" she asked.

"It's about this issue with Alabaster. It's not getting any better and I'm worried."

"I know you are, love, but I'm sure it will sort itself out eventually."

I shook my head. "I'm not so sure as I think it's too deep-rooted. It's like he's completely lost his Christmas joy, and I don't want to sit around and wait for him to continue spiralling out of control and see him and Christmas fall off a cliff." I stood up and paced around the kitchen. "So… I've been toying with an idea about something, which is… radical."

Mrs C watched me as I ran my hands over my face. "Radical?" she asked, frowning.

I stopped pacing and sat back down so I could look her in the eye. "Do you remember that little girl and her father who we delivered a letter to?"

"How could I forget? I can't stop thinking about them," she said.

"You can't?" I asked, raising my eyebrows.

"No, it's the weirdest thing. Something really hit me when I met them, like I wanted to help them."

I paused in shock. "I know why you feel that way. It's because of Pepper. She's used one of her elf charms to make us feel like that."

Mrs C frowned. "I don't understand. Why would she manipulate us like that?"

"It's a long story, but she might have a point. I can't help but think they could be the answer to what we need, so I'm thinking about inviting Pip and David to come and stay with us and visit the North Pole."

Mrs C jumped to her feet, her hand on her stomach. "Stay with us! We've never had people stay with us."

"I know. But I can't stop thinking about it. I think it might do everyone some good to have some fresh faces around here. The elves have never met a child in the flesh and I think it might help restore some of Alabaster's joy and encourage him to remember why we do what we do."

"You weren't joking when you said radical." She then looked around. "You're honestly going to invite them here, into our home?"

"It was Pip's Christmas wish. I feel like I want to honour it."

Mrs C looked stunned, but then she grinned and sat down. "Very well. You're the only person who can say yes to this."

"So, you're okay with it?" I asked.

"Okay with it. I can't think of anything more exciting."

"Phew. Although, I'm not sure how to go about inviting them. I doubt David would believe me if I just turned up at his house again and told him to come with me."

Mrs C chuckled. "No, and he would need to take time off work during the school holidays." Then, as if a light bulb appeared above her head, she looked at me. "I know what we can do."

I raised my eyebrow in relief because I was stumped.

"They said they were potentially looking to go on holiday to Lapland this year."

I scoffed. "Yes, I heard what they said about Lapland."

Mrs C smiled. "Well, I doubt David could afford it. I got the impression he was having some financial difficulties, but I could set up a competition for a free trip to meet Santa at Lapland. I'm certain he would enter it, with how much Pip wants to go."

My eyes lit up. "Oh, I'm sure of it, but then he'd be in Lapland, with Him, not here with me."

Mrs C laughed. "Yes, but it would be an easier ask from Lapland. At least they would have made their own arrangements to be away from home and would be excited about meeting Santa. You can just meet them there."

"That's genius!" I gasped. "Plus, it would give me a chance to do my annual catch up with Him. So, how would you ensure David entered the competition?"

"Well, that's where I will need to know a bit more about him, what he's into and passionate about to tailor it to him."

"Oh, I know! He always requested books on antiques and also old retro style toy cars for Christmas. You know, the collectible types."

Mrs C looked surprised. "Well, it's an odd one, but I could make it work. Leave it with me."

I sat back in my chair, feeling chuffed and excited.

19

Over the next few days, Mrs C kept me updated on her progress. She had managed to find a reputable retro car dealership catalogue website that David had already signed up to and got regular emails from.

She then used some extremely impressive computer skills to send a string of emails out to David from the company about a competition for a free trip to Lapland to meet Santa during the Easter holidays. Mrs C was convinced that David wouldn't pass up such a great opportunity for Pip, so it was only a matter of time before he took the bait.

One afternoon, a few days later, I was sitting with my feet up, sipping on a sherry, whilst watching my favourite film, Miracle on 34th Street. It was, of course, a film about me being taken to court.

I loved it, because I liked to compare and contrast the depiction of me and the real me. "I would never do that," I would cry every time I watched it, whilst smugly sipping my drink. "All of this is just crazy. I would never go to prison because I would just use the time-warp to throw people off and return to the North Pole. Also, I would never get so attached to one girl. It's just ludicrous and unfair. Not to mention I would never carry a cane, at least not one that isn't made of sugar."

Then suddenly, a loud shriek from Mrs C made me throw half my drink over my sleeve.

"What's wrong?" I asked, rushing into the small study area where the computer was. I glanced around, unsure what would cause her to shriek. We didn't get mice or spiders, or burglars in the North Pole, so I wasn't sure what I was about to fight on her behalf.

"It's David! He's finally responded to my competition."

"Crikey, is that it? You scared me half to death," I panted, grasping my chest. "Are you trying to give my ticker a shock because you could kill me?"

"Oh, don't be so dramatic. I doubt much could kill you, which means I'm going to have to put up with you for at least a few more centuries," she teased. "But isn't this great news?"

"Yes, fantastic news. So, what happens now?"

"Well, I'm going to wait a few days before I contact him and tell him he's the lucky winner. Then I will make the arrangements for them to fly to Lapland during the Easter holidays. You can meet them there and break the news to them that the actual intention of the competition was for them to come here. And did you mention you were going to go a day earlier to have your annual catch up with Him?"

My smile slipped as she reminded me. "Yes, that's correct," I said, narrowing my eyes in determination.

I was already calculating how the visit was going to play out. I ran my thumbs down my trouser braces, as a rush of adrenaline went through me, for more than one reason.

Mrs C narrowed her eyes in suspicion. "I never know exactly what you discuss with Him. But you always get that look on your face."

"It's just business." I didn't really want to tell Mrs C what actually occurred in my meetings with Him.

"Well, I best finish watching my film." I returned to my throne, but I had lost all my focus. I was too distracted thinking about…. business.

Later I went to have a catch up on progress at the workshop, and true to form, Alabaster was still slamming things down, making the tension thick.

I'd not told the elves about our plan to invite guests to the North Pole, but I wanted to let Pepper know. Seeing as every time I saw her, she looked like she was holding her breath, waiting for some news.

I stepped close to Pepper while the elves were busy. "Easter," I muttered out the side of my mouth. "Expect visitors."

Pepper gasped and stared at me. "Seriously?" she asked.

I nodded. "But I'm sure you knew this would happen." I slowly looked down at her and smiled.

"Well, I.." she said, pulling her sleeves down.

I laughed and shook my head. "If you want to tell the others, go ahead, but perhaps best not to in case something goes wrong."

"I won't say anything," she whispered, looking stunned, before she stumbled back to her workstation.

A few weeks later, I dressed in my finest fake suit and stared at myself in the mirror. I raised my chin and gave myself a defiant stare. There couldn't possibly be any confusion about who the real Santa was, and it wasn't just Pip and David who I wanted to prove it to. He could always do with a reminder as well.

I finished packing my small case with my pyjamas, slippers, a few toiletries and my special hat and went downstairs.

"You look like the perfect Santa," Mrs C stated and smiled reassuringly. She knew exactly what I needed to hear, and I grinned back at her. "Now, good luck. I'm sure it will all go smoothly." She clasped her hands together and looked around at her home. I could tell she was nervous, too.

"Thanks love." I gave Mrs C a kiss on the cheek.

Moments later, I drove the plane out of the hangar, picked up speed and took off into the air. I steered the plane into the tip of the North Pole and the plane shot off into the vortex and within a few seconds; I arrived in Lapland. I flew over a beautiful blanket of white grounds, with conifer trees draped and dusted in snow, and landed on a snowy plain.

Directly in front of me was a sign. "*Welcome to Lapland, the home of Santa Claus.*" I raised an eyebrow and sniggered. I had seen it several times before, but I still wondered who believed it. Everyone knows the real me lives in the North Pole.

At least the temperature was pleasant. I drove my plane into my usual spot in a private shed and then trudged along the thick snow towards Santa Claus's Village.

There were plenty of people heading in various directions, all dressed in bobble hats, thick coats, and snow boots, and I marvelled at how happy everyone looked. I knew these people were my committed fans, and they all seemed to be delighted to be in a place where they could continue to celebrate Christmas and honour me and my traditions, even though Christmas had fizzled out over three months ago.

I waved cheerfully at some passersby who were holding steaming cups of cocoa, and others who were in the middle of eating food.

One man paused with his bratwurst, dripping in onions, mustard and sauerkraut, halfway to his mouth, before he waved frantically at me. "Hi Santa," he called, as several onions fell off the sausage, down his front and onto the floor.

His delight simply made me bellow out my usual laugh, which only caused more people to stare at me. I relished the attention, and it was the reason I loved visiting so much, because although Lapland was a facade, it was like home from home, where I could be myself with no pretence, and no one questioned it.

I reached Santa's main hut, and walked past a large snowman which bore little resemblance to Mr Frosty, but I could appreciate the attempt and its rustic look.

Inside, a grown lady pretending to be an elf, dressed in a green and red costume, with a floppy hat, greeted me with a wide smile.

"Warm greetings, and welcome to Santa Claus's village," she chorused, as if on autopilot. "Are you here to see Santa?" she asked, before her eyebrows creased into a frown. "Wait, sorry, are you a stand in?" she asked quietly, as if she wasn't sure whether to ask, or if I was just a big fan.

I shook my head and chuckled, suppressing the urge to tell her the truth. "I'm not a stand-in, no."

She raised her eyebrows. "Oh, so you don't work here then?"

I laughed again, which only made her look more confused. "No, I don't work here, but I am here to see Him though."

The fake elf looked unsure how to proceed before she plastered a smile on her face. "Very well. It's quieter today for some reason, so I'm sure we can go straight through, unless you would like a tour of the postal room first."

I stopped in my tracks. "Yes, actually, that would be good."

"Great, this way." She escorted me to another room and gestured to a shelving unit spanning the wall. "Here are the letters we receive from around the world." The shelves were divided into sections to correspond to each country and they were full of letters, all addressed to me.

I swallowed the guilt, knowing that the intent of every child who wrote one of these letters was that it landed with me. And whilst they arrived here to Him, which had its own unique special touch, I couldn't help but feel like I was cheating them.

"We receive over 30,000 letters a day on the run up to Christmas," she boasted. "It takes a lot of work, but we read every single letter."

"You should try fulfilling each letter's requests," I mumbled.

"Excuse me?" she asked. "I didn't catch that."

"I said, it's lovely that each child's letter gets read."

The fake elf nodded and I could sense her studying me, as my eyes trailed over the rows of shelves. I refrained from running my fingers over them as emotion rose inside me at being next to their physical presence.

"Shall we head over to Santa's office now?" she asked after a few moments. "I'm sure he'll be free."

"Please," I swallowed. I felt a lump in my throat as I pulled my eyes away.

The fake elf then led me away to a room that was labelled '*Santa's office*', where she knocked before she turned to me. Her eyes roamed over me, curiously. "Can I ask something?"

"Sure," I smiled.

"You're not who I think you are, are you?" she asked.

"I guess that depends on who you think I am," I replied, winking at her.

Her smile widened in understanding. She didn't need to ask anymore. "I'll leave you to it," and she walked away.

I straightened myself up, stood up taller and entered the room to face The Man sitting in a large chair by a crackling fire.

20

"Hello you," I said, keeping my distance.

The Man got up from his wooden chair with old-styled padded red upholstery, which was centrally placed in the room. "You took your time. Did you have issues getting through border control or something?"

I rolled my eyes. "I'm not that late." I glanced around the cosy, wooden cabin styled room which was decorated thoughtfully with traditional Christmas taste.

"Well, I've had to find other ways to distract myself this morning, seeing as I've miraculously had no visitors today. I take it you had something to do with that?"

I shrugged. "I thought it would be best to give you the day off so we can talk business."

"Ah yes… business," The Man retorted, glancing towards the wall behind him.

I clocked his eyes, knowing what he was looking at, but I wanted to remain in control of our meeting, so instead of jumping into official business, I nonchalantly walked over to the Christmas tree to admire the ornaments on it. I picked up a red and green bauble hanging down from the bottom branches, rubbed it with my sleeve and hung it back in the centre. It looked better in that position.

The Man remained where he was, watching my every move, as I inspected a few other ornaments, before I walked over to Him and my eyes trailed up and down his body. "You've lost weight!"

The Man pulled on his large, loose belt, and patted his belly. "That I have.

I've been off the sugar since January."

I frowned. "But why would you do that? The children know me as a happy, fat, jolly man, which means you need to be too." I'd come to terms a long time ago that whilst there was me, there was also Him, and I had to accept that. But only on the condition that He didn't make a fool out of me.

"Yes, I thought about this, and lots of people who pretend to be you stuff a cushion up their coat. I'm sure I can make it work."

"A cushion! Like a generic shopping mall Santa? You must be joking. You are actually supposed to be me. You are the face of what I do. You connect these children to me and make their dreams to meet me come true."

The Man sighed. "Yes, I know who I am."

I stared at Him, wanting to protest even more, but I wasn't in the mood for an argument, so I begrudgingly accepted The Man's new appearance. "Look, you do an excellent job of being Santa, and if you think you can make it work, then I trust you," I acquiesced, hoping he wouldn't go too far with his crazy weight loss. "Anyway, moving on, I wanted to catch up on how your season went." I pulled a report out of my pocket. "I see it went well. The turnover of children was good, without each session being too fast, allowing each child to have their dream of meeting Santa fulfilled. The children's happiness radar was high, and you actually saw more children last season than the season before."

The Man nodded and straightened himself. "Yes, it went well, thank you. Did you have any concerns it wouldn't?"

"No, I guess not. I also can see that people find you charming and authentic, and appreciate your deep, soothing voice, but I have a little critique."

"And what's that?" he asked, folding his arms.

"Well, it's the laugh. Yours doesn't quite have the same baritone as mine. You need to project from the core to get the right bellow. Let's have a go together."

The Man stared at me in silence and I held his gaze back, waiting for Him to realise I wasn't joking. Eventually, he sighed. "Fine," and together we gave our best laugh.

I shook my head. "Not quite, it's more like this." I demonstrated my laugh.

The Man rolled his eyes and tried again, making me cringe inwardly. It was completely wrong. "No, let's go again. You have to laugh from here." I pointed to my belly.

"I am!" The Man declared, looking exasperated.

He tried again, and then again, but I was determined for Him to nail it perfectly.

Eventually, The Man shook his head. "Look, I don't really hear the difference if I'm honest, and I'm pretty sure the kids won't either. Plus, I've had no complaints."

I raised an eyebrow at Him, amazed he couldn't hear how obvious it was. "Fine. We'll leave that for now."

"Is there anything else?" The Man asked.

I inspected his current ensemble, a red waistcoat and white shirt. "Well, it's your outfit. I know you can't have one as excellent as mine, but I think you should at least wear the same style as me if you're going to be me." I knew his red overcoat, which he wasn't currently wearing, reminded me of a cloak.

"Not this again," The Man said. "I think it's important that I wear a different outfit so the children see a difference. Deep down they need to know I'm not the real Santa, but that I'm definitely the second best, and magical in my own right."

"Very well," I said, frustrated with The Man. I wanted Him to listen to me and remember who I was and my authority, but He had a point. "I guess it is important for people to know you're not quite playing in my league."

The Man pushed his glasses up his nose and glanced at the wall behind him again. I followed his gaze at the lines etched into the wood. "Not quite, but then I can hold my own," and he lifted his head to stare at me.

I raised my eyebrow, as clearly the etches proved otherwise. "Is that right?" It was time! "So, are you ready, then?" I challenged.

"Oh, I'm ready," The Man replied. "Let's do this."

The Man walked past me, out the door, his steps wide and determined. I straightened myself up and followed behind him. We marched past adults pulling their excited children on sledges and I smiled politely at them, but I couldn't allow myself to get distracted. I needed to focus.

We arrived at the reindeer pen and The Man turned abruptly to me. "Which one are you going for then?"

I squinted at the reindeer roaming around in and amongst the trees in the snow-covered paddock. I quickly analysed each one, their muscles, stature and personality, and spotted the stud of the pack. "I'll go for fake Prancer." I pointed to the one scraping his antlers against a tree and found it amusing just how different his stature was from the original.

"Good choice. I'm going for Olive," The Man declared, a small smile creeping over his face.

I scoffed. "Olive, how… modern."

We both collected our chosen reindeer. Prancer trotted across to me straight away, listening to my call, whilst He had to grab Olive by her harness, and guide her in the right direction.

We then each attached our reindeer to the two little wooden sleds, which were already in the starting position on the track.

"Shall we get on with this?" The Man asked.

I gave a curt nod as I climbed up onto the back of my sled, and He climbed up onto his. I took a deep breath, gearing myself up and stared ahead at the long, winding snowy track. This was the moment. This was what I had come here for and this was the business Mrs C never knew about. I needed to win, and show this Man who the best Santa was.

"I'll count down," The Man called. "On three. Ho. Ho. Ho!"

I lifted my reins and gave fake Prancer the nudge he needed and we shot off along the snowy trail. I could see Prancer putting his might into it, but he was a fraction of the speed I was used to, as the trees filtered past us, in what felt like slow motion.

"Come on," The Man shouted as his sled came level to mine. "I thought you were the master." He then pulled ahead of me.

I thrashed my reins again, but as much as I encouraged Prancer, we still didn't move any faster and I wondered why. Every year we challenged each other to this test, and I always won. I could read reindeer better than anyone. I was a pro with the reins. I could whisper encouragement and instructions to them in ways that only I could do, and I had a magical lightness that the reindeer could benefit from.

The Man twisted round and gave out a loud astonishing cackle. I frowned and watched as moments later, his sled crossed the finish line, before I trailed over it behind him.

I stomped off the sled and placed my fists onto my hips and studied The Man's smug, beaming face.

"Looks like I won," he boasted. "You might have lost your touch, but don't worry, I'll make sure we officially mark the occasion as usual."

"That race didn't feel right. I'm sure that reindeer was slower than normal."

"Hey, if you can't hack it…" he shrugged.

I shook my head. "Something was off. I'm sure of it."

"Well, it might be because all this lot has disappeared," he said pompously, patting his belly. "It's just made me a phenomenal opponent."

I narrowed my eyes as he flounced back to his office. I turned to look at the fake Prancer and stroked his neck and head. "What was up with you? I really thought you would be a sure win." I detached his reins from the sled, then fake Prancer leaned his head closer to mine, before he trotted off to join his companions in the large snowy woodland pen.

I pushed the sled to one side and then felt an unexpected resistance. "What the…?" I lifted the sled up and discovered two concrete bricks underneath, weighing it down. Not only that, there were rubber strips along the runners to create additional friction on the snow. I dropped the sled back down and marched after The Man. I closed the door to his office with a little extra force, just as He extracted his pocket knife.

"Not so fast," I said.

"Sorry, it's too late," he smiled smugly, as he pressed the knife into the wall. "I won this time, and it's not my fault you're a sore loser."

"I'm a sore loser? You're the one who resorted to cheating because you can't cope with the fact that I'm better at this challenge than you and win all the time, except for the handful of occasions you got lucky."

"You're Santa Claus. Of course I'm never going to beat you with something like this. How do you think I won those other times, because it wasn't through luck?"

I stared at Him in amazement. "Wait, have you been trying to cheat this whole time?"

"Yes! It gets boring with you constantly winning. Plus, you are in my territory, so I'd say all's fair in love and war."

I tried to say something, but then I smirked. "You're right, you crafty sprout." I walked over to inspect the overwhelmingly one-sided tally we kept. "Where is the fun with me always winning? Here, let me do the honours."

The Man handed the knife over to me with a subtle look of suspicion.

I then carved out a deep etch into the wood on the left side to add to his limited tally. I grinned at him. "There you go. That's one more to add to your collection. I still don't know how you cheated those other times, though."

The Man shrugged. "A variety of ways. I've had my elves distracting you. I slipped a sedative to your reindeer once, and there was also that time your reins snapped. That was me too."

I stared at him open-mouthed, then grinned again. "Well, let's see what sabotage you can come up with next year. I'm quite looking forward to it."

The Man smiled back, his animosity evaporating. It was the first time both of us dropped our guard.

"Anyway, now all that business is over. Tell me, how's your wife?" The Man asked, as he settled back in his chair.

"She's great, except she's trying to sneak more vegetables into my diet all the time."

"You see, even she thinks it's important to keep healthy."

I rolled my eyes. "Please don't gang up on me."

The Man laughed. "So, she mentioned that you have concocted this elaborate plan to entice a man and his daughter here to Lapland so you can whisk them back to the North Pole. It seems like a lot of trouble for one kid.

How special is this girl?"

"I think she's very special, and pivotal to putting Christmas back on track."

The Man frowned. "Are you having problems?"

"Well, I guess. We can't seem to pick the big go-to toy this year, and Alabaster and the other elves, well, they've been having some... issues."

"Oh dear. Should I be sending out warnings to the children?"

"No. Please don't panic the children and make them think Christmas could be cancelled or anything. That would never happen." My heart raced at the thought. "We'll manage. We always do."

"Phew. That's good then. I still can't believe you're going to whisk them off to the North Pole to see all your magical secrets. Doesn't that go against the Christmas Law?"

"I'm making an exception," I confirmed.

"I see. So, all you need me to do is disappear tomorrow, so you can be the one to greet them?"

"Yes, please." I eyed up his uncomfortable looking chair.

"Well, you're the boss, but don't take too long. You've already created a dry spell today. I don't need another day like this."

21

That evening, I returned to my cabin at the far end of Santa's village. It was a quaint cabin, standing by itself on a snowy plain surrounded by conifer trees. It was never rented out to the public in case I arrived, and whilst I liked it being relatively secluded, I also missed being able to absorb the action, and the comings and goings of the parents, children and groups of friends.

I opened the door to find it had been cleaned since I left it, lifting the smell of timber, but it still had all my possessions and everything I was familiar with. There was a Christmas tree in the corner decorated with handcrafted baubles and ornaments. There were light fittings on the wall in the shape of antlers, random Santa dolls on a bench, and the floors were wooden with thick, red, fluffy carpets.

I headed into the bathroom where there was a wooden sauna. I hesitated, wondering whether to use it, when I decided against it. The steam room in London was enough intense heat for one year. Instead, I simply changed into my pyjamas, flopped into bed and started scoffing some Finnish chocolate from a basket on the bedside table while I watched a flurry of snow land on the white conifer trees outside.

I dozed off when a loud commotion made me jolt my eyes open. Outside, four young lads had sneaked through to my private area and were having a late-night snowball fight.

"What the…" I muttered, unable to comprehend how they had ended up there. I watched the chaos for a while, listening to their loud, off-putting screams and shouts, whilst getting increasingly worked up.

After a while I couldn't take it any longer, and shoved the duvet off me. I was ready to sort this out once and for all. I wrapped my coat around me, pulled my boots on and yanked the door open, causing the boy closest to me to startle. "I can't watch this charade all night!" I growled.

"Leg it, it's bloody Santa," the boy cried.

"Not without joining in," I shouted and scooped some snow into my hands and launched it at the boy who had run away. It hit him square in the back, causing him to stop and turn around in shock.

"Wow, that's a good aim," another boy responded, rising from a mound of snow he had dropped behind at the sight of me.

I puffed out my chest and laughed. It was a skill I was proud of.

"What do we do?" the boy inquired to his mate.

I stood firm. "Well, you can't have a snowball fight on my patch and not include me."

The boys looked at each other and all seemed to agree in unison as they scooped up balls of snow and launched them at me.

I laughed as the snow from three balls sprayed my coat and dusted off to the floor, whilst the other ball landed beside my boots. I scooped up more snow to form two snowballs and hurled them in quick succession at two of the boys, then repeated the move to get the other two boys. They leapt away, but the snowballs hit them, anyway. Then it began. War; as the four of them took me on.

They scooped snow and threw it, whilst running and stomping through the snow. They ducked and dived, with some taking it seriously enough to do commando rolls to escape the path of my snowballs. They strategized with silent signals to each other to attack me from all angles, but I thwarted each one.

Eventually, after I rained a shower of snowballs on each of them, they held their hands up in surrender. "We give up," one of them shouted, as they gathered together around me, grinning and laughing.

"You're like a machine," another one panted.

"Well, I am the best snowball fighter the world has ever seen. Only my elves can give me a run for my money." This caused the boys to laugh as if

I was joking. "Anyway, it's been a blast. Now you best head back to your cabins to get warmed up."

They grinned and skipped away, whilst turning back to wave enthusiastically at me. I returned the wave and watched them for a moment, before I entered my cabin, removed my boots and coat, and climbed into bed. I fell asleep smiling.

The next morning, I woke up feeling excited to see Pip and her father. I went to the restaurant and ate breakfast beside a crackling fire, pondering how the day would unfold.

After finishing my meal, I strolled around the area, wondering if I would prematurely run into Pip and David. I watched some huskies racing along deep snowy tracks and drank more hot chocolate, then made my way to Santa's office. The Man stood up from his chair when I entered. "Sleep well?" he asked, an accusation in his voice, as he hitched up his trousers before tightening his belt notch, much to my dissatisfaction.

"Yes, very well, after I had some fresh air." I twitched my lips as memories came back to me.

The Man raised an eyebrow. "Interesting. Is that why I heard a rumour that I was having a snowball fight last night, even though I don't recall it?"

I shrugged. "I thought I'd show these young ones a thing or two."

"You're giving me even more of a reputation around here than I already have."

I stared back at Him. "You're welcome. I doubt you'd have had the skill to pull it off yourself," I muttered under my breath.

"What was that?" The Man asked.

"Nothing, let's proceed."

The Man cast his eyes to the clock. "Right, I've told my elves to greet this girl and her father when they arrive, give them a tour, and bring them here, which should be at any moment. You can take my seat and get settled. I'm going to check on the Christmas post."

I sat down on the slightly padded wooden chair by the fire and waited, drumming my fingers on the arm. I shuffled to adjust my red coat and smoothed out my beard. I grew restless waiting, but it was important I greeted them in an official capacity as Santa, otherwise they might think I'm a crazy lunatic trying to take them away in my plane.

Eventually, the door opened, and I heard voices before I saw who was approaching.

22

"Come on, Pip, please cheer up. We've come a long way," I heard David's tired voice say.

Then a lady dressed in an elf outfit came into view. "Here we are. Let me introduce you to Santa." Her smile was exaggerated as she pointed at me.

Pip was clutching David's arm as she stepped inside the room, looking confused and lost, as if something wasn't right. Then when she saw me, her eyes widened. "Santa!" she cried.

David was rubbing his forehead, looking exhausted, when he took a double glance at me. "It's you," he declared.

I grinned. "Yes, it's me. Don't worry. Your eyes aren't deceiving you. We have met before."

"Right, you work for the postal service, but I'm confused. Don't tell me you have another letter for me and it's now a service you guys do, to hand deliver letters anywhere in the world."

I chuckled. "Not quite."

"No Daddy, it's actually Santa," Pip stated. "I told you it was."

I smiled warmly at her, marvelling at just how often children could see the truth when adults couldn't. "Pip's right, I don't work for the postal office and I am in fact Santa."

David took a deep breath and forced a smile. "Of course you are." He looked as though he didn't believe me. "It is strangely coincidental, though, to travel all the way around the world and run into you again. I would say it's a small world, but that flight didn't feel like it."

"Oh dear! Not a pleasant journey, then?" I asked, feeling guilty.

David stared at me. "No, it wasn't. You know how it is, screaming kids, busy queues at security, being told off because I forgot to put my liquids in a plastic bag. The flight was delayed. I had to sit in a cramped seat, on a long flight, made worse by the person in front of me reclining their chair, plus dealing with a fidgety seven-year-old," he grumbled, causing Pip to stare at him and sulk slightly.

"That does sound horrendous. I'd forgotten what airports and aeroplanes can be like for everyone."

David frowned in confusion. "Anyway, let's just say, if I'd known it was you a few weeks ago, it could have saved us a trip."

"Where's the adventure in that?"

David's expression flickered. "I can't say I'm much of an adventurer. It was always my wife who…." David trailed off and covered his mouth. His eyes were full of emotion, making me wince inwardly about raising sensitive memories.

"Anyway Pip. You finally got your wish to meet Santa. Are you feeling happier now?" he asked, forcing a faint smile and placing a hand on her shoulder.

Pip stared at me, her brain working hard and her eyes roaming over me. "Yeah," she replied, her frown flickering. She then grew distracted as she stared around at her surroundings with her nose wrinkled, still looking confused.

David sighed. "Pip, can't you be a bit more enthusiastic?"

Pip glanced at him, before she returned to her perplexed, sad expression.

David ran a hand over his face and changed the subject. "So, how long have you worked here?" He darted a glance at Pip and quickly covered his tracks. "I mean, how long have you lived here…. Santa?"

I adjusted in my seat, feeling affronted. He genuinely thought I was Him. I was about to tell him I wouldn't dream of living here, nor work here, when Pip tugged on David's arm.

"Daddy. This isn't Santa's real grotto," she whispered.

David sighed. "Pip, we've been through this. I know it wasn't what you were expecting, but it is Santa's real grotto." He swallowed as if the whole experience was tough on him.

Pip frowned. "But…"

"Pip, please," he said, exasperated. "We've travelled all the way to the North Pole to see this place and meet Santa in his home village, and here we are. So, let's just focus on making it a great trip."

Pip's frown creased even further, and I smiled again at her perceptiveness. It was just David who needed convincing, and from his reaction, I wasn't sure how receptive he would be to what I needed to tell him.

"Pip," I called, rising from my chair. "Why don't you have a look at that Christmas tree, and see if you like any of the baubles on it? I need to speak with your father."

Pip nodded and glanced at David for quick reassurance, who gave her a small nod. "Okay, Santa." She shuffled across to the Christmas tree at the side of the room. She scanned the variety of baubles and decorations when suddenly she stepped closer and gazed at the bauble I had polished and moved earlier.

David watched her for a moment before he shook his head in dismay. "I'm sorry about that. It's always been a dream of hers to come to the North Pole and meet Santa, but now we're here she seems disappointed. I mean, we were given a quick tour of the place before we came to meet you and she looked close to tears at one point and kept saying everything was wrong. I think she thought there would be a real Rudolph and flying reindeer, and millions of little elves in a workshop."

"Kids and their imaginations, aye. I can barely cope with six elves, let alone millions," I muttered.

David frowned at my response, but I quickly changed the subject. "So, what did you think about this place?"

"It's great," he said, although his mood didn't match his words. "It's busy. In fact, I thought I'd be queuing for hours to see you in your special office, but we just walked straight through."

I smiled. "Well, of course. You are the winners of our competition, so you get special treatment and lots of extra perks."

"Oh, I thought the prize was just free accommodation and flights here. I didn't know there would be other perks as well. What else does it include?"

"Well, you get to see backstage secrets about Christmas," I smiled, smoothing down my coat. "And that includes you learning and understanding who I actually am."

David raised an eyebrow. "Well, we've already established you have multiple identities. One moment you're in Scotland working as a postal worker, the next you're sitting here in a Santa costume. What's next? I'm going to go to my local supermarket and find you serving me from behind the counter, or are you going to turn up at my house as the local plumber with a bag of tools?"

"No. Now brace yourself... I actually am the original Santa Claus."

David glanced at Pip, who was completely transfixed by the red and green bauble and was ignoring our conversation. "Of course you are. We've already established that," he said, his expression full of irony.

"No, you don't understand." I realised I wasn't getting anywhere, so I stepped closer to him, forcing David to look me in the eye. Our eyes locked, and I deepened my voice, so it was assertive and commanding. "I'm not the fake Santa who lives here in Lapland. I'm me, the real Santa. The original."

It took a second before David's pupils dilated as his eyes remained glued to mine. I saw his chest inflate as his breath caught. I could see the message travelling through his body and the realisation of who I was dawning on him. "No, you can't be," he whispered, his eyes moving up and down me. "It's impossible."

I puffed myself up even more and stood straighter. "It is possible. I am Santa, and I know you can feel it now."

His eyebrows flickered, and he swallowed. "The real Santa?" he muttered, blinking rapidly.

"Yes, and I have a proposition for you."

"What's that?" he whispered. It was clear he could barely process the information.

"I want to make you an offer to spend a few days at my home in the real North Pole, where you and Pip can visit my workshop, meet my elves and reindeer, and learn about everything I do."

David opened his mouth, then closed it before opening it again. "Do you do this often, inviting people to visit you?"

I cleared my throat. "No, no one has ever visited our home and workshop before."

David's frown deepened. "Then why would you make an exception for us?"

I hesitated as my hand automatically went to my waistcoat pocket, where I still had Holly's letters, before I dropped my hand. The actual reason could wait. "Well, it's just one of the perks of the competition."

"Oh, of course, the competition. If I'm honest, I would have thought the extra perk would be some free food vouchers to use at the kiosks and restaurants, not to leave Lapland and explore the real North Pole."

"I doubt that would be as special, although the hot dogs here are decent," I chuckled. "But now it's up to you. Of course, if you want to stay here you can, but if you want the chance of a lifetime to meet the real heroes of Christmas, then all you need to do is say yes."

David glanced at Pip, who was now running her fingers over the bauble. A haunted expression came on his face and he started to shake his head. "I… I think it might be a bit too much… I'm not one for spontaneous adventures."

I raised my eyebrow. "You got all the way from Scotland to here. Why not go further?"

He looked down at the ground, then back at Pip, and he then looked at me. He hesitated some more before he spoke. "I can't believe this, but I think I need to say yes, don't I? For Pip's sake," he whispered.

I grinned. "Is that a yes?"

David nodded, looking pale. "Yes. I guess it is. So, what happens now?"

"Excellent. Now we just have to take care of the formalities." I reached into my pocket and pulled out a scroll tied with a red ribbon. I unrolled it and placed it on a table.

"I just need you to sign this."

"What is it?" David asked.

"It's a Christmas contract. Anyone who signs it is bound by the Christmas

Law, so you can't publicise what you see."

"And what happens if we break the contract?" David asked as he tried to read the print.

"If you sign this, you physically won't be able to."

I handed him my gold quill. He hesitated, looked over at Pip, sighed, and signed his straight, neat signature on the page, and he then signed it on behalf of Pip.

The wet signature sparkled and glowed red before it turned green and settled and dried on the paper.

Pip blinked and pulled the red and green bauble off the branch. "Look Daddy, I love this bauble."

I smiled. "Why don't you keep it? I'm sure the elves here won't mind."

Her eyes lit up. "Really?" she asked. I nodded, causing her to giggle. She then handed it to David to slip into her little Rudolph backpack.

"Well Pip, it looks like we're not staying here," David stated. "We're going to go with Santa to the real North Pole."

Pip's eyes widened, and she gasped, "I knew this wasn't the North Pole."

David cleared his throat. "So, what happens now?"

I smiled. "Well, we best get going. I already took the liberty of asking the elves to load your suitcases into my plane so we can leave right away."

I led the way out of the office, past the human elf, who smiled and waved us away. Pip held David's hand and skipped next to him.

We passed the reindeer field and Pip waved at them. "These ones can't fly, Daddy, but we're going to meet the ones that can," she shrieked, looking delighted.

"Yes," David frowned, looking slightly numb. "I guess we are."

"Here we are," I said as we arrived at my small plane.

"Are we all going to fit?" David asked.

"Oh yes. It's deceptively spacious. Now, in you both get."

David helped Pip climb into a small gap behind the two seats at the front before he settled in the passenger seat.

"Everyone comfortable?" I asked, as I heaved into the pilot seat, and handed Pip and David some goggles.

"Very," Pip replied, as she bounced up and down in her seat.

"Everybody ready?" I asked, starting the engine.

"Ready," Pip shouted so loud it made me jump, and David nodded tightly.

I grinned, drove my plane along the inconspicuous runway and took off into the sky.

Pip glanced from left to right, eagerly peering out of the plane, whereas David looked more anxious and gripped his seat firmly.

"Hold on," I called, and I pressed the button next to my steering control. A vortex appeared in front of us and we suddenly shot off, travelling through the twisting colourful lights circling the plane, but within seconds we slowed down as we emerged out the other side.

"This is the real North Pole," I declared, as we flew across the barren snowy land.

There were no humans in sight, just the occasional sighting of a polar bear getting on with its own business, which Pip happily pointed out by shooting a finger across my face and screaming. "Look!"

"Wow." David blinked as if he couldn't quite believe where he was. "This is crazy!"

23

I lowered the plane and guided it to the ground with a delicate landing, and drove it straight into the hangar. We climbed out, grabbed the luggage, and I led them across the snow to our house. I noticed Mrs C had added a few extra garnishes to the wreath on the front door, and it smelt of orange and cinnamon.

I opened the door to find Mrs C hovering in the entrance with a plate piled high with her best cranberry and nutmeg cookies.

"Hello," her voice contained a noticeable wobble of nerves. "Welcome to our home."

"Hello, I forgot I'd be meeting you again too," David said, with a questioning eyebrow, as if he still couldn't believe it. "You must be Mrs Claus."

"Call me Mrs C. It's a name that seems to have stuck, and I'm sorry we lied to you before about who we were." She then bent down to Pip's level to hold out the plate to her. "It's so lovely to see you again," she smiled.

Pip's face lit up at her expression. "You too, and thank you." She was clearly delighted to be here and took two cookies.

David glanced around our humble home, at the wooden beams and cosy snug lounge. "Nice place, very quaint."

"It's perfect," Pip gushed. "It's just how I imagined, and it smells just like Christmas."

Mrs C's smile widened. "I'm pleased you like it. Now, why don't you get unpacked and then you'll feel more settled?"

"Yes, I'll show you to our guest room," I offered.

I grabbed David's large suitcase in one hand and Pip's smaller one in the other and led them up the narrow staircase which creaked underfoot. I hadn't thought through the difficulty of carrying both the suitcases, so on every step, I either scraped or crashed them into the wall.

"Do you want me to help with that?" David asked, concerned, after I momentarily got wedged.

"No, certainly not. You're our guests." I finally squeezed through onto the landing. "Now, here we are." I proudly opened the door to the guest room.

There were two neatly made single beds that were pushed up against the far sides of the wall, which were dressed in tartan bedspreads and laden with an obscene amount of green, red, and tartan cushions. An evergreen banner ran along the headboard, as well as additional evergreen foliage trellising the wooden beams.

I dumped the bags on the floor at the foot of one bed. "The beds don't look much, but I can assure that you will have the best night's sleep of your life in this room."

"This is lovely," David swallowed. "It reminds me of how my wife would decorate at Christmas."

"Is that my bed?" Pip asked, running across to the other bed, where Mrs C had left a white teddy wearing a little red scarf, nestled into the cushions.

"Hello Mr Stuffy." She scooped it up to give it a massive hug.

"I'll leave you to get unpacked and freshen up."

When I returned downstairs, Mrs C was pacing back and forth in the hallway.

"Did they seem happy?" she fretted.

I nodded. "They were delighted."

"That's a relief. Is the place tidy enough?"

"It's perfect." I wrapped my arm around her waist to calm her down. "We're going to have a lovely few days with them."

A little while later, the tiny patter of feet, along with David's heavier footsteps, came down the stairs.

Pip was now wearing a pretty pink dress, with frills around the short sleeves and the hem. It was lovely, but it looked slightly too small and tight on her, and I also wasn't sure it was suitable for the climate.

David noticed me looking at her. "I know. She really wanted to dress up for the two of you and this is her favourite dress, which she insists on taking everywhere."

"It's my happy dress," Pip beamed, twirling around.

"You look lovely, dear," Mrs C smiled.

Pip grinned and smoothed out her dress proudly. She then spotted a picture on the wall of the reindeer and hurried over to it. "Is that... the real reindeer?"

"Ah yes, that's them."

Pip's eyes lit up. "Can we meet them?" she asked.

"Of course," I said. "Let's head over to the shed now."

David told Pip to fetch her coat and scarf, so after she scampered off and returned with it trailing behind her, requiring David to tell her she also needed to wear it, we all headed out to the shed.

When we arrived, I pulled open the door, causing Rudolph to bolt out of the herd and knock his antlers onto the wooden fence.

"He's saying hello," I said, as Pip took a fearful step backwards.

I turned back to Rudolph. "Aye up, lad." I scratched his head next to his antler, and he pressed his head into my hand.

David was staring at Rudolph incredulously. "I still can't believe this is happening. That this is '*the*' Rudolph. He's more famous than....," he struggled to find an analogy. "Elvis," he finally settled on.

"Ah, are you an Elvis fan?" I asked, looking delighted and hopeful.

David shook his head. "No, not really. But I wouldn't mind coming across his Gibson Guitar, which was sold at auction," he claimed, his eyes momentarily lighting up.

I should have known that David would be more passionate about any antiques or valuable memorabilia.

"Can I stroke him?" Pip asked, inching closer.

"Of course. He's friendly."

Pip cautiously lifted her hand and moved it towards Rudolph. Eventually she touched his bright red nose, and Rudolph licked her hand, causing her to jerk her hand away.

"It's fine," I reassured her, as David stared at her with concern.

Then Cupid waltzed up to David, poked his head through the fence, and licked his hand, causing David to gasp and spin around. He laughed at Cupid's intrigued expression and began petting him whilst his eyes strayed back to watch Pip again.

Pip took a deep breath, fixed a determined expression on her face, and reached back to stroke Rudolph again. She trailed her small fingers across his nose. "Why is Rudolph's nose different from the others'?" she enquired.

I hesitated, slightly thrown by the question, and then after a moment's thought, I came up with my answer. "It's because he eats up all his carrots. He gets loads on Christmas Eve."

Pip frowned. "I thought carrots made you see in the dark, not make your nose red."

"Ah, right…" I pondered again, and then it hit me. "Actually, I know, it's because me and him have such a special bond that eventually his nose turned the same colour as my coat to match." I heard a sudden snort come from Mrs C.

"That's what he would like you to believe," Mrs C retorted, shaking her head. "A long time ago, Alabaster gifted Rudolph the red nose. It was after Santa got lost in the fog one terrible Christmas." Mrs C turned to me. "Do you remember? It was a mess. All the reindeer kept banging into each other, and into buildings. That's when you got a huge scrape down the side of the sleigh and then moaned about it all year."

I frowned in confusion, and rubbed my whiskery chin, still not recalling.

Mrs C sighed. "Gosh. Your memory must be as foggy as that night."

"Well, it was centuries ago, wasn't it, lad?" I muttered, patting Rudolph on the head.

"Not quite that long, but perhaps you can't remember because you still manage to come back with a beaten-up sleigh every year, which I can't for the life of me work out why. I guess Rudolph's red nose still doesn't prevent drunken driver mishaps," she quipped.

"Anyway, moving on," I blurted. "Does that answer your question, Pip?"

"Erm, I guess. My mum told me he might have been born that way and the red nose helps Rudolph control his body temperature better, which makes his brain warmer, and that is why he's the cleverest."

Ms C and I stared at Pip for a moment in amazement, whilst I contemplated if she was onto something.

David cleared his throat, clearly wanting to redirect the conversation. "So, tell me, which reindeer is which? I can never remember all their names, and it's always a question in a Christmas pub quiz."

"That's quite typical. There's at least one that people forget. Now, then, the one nuzzling into you is Cupid. He's an affectionate type and likes to be stroked a lot."

Mrs C nodded. "Yes, he is a softy, but watch out for the drool."

"What?" David yanked his hand away, and wiped it on his trouser leg.

I pointed at a reindeer at the back of the pen. "That one is Comet. He has a fetish for sniffing the other reindeer's backsides, so you will always find him trailing behind the others."

"Ah, I can see why you called him Comet, brilliant," David agreed.

"The one he's sniffing is Donner, who is perhaps the most, shall we say, fragrant of the reindeer, and next to her is Blitzen. Those two are never apart from each other. They also like to stamp their hooves a lot when they want something."

Mrs C nodded. "It's true. As soon as one starts, the other joins in and they can create quite a racket."

"Over there is Vixen," I pointed to the biggest of the herd, just as she let out a grunt of air. "She can be quite bossy and do not mess with her when she's in a huff as she'll barge right into you."

I then pointed to a reindeer who was shuddering his head and flinging it around from left to right. "This peculiar one is Prancer." He trotted a couple of steps forward, then stopped, then trotted forward again.

"We don't know why he does this, but he seems to go into his own world sometimes." Mrs C smiled affectionately. "And when he's looking forward to something, he shimmies around the place without a care."

David laughed. "How strange, but I'd have thought Dancer would be the one shimmying around."

"Oh no. Dancer wouldn't shimmy! No, no, no. She has a regal elegance to her and walks with a kind of smooth poise. You can always tell Dancer by her somewhat condescending expression," I said, pointing towards Dancer.

She was currently in the corner scanning the room and looking at all of us with a look of disdain. She was above begging for a stroke, she wouldn't dream of sniffing another reindeer's behind, and she wouldn't move so wildly as Prancer.

David chuckled. "Oh yes, I can see exactly what you mean. Now, who's the last one? I think it must be the one I always forget."

"That will be Dasher. The lazy one." I pointed to Dasher, who was curled up on the ground, barely acknowledging our guests.

David frowned. "I'd have thought he would be the least lazy one."

I grinned widely. "Ironic, isn't it? Everyone in the world probably thinks the same as you."

Pip looked between everyone. "I think Prancer is my favourite." She beckoned Prancer over to her to stroke.

David laughed and stroked her head. "You've always liked Prancer. Just like your..." he cut off and looked away.

I scratched my head. "Err. I guess Prancer has his quirks." I frowned at her choice, wondering why it wasn't automatically Rudolph.

"Can these reindeer fly anytime, like now?" Pip asked.

"Well, technically, they have the ability to fly around the North Pole or anywhere else, but they are only supposed to do so on Christmas Eve or when they are preparing for Christmas Eve."

Pip looked disappointed. "That's sad. I wanted to go for a ride." Her eyes then lit up. "Oh, are your elves preparing for Christmas Eve? Are they making presents right now?"

"They'd better be. Let's head over to the workshop so you can meet everyone."

Pip's mouth opened as she raced across to me, barely able to contain her excitement. "Bye Prancer," she called.

David smiled as he followed us.

"I'll leave you all to it," Mrs C said. "I need to make a start on dinner."

24

I led the way across the snow. "This is Mr Frosty. He watches over the place." The snowman was now wrapped in a brand new yellow and black scarf and wearing a bobble hat. Mrs C must have changed him whilst I'd been in Lapland.

"Wow, he's very impressive," David commented. "His eyes look like they are constantly following you."

I smiled. "I know. The elves gave the coal a special shine."

"Does he talk and walk?" Pip asked.

I smiled and shook my head. "No, he's just a snowman. But he's still precious."

We arrived at the workshop, where the sign on the door read. '*Elves Happily Busy Building Toys.*'

I pushed open the door to find the elves were in full flow, running around, heads down, determined to keep working hard and building up their piles of toys, but there also seemed to be a fraught, overly focused energy coming from them as if Alabaster had recently shouted at them all.

"Wow," David exclaimed, as he witnessed the elves racing around, carrying mounds of gifts that equated to about fifty times their body weight, and doubled, then tripled the piles of toys beside their workstations within seconds. "This is…." David looked somewhat overwhelmed by the scene. "This is incredible."

Bushy was running along, fully focused when she glanced towards us, before she did a double take, her mouth dropping open, and collided straight into the back of Shinny.

"Hey," Shinny cried, as he knocked over a pyramid of Monopoly money, but he then followed Bushy's stare. "Oh my holly brambles." His mouth popped open, and he straightened up rigidly, his eyes wide, looking somewhat terrified and shocked. He looked at Bushy for reassurance. "It can't be…" but Bushy had already started racing towards us.

Shinny followed behind her, looking nervous and unsure, as he fiddled with his hat, and pulled the sleeves of his little shirt down.

Pepper also noticed, and she seemed to take a deep breath and closed her eyes as if to calm herself, before she placed everything down and slowly approached.

Then a loud shriek caused everyone to spin round and look over at Sugarplum. "A child! A wonderful, glorious child!" She raced over, and even beat Shinny and Bushy to stand in front of Pip. "What is going on? How is this possible?" Sugarplum looked flabbergasted. "Here," she thrust a handful of candy canes at Pip. "Whoever you are, welcome to our workshop."

Pip looked both gobsmacked and delighted. "Thank you."

As Pip's hand touched Sugarplum's, Sugarplum shivered with excitement and delight before she held up her hand to inspect it. "I just touched a child. I'm never washing my hands again."

"I hope you do," Wunorse grunted. "Your hands get rather sticky at the best of times."

He then bowed to Pip and David. "Welcome, what brings you to our workshop?" he asked, darting a glance at Alabaster, who had remained at his workstation and was clearly doing his best to appear that he wasn't listening to the conversation.

"I thought it was time we had some visitors." I glanced at Pepper, who had not told the others about the surprise.

Pepper gave a small smile back at me, before she turned to Pip. "It is a pleasure to meet you." Her voice was coming out thin, and full of nerves.

"This is amazing," Pip gasped as she gazed around with her mouth wide open. "This is just how I imagined."

Sugarplum looked giddy. "I still can't believe you're really here. Do you want to see some toys we have created?"

"Yes please," Pip said. She was still cupping all the candy canes, which were warming up in her hands, so she turned round and thrust them towards David to hold, before she rethought and took one back to suck on.

Sugarplum and Bushy dragged Pip away, with the others following closely behind.

David glanced at his hand with a subtle sign of disgust before offering me a candy cane, which was now a lot stickier than usual, but I gladly took it.

"So, err, is it just these six elves that make everything?" David asked, incredulously. "I was half expecting an entire army of them."

"Yes. It's just these six. It always has been, and every year they never fail." My words caught in my throat as I wondered if my elves would continue to be successful with the way things were going. "They can do incredible things. As long as they keep up the energy and Christmas spirit, nothing can stop them." I glanced at Alabaster, who was now banging his toys down on the workstation as he watched the others with Pip.

"Is he alright?" David whispered.

I cleared my throat, not sure how to answer that. "He'll just take a while to warm up. Now, let me show you around."

David nodded, as he momentarily became mesmerised watching Pip gasp as Shinny presented a stuffed octopus to her. "It's so soft and squishy," she cried.

David tore his eyes away as I led him around the elves' work stations, which all came with a platform for them to stand on. "Each elf has their own main workbench, but there are some more benches at the back of the room for when the elves need to start multi-tasking during the busy season," I said, gesturing to the six benches towards the planning board.

"Each workstation has a selection of tools they can use." I pointed out the needles and threads, plastic moulds, paintbrushes, hammers, screwdrivers, glues, glitters, and tonics to make the toys shine brand new. "There is also a pantone banner across each workbench displaying every colour in existence so the elves can mix and match and apply it to their toy ideas. Beside each workbench are buckets and pallets to collect the toys they make, along with a scanner which automatically logs each toy so they can keep track of the production numbers and stock requirements," I said, as David nodded along.

"Each elf has their own list of toys to make. Shinny makes single component type products such as bouncing balls, buckets and spades. Sugarplum and Bushy both work on dolls, teddies, and accessories. Pepper works in the arts and crafts section, and specialises in more… personalised gifts. Wunorse works on board games, whilst Alabaster works on the complex toys, such as electronics, anything that moves or talks, or requires intricate parts. Of course, everyone mucks in where they are needed."

"It sounds like a well-oiled machine," David noted.

"Yes, it works perfectly," I replied, slightly forced. "And of course we have the countdown clock on the ceiling to keep us all on track for the big day."

"Fascinating," David mumbled, but he was distracted as he glanced across at Pip. She had now removed her coat and was twirling around to show Sugarplum and Bushy her pink dress.

"Oh my goodness, what a gorgeous dress," Sugarplum gushed alongside Bushy's vigorous nods of agreement.

"It's my mum's favourite colour," she grinned, before her smile dropped slightly. Seconds later, her face glowed again, and she skipped across to look at another toy.

I looked at David, whose jaw had gone taut at the mention of Pip's mum, and he roughly turned his face away. "What's that?" David asked as something caught his eye.

25

David was pointing to the wall, where a ten-foot list of swirly gold writing twinkled in the light.

"Oh, that's the Christmas Law. It's all the rules I need to abide by to ensure I can deliver presents every year on Christmas Eve. It's an old constitution which was agreed by the world's governments and leaders back when I started out."

"The world's governments? I didn't know they had a say in what you do each year," David queried.

I laughed. "Of course, they do. Each one has given me a pass to enter their airspace on Christmas Eve night."

"So, what else does it cover?" David asked.

"Well, the top ones are the serious regulations, then the lower half are more directives."

"Ah, that makes sense, gives you a bit of flexibility. So, what's on it?" He stepped closer to inspect the list. "Do not provide weapons of destruction to any individual," he read. "Wow, it starts off pretty heavy."

"It also goes hand in hand with the one underneath."

David squinted at the list. "Must not work directly with any government or country to give them any additional advantage. Like what?"

I shrugged. "Like allowing my elves to share their charms and skills with them, or designing some kind of sophisticated tool."

"It really sounds like these governments were very concerned you were going to play countries against each other." He continued reading. "Must not steal from people's houses."

"I would never do that. I'm there to give not take… well, except for the treasures they leave out for me like a glass of whisky and a mince pie."

"Each child must be given gifts within the economic means of both the family and country they live in," David read. "I guess that makes sense. It would be odd if someone from a poor environment was suddenly walking around with a diamond encrusted Gameboy."

"True, but it's the poor I want to give more to as they are the ones who need it most."

"What's that one, under the blue line?" David asked, squinting. "Must not warp or alter time except on Christmas Eve."

"Ah yes, you're onto the directives now. I may have broken this one a few times, but as I don't break it too often, I'm hoping I can get away with it."

David nodded. "I can imagine that would come in handy at certain times."

"Oh yes, very handy," I agreed, thinking about Sugarplum's missions.

David continued reading. "Must not get caught on camera whilst delivering presents… Hmm. That must be a difficult one these days."

"That's why I take my Santa toolkit with me, to protect myself from these sorts of things."

David raised his eyebrow and looked confused, then turned back to the list. "Must not snoop around people's houses."

"Yes. One I would never do," I fibbed, trying to hide my smile.

"Really?" David asked, raising an eyebrow.

"Yes, I certainly wouldn't snoop, but it's not to say I haven't seen some very interesting things," I chuckled.

"It sounds like you have some stories to tell," David queried, but my lips were sealed.

"So, what happens if you break these laws? Surely, they can't send you to prison. You'd be able to escape easily, or do you always need a chimney?"

"Chimneys are useful but not a necessity, and it's true. It wouldn't do much good trying to lock me up," I boasted. "When it comes to the regulations, I physically can't break them as the elves placed an agreement charm on me, similar to the one on the contract I had you sign. But when it comes to the directives, I will most likely get a slap on the wrist. At worst, they could stop me from entering their country. But who really knows? I've not been told off yet."

David turned his attention back to the list. "Must not reveal yourself and share the secrets of Christmas with anyone in full." He looked confused. "It looks like you've breached this one."

I nodded. "Yes, it's one of the rules I've bent to get you and Pip here. However, I put in place safeguards with the contract you signed." I momentarily fretted that I had stepped over the line, then shook my head, certain I was well within my limits.

David watched my expression before turning back to the wall. "And what's this underneath?" He pointed to a very long list.

"It's a list of the gifts I'm not allowed to give, such as new jobs, love, babies, unwarranted success, unique and priceless items, and new parents. I get asked the latter a lot from teenagers."

David frowned. "What do you mean by unique and priceless items?"

"Oh, you know, I can't give anyone anything that's a standalone and can be considered of great value, like, for example, the original copy of Pride and Prejudice, or an original Monet painting."

David looked thoughtful. "Ah, that makes sense."

"But having said that, I always find a loophole if I want to," I grinned.

"I see joy rides on Rudolph, and tours of Santa's workshop are also on the list," David noted. He then turned to me, shaking his head. "I still don't quite understand why you have invited us here, particularly when you're breaking so many rules."

I shrugged. "I just thought we needed some reinvigoration." It still didn't feel like the right time to go into detail, so I ignored David's suspicious look. "So, what do you think so far?"

David glanced around the workshop, moving from the Christmas Law where his eyes lingered on Alabaster, who was continuing to churn out thousands of toys in seconds.

"It's great. But it does bring it home just how much effort has gone into one day. You've got all these laws that the governments have set out, then you've got your elves constantly churning out presents all year round, then there is the day itself, where you and your reindeer must work tirelessly to get around the world in one night, and I guess it makes me wonder why you do it?"

I frowned. "Why do I do what?"

"Go to such efforts for one day? I mean, it's not just you, the whole world has to do so much to prepare for it. Everyone's routines have to change. Loneliness and grief become more intense at this time of year, and emotions go up and down, particularly for children. They have so much unrealistic expectation of their hopes and dreams coming true, that there is potential for huge disappointment." He then sighed. "It leaves them getting hurt."

I studied David, noticing the anger seeping out of him, as if he was speaking from experience, and it made me feel sorry for him. I opened my mouth to respond when a shriek occurred, causing David to immediately look around at Pip, clearly panicked. Pip and the other elves were standing beside Pepper's workstation. A jar of glitter was now on its side and the glitter was covering her dress.

"Pip!" David shouted, racing towards her, whilst Pip giggled as she tried to wipe the glitter off. "What have you done?"

Pip looked up at the sound of his anger, and the natural smile disappeared from her face.

"I've told you not to be so clumsy." He crouched down and roughly tried to swipe away every flake clinging to her. "You know glitter is difficult to get out, it's never ending and we'll be seeing glitter on your favourite dress for weeks!" He stood up and ran his hands over his face, as if he was in distress.

I stared at his overreaction, surprised he was so angry about the situation. I then glanced at Pepper, who also looked concerned at just how much David was struggling.

Shinny stepped forward and wrung his trembling hands together, looking uncomfortable. "I'm so sorry, sir, but it wasn't Pip's fault. I knocked the jar over." His face and ears were now crimson.

"It's fine, Shinny. Don't worry yourself about it," I reassured him. "No damage is done and I'm sure Mrs C can remove the glitter in no time."

David let out a sigh, and all the energy seemed to slump out of him. "I'm sorry. It's just that it's Pip's favourite dress, and if anything happened to it, I'd be devastated for her. I get terrified every time she goes out in it. I'm even scared every time I wash it." He shook his head in exasperation.

"It's understandable," I sympathised. I could see that it was more than just a dress. It was a dress Pip associated with her mother.

Pip was now looking down at her dress, clearly upset. Pepper was pointing at it and telling her she liked the way the glitter made the dress sparkle, and Sugarplum was trying to thrust another candy cane into her face to make it better.

"Pip, come here," David said curtly, as he knelt down and Pip walked over to him. "I'm sorry, I shouted at you. You know I love you, don't you?"

Pip nodded, still sulking, so David opened out his arms. They had a brief hug, before David stood up and held her hand in an effort to stop her going off again with the elves.

Pip then looked up at me. "Do you still have the letter I sent you?" There was a pleading expression behind her eyes, and I understood why. She was still desperate for her full Christmas wish to come true.

"Actually, that's a good question," David said, before I could respond. "I always thought when Pip addressed her letter to the North Pole, it ended up in some random post office in the UK. Do they forward the letters on to you?"

"No, they don't get forwarded on. Let me show what we use to find out children's Christmas wishes." I beckoned them to follow, and everyone, bar Alabaster, hurried along with me. I led them past the elves' workstations to the centre of the room, to an enormous glass dome on the floor, surrounded by a gold ledge.

26

"This is the Christmas looking glass. It is our window into not only the world below us, but into the minds and workings of every child. Every time a child wishes or dreams about something they want for Christmas, the looking glass will detect that and automatically compile a report of who wants what, which the elves can work from."

Wunorse nodded. "Yes, it's much more reliable and flexible than the postal system. If a child sends a letter at the beginning of the festive season and then wants something else closer to Christmas, we don't have to wait several days for a new letter to get here. We can react as soon as they wish it."

Bushy nodded enthusiastically. "It means we can add extra presents right until Christmas Eve. It's tight, but we always do everything we can to make children's dreams come true," she gushed, looking proud.

David peered over into the looking dome, which looked like it was full of swirling clouds. "Wow, so you can literally read children's minds?"

The elves nodded happily and Pepper looked at Pip, who appeared a little overwhelmed.

"So, is there any point in asking children to write letters to you if you don't need them?" David asked.

"Of course there is," Pepper replied firmly. "Letters are a wonderful expression of what children really want for Christmas. Writing a letter encourages a child to focus and think about exactly what they want before sharing them with us."

"Yes, and it is those decisions that we can work from," Wunorse agreed.

"If a child doesn't write a letter, we get wishy-washy ideas about what the child wants, and we then have to guess what would be the best gift to give, then there's the risk that we get it wrong which leads to disappointment."

Sugarplum clasped her hands together to her chest. "Also, hand-written letters by children, who have excitedly skipped to their local postboxes and sent their requests out into the world, has a much more personal touch, and adds to the Christmas magic."

"So, did you read my letter, then?" Pip asked, looking concerned.

Pepper glanced at her. "Of course we did. Whenever a child writes a more unique letter to us, we get an alert to it, so I can assure you that we read every word, and we saw the lovely drawings you did."

Pip smiled and looked relieved, whilst David glanced at her suspiciously. "I didn't see you do any drawings on the letter we sent."

"I sent another one with Grandma." Pip's cheeks turned rosy.

David frowned and sighed. "What did you ask for, Pip?" his voice rising an octave.

Pip shrugged and looked back at the dome. "Can it read all my thoughts?" she asked, sounding concerned.

Wunorse smiled. "Well, it can, but the Christmas Law stops us from prying into anything that doesn't relate to your Christmas wishes or the odd idea for a new toy. It does, however, track each child's behaviour throughout the year, in order to produce the two different lists. The red list and the green list."

Pip swallowed. "What do the lists do?"

"The green list is for those children who have been good all year," Wunorse confirmed.

"Well, generally," I chimed in. "What child doesn't have their cheeky moments?"

"And what's on the red list?" Pip asked, looking anxious.

"The red list is for those children who have been consistently naughty and not very nice," Wunorse continued.

"Ah yes, is this when you give them coal to teach them a lesson?" David asked.

I shook my head. "Oh no, those days are over. The coal didn't really have the desired effect we had hoped for, and instead it just caused the children to act up even more. There were even a few occasions where the children would throw the coal in a frenzied attack, smashing windows and ornaments."

"Yes, that's why we came up with a new idea," Wunorse said. "So now, Pepper creates a gift of personalised elf dust, which Santa sprinkles over them. The dust helps them see the error of their ways through either karma, empathy, or realisation."

"Wow, that's incredible," David commented.

Wunorse nodded. "Yes, sometimes it's very effective, but sometimes, no matter what we do the children just need time to grow out of it. But we try!"

Pip looked down at the floor, and she wrung her hands together. "Am I on the red list?" she asked.

Wunorse blinked. "Why would you be on the red list?"

Pip looked at her dad, then back at the floor. "I... I was playing with my dolls and one of Daddy's model cars. The green one without a roof, and I accidentally broke the door off it."

David's mouth dropped as he stared at her in horror.

"I'm so sorry Daddy, it just broke off in my hands, so I hid it down the back of the sofa."

Pip looked close to tears and I could see David was trying his hardest to recalibrate his reaction and calm down.

"Are we talking about my 1964 mint green Buick Skylark car?" he choked, his face pale.

Pip stared at him, unsure if she should nod.

David appeared to count to three before he took a deep, steadying breath. "Pip, I have told you that those cars aren't to be played with."

"I know, which is why I'm certain I will be on the red list." Her voice quivered before she looked at me questioningly.

I chuckled at her sad, scared, hopeful eyes. "Whilst you should listen to your dad and not play with things you shouldn't, it takes more than that to get on the red list."

"Phew," she looked relieved, whilst David ran his hands over his face in frustration.

"We'll talk about this later, Pip," he warned.

Pip nodded meekly before David turned his attention back to the dome. "This tool is pretty mind blowing to track children like this." He then looked back at the wall where the Christmas Law shone in gold and he scanned the list again. "Does this relate to the law that states 'Will not share the insight of any child with anyone, and the knowledge of a child's character will only be used for Christmas present related purposes?"

I nodded. "Yes, it does. When the world governments first recognised that I had this ability, they wanted to know who the naughty children were in order to keep a closer watch on them because some could go on to committing more serious crimes. However, it turned out that certain groups were only interested in the naughty children, as they wanted to recruit them for their own gains. Even now, I still find it hard to believe that this happened."

"Wow," David gasped. "That's pretty scary."

"Yes, it is. So, I put a stop to it and I added it to the Christmas Law so that no one except me and the elves could access this knowledge."

Pip hopped up onto the ledge. "Molly Humphrey!" She stared down into the dome, but the dome remained blank except for a few wisps of white moving across it like clouds.

She then bent down to touch it when David stopped her. "Pip, get down from there," he shouted, pulling her back. "I told you to not go climbing on things you shouldn't. You could get injured or break something."

"Sorry," Pip replied, looking at her shoes. "I just wanted to check if she was on it, as she's mean to me at school."

"Only an elf or Santa can use the looking dome," Sugarplum said. "But I'll do it for you." She hopped onto the ledge and peered into it. "Molly Humphrey," she whispered. Then several names saying the same flitted across the glass. Streaks of green went past until one name emboldened into a dull red colour. "Ah yes, Molly Humphrey from Plockton. She's definitely on the cusp of red."

"I thought so." Pip glanced at David, and looked appeased.

David sighed and ran his hands over his face. "Pip, you shouldn't concern yourself with other people, just focus on being good yourself."

Suddenly Alabaster stomped past us, carrying a pile of remote-control racing cars, whilst shooting an uppity, annoyed look at us. He opened the door to the storage room and placed them inside before he stomped back again.

"Is that where you store the toys?" David asked, gesturing to the cupboard which Alabaster had just closed.

Wunorse nodded. "Yes. We keep all the toys in our storage cupboard." He then consulted the tracking device he had around his neck which looked like a stopwatch. "Currently, we have four hundred million, six hundred and sixty-six thousand, eight hundred and fifty-six toys already made."

"We're a little behind," Bushy confessed, and darted a glance at Sugarplum, who shrugged as if she didn't seem to care, which caused Pepper to close her eyes briefly and cross her fingers behind her back in hope.

"Wow. That storage cupboard must be massive," Pip gulped, opening her arms wide.

"It's just a normal storage cupboard size, with an excellent sorting system. Here, let me show you."

I led Pip and David across to the storage room and opened the door to the shimmering barrier, which looked like a layer of water was hovering across the entrance.

"Ah, what is that?" Pip asked, instantly taking a step backwards, as if it might attack her.

Pepper smiled. "This is called a span-warp field. It creates a never-ending space for all our presents, along with a protective barrier to prevent any damage happening to the toys."

"Can I touch it?" Pip asked.

"I'm not sure," Wunorse said. "I think only elves and Santa can penetrate the field."

Pip grinned. "Can I try?"

Wunorse shrugged. "I can't see the harm."

Pip stepped forward and placed her hand against the shimmering barrier, unable to go any further. She gasped. "It's like it has a heartbeat."

"Of course it does," Sugarplum said. "Those presents are the heart of Christmas."

Pip frowned. "I thought the heart of Christmas was spending it with family and loved ones. That's what my mum said."

Sugarplum looked like she was about to object when she snapped her mouth shut, whilst David took a deep breath, and looked away from Pip in pain.

"Why don't we head over to the planning board so we can show you what toy ideas we have for this year," I suggested in order to change the subject.

"Excellent idea," Wunorse agreed.

Once we were all standing in front of the huge board, Wunorse adjusted his collar and cleared his throat as though he was ready to do a presentation. "So, this is where we plan the toys for the year, and as you can see, there is an eclectic array of ideas."

Pip looked excited as she studied the board. "What's that?" she asked, pointing to one squiggle.

"It's a helicopter that transforms into an enormous spider," Wunorse replied.

"A spider?" Pip shuddered. "Why would anyone want that?"

"One boy dreamed it up, so I thought it would be a good idea," Shinny uttered, rocking on the balls of his feet as he spoke to the floor.

"That boy must be strange," Pip said.

"Perhaps to you," I replied. "But every child has their own personality with unique flairs and dreams, which means one child's junk can be another child's favourite toy."

Pip nodded. "I guess that's true. One boy in my school likes flicking elastic bands at the teacher, and I find it boring. What's that one?" she asked, pointing at the board.

"That is an alpaca that you can take for a walk," Wunorse stated.

"Does it spit?" Pip asked.

"No, not this one," I chuckled, but it made me wonder if we should include it as an additional feature.

"What's that?" she asked, pointing to another doodle on the planning wall.

"That is the world champion sausage eating game," Wunorse confirmed. "You play against your opponent to see how many of these plastic sausages your player can eat."

"Do the sausages come with ketchup?" Pip asked.

Wunorse looked startled. "No," he spluttered, looking somewhat confused whether they should.

Whilst Pip studied the wall, I watched her reactions to see which ones she found interesting. She would grin, jump up and down, or frown and move on.

"You have a lot of ideas here," David commented. "It must take a long time to come up with everything, then design and make each one."

I nodded. "It's a lengthy process. Of course, not all these ideas will get used, but as we get closer to the date, we will work out which ones to move ahead with."

Pip then danced around. "These all look so exciting."

"Maybe tomorrow you could try out some prototypes," Pepper suggested, darting a questioning look at me, to which I smiled and nodded.

"That would be so much fun," Pip agreed.

"Oh, that would be perfect," Sugarplum gushed. "We never get to see the children play with the toys we make."

"That's sad. But I will definitely be your toy tester," Pip promised.

"Well, I think we should head back. Mrs C will kill me if we don't get back in time for dinner."

Sugarplum clasped her hands together before she suddenly burst out. "Oh my cinnamon buns, I'm so excited to have you here. I can barely believe it's happening."

"Me too," Bushy added.

I smiled at how happy they appeared. "Come on," I beckoned to David and Pip.

I guided them to the door, where David helped Pip put her coat on, and wrapped a scarf around her neck. Meanwhile, all the elves, apart from Alabaster and Wunorse, stared at us, whilst appearing to hold their breath. We stepped out into the cold and the door had barely shut, when I suddenly heard an outburst of screams and shouts, making me jump.

"What the..." I pushed the door ajar to peer back into the workshop.

Bushy, Shinny and Sugarplum were holding each other's hands, jumping up and down and round in a circle, dragging Pepper with them, who seemed happy to join in but also slightly more reserved and thoughtful.

"Candy canes and gingerbread. Presents and bows. Nothing compares to a child, and the joy she sows," they sang together.

This chorus was new to me, but I was amazed by how they all sang in unison. I then blinked as they started screaming and twirling in delight, whilst Bushy grabbed some glitter from Pepper's kaleidoscope station and threw it up in the air so it showered down on all of them. It settled on their hats and green outfits and they sparkled just like Pip had earlier.

"Do they normally behave like that?" David asked, peering in next to me.

"No! Only when we have you here," I muttered.

David forced a smile. "Well, it seems like Pip is a big hit," he said, stroking her head.

Pip grinned widely, and I smiled in return, feeling happy. I'd not seen the elves with so much energy in a long time. "I think you're going to be a wonderful influence on them," I said as I closed the door.

27

We entered the warm house, and I stomped off my snow-covered boots and sniffed the air to inhale Mrs C's cooking. Instantly, I recognised the intoxicating, rich smells, and I grinned joyfully.

"Something smells good," David muttered.

"It certainly does." I felt excited as my tummy rumbled.

Mrs C appeared from the dining room. "Great timing. I've just finished laying the table. I hope you're hungry."

She held open the door, allowing us to step inside, and instantly Pip and David gasped. The dining room table was dressed with green and red tartan napkins and tablecloth, along with our posh plates, which were white with a red rim around them, and there, in the middle of the table was my all-time favourite feast, a glistening, golden brown turkey. Beside it were silver serving dishes containing roast potatoes, cauliflower cheese, mashed potatoes, green bean casserole, brussels sprouts, pigs in blankets, and honey roasted carrots. There was also a bottle of red wine on the table and a jug of milk for Pip.

"It's Christmas dinner," Pip shrieked.

David's face paled at the sight, and he pulled his collar away from his neck, looking uncomfortable.

"Well, it's not Christmas now, but I thought what better way to celebrate having guests than to have a feast like this," Mrs C smiled, and gestured for everyone to sit down.

"You really didn't need to go to so much fuss," David said, reluctantly walking around to take his seat.

"Don't say that. I could eat this meal every day, but Mrs C only does it for me a few times a year, so I have to savour every one."

"A few times? You eat way more than your fair share of turkey, and it's still not often enough. But speaking of which, you can do the honours and carve." Mrs C handed me the knife and sharpener.

"Gladly." I stood beside the turkey, scraped my knife against the sharpener a few times, before I slowly sunk it into the turkey and shaved off a slice for each person.

Mrs C then began passing around the side dishes for everyone to help themselves. David helped Pip load food on her plate. Whilst I only stopped spooning out the mashed potato onto mine when Mrs C cleared her throat, and I begrudgingly put the spoon back in the bowl.

Pip was so excited that she kept climbing in and out of her seat. "I can't believe I finally get to have a Christmas dinner," she squealed, now kneeling on the chair and hugging the side of it.

"Pip, calm down and sit still," David said sharply, looking frustrated with her.

Pip's smile flickered as she shuffled into the right position.

"Did you not have Christmas dinner this year, then?" Mrs C asked as she poured out the drinks for everyone.

"No!" Pip glanced at David with a look of accusation. "We ended up having chicken, burnt lumpy potatoes and soggy cauliflower. It was awful." She leaned towards Mrs C, her eyes wide. "It was the worst Christmas ever."

David opened his mouth to say something, but instead, he just stared at Pip.

"Well, tuck in everyone," Mrs C said to change the mood. "There's plenty for seconds and thirds."

Pip instantly shoved a loaded forkful into her mouth. "Yum! These mashed potatoes are so creamy," she remarked gleefully with her mouth full. "This is the way my mummy used to make them…, without lumps." She looked up at David and pointed at her plate before she scooped up more food.

David sighed. "Come on Pip, I did try. It's just that it was always your mum who was the good cook and made the Christmas dinner." His voice quivered slightly as he spoke.

"Cooking isn't easy, is it?" I chimed in. "That's why I leave it all to Mrs C."

David nodded, looking forlorn. "It definitely isn't easy. I mean, I'm not lying when I said I tried to have a turkey this year. I went online to read up on it, but it was so overwhelming. There were so many different instructions and ideas on how to cook it, such as soaking it in a bath overnight, wrapping it in bacon to keep it moist, cooking it upside down first before rolling it over, basting it in oil or butter, or even lemon juice, or just shoving it in the oven and being done with it." He shrugged and shook his head. "I didn't know where to start, so I just decided chicken was easier."

"Wow, I didn't realise cooking a turkey could be so complicated," I remarked.

David nodded. "Most things are complicated. That's why I tend to stick to things I can shove in the oven, like fish fingers, chips and jacket potatoes."

Mrs C smiled sympathetically. "If you like, I can give you some cooking tips and walk you through some recipes whilst you're here."

"Oh," David said, surprised. "That would be great."

"Is there anything in particular that you wish you could make?" she asked.

"Mummy used to make a really tasty pasta sauce," Pip muttered.

David sighed and nodded. "She did. I've tried to recreate it, but I've never been able to do it justice."

"Definitely not," Pip agreed, sticking her tongue out and wrinkling her nose.

"Fine, it was a disaster," David admitted.

"And so was the chilli, and the stew, and that strange vegetable soup, and the…" Pip continued.

"Okay Pip," David interrupted. "We're all getting the picture that I'm pretty hopeless at cooking."

"Well, I suggest we have a look at this pasta sauce recipe first and see how close we can get to the original, and then go from there," Mrs C said, giving a wink to Pip, who suddenly looked happy and satisfied. "Now, Pip, have you had a good day so far?"

Pip nodded. "I really enjoyed meeting the elves. They were a lot of fun. They even screamed when I left the workshop and then they started singing about me."

Mrs C chuckled. "Gosh, they must have loved meeting you, but who wouldn't?"

"I don't think Alabaster did. I don't think he liked me very much at all." Pip's smile slipped, and a frown came across her face, before she quickly brightened. "It's okay though, because I'm sure one day we will be best friends."

Mrs C exchanged a look with me, both of us surprised by her resilience and determination. "Sweetheart, it might be best not to get your hopes up about Alabaster. He takes more time to warm up than the others," Mrs C said.

Pip nodded and wiped her lips on the back of her sleeve. "I guess I better spend more time with him then."

I pressed my lips together, unsure what the best approach to Alabaster was, but deep down I knew I needed to let things take their course. I just hoped Pip wouldn't get hurt in the process.

David watched us with intrigue, before he placed a hand on Pip's back. "Just be careful, Pip," he warned, making me wonder if he knew the real reason we had invited Pip to stay.

Pip didn't seem to notice the concern, and soon she was happily retelling us stories in elaborate detail about what she had seen in the workshop, during which David had to keep telling her to sit back down and stop spraying food everywhere.

Once I had finished my second helping of food, and David had had a few extra nibbles, Mrs C brought out a Chocolate Gateau, which delighted Pip even more, and then finally Pip sprawled out over the table.

"I'm stuffed," she yawned.

"Like a teddy bear?" I chuckled.

Pip giggled and nodded. "Yes. I'm squishy, just like a teddy bear." She poked her stomach before her eyes closed.

David stood up. "Come on, Pip, you've had a really long day. I think it's your bedtime."

Pip opened her hazy eyes. "But I'm not tired, and the reindeer need a midnight treat."

David pulled Pip towards him and picked her up, her head resting on his shoulder. "The reindeer can have their midnight treat in the morning."

"I've had the best day. And this time it wasn't a dream, was it, Daddy?"

David's breath hitched. "No sweetheart. It wasn't a dream."

As David made his way up the stairs, Mrs C started to clear the table.

"Poor man," she sighed, scraping Pip's plate onto David's. "He looks so miserable and tense all the time. He's clearly struggling to be here without his wife."

"I know. It's such a shame, because he and Pip should be loving this opportunity, being here together. It is Pip's Christmas wish, after all."

"I would hate for it to get to the end of the trip and David looks back with regret," Mrs C said. "Perhaps now is the time for you to talk to David properly, and tell him why he's here."

"What, now?" I asked, just as David returned downstairs.

"She was asleep as soon as her head hit the pillow. I think you were right about those beds being comfortable."

"Oh, you won't be disappointed. It's not just the beds. The North Pole always ensures a good sleep and a good appetite, so what can be better than that?" I smiled, but as my eyes strayed to Mrs C, I could see her nudging me with her expression. My smile slipped, and I frowned back at her, not knowing what to do.

"How about that sherry for a nightcap?" she suggested, as she hurried to the drinks cabinet.

She returned in seconds with two glasses of sherry with a candy cane poking out of each glass.

David looked surprised by the concoction, and he gave her a tight smile. "Thank you."

Mrs C then shoved the other glass into my hand, and accompanied it with another purposeful look, but I remained bewildered.

"Why don't you both take these to the rooftop? It's a wonderful clear night," she hinted, casting her eyes back to me.

"Rooftop?" David asked, confused.

"Ah, yes, good idea," I said, getting afraid of Mrs C's glares. "Let's make our way up there."

I led David up the stairs, past the guest room, to a door at the end of the corridor, which led to another set of steps. A coat rack holding two long fluffy red coats was on the wall beside the steps.

"You might want to wrap up." I handed him Mrs C's coat.

David pulled it on and followed me up the steps. At the top was a skylight window that opened up and allowed us to climb out and step onto the roof.

"Wow," David gasped, instantly taking in the scene of the Northern Lights. The view was fabulous from the roof and spoke a thousand words and hung a thousand paintings with the way the lights danced across the sky. "This is magical," David exclaimed.

28

"Mrs C and I like to come up here and just absorb the atmosphere. There really is a wealth of beauty in the world when you find it, isn't there?"

David nodded as he tugged his coat tighter around him. "There truly is," he whispered as he frowned perceptibly at the sky.

I gestured to the two wicker armchairs on the roof and as we sat down; I took a swig of my drink. Mrs C clearly expected me to get him to open up, but I wasn't sure if I could measure up to Mrs C's natural ability to get people talking. She would have been better positioned to handle this. I turned my head to the door, wondering if I should go fetch her, when I took a deep breath, and told myself I could do this.

A moment of silence passed as David stared into the sky, lost in thought, whilst I racked my brains for a way to break the ice. "So, is your competition prize living up to expectations?" I asked.

"Huh?" David blinked as he adjusted to the present. "Oh, yes. It's great."

"That's good," I said, although half the time I wasn't sure David was enjoying himself.

Silence fell again, and I mused what to say.

"Good sherry, isn't it?"

David took a sip and nodded. "Yes, very good."

I returned to thinking which direction to go down and I could feel the pressure from Mrs C to get everything out in the open sooner rather than later. It was like a telepathic power of hers. I took a sip of my sherry and decided there was nothing better than to just go for it and to rip the band-aid off.

"Pip's a sweet girl. It must be hard for both of you since your wife passed away," I said, bracing myself.

David froze. His body tensed and he gripped his glass tightly, making me wonder if I should have gone in more gently, but I thought starting on a positive note about Pip was gentle enough.

"It's been really hard," he muttered.

I waited, hoping he would fill in some gaps. The silence eked out further, and it felt like a test to see if I would cave and speak first, but I knew some of Mrs C's tricks to make people open up to her. She always played with the power of silence, even when it grew uncomfortable. I sipped my drink to prevent myself from speaking, causing the candy cane to tinker against the glass.

David swallowed and stared at the sky. The aurora borealis held so many hidden and powerful secrets, but it also had a hypnotic and relaxing quality to it, which aided my difficult task.

Eventually, he spoke. "I can't help but think that it would have been so much better on Pip if it was Holly who was still around rather than me. She needs her mother so much, and I can't do what Holly did. I'm failing abysmally at being a father, let alone a mother as well. I just can't do it without her."

"What makes you think that?" I asked, trying to hone Mrs C's tactics by using open questions to make people talk.

David shook his head a little. "Holly was incredible. She was so capable, and nothing seemed to phase her. She was the one in a stable job, supporting me and Pip whilst I tried to get my business off the ground. It was her who would take care of the household, the cooking, the cleaning, running Pip around, showing her all the love and care in the world, whilst I ploughed my time into my…. business. It was like she was juggling the world and never once did she complain."

I nodded along. "She does sound incredible."

David took a deep breath. "Sometimes I wondered if I was being selfish going after my dream and spending too much time trying to make something work that ultimately might very well be a waste of time, but

Holly was the one who insisted I keep pursuing it. She believed that if you want something badly enough, and you work at it, it will happen."

I smiled, knowing all too well the power of what can happen if you ask for something, but I was keeping my cards close to my chest for a little while. "She seems like a bright and insightful woman."

"She was, she was so full of life. She gave me the belief I could do anything, as she did to Pip as well." He looked down at his glass and spoke to it. "Yet without her, I feel so helpless. I feel like I'm drowning in everything and struggling to come up for air."

"It's always difficult losing someone so close, but I'm sure you're doing a better job than you think you are."

David shook his head. "I'm not and I'm ashamed of it. I've been too busy trying to make ends meet and struggling to get the motivation to pick myself back up, that I've been finding it difficult to focus on Pip. I thought that making my work a priority and throwing myself into it in order to provide a better future for both of us would be in Pip's best interests, but it's causing issues."

"I'm sure Pip understands you're doing everything you can for her. She's a bright girl."

David nodded. "She is, but she doesn't deserve this." He sighed and clenched his glass, taking a moment to gather himself. "She certainly didn't deserve what happened at Christmas."

"Do you mean about the chicken dinner?" I asked. I couldn't help but sympathise with Pip on that one. "Well, I guess chicken is a decent substitute…," I muttered.

David shook his head. "That farce of a Christmas dinner was just the tip of the iceberg. I also committed the most cardinal sin imaginable and I don't think I will ever forgive myself for it."

"That doesn't sound good. What happened?"

"I missed her Nativity play," David said, his voice sounding rough. "She was a shepherd, and she'd been running around pretending to herd sheep and reindeer all along the run up to it. She was so excited, but I had a meeting and I couldn't go. A meeting that turned out to be a waste of time, and another rejection," he said bitterly, shaking his head.

"Ah, I've heard about these plays the schools put on. It seems to be a way to make working parents feel terrible, but so many parents don't get to see their children in their Nativity play, so you really shouldn't beat yourself up."

"I don't know," David muttered. "She was so disappointed. You see, her mother would never have failed to turn up. She would have been front and centre, beaming with encouragement at her, so the fact it went from that to nothing, makes it even worse. Then, the rest of the run up to Christmas hardly made up for my failings about the Nativity play."

"What happened in the run up to Christmas?" I asked.

He shook his head, took a sip of his sherry, and stared up at the sky. "Nothing, and that's the problem. I failed to buy her an advent calendar. I didn't stock the cupboards with any festive foods. I didn't bake anything with her. And I didn't put any decorations up except a few measly ones a few days before Christmas."

"Oh… well… at least you put in a bit of effort at the end," I said, trying not to squirm at the thought.

"It was pitiful. I wanted to give Pip a special Christmas, but money was tight, and I just couldn't bring myself to do it. You see, Holly was always the one who made it magical, not just for Pip, but for me as well. Before I met Holly, I was never into Christmas. No offence," he uttered, as my mouth dropped open slightly.

"That's fine. Many people aren't for some strange reason," I muttered. It always baffled me, but I had to accept it.

"But Holly converted me. She would get excited as she hung tinsel in every place imaginable and arranged the baubles on the tree with absolute delight. She would bake mince pies and cookies, and all the while, she'd be dancing around in her hideous Christmas jumpers and singing the same Christmas songs on repeat. It was difficult not to get swept up in the Christmas spirit, and I guess this last Christmas a huge part of me just couldn't bring myself to do it without her." David took a deep breath. "Everything was so painful, seeing all the decorations in the village, and smelling those familiar smells. It just made me miss her so much and I continuously felt this incredible guilt." He fiddled with the candy cane, lifting it from the glass and using it to stir the drink. "Every time I smiled, or had something nice to eat, I felt it was wrong. She should be celebrating Christmas and watching Pip laugh, play with her toys, and grow up."

I took a sip of my sherry. "I guess being here in the North Pole must be constantly reminding you of Christmas and Holly."

David nodded. "I knew a Christmas themed holiday would be difficult, but I didn't think it would be this painful. I mean this place is incredible and we've been given a once in a lifetime opportunity, that no one but us will get to experience, and yet I'm wracked with this horrible feeling in the pit of my stomach, one of intense grief and guilt. I wanted to do this for Pip to make up for the disastrous Christmas, but it feels so wrong that Holly is missing this."

I sipped my sherry and pondered for a moment. "Guilt is a strange emotion to feel when something isn't your fault, and it's not your fault Holly isn't here in person. Life goes on for the living and it's worth making the most of it, don't you think?"

David opened his mouth to say something, when we both suddenly looked at a movement down below. Sugarplum and Bushy were hurrying out of the workshop, across the snow, carrying a ladder between them. Their feet were so light they didn't leave any footprints and they stopped beside Mr Frosty. They both smoothed out the snow on his sides, and then Bushy climbed up the ladder to be level with his head, where she smoothed out his head and brushed a covering of snow from his hat.

Once they had finished, they stood in front of him and appeared to be chatting with him. Not only that, they were laughing, as if he was telling them a joke. Seconds later, both Bushy and Sugarplum jumped around him and gave him a big hug before they picked up the ladder and hurried off back into the workshop.

David blinked, and a faint smile came across his lips at the elves' delight. It was impossible not to.

"I often wonder what they say to Mr Frosty," I said. "They always look so excited whenever they fix him up, but I'm never close enough to hear them."

"I assume they are telling him they love his hat and scarf, but really he should put some actual clothes on in this weather," David joked, his lips twitching into a half smile.

I chuckled, wondering if he was trying to be funny. "That's an excellent point. I had no idea that Mr Frosty was potentially suffering from the cold; and that he might be desperate for Mrs C to knit some trousers and a coat."

David's smile then slipped, and his expression suddenly clouded over.

I could see that the guilt had reared itself again. I was pleased that he had opened up to me, but it was clear that he certainly hadn't been fixed.

"Do you know what I love about my elves? They take such delight in the little things. I mean, they spend their whole lives building toys, but they find ways to love it. Sometimes it's a hard slog, but they always find a rhythm, smile, find joy and continue because it's the right thing to do," I said, forgetting about Alabaster's new attitude for a moment.

David took a deep breath and took a sip of his sherry.

"I get you are processing the loss of your wife, but you have to realise that Pip is here and whilst you're missing the moments that you should be sharing with your wife, you're also missing the memories you should be creating right now with your daughter." I decided it was time to lay my cards on the table.

David looked uncomfortable. "It's just so hard."

"Of course it is. Grief is hard, but don't forget Pip's grief is compounded. Like you said, you're struggling at being a father, let alone a mother as well, which means Pip has lost both of you, along with her favourite things."

"Like Christmas," David retorted.

"No, not just Christmas," I remarked. "You! Your company and the things you do together, like days out, talking and laughing. She misses your lightness and fun. I know all Pip desperately wants is to have you back, so you can share memories of Holly together. I know that because she told me so in her Christmas letter."

David frowned and paused. "Is this the one she sent with her grandma?"

I nodded. "She put a lot of time and thought into it."

"What did she say?"

"What was it now…" I thought, recalling what Pepper had shown me.

"Oh yes. '*Dear Santa, all I want is my daddy to spend time with me, for him to smile more, and for us to have the perfect Christmas the way we used to.*

I know he is busy with his job, but I wish he would win lots of money so he never has to work again. Then he can take me for ice cream and walks in the park to see the reindeer, just like daddy used to when mummy was here.

I miss my mummy so much. I miss her cooking, the smell of her perfume, and how she would pick me up from school and ask me about my day. My Daddy gets sad when I mention her, so I try not to, but I'm scared that I've already forgotten what my favourite dress of hers looked like. I think it was red and black, but I'm not sure. I wish I could keep all my memories of her in my fairy box, so that I never forget her.

Also, my mummy used to tell me so many stories about you, and I have so many questions that I would love for you to answer, so I'd also love to meet you and visit you, the elves and the reindeer. Mummy always told me to write to you when I was feeling sad, because you would listen. Is that true? Love from your biggest fan, Pip'."

David smothered his mouth, looking like he wanted to cry. "Did Pip really write that?"

I nodded. "Yes. Of course, the punctuation was all over the place, and there were quite a few spelling mistakes, but that's what it said. Plus, the picture she drew of me was rather questionable. I know my belly is rather round, but I was a little horrified that I looked like I was devouring my own head."

He shook his head. "I feel terrible. I had no idea she was worried about forgetting her mother." He scratched beside his eye, trying to prevent the tears from forming. "I just struggle so much to talk about her, as I miss her terribly."

"I get that, but I also know that Holly never wanted you to be sad. She certainly didn't want her death to put a thorn in your relationship with Pip."

"How can you even know that?" David whispered.

"I have to be honest with you and tell you the real reason you are here. You see, it actually goes back to Holly."

"Holly?" David looked surprised.

I nodded. "She used to write thank-you letters to us, which are the only physical letters we receive here, when I collect them on Christmas Eve. She would write every year to us about how she loved Christmas, and that she was always grateful that we created a magical time. Her letters were so full of love, and they spoke so highly of you both, that Pepper grew attached to them, and to Holly." The waves of light above us started to move faster, twisting and dancing in the sky. "Then, when she saw Pip's letter, she insisted we do something."

David's eyes widened in shock. "I knew she wrote letters and left them beside your mince pie and carrot, but she always sealed them."

"Well, perhaps you should read them." I slipped my hand into my inner coat pocket. I pulled out the letters Pepper had handed to me, flicked through them to find her last one, and passed it to David.

David's fingers shook as he took the letter from me and read it.

"Dear Santa,

Thank you for all the presents you bring to my family every year. I know they come from a special and heartfelt place, and they bring so much joy to us. I do hope you, the reindeer, and the elves are enjoying the North Pole and not working too hard, but either way, please know we all appreciate it.

This Christmas period has been special to me, and I am looking forward to seeing what tomorrow brings. I may not be around to see the next Christmas, but I hope you continue making Christmas magical, so my family can continue to enjoy it as much as I always have, when I'm not around. They are the world to me, and I would hate for the magic to leave them during these wonderful festive periods.

Please do keep a watch over them when I'm gone, even though I know

160

you will. I want them to keep living, smiling and be happy until we are
reunited again.

Thanks again for everything.

Your biggest fan,

Holly."

David's eyes were brimming over with tears as he lowered the paper. "I can't believe you have this," he whispered as the colours of the sky changed. Sections of the lights danced from green to purple, then to pink.

"Well, Pepper kept it and pored over it daily, but I wanted you to see that you shouldn't feel guilty about continuing without Holly. She wanted you to enjoy yourself, to laugh without her, to embrace Christmas and to have a wonderful life. She wants you to go on living, to go on adventures, and she certainly wants Pip to be happy too, particularly at Christmas."

David nodded and sipped his sherry as he stared up at the sky in silence. A reflective look crossed his face as the words sank in and he wiped his eyes. "You're right. I've been too busy thinking about how much my wife would love this, instead of enjoying myself on her behalf. I've stopped myself from letting the experience in and I've stopped letting Pip in too." A tear rolled down his cheek. "But enough is enough. I need to embrace every moment, not just for me, not just for Pip, but for Holly as well."

I smiled, feeling happy that he had finally come to this realisation and would approach things differently and more positively. "I'm so pleased and I'm pretty sure Holly is, too."

David glanced at me, then back at the sky. "Wow," he exclaimed, as the pink colour in the sky had become more defined and had spread out across the sky. "The sky looks even more beautiful than it did before. It makes me feel like she's with us, spreading her angel wings, as she looks down on me and Pip." He suddenly shivered. "I know it sounds weird, but I feel closer to her right now than I ever have since she passed away."

I smiled contentedly, feeling happy that he was attuned to what was around him.

David returned his attention to the sky and as he watched the lights, a smile came across his face. He pressed his fingers to his lips and then placed his hand over his heart.

29

The next morning, I came downstairs to Mrs C's breakfast spread. She had made banana muffins, croissants, stacks of pancakes with bacon and a pot of coffee, ready for our guests.

"So, how do you think David will be today?" Mrs C asked as she poured me a coffee.

"I'm not sure, but our conversation seemed to go well."

Mrs C smiled. "I'm just glad you didn't make him pack his bags and demand to be taken back to Lapland."

"Eugh, not that place. No one would choose to go there if they had the option to be here."

Moments later, we heard the patter of excited feet racing down the stairs. Pip stopped dead in the kitchen doorway, her eyes wide as she scanned me and Mrs C. "It's still true."

Mrs C grinned at her. "Yep. We're still here. Now, what would you like for breakfast?"

Pip's eyes lit up at the sight of the food. "Pancakes," she cried.

David appeared in the doorway. "Did I hear you say pancakes? Your mother used to make them with mascarpone and lemon."

Pip's eyes lit up at the mention of her mother.

David smiled. "She then used to pretend to be a blindfolded horse, and she'd gallop and neigh, then bump into something."

Pip looked thoughtful for a moment, trying to recall. "Oh yes, I remember that. I never understood why."

David laughed. "She was pretending to be Mask-a-pony. She had a great sense of humour."

Pip still looked confused, but she giggled anyway, happy to be talking about her mother.

I exchanged a look with Mrs C, who appeared delighted at David's change of mood.

"I can whip that up for you if you like," Mrs C said.

David looked momentarily surprised, then he smiled. "That would be lovely."

Mrs C served Pip and David some lemon and mascarpone topped pancakes, whilst I drizzled some syrup on mine.

"This is perfect, just like she used to make them. Thank you!" David said.

"You're welcome," Mrs C replied.

Pip bit into hers, and her eyes suddenly flickered to her dad. She looked at him excitedly. "I remember this. And mummy always smelt of perfume at breakfast time."

David smiled back at her as he tucked in. "She always wore perfume from a bottle with a daisy on it."

Pip grinned, loving the story. Once she finished her pancakes and wiped her mouth on the back of her sleeve, she jumped to her feet. "Please, can I go play in the workshop?"

"Sure, you can. The elves will be delighted to have you visit," I said.

David slowly stood up. "I guess I best escort you."

"She'll be perfectly safe going on her own, trust me."

"Yes, I can go on my own. I am seven, you know," Pip boasted.

David raised his hands up in surrender and sat back in his chair as Pip raced out of the kitchen. "Make sure you put your coat and hat on," he called, as the front door slammed. He shook his head. "I have no idea if she actually did or not, but right now, I'm enjoying this coffee far too much to check." He picked up his mug and took an indulgent sip. There was definitely a relaxed nature about him that hadn't been there the day before.

"You know what?" he said to me, as he grabbed a banana muffin. "I really want to thank you for last night and our talk. I know Pip and I still have a difficult road ahead of us, what with balancing work on the business and trying to spend more time together, but I've decided that the least I can do is to be completely present for her when I am around." He took a bite of his muffin. "I'm sure I can give 100% to my business, during work hours, and 100% to Pip outside of that," he pledged, as if convincing himself.

Mrs C picked up her coffee. "That's a lovely idea. It's important to remember that quality time is sometimes better than quantity, so I'm sure Pip will appreciate it."

David nodded, and after he finished his coffee, he stood up. "I think it's time to check on Pip."

"Noo," Pip cried, as soon as we opened the door to the workshop. "My sausage shot off early and in the wrong direction."

"You missed my mouth by a mile," Bushy giggled.

"I'll get it for you." Shinny raced over to collect the sausage to give back to Pip.

"My go," Pepper sniggered, as she flung her sausage against the board and Pip tried to wind her character's mouth shut before it landed inside.

"Missed," Pip squealed in delight, as the sausage flopped against the character's forehead and bounced off.

David was studying the game with a slightly amused frown on his face. "What is this game?" he asked. "It looks…interesting."

"It's the World Champion Sausage Eating Contest. It's a prototype for this year."

Wunorse was staring longingly at everyone playing as he dutifully remained at his station, whilst Alabaster firmly kept his eyes on making toys, but I spotted him glancing over several times to watch.

As they carried on playing, none of them noticed David or me standing nearby, until Pip's sausage flung towards David's shoe.

"Daddy!" Pip called, and skipped over to us. "Do you like my new badge?" She pointed at her chest. "It's a daisy. Pepper helped me make it."

David smiled. "It's wonderful. Your mother would have loved it."

Pip's smile grew before she hurried back to the game. "Do you want to join us, Alabaster?" she asked.

Alabaster stopped midway through twiddling the mechanics of a Gameboy and scowled. "No, I don't have time, and neither do the others!"

"Oh, don't get your striped tights in a twist," Sugarplum snapped. "We'll be fine as long as you stop nagging us all the time."

"Well, maybe if you weren't idle on the job, I wouldn't need to nag."

Bushy looked sad. "He used to be fun," she whispered to Pip.

"Yes, he used to be the most cheeky and adventurous out of all of us," Sugarplum said. "Now he's turning into the Grinch."

Pepper gasped, whilst Shinny quickly slammed his hands over his large ears. "Don't say that."

"Well, he is," Sugarplum huffed, folding her arms. "He's ruining the Christmas buzz we usually get, and he's upsetting our guests."

Pip walked over to Alabaster. "I'm sorry for being here, Alabaster. I don't want to upset you."

He stared at her, surprised she was addressing him. He was about to say something when Sugarplum cut him up. "Don't apologise to him. He should be the one apologising to you for being rude."

After a moment's hesitation, Alabaster turned his back on her. "I won't be apologising to anyone."

Sugarplum's face turned bright red with anger. "If anyone should be on our naughty red list, it's you."

"Hey," I cried. "Enough arguing, everyone."

The elves went silent as Pip shuffled over to David, with her head bowed, looking deflated.

I took a deep breath, wondering what to do. "I know." I thought about my trusty manual of jokes, which was a necessity to diffuse any tension. "What did the snowman say to the polar bear?"

"Ooh, I know!" Bushy shot her hand up.

Sugarplum frowned and yanked Bushy's hand down. "You're not supposed to tell anyone about what Mr Frosty said."

"Oh? But he asked…" Bushy looked confused.

"Wait! It's not literal, it's a joke, and the punchline is… I have snow idea," I smirked.

166

The elves frowned, but Pip began giggling. "Snow idea! So, it's meant to be no, but instead it's snow because he's a snowman," she explained, laughing even harder.

The elves stared at Pip and began nervously giggling along with her.

Shinny stepped forward. "I... I know a joke."

"Fantastic! Please share," I pleaded.

Shinny's cheeks turned rosy. "What do snowmen eat for dessert? Ice crispies," he blurted.

I shook my head. "You're meant to pause for people to guess before giving out the answer."

Pip cackled louder this time. "Ice crispies, not Rice Krispies. You know, like the cereal," she explained to David again.

Shinny grinned proudly, whilst David and the elves started laughing at Pip's infectious childish charm. I even spotted Alabaster give a quick chuckle before he forced his serious expression back on his face.

"Okay, okay, I've got a good one," David grinned, as Pip calmed down. He cleared his throat and looked around to ensure he had everyone's attention. "What do you call an obnoxious reindeer?"

He paused expectantly. "Rude-olph," he laughed into the silence.

Pip looked confused, possibly because she didn't understand the word obnoxious, and the elves stared at me, as I frowned and folded my arms.

"Rudolph isn't rude. He's my best mate!" I stated.

David's face dropped before I grinned. "Only joking," and I laughed in my deep booming laugh, as the elves joined in. "It's a good one, although if any of my reindeer are rude, I would say it's Vixen or Dancer."

David sighed. "Phew. I thought I'd offended you then."

"Nah, not at all. I have a whole manual of Christmas jokes, and a storage cupboard full of stocking filler books on them, which we wrote. In fact, I think it was me that came up with that one."

David looked relieved. "You got me then; I really thought you were angry."

I chuckled and placed my hand on his shoulder. "It takes more than that to offend me. I usually only get offended when I eat a mince pie with a soggy bottom. Actually, even that would be a delight."

30

While David and I were chatting, Pip had wandered around the workstation. "What's all this?" she asked, stopping at Sugarplum's station, which had bald and faceless doll heads lined up on it, a fabric flip book, along with the pantone colour bridge on the back wall of her bench.

Sugarplum skipped over to her. "This is our doll creation station, where we can design our dolls' outfits and appearances."

"Wow, that looks like so much fun. Can you do anything you like?" she asked.

"Of course," Sugarplum said proudly. "I know. Why don't we create a special doll for you, so you can see how I do it?"

Pip gasped. "Wow, that would be amazing."

"Right." Sugarplum grabbed one of the doll heads. "What colour hair shall we go for?"

"Orange, with streaks of yellow," Pip said.

Sugarplum nodded. "Orange is interesting. Which orange and yellow would you like?" she asked, pointing to the collection of orange variations on the colour bridge.

Pip tapped her chin thoughtfully. "All of them!"

Sugarplum laughed. "Okay, let's see what I can do." She took a doll's head and within seconds, strands of different orange and yellow colours appeared out of its head.

"It looks like the sun," Pip said, happily.

"What colour eyes and lips shall we give her?" Sugarplum asked.

"Green eyes, with pink eyeshadow and bright pink lips because pink is my

169

mum's favourite colour!"

Sugarplum picked up a paintbrush and dabbed at the doll's head, revealing a perfectly drawn face, as Pip jumped up and down, looking like she might burst with excitement.

"Now, what shall we get her to wear?"

"An orange tutu, pink knee-high boots, and pink leotard," Pip chanted, as she spun around in a wobbly pirouette.

Sugarplum stared at Pip for a moment, before she broke out into a grin and turned back to the doll to finish it. "Here you go, one doll designed by Pip."

Pip squealed as she took the doll off Sugarplum and stroked her hair. "I love her already, and I'm going to call her… Delilah Sunrise," she exclaimed, holding her upwards to look at her. "Can I go play with her?"

"Of course you can," Sugarplum said.

Pip gasped and raced over to a box on the floor, sat down in front of it, and started walking the doll back and forth along it. She began mouthing something that the doll was supposedly saying, and Pip looked completely absorbed.

David stepped towards me. "Wow, Pip really loves that doll."

I watched Pip's radiant smile. "Yesterday you asked me why I do what I do," I reminded David, unable to take my eyes off Pip. "Well, this is why. The way each child interacts with a toy is entirely unique. It not only brings them joy, but it helps develop their imagination, and it unashamedly gives them the power and control to be who they are in the world."

Then my smile slipped. Pip's ear splitting tuneless tones were travelling across the room as she now made her doll pretend to sing into a microphone and destroy my favourite song, Jingle Bells.

David blinked at the noise. "Yes, the joy of children is truly… wonderful."

We were both relieved when Pip's tune veered away on a long deafening note, before she stopped, having become distracted by the box she was using as her stage. She opened it up and inside were some of the craft items the elves had used to decorate the room and the tree. There were lengths of tinsel, bows, glitter glue, baubles, stickers, little jewels and sequins, stencils, and paints.

Pip gasped. "Please, can I make some necklaces for the reindeer?"

I blinked, surprised by her request. "Sure, go ahead."

She tipped the box of items out onto the floor, then sorted out nine long pieces of tinsel and got to work, glueing sequins everywhere, with her tongue sticking out the side of her mouth as she concentrated.

"I've got some mini plastic penguins, you could add," Bushy offered.

"Yes, and I've got some little ruby and emerald birthstones." Sugarplum skipped across to her with a box of jewels.

"Excellent. They will look very Christmassy," Pip chuckled.

Then shortly, with the elves' help and using their drying guns to dry the glue and paint, Pip held up her tinsel necklaces, which were covered in a scattering of random items.

"Very nice," David said, exchanging a look with me. They were garish and gaudy, and anything but nice.

"Can we put them on the reindeer?" she asked.

I hesitated, but I could see how happy it would make her. "I'm sure they will love them," I lied. "Let's do that now, before lunch."

Pip scampered to her feet, grabbing all nine tinsel necklaces, which clinked and rustled loudly as I led them out of the workshop.

Just as I closed the door, I heard Alabaster. "I hope you are going to clear that mess up after her."

"Of course I am," Sugarplum promised, as this time, even Alabaster's mood would not affect her glee.

We entered the reindeer pen, with Pip looking chuffed with herself. "Dancer," she called, as she was the closest to the entrance. "I have a present for you."

She rattled the necklace in front of her, causing Dancer to retreat.

"Come on you! Pip's got a lovely gift for you," I teased, over enthusiastically.

Dancer slowly stepped forward, her expression full of disdain, as she reluctantly bent her head towards Pip, and with David's help they looped it over her antlers and head, so it rested around her neck.

"It looks amazing," Pip clapped.

Dancer scowled at me before she trotted away into a corner.

"Sorry," David mouthed at me, and a part of me wondered if this was too cruel, but I shrugged. They could cope for a couple of hours until I came back and removed them.

"Prancer, you're next," I called. He'd been watching the scene with his head slightly tilted to the side in curiosity. Pip eagerly beckoned him across, so he strutted towards us, and Pip and David placed the necklace over him. Prancer shook himself, causing the necklace to rattle loudly, before he went to inspect his reflection in the water trough.

We got through them one by one, but when it came to Rudolph, and he looked at me with his big pleading eyes, I hesitated, unsure if I could do it to him.

Pip nudged me, so I sighed and reluctantly helped her put it on. "Sorry about this, lad." I gave him a pat on his snout, feeling guilty.

"Well, don't they all look lovely," Mrs C gushed from the doorway. "I came to tell you that lunch is ready, but after witnessing this delight, I think it calls for a photo." She waved her large camera at me with an amused smile. "Come on, everyone, gather round." She signalled for us to squeeze together.

I glared at Mrs C, knowing that the reindeer would not be happy to have this moment immortalised on a photograph. However, Pip looked delighted at the idea.

We got into position, including the reindeer, and once Mrs C was satisfied, she called, "Say cheese!"

"Cheese!" Pip screamed above mine and David's mumbles, before we forced our grins for the photo.

Mrs C snapped a few pictures. "Lovely. Now, I hope you're all hungry as lunch is ready, and then after lunch, David, we can do some cooking."

David grinned. "Fantastic! I've been looking forward to it."

31

After lunch, which consisted of sandwiches, quiches, sausage rolls, pork pies and my favourite; mince pies; David put on Mrs C's apron and disappeared into the kitchen, leaving me and Pip to head over to the workshop. When we entered, there was a strange, eerie silence as the elves glared at each other.

Pip looked up at me, and I patted her head. "Why don't you play by yourself for a moment?"

She nodded and ran straight over to find Delilah Sunrise and started playing.

"Everyone, meet me at the planning board, now!" I called. "Right," I hissed as everyone gathered around. "What on earth is going on now?"

Sugarplum glared at Alabaster. "He called Pip a nuisance."

Alabaster glared back. "She is a nuisance. She's distracting everyone and making a mess."

"You're just sensitive because it's you that can't handle your own station," Sugarplum snapped.

I sighed. "Enough, both of you! Alabaster, whether you like it or not, we have company for the next couple of days, so you need to be polite and deal with it. And as for everyone else, if Alabaster is struggling to make and create his complex toys, then it is not Alabaster's fault. We are a team, and if we fail, we all fail." I glanced over at Pip, who was now rummaging around in another box beside Shinny's workstation. "Now, have you come up with any fresh, exciting toys since we last went through it?" I asked, scanning the board and not seeing anything new.

"Unfortunately not, but I'm sure we will find something soon," Pepper said, glancing over at Pip, as she extracted a Velcro dinosaur shaped mitt and ball set and began playing catch with it.

I cast my head up to the ceiling to take in the daily countdown and took a deep breath. "I hope so, because we are fast approaching the half-way point, which is when we need to have nailed down our new products for the year; and whilst there are some good toys on here, I'm not convinced we have anything yet that will take the world by storm."

"Perhaps if everyone stopped messing around, then we would be further along and have something better than what we have," Alabaster grumbled.

"Let's not start an argument again. All I can say is keep trying and we will reconvene in a couple of days." I noticed Pip had found some green silly slime on Shinny's workbench. Then, to my horror, she started using it instead of the felt ball to throw up in the air and catch on her mitt. I could see the silly slime was now covering the mitt and matting in with the fibres of the Velcro. I shuddered to think what Alabaster's reaction was going to be, so I quickly ended the meeting and hurried over to protect her.

The elves got there before me, and I wasn't fast enough to stop Alabaster from shouting. "What do you think you are doing?" as Pip thrust her dinosaur mitt into the air to dislodge the slime.

"The silly slime is stuck," she cried, wafting it upward again.

"You're ruining our stock," Alabaster yelled.

Shinny moved forward, looking both intrigued and pained by what she was doing. "You're, err… You're meant to use the fuzzy ball with the dinosaur mitt."

"But I like the slime," and she wafted the Velcro mitt around with more vigour.

I felt frozen, not sure what to do, as she kept jabbing her dinosaur mitt upwards, when suddenly the slime launched across the room and landed on Alabaster's face. The shock on his face and the green slime which was left dangling questionably from his nose made me choke out a snort of laughter, which I quickly covered up with a cough.

The elves weren't as polite as me. Sugarplum and Bushy giggled hard. "It looks like snot," Bushy sniggered, her ears flapping back and forth as she laughed.

Pip gasped, horrified. "I'm sorry Alabaster!"

Alabaster slowly lifted his hand to his face to wipe the slime away, which caused it to dangle from his chin like a little elf beard.

He opened his mouth when Pip spoke. "You can throw it back at me if it makes you feel better."

There was a strange silence as everyone stared at Alabaster, wondering how he was going to react when suddenly, another ball of slime flew through the air and landed on Alabaster's shoulder. Everyone spun around in surprise to see Shinny looking more shocked than anyone, his hand still covered in green slime.

"I...I...I'm sorry," he blinked. "I...I just thought it looked like fun."

Sugarplum's eyes widened. "It does look like fun. Can I have a go?"

"Don't you dare throw it at me again," Alabaster snorted as he wiped the slime off his shoulder and flicked it to the floor in irritation.

"You can throw some at me," Pip screeched, looking excited.

Sugarplum raced over and grabbed some silly slime from the bucket next to Shinny's workbench and threw it at Pip, who tried to dart out of the way, but it landed on her back, causing her to giggle. Shinny raced over to Pip and handed her a whole bucket of silly slime, who happily tried to throw it back at Sugarplum, but Bushy ran into the path of it, desperate to join in. Then chaos erupted, as all the elves besides Alabaster and Wunorse began racing around, throwing silly slime at each other.

"Will you join in?" Pepper asked me, as she darted out of the way of some coming towards her, her face flushed with excitement.

I held my hands up. "No, don't get me involved." I knew how seriously I take these games and get carried away. Although that was normally more when snow was involved, not slime.

Wunorse was watching the chaos longingly when he eventually turned to Alabaster. "Can I...?" he asked hopefully, pointing towards the others.

"Do what you want," Alabaster sighed, clearly giving up trying to stop everyone.

Wunorse grinned and instantly gathered some slime that had landed near his workbench and joined in.

I was keen not to get any slime on my chequered trousers, so I quickly made my way towards the safety of the gingerbread styled armchair beside the Christmas tree. I sank into my chair with relief and even from the comfort of my armchair; I found the chaos draining to watch.

The elves darted back and forth, and soon the game started getting confusing. One moment Pip and the elves were darting out of the path of oncoming slime, the next, Pip was doing everything she could to jump in front of it. Even Alabaster had paused several times in his toy making as he got distracted by the scene, and the glare in his face grew softer. In fact, I was certain I saw his hand move around a fist of slime as if he was itching to throw it and take part, but he stopped himself.

Suddenly Pip stopped moving, looking breathless, and she scanned the area. "Everything is green. I can't see which is my slime and which is everyone else's."

Sugarplum's eyes lit up. "Good point. Throw some at me. I have an idea."

Pip launched some at her and as she did, Sugarplum grabbed some colour dust from her bench and threw it onto the ball of slime and when it landed, the slime was red, standing apart from the sea of green.

"Wow," Pip exclaimed. "Can you do that again?"

Sugarplum nodded. "We all can."

Then Pip began throwing more slime at the elves, and each elf changed the colour to red.

"Alabaster, will you do it too?" she cried, launching some at him.

Alabaster sighed, and nonchalantly threw some colour dust at it to turn it red, making Pip jump up and down and clap with glee. He rolled his eyes and continued to work. It was then I decided to put an end to things before she pushed him too far.

"Okay, everyone, enough is enough," I called. I scanned the area. There was green and red slime everywhere, on the walls, across the floor, on all the workbenches and mixed into work in progress buckets. The elves finally lowered their weapons and faced each other to see what they all looked like in the aftermath.

Pip giggled, and she walked over to Alabaster, covered head to toe in green slime. "At least now you're not the only slimy one," she said sincerely.

Alabaster's lips twitched into a faint smile, which he quickly covered up. "I should never have been covered in slime in the first place. Now, who is cleaning this lot up?"

"I'll do it," Shinny offered.

Alabaster shook his head. "Not you. You need to spend your time redoing the silly slime that you've all wasted."

Sugarplum rolled her eyes. "We'll all clean up. We'll be back to normal in no time."

Wunorse, Sugarplum, Bushy and Pepper quickly raced around, cleaning the room. Shinny returned solemnly to his bench to make more slime, whilst Pip spun and twirled, still hyper from the game.

"Alabaster, why don't you ever play with us?" she asked.

"I don't have time to play," he grumbled.

"I think everyone should make time to play," Pip said. "If I never played anything, I'd be very miserable. It makes the world more colourful; don't you agree?" She glanced around the red and green room with a look of happiness on her face.

Alabaster frowned and opened his mouth, then snapped it shut and stared at Pip's earnest face.

"All Alabaster does these days is work and sleep," Sugarplum declared.

"That's very sad. Do you sleep on your workbench?" Pip asked, staring at the bench, looking disturbed, and no doubt imagining Alabaster lying on the hard surface.

"I bet he would if he could," Bushy sniggered. "He'd happily carry on working whilst sleepwalking."

"We all sleep in our dorm room," Pepper said gently, as she found some slime under her chin and wiped it with the back of her sleeve.

"Wow. Can I see it?" Pip asked, looking excited.

"Sure, you can," Sugarplum agreed. "I think we all need to get changed, anyway."

Sugarplum led the way, and we all followed apart from Alabaster, with

Pip skipping and waving the skirt of her slime covered pink dress around. Shinny was by her side. "Did you like the red slime or the green slime better?" he asked anxiously.

"I like them both equally. I like all colours, but pink is my favourite."

Shinny looked thoughtful as his powerful little legs matched her stride.

We exited the workshop through a side door and instantly Pip gasped. "Wow. It's like a magic tunnel out here."

The corridor was draped in sparkling red and green lights, and the walls were painted to look like they had hundreds of green and red tinsel ribbons and bows running along it.

"I've never seen anything like this before." She stared up at the lights like she was hypnotised by them, as she walked down the corridor, with everyone leaving slimy footprints behind them. "These fairy lights are really pretty."

Bushy spun around to face her, looking as though she'd been slapped in the face. "These aren't fairy lights. They are elf lights and the fairies stole our idea."

"Yeah. Stupid fairies," Sugarplum scoffed.

"What's the difference?" Pip asked, confused.

"Elf lights shimmer and twinkle. Fairy lights… well, they just sit there or they flash," Bushy stated.

"Yeah, elf lights are far more magical and special, so we win," Shinny boasted.

I shook my head to myself and chuckled. This was a debate I always tried to stay out of.

Sugarplum opened the door to their dorm room. "Here we are."

There were six small beds lined up next to each other with their names embossed on the wooden panel at the foot of the bed. Each one had a duvet cover displaying an accurate image of an elf body with elf red and white tights and shoes on it, so when the elves slept with their heads poking out, they barely looked like they were underneath it.

The beds displayed different stages of disarray, beginning with Alabaster's, which was neatly made, with the corners tucked in and no sign of a crease. The beds then progressively became messier through Pepper, Wunorse, Shinny, and Bushy, culminating with Sugarplum's bed at the end where her duvet was screwed up and her pillow had been haphazardly thrown on top. There was also a pair of balled up striped tights and some sweet wrappers under the bed.

Pip stared around the room and hugged herself. "This looks wonderful. I bet you stay up chatting all night, telling stories and laughing like a sleepover."

Shinny nodded. "Yes, we do."

"Well… we used to," Bushy recalled. "Now Alabaster tells us to be quiet, so Sugarplum, Shinny and I gather under the duvet cover to talk and eat chocolate treasure, whilst the others sleep."

Pip grinned. "That sounds fantastic. I've never had a sleepover before and I've always wanted to go to one."

"Well, I'm sure you will when you're older," I said.

Alabaster suddenly appeared and stomped across to the red chest, pushed up against the foot of his bed, and took out a fresh uniform. "Is no one doing any work today?" he grumbled.

Sugarplum sighed and marched past us towards her own chest, and opened it. "I see your Grinch mood is back!"

"Well, Pip," I said loudly to cut over the tension. "I think we best get you cleaned up before dinner, too, as I dread to think what your dad is going to say about your dress." I glanced down at her special dress and fretted about the state she was in as I recalled how David had reacted to the glitter incident.

"Maybe we shouldn't tell him!" she remarked.

I chuckled. "I think it will be hard to miss. Come on."

We left the dorm, and Pip waved goodbye to the elves. "Bye Alabaster," she called, and to my amazement Alabaster gave her a curt nod of goodbye, and half a wave.

32

Pip and I made our way to the house, and I braced myself for David's reaction. When we entered, David instantly appeared from the kitchen, still in his apron. His face glowed, and I'd never seen him look so happy and relaxed. "Wow. What's happened to your dress? Where has all this slime come from?"

Pip grinned. "We were playing with silly slime, and it was so much fun. Even Alabaster wanted to play with us, but he pretended he didn't!"

"It sounds like you've had a great time. Now, why don't you go upstairs to get cleaned up and changed, because right now you look like you've been busting ghosts," David laughed.

Pip frowned in confusion, before she nodded, and made her way to the stairs.

"Don't forget to bring your dress back down with you. Mrs C can get it cleaned up in no time," I said.

"Yes, and then I have a surprise to show you," David said, smiling happily, and at the mention of a surprise, Pip bounded up the stairs.

"Have you had a good time cooking with Mrs C?" I asked, smiling at his cheerful expression.

"I've had a great time. Mrs C has taught me how to cook so many things, all with secret ingredients or techniques to make it all taste amazing. I feel like I've had a life lesson in just a few hours."

Mrs C smiled as she emerged from the kitchen, drying her hands on a dishcloth tucked into her apron. "Well, you've been a brilliant student and we've talked a lot as well, haven't we?"

"Yes, it's been great. I feel like I've also had an incredible therapy session on top, which I think I've needed for a while now." He gave Mrs C a grateful smile and I knew they would have been discussing Holly and Pip; and that her advice and guidance would have been on another level to what I was capable of. His eyes then lit up. "Plus, she's giving me a special recipe booklet to take home so I won't forget anything, including her recipes for the perfect turkey and mince pies."

"You're giving him a recipe book full of your secrets," I glanced at Mrs C, who nodded happily. I frowned and turned back to David. "But of course, you won't be able to share any of it with anyone. You'll be stopped by the Christmas Law and the contract you signed."

Mrs C shook her head. "Yes, don't worry yourself. David knows the contract also governs my cooking secrets. These are just for him to share with Pip."

I breathed a sigh of relief.

Pip then scampered down the stairs now dressed in her pyjamas and a little unicorn styled dressing gown, carrying her slime covered dress. She looked a little cleaner, but there was still some green goop in her hair.

"Don't you look adorable? I'll take that off you and clean it up in no time," Mrs C offered.

"Thanks Mrs C." Pip then turned to her father. "What's the surprise?" she squealed.

"Well, there's more than one," David replied. "For starters, Mrs C taught me how to make gingerbread, and we made so much of it we didn't know what to do with it." He opened the door to the kitchen. "So we built a house."

Pip poked her head inside and gasped before she ran in. David and Mrs C followed her, smiling happily. There on the countertop was a replica of our house here in the North Pole. It was carved and constructed so perfectly, right down to the wreath on the front door, and the wicker chairs on the roof terrace.

"It's here," she screeched, inspecting the scene. Beside the house was a replica of the workshop, the reindeer pen, and the shed. "Oh my goodness, are they the elves, reindeer and Santa?" she asked, pointing to a range of gingerbread figures they had made.

"Yes, plus we built a sleigh." David pushed the sleigh towards her, which was parked inside the hangar.

Pip jumped up and down and squealed with delight. "This is amazing."

"That's not all," David whispered. "Look behind you."

There on another counter top was a second gingerbread house, carved and designed into a quaint-looking cottage, from the smooth walls, the flowerbed at the front, an oak tree at the side, and the picket fence and gate at the end of a cobbled path.

"It's our house," she shrieked so loudly, Mrs C jumped.

David nodded. "And look who's in the garden?"

Pip squealed. "It's me and you."

David chuckled at her reaction. "Mrs C has an incredible talent, doesn't she?"

Pip nodded eagerly, her face beaming. "Can I play with it?"

Mrs C smiled. "Of course you can, but after dinner. Why don't you both go into the dining room? David and I will serve."

I led Pip into the dining room, where the table had already been laid, and drinks were waiting for us. Pip sat down in her seat and instantly she was wriggling and bouncing up and down impatiently. I took a sip of my beer and wondered how parents coped daily with excitable children. Then I contemplated how my antics at Christmas must hype children up so much it must sometimes be unbearable, and I took another swig of my beer, and chuckled. At least I didn't have to deal with it.

Moments later, Mrs C arrived, holding the door open for David, who was carrying a large bowl. "Pip, this is surprise number two." Pip stared at David as he placed the bowl down on the table. "It's taken us a while to perfect, but with Mrs C's expertise, I think it's pretty accurate."

Pip peered into the bowl. "Spaghetti and sauce," she announced.

"Just the way your mum made it," he grinned, as he began spooning some out onto a plate for her.

Once David sat down, we all tucked in. Pip twirled her spaghetti around on her fork and flicked sauce in several directions, making me even glance up at the ceiling to see if any had landed there.

She then took a bite. "Yum. This is just how I remember it!" and she slurped the spaghetti into her mouth.

"I'm glad you're enjoying it, and now I know how to make it, you can have it whenever you want," David promised.

Once Pip devoured her food and downed her milk, she jumped up from the table. "That was scrumdiddlyumptious. Now can I play with the gingerbread houses?"

David chuckled and nodded, as Mrs C dabbed the corners of her mouth with her napkin. "I'll help you." She gathered the plates together and went into the kitchen with Pip.

"Shall we have a drink in the lounge?" I asked David.

I led the way into the sitting room and David sank into Mrs C's armchair, already looking comfortable, whilst I got to work building a fire. Within a few minutes, the fire was roaring and crackling, warming the room to make it cosier.

David smiled serenely as he relaxed in his chair by the fireplace. "I can't believe how much of a success that pasta sauce was. You know, I've spent so long trying to push Holly out of our lives, but you and Mrs C have made me welcome her back into our hearts and lives, and I'm so grateful for that."

"I think it's great news that you now feel comfortable doing that. For both you and Pip's sake. In fact, I think it calls for a little celebration. I'm going to open one of my bottles of whisky that I've been keeping for a special occasion."

I walked over to the drinks cabinet and opened a cupboard. A span-warp field shimmered in front of it, and David sat up to peer at me curiously. "Now where is it?" I stuck my head inside, and pulled out a few of the thousands of bottles that had been given to me as thank you gifts over the last few centuries, and placed them on top of the drinks cabinet and the floor. Eventually, I spotted the one I was after and pulled out the dusty bottle to show him. "I thought we'd give this a go." I popped open the cork, causing the whiffs of woody notes to hit my nostrils.

David was now on his feet, his mouth hanging open. "Hang on," he exclaimed, looking in disbelief. "What year is that whisky from?"

"Err," I squinted down at the bottle. My reading glasses were probably next to the computer somewhere. "This one is from 1926." I grabbed a couple of glasses and poured a dash of whisky into each glass.

"Single malt?" David asked, staring at me in what appeared to be a numb surprise.

"Of course!"

David's mouth popped open. "Wow, that bottle is probably worth a lot of money." His eyes lit up. "One second!" He raced from the room towards the coat-rack, where he rummaged around in his coat pocket. He returned holding his mobile phone. "May I have a look at that bottle?" His eyes were wide and there was an excited buzz around him.

"Sure," I said, perplexed by what he was about to do.

He held up his phone in front of the bottle and moved it around the sides, as if he was taking a video of it. When he glanced back at his phone, he shook his head in astonishment. "This bottle could be worth 1.5 million pounds, if sold to the right bidder." He spun his phone around for me to look at the figure, large and bold, on his screen and surrounded by some other text.

"Oh wow, that is interesting." I passed him the glass to sip.

"Are you actually going to drink it?" David asked in disbelief.

"Well, eventually someone has to, don't they? Otherwise, what's the point of the bottle containing whisky, if all anyone does is look at it?"

David stared at me in horror. "To preserve something that is incredibly rare in the world."

I chuckled and shrugged. "But then I'd never get to drink any of my gifts. And I thought, what better person to share it with than our first guest in centuries?"

David smiled and looked down at his glass. His hand trembled slightly. "I can't believe I'm about to try such an old refined whisky."

I'd never seen anyone look so emotional and excited about the prospect and it made me more excited, too.

He swirled his glass around, gave it a sniff, then brought it to his lips as he closed his eyes. His eyebrows came together in a frown as he swallowed and then let out a breath. "It reminds me of medicine," he deduced, smacking his lips together to prolong the taste.

I gave mine a sip, and it was smooth as it went down, but I could understand David's association with medicine. "Very nice. That should clear the sinuses. So how did your phone know how much this would be worth?" I asked.

"Oh," David said. "Well, that's what my business is."

"Whisky valuations?"

"Not quite. I've invented an app called 'Vintique Scanner' which can identify valuable and rare items of any kind, by processing the shape, distinct patterns or features, any hallmarks, along with a whole range of other identifiers." His eyes glowed with excitement as he spoke about it. "It then provides you with the history of the item, including its place of manufacture, year of production, and other items made during the same period. Then, it calculates everything, including the last time a similar item was sold, the market interest for such an item and the current demand, including where the hot spots are for potential buyers. It generates a predicted range, including a high, low and average price, and it shows the likely probability it could sell at each value."

I sipped my whisky and listened intently. "That sounds like a great tool. What made you decide to launch that?"

"Well, alongside my technical engineering background, I've always been interested in antiques, vintage and retro items, and I used to go to pawn shops, car boot sales, and auctions all the time. But I often witnessed people getting low offers from experts in the field. I could see their eyes light up with pound signs in them and I hated it." He sipped his drink and wrinkled his nose a little at the strange taste. "It inspired me to create this mobile app, so that you didn't have to be an expert to recognise if you own something valuable. It would put the control back onto the seller, who is your everyday person, and they would know the real market value."

"It sounds like you're doing a good deed, so I take it the business isn't going very well?"

David's face was lit up talking about his invention, but his expression suddenly darkened. "No, it's not. I've thrown a lot of our savings and resources into it. I've got the product, and it works exceptionally well, but I'm struggling to get it launched and find an investor who can help get me to market. It's so frustrating because I truly believe if I can get it out there it will be successful, but I keep getting rejected, time and time again. Even that letter you delivered to me when we met was another rejection letter to add to the pile."

"Oh, yeah, sorry about that. So why do you think you keep getting rejected?"

He ran a hand through his hair. "I don't know. Perhaps I'm approaching the wrong people, or I'm pitching it wrong. I get anxious during presentations and interviews, so I stumble over my words and I get flustered." He sighed. "You see, I've never been that great with the business side of things. I was counting on Holly to help me with it once the product was ready, and now the product is ready Holly isn't here."

I nodded in understanding. "Well, do you know who's fantastic at presentations?"

"Who?" David asked, as his eyes darted to the other bottles I had removed from the cabinet and left on the floor.

"Someone who helps me all the time, Mrs C. She could help you put a plan together."

"Do you think she would?"

"Of course," I replied as I wiggled my toes in front of the fire.

"That would be incredible. I've been navigating my way through it all by myself for so long that even just talking it through with someone would help."

"Oh, I'm sure she'll do more than that," I muttered, smiling into my drink.

David's eyes then darted back to the bottles, and he shifted in his seat. "May I have a look at those more closely?"

"Be my guest. They have been in my cupboard for ages now."

David's eyes lit up with excitement again and he jumped out of his seat and went to sit on the floor, where he began scanning each bottle.

"Wow. You have quite the collection. Some of these are worth over a hundred grand each."

I shrugged. "It's because I'm a hoarder, I guess. That's the problem when you can use span-warp fields. You never have to chuck anything out."

David then gasped. His eyes bulged at a dusty bottle he was holding. "No," he whispered. He'd turned ghostly white. "No way."

"What is it?" I asked.

"Th… this bottle. It's from the 1400s, one of the first ever bottles of whisky to be made. My app says its value is unlimited. Is that right?" he asked, his eyes still bulging, and he swallowed as if his mouth was dry.

"Let me see that." David spun the bottle towards me and then realisation clicked. "Oh yes, that's correct. It was a gift from Henry the eighth. He was more of a mead guy, but he gave this to me more out of courtesy than his generosity."

"Henry the eighth. '*The*' Henry the eighth?" David looked astounded.

"Yes. The one and only. I met him a couple of times. I must say, though, I was never a fan of the way he treated his wives; arrogant, obnoxious bloke," I muttered, shaking my head. "Plus, I'm surprised he got away with it. I mean, if I chopped Mrs C's head off, she'd kill me."

David was barely listening to me as he stared at the bottle in silent disbelief. "I never thought I would ever get to see and hold something so incredible." He then gently placed it back down on the floor and wiped his hands on his trousers. "I should probably wear white gloves to handle it."

"To be honest, I'm not that excited about opening that bottle. Whisky back in those days certainly wasn't what it is now. It tasted more like a mix of bleach and pet…" the sound of a small tap at the front door cut me off.

33

I raised my eyebrows in surprise as we never had visitors, let alone at this
time of night. I clambered out of my seat and made my way to the door, just
as an exhausted-looking Mrs C also emerged from the kitchen to
investigate.

"Who could that be?" she muttered.

I opened the door to find Shinny and Sugarplum clutching each other's
hands, looking anxious.

"Is everything alright at the workshop?" I asked, suddenly concerned.

"Yes," they squeaked together.

"Shinny has something to ask. Go on," Sugarplum said, encouraging him
to speak.

Shinny squeezed Sugarplum's hand even harder, as he looked down at his
little shoes with his upturned toes and red pom-poms dangling off the tips.
"We were wondering if Pip wanted to come to our sleepover."

A toying smile crept across my face. "And what does Alabaster have to
say about this?"

"I'm sure he's fine with it," Sugarplum said.

I exchanged a look with Mrs C, who seemed to find the situation rather
amusing. "Well, it would be up to Pip and Pip's dad."

David came over to investigate, and I spotted Pip poking her head out
from the kitchen. "What's going on?" David asked.

"We're here to ask Pip if she wants to come for a sleepover," Sugarplum
said, lifting her head confidently.

David was clearly shocked at the request. He then looked at Pip, who stepped towards us, clutching a gingerbread man, looking both terrified and excited. "Is this something you would like to do?" he asked.

Pip took a deep breath before she nodded enthusiastically.

David ran his hand along his chin. "Are you sure? You've never slept anywhere by yourself before."

Pip's eyes were wide. "I'll be alright. I'm seven now. I'll be fine."

David looked at his watch. "Very well, if you're sure. It's still a couple of hours before your bedtime and we are on holiday, so run upstairs and fetch your toothbrush and Mr Stuffy."

Pip gasped, and then hurtled herself to the stairs, with David following her.

I lowered my head to Sugarplum and Shinny. "Make sure you look after her, and don't forget, she's not an elf, so she needs more time to get ready for bed and she needs more sleep than all of you."

Sugarplum nodded, almost ready to burst with excitement. "We'll look after her, Santa, sir."

I glared at them and whispered. "And not too much chocolate treasure, either."

Sugarplum and Shinny both nodded, then looked at each other and grinned.

Pip raced back downstairs, hugging her teddy, Mr Stuffy, along with a mound of clothes.

"Pip, I don't think you need to take all of that," David was saying behind her, but Pip locked her arms tighter.

"Ready?" I asked, and Pip nodded.

"I'll be over to check on you in a couple of hours," David promised, as Sugarplum and Shinny both held onto each side of Pip's dressing gown to guide her away. David stood in the doorway watching for a moment, before he closed it silently. "Her first sleepover," he whispered.

"The elves will look after her," I said, despite feeling slightly worried that chaos could ensue.

"Yes, I'm sure they will, and after all that, I don't even think she took her toothbrush," David mumbled. He then shook his head. "Now I really do need that whisky."

"Whisky?" Mrs C asked, her eyes lighting up. She tapped the top of her head and noticed she had hair sticking out in places it normally wouldn't. "That sounds good right now."

I smiled and poured another glass and gave it to Mrs C, who sank onto the sofa. "How was it playing with the gingerbread houses?" I asked, smiling as she closed her eyes for a moment.

"Exhausting. Apparently, we forgot to build the aeroplane that she arrived on, so I made one for her and spent all that time flying back and forth from her home to the North Pole," she grumbled, despite a smile dancing behind her eyes.

David chuckled. "Yes, she does like to play the same game over and over."

"I don't know how people do it," Mrs C said, taking a sip of her whisky. She smacked her lips together and frowned. "This has a strange taste to it."

"Medicinal?" I asked.

"I guess so. It's very smoky." She then spotted all the bottles scattered across the floor. "Were you two having a party?"

"Not quite, just a mini celebration before David started telling me about his business, which currently isn't going so well, and we were thinking you might help him."

David looked momentarily lost as he stared at the bottles on the floor, whilst sipping his drink quietly. I couldn't tell if he was thinking about Pip or my bottle collection.

"Of course," she agreed, smiling warmly. "Why don't you tell me all about it, David?"

David blinked, then turned his attention away from the bottles onto Mrs C. "Okay, well, I've invented an app called Vintique Scanner." He then explained exactly how it worked, his reasoning behind setting it up and the trouble he was having finding an investor and getting it to market.

"Well, Vintique Scanner sounds like a fantastic app," she agreed once David had finished. "It's definitely something every single person should download, just to wander around their own house to discover if they own

190

anything valuable."

David nodded. "That's the dream."

Mrs C smiled. "Well, I will be delighted to help you. I think the first thing we need to do is for you to show me your current presentation slides, and demonstrate to me how you've been pitching it and to whom."

David grinned, and a look of pure excitement came across his face. "Wow Mrs C, you've already helped me so much today, but that would be incredible. I actually have everything saved in the cloud. I could show you now if you like."

Mrs C suddenly seemed less tired. In fact, energy and excitement seemed to flow back into her. "No time like the present," she grinned.

They both looked at me, and I shooed them away. "You two go for it. I'll be right here, minding my own business." Me, whisky, and sole possession of the remote control suited me fine. I knew exactly what film I was going to watch again.

Mrs C and David left the room to sit beside the computer. For an hour, I could hear their murmuring as they discussed David's business model. I then heard him nervously presenting it to her as if she was an investor, and she asked him tough questions that he stuttered over. I could hear Mrs C providing her advice, suggesting alternative ways of phrasing things. I could hear the tapping of keys on the keyboard as they verified data and wrote up notes. Then I heard David presenting it back to her a few more times. His answers sounded stronger on every round, and I could hear his voice growing more confident.

I knew Mrs C was revelling in being able to offer her advice, and giving him the tools he needed to succeed. It was how she often helped me with interviews, meetings, and business cases. She was the brains behind it all, and so I knew just how much she was helping and how invaluable it was.

Eventually, Mrs C and David returned to the lounge. "I really can't thank you enough, Mrs C. You've made me look at things completely differently," David said.

"It was my pleasure, and I really think you will smash it, if you remember everything we've talked about," Mrs C replied.

David's smile widened as he cast his eyes down to his watch and his eyebrows shot up. "Gosh, is that the time? I think I should check on Pip."

I downed the rest of my whisky. "I'll come with you and make sure the elves are behaving."

David and I headed across to the workshop, which was empty and quiet. I led David out the opposite door and we quietly approached the elves' dorm, along the elf lit corridor. As I opened the door to the dorm, there was a scuffle.

"Quick, someone is here," Bushy cried, and all the elves, apart from Alabaster, moved from a huddle into some strange attempt at a pyramid. Sugarplum leapt onto Wunorse's shoulders and Shinny leapt onto Bushy's. Pepper seemed to hover in front of both of them as if they were blocking our view of something.

"What's going on?" I asked.

"Nothing," Bushy and Sugarplum declared at the same time.

I darted a glance at Alabaster, who was lying down in bed having swapped his elf hat for a red and white striped nightcap, and was clearly watching what the elves were up to.

"Where's Pip?" David asked, sounding concerned.

The elves looked at each other before they sighed, and Wunorse and Bushy stepped apart.

"Daddy!" Pip was grinning as she appeared between the two elf towers.

I pressed my hand to my mouth to stop myself from laughing.

"Oh, my!" David stared at Pip in shock.

"I'm not Pip anymore. My name is Pipshine now."

David laughed. "Is it now?"

Pip was now dressed in an identical outfit to the elves. She was wearing a green coat with large yellow buttons down it, which was far too tight, making Pip stand there like a stuffed doll. Her feet were scrunched up into a pair of far too small elf shoes that curled up at the toes, and a green hat with a red trim was stretched tightly over her head. Her cheeks had been painted with red circles to match the elves' natural rosy cheeks and her nose had also been painted red as well.

"Do you like it, Daddy? I'm an elf now."

David bit his lip. "You look fantastic."

Pip moved to clap, but stopped as she couldn't meet her hands together in the tight outfit. She turned around to look at Bushy. "I love being Pipshine, but I think I need to get out of this now."

Sugarplum raced over and both she and Bushy assisted her in squeezing back out of the coat to reveal her Rudolph pyjama top, which I was secretly admiring and felt chuffed about.

David appeared to be trying to stop himself from laughing. "Well, Pip, or Pipshine, whichever you prefer, have a good night, but make sure you get some sleep. I'm sure one of the elves will bring you across for breakfast tomorrow," he smirked, sharing an amused look with me.

We left the dorm and both let out a small laugh. "She looks so happy," David said. "This is her dream come true, to be here with the elves, and go to a sleepover with friends."

The following morning, I trudged down the stairs, rubbing my eyes. I could hear the sizzling sound of bacon cooking and I was eager to follow the mouth-watering smell, when there was a tap at the door.

It was Pip with smudged red cheeks and nose, hugging all her clothes to her chest, standing next to none other than Alabaster, who was holding Mr Stuffy for her. Instantly, I was concerned that he'd blown up and dragged her home, but whilst Pip looked tired and exhausted, she also looked sincerely happy.

"How was last night?" I asked her.

"Wonderful," she yawned. "We played, sang, and talked. It was the best night of my life." Her eyes were drooping, and she looked like she could fall asleep standing up.

David then appeared behind me and hurried over. "Pip, are you alright?" he asked, to which she nodded with her eyes closed. "Come on, let's get you to bed, and you can wake up in a few hours and tell me all about your sleepover."

Pip nodded sleepily. Alabaster then handed Mr Stuffy to David, as he guided Pip away upstairs. Alabaster watched her go with a surprisingly calm, intrigued expression.

"So, how did it really go last night?" I asked, curious about his reply.

Alabaster shook his head. "It was terrible. They giggled and chatted until the early hours. Bushy and Sugarplum don't seem to realise that a duvet cover isn't soundproof. Then Shinny fed her chocolate treasure, which caused Pip to have a wave of energy and run around with the others in the middle of the night, playing obstacle courses and who could jump the highest on the bed."

"That sounds like the perfect sleepover," I said.

"Well, maybe for them, but I didn't sleep at all. That girl can talk and she continuously kept asking me questions." He looked irritated, but when I looked more closely, I could see his lips were slightly curled up in the corners and I wondered if he was as irritated as he claimed to be.

"What did she ask you?"

"Oh, all sorts. How come we are so fast? How do we turn out millions upon millions of presents per year? Where did we originally come from? Do I enjoy what I do? Why am I in charge?" He shook his head, trying his best to look annoyed. "She doesn't stop."

I chuckled. "She's quite a character. Did you answer all her questions?"

"I had to," he cringed, exasperated. "She didn't give me a choice."

"Well, she said in her Christmas letter she wanted to ask questions."

"She certainly accomplished that," Alabaster grumbled. "Anyway, she's safe and sound back here now, so I'll crack on." He dipped into a slight bow and hurried back across the snow to the workshop.

As I turned around, I found Mrs C watching us with an amused smile.

"Something tells me he enjoyed Pip's company, after all."

I smiled back at her. "Me too."

34

A few hours later, Pip woke up, and we all heard her jumping around before she bounded down the stairs.

"I'm awake!" She raced into the kitchen wearing her pink ruffle dress that Mrs C had cleaned for her. There was no hint of slime anywhere on it. "Can I go to the workshop to play with my friends now?" she asked.

"Sure, you can. David and I will escort you. I need to check in on the elves and then do a couple of chores, anyway," I said, placing my mug of tea on the table.

Pip grinned, grabbed her coat and raced out of the house, slamming the door behind her so that the wreath banged haphazardly against it.

I looked at David and frowned. "She heard me say we were going with her, didn't she?"

He shrugged. "She has a secret power called selective hearing."

We hurried after her and caught up with her before she burst into the workshop. The elves were busy working, but looked slightly more sluggish and wearier than normal. Bushy and Sugarplum grinned when Pip arrived. Shinny, however, didn't look up. He was concentrating intently and bent over his workbench to the point he was barely visible, whilst different clouds of colour kept wafting upwards around him.

"Hello Pipshine," Sugarplum greeted, as Pip skipped over to them.

"Hello fellow elves," she called, looking delighted. She then turned to Alabaster. "I'm at your service, master Alabaster. How can my elf hands help with Christmas?"

Alabaster rolled his eyes. "They can't. Just go play with your toys," he said, although his expression was now looking softer.

"No problem, master. I will be the toy tester," she saluted. She grabbed Delilah Sunrise and started singing tunelessly as she brushed her hair, which finally made Shinny look up from his workbench.

"Alabaster, will you sing with me?" Pip asked. "Bushy said that you used to sing all the time."

Alabaster stared at Pip. A flicker of longing flashed across his face, before he then glared at Bushy and shook his head. "No, I'm busy," then he started fiddling with some motherboards to go into a games console.

I stepped close to Pepper. "Is everything alright in here?" I asked.

Pepper continued to stare at Pip with an affectionate, hopeful expression. "We're getting there." A small, perceptive smile played on her lips.

I gave her a calculating look and then smiled. "Well, I think David and I will leave you elves to it."

We turned to leave when Pip suddenly gasped. "Oh, no! Delilah's head has come off." She was holding the head in one hand and a little hairbrush in the other.

Sugarplum and Bushy gasped and lowered their toys, ready to assist her, but stopped in their tracks. Alabaster had instantly dropped the motherboard he was holding and raced over to her on impulse. "Let me look at that," he said assertively.

Pip handed it over to him, tears forming in her eyes. "I'm so sorry, it just came off," she whimpered.

Alabaster shook his head. "It's a simple fix."

"She was about to go on stage for the concert. Now she'll be nervous that her head will fall off again." Tears were now rolling down her cheeks.

Alabaster looked at her. "Perhaps she needs a support group to make her feel more comfortable, so that not all the attention is on her."

I stopped and stared. Something was happening that was completely captivating.

Pip nodded and wiped her eyes. "I think that would be a good idea. She should be in a girl group."

"Well, maybe Bushy can help you create some more, whilst I fix Delilah."

I glanced over at Pepper, who was staring at them with her mouth hanging open. Bushy was also in shock and cleared her throat, as Pip nodded and walked over to her. I nudged David. "Come on." I was cautious about interfering with the mood. "I could do with your help to muck out the reindeer pen."

David nodded. "Sure," he muttered, staring at Alabaster, before he blinked. "Wait what?" he said.

I smiled and led him away. We made our way over to the reindeer shed. "So how come Alabaster is the head elf?" he asked.

"He's the best. He's the most intelligent, a great leader, and he's so talented that I actually think he could pull Christmas off all by himself if he had to."

David raised his eyebrows. "That is impressive."

"Yes, it is, but it's just that he's lost himself along the way. Although, I think we're now seeing signs of the real Alabaster returning."

I pulled open the shed door, and instantly my heart dropped. The reindeer were still wearing their hideous tinsel necklaces covered in beads and baubles.

Rudolph instantly looked away from me. "I'm so sorry, lad, I completely forgot. Let's get that thing off you." I approached with caution, but Rudolph let out a huff of air and backed away from me, giving me a piercing look. My heart sank. "Please don't be mad at me. I've been distracted, and I didn't mean to leave you in that thing for so long." I was feeling terribly guilty.

David approached behind me. "I'm really sorry you're in the doghouse with Rudolph. I feel like it's my fault for letting Pip get carried away."

"No, it's not your fault. It's mine. I promised him I'd come back and remove them," I said, as Rudolph moved towards the opposite end of the pen. I hurried after him. "Come on, pal. Pip was just having a bit of fun." I reached out to unhook the necklace, but as my fingers grasped the tinsel, Rudolph shook his head, letting out a snort which meant no, and backed further away from me. I stood up and stared at him. "Wait, have you decided you like it now?"

Rudolph knocked his antlers onto the wooden panel, causing his necklace to rustle and jangle, and I chuckled, feeling relieved.

"Very well, you can keep it. Does that go for all of you?" I asked, looking around at the other reindeer's defensive stances. I laughed again and held my hands up in surrender. "Don't worry, you can all keep them."

The reindeer instantly relaxed, dropping their taut, heightened statures and carried on as usual.

"Wow, I think Pip has a talent we didn't know about, designing necklaces for reindeer," David smirked.

"It looks like it. Perhaps they remind them of their Christmas Eve collars and harness. Now, let's get to work," I said as I hitched up my trousers.

At the back of the pen, there was a mix of straw and reindeer droppings, all piled together. I picked up a broom and a heavy-duty dustpan and handed them to David. I grabbed the wheelbarrow and wheeled it over to the pile, with David trailing behind me as all the reindeer watched us.

"Woah, this pile is even bigger close up," David muttered. "I can tell you're feeding them well!"

"Yep, they like their food, particularly Donner. You have to watch out for her, because when she goes for a number two, it's lethal and I'm always astounded by how much comes out."

"Nice," David said, wrinkling up his nose. Then, following my instructions, David started sweeping up the excrement and used straw into the dustpan, and emptied it into the wheelbarrow. "Phwoar," he exclaimed, as he lifted a fragrant mound. He wafted the air in front of his nose, his eyes watering. "That's a doozy."

I chuckled. "Sorry, I guess I've got so used to it over the years that I forget how bad it can be for newcomers. But you're doing an excellent job."

"Thanks. It's something I can now put on my resume," he chuckled. "Shoveller of... Hey" he cried, as Prancer came over to investigate and nudged David's arm. It was clear he just wanted attention, because he then shimmied away, wiggling his behind eccentrically.

Once we had finished loading up the wheelbarrow and I shoved a heap of fresh straw down, I went over to pet Rudolph, who was slumped on the floor by himself in the corner, licking his tinsel necklace. "There you go, lad. It's all nice and clean for you." I gave him a scratch behind the antlers as the other reindeer stepped to the side and watched our interaction.

"Out of curiosity, do you think the other reindeer are at all jealous of your relationship with Rudolph?" David asked, studying the herd as he went to lean his broom against the wall.

"Nah, not at all. They all respect it."

David nodded. "I see." He glanced around at them looking slightly sceptic. "It's just funny, because some rumours go around that the other reindeer bully Rudolph and don't let him join in with games and things."

"Oh no, not at all. Everyone adores Rudolph, even the other reindeer." I winked at Rudolph and gave him a good scratch under his chin. "Isn't that right, lad?"

David paused for a moment. "That's good then. So, you're all one happy bunch together."

"That we are," I said, feeling chuffed. I looked up and happened to notice both Vixen and Blitzen staring at us with a strange expression. I couldn't work out if it was distaste, curiosity, or admiration, but then I shrugged it off. I grabbed the wheelbarrow and wheeled it into the corner, before David and I filled their water and food troughs.

We were just about to leave when Dancer strode across the pen into the corner, and let out a long stream of steaming pellets. She then lifted her head to us, and it was impossible to ignore the smug, satisfied look she gave us.

I shook my head. "Typical," I muttered.

"Bye, lad," I called to Rudolph. "Until next time, everyone," and as I closed the door to the shed, my stomach growled. "That job always works up an appetite."

David raised an eyebrow. "Does it? My stomach feels a little tender after that."

"You'll get over it after a bit of fresh air. Now, let's head back to the house for some cookies, tea and eggnog."

"That sounds like a great idea," David agreed.

35

David, Mrs C and I sat down to have our afternoon tea. It was nice to have a civilised conversation without Pip as I filled Mrs C in on what we had witnessed earlier with Alabaster.

"Sounds promising," she smiled.

"I best take a sandwich across to Pip," David said after we finished eating. "She must be hungry, and her routine will be all over the place today." He picked up a cheese and pickle sandwich and some carrot sticks and we headed over.

I opened the door to the workshop cautiously, not wanting even a creak of a footstep to potentially disturb what could be happening inside. We entered the workshop, and I knew instantly I was right to be silent. Wunorse had paused with a paintbrush in his hand, and the other elves were pretending to work, but were actually fixated on watching Pip and Alabaster sitting on the floor, playing together with a mended Delilah Sunrise, and three other brand-new dolls. Bushy spotted me and quickly reaffirmed the situation by placing her finger on her lips.

David held up the cheese sandwich and carrot sticks at me helplessly, not knowing what to do, so we approached carefully.

"Sunflowers and daisies, buttercups and tulips. We shine in the sun and bloom like flowers. We look amazing in our outfits, and eat cookies and ice cream, because we can do what we want before going on stage." Pip sang in her usual out of tune voice, whilst parading Delilah Sunrise and another doll around on top of a box. She was clearly making her song up on the fly. Alabaster smiled as he tried to keep up with her, whistling along as if he was her backing singer, throwing in some odd 'doo-doo-doo' sounds, whilst waving the other two dolls around.

"And we all love one another and will rocket to success, because we are the stars of the universe," she sang, on one long warbly note, which caused Shinny, who hadn't been listening, to dart his head up, just as a plume of purple dust rose around him. The song wasn't great by any means, but Pip grinned mightily when she had finished.

"That was great," Alabaster said. "I think the song will be a big hit."

"Thank you, master Alabaster. Bushy was right. You have a lovely singing voice."

I cleared my throat and Alabaster looked at me and smiled. The lines around his eyes had relaxed for the first time in a long while.

"You two look like you are having fun. So, who are these interesting new characters?" I asked, gesturing to the dolls.

Pip grinned. "Let me introduce you because Delilah Sunrise is now in a girl group. This one is Ethel Wilde." Pip pointed to one that Alabaster was holding, which had bright blue hair, stuck out at all angles, and was wearing red dungarees and red ankle boots. "The other one is Shandy Smiles." She pointed to the other doll Alabaster was holding which had streaks of every colour of the rainbow mixed into her hair, and was wearing a multi-coloured A-line dress and matching multi-coloured platform shoes. "And this one," she held up her other doll, which had half red and half green hair, and was wearing a dress which was also half red and half green, reminding me of Christmas, "is called Holly Berry." She darted a quick glance at David.

His face changed instantly at the mention of the name Holly and he suddenly looked emotional as he lowered the cheese sandwich and carrot sticks by his side.

"Together they are the Fashion Factor," Pip declared loudly.

"Wow, well, it's wonderful to meet them all." I smiled at the eclectic group of characters.

Pip grinned proudly. "They have all sorts of outfits that they can wear when they perform."

"Art is part of their music," Alabaster mumbled, as if he was being forced to repeat those words.

Pip nodded appreciatively. "Yes, it is."

"Well, they all have interesting and unique appearances." I frowned peculiarly at Alabaster.

Alabaster shrugged. "It's what Pip wanted. She put the band together."

David cleared his throat. "I like Holly Berry," his voice was a little rough with emotion. "She obviously loves the Christmas vibe, just like your mum. Now, Pip, I have some food for you." He raised the sandwich and carrots again.

Pip nodded, stood up from the floor and passed the dolls to Alabaster. "Thank you for playing with me, master Alabaster. You were a great Ethel Wilde."

Alabaster smiled. "It was my pleasure. I'm sure Fashion Factor will be superstars."

Pip ate her sandwich and carrot sticks, then turned to David. "Can I carry on playing here?" she asked.

David glanced at me with a questioning eyebrow.

"Erm," Shinny called, as he inched forward from his workbench carrying a small bucket.

"I guess so. As long as Alabaster doesn't mind," I looked at him for approval.

Alabaster smirked. "I don't think I have a choice."

I glanced over at Pepper, whose eyes were watery with emotion and she smiled back at me and gave me a subtle nod. She looked so pleased to hear Alabaster's lifted mood.

"Erm," Shinny called again, shuffling towards us.

"Can we play a new game?" Pip asked.

Shinny then gave out a strange little yelp. His eyes opened wide, and he held his bucket out in front of him in both hands. When everyone turned to look at him, his face turned bright red. "Sorry. It's just that I made something."

"What is it?" Pip asked.

Shinny looked around at everyone, before he leapt forward, reached into the bucket and then shoved something into Pip's hand.

She shrieked, before looking down at her hand. "Silly slime!" she cried.

Shinny shook his head. "I made it different. When you throw it, it lands as a different colour, just like you asked for."

"Wow. Can I throw it?" she asked, glancing at me.

I nodded. "Go ahead," I said, intrigued to see this new slime in action.

Pip lobbed the green slime at the wall, and as it hit, the slime changed colour. "Purple!" she shrieked.

My eyes widened. "That's pretty impressive." I looked at Shinny, surprised that out of all the elves, he had come up with something like this.

Shinny's cheeks turned redder. "There are seven colours: red, orange, yellow, green, blue, purple, pink and black. Each time you throw it, a random colour will appear."

Pip jumped up and down. "It re-styles itself, like my Fashion Factor dolls." Pip was beyond excited, her eyes wild. "Oh, I know, let's play a game where you have to shout out the colour you think it will be as you throw it at someone. If you get the colour right, you win a point."

"I'm in," Sugarplum shouted.

"Me too," Bushy cried.

Pepper walked forward, looking like she was floating on air. She was so happy. "Me three."

I turned to David. "What do you say?"

"Why not? We're only on holiday once," he grinned.

"Okay, count me in too, but I must warn you, I take these games far too seriously."

Shinny gasped, ran back to his workbench and returned with several buckets of slime, which he handed out to everyone, and he hesitated before he nervously placed a bucket down next to Alabaster.

"Everyone, spread out," Pip ordered. "On your marks, get set, go."

Then, suddenly, chaos ensued. Everyone started jumping around, shouting colours, lobbing slime at each other, missing, and stealing other people's slime.

I tried to control my competitive streak and not get carried away, but it was difficult because David's competitive side came out. He constantly aimed his slime at me, finding me an easier target than the smaller, faster elves, and tried to get as much slime on me whilst repeating the word Blue. I thought his tactic was cheating, but unfortunately luck was in his favour though, because un-statistically four of the nine slime balls he hit me with were in fact blue, which made him laugh in smug delight.

Pip once again, seemed to want to be hit by everyone, and kept spinning around in the middle trying to get them all on her, whilst the elves, including Alabaster, jumped from counter to counter, rolled on the floor and leaped over oncoming slime balls. Sugarplum, at one point, slid face down, across the entire room, in order to grab some more slime before she leapt to her feet to continue.

In the end, Shinny won. He seemed to know which colour it would land as and kept shouting it out correctly. Each time he got it right, his eyes would dart around uncomfortably, as though he felt guilty.

Once we all stood there catching our breath, having giggled and screamed so much, we took stock of the room, which looked like a unicorn's wonderland, with colour everywhere.

"Who is going to clean this up?" I asked.

Pepper glanced anxiously at Alabaster, waiting for him to bark his orders, but he looked calm and the elation was clear on his face.

"I'll do it," Sugarplum offered, with slime dripping from her chin, nose and eyelashes.

"We can all do it," Alabaster responded.

"Come on, Pip," David said. "We best get ourselves cleaned up before dinner."

Pip nodded and skipped to him, looking happy. "I like it that Alabaster is happy now." She then looked up at me. "I told you I'd make Alabaster be my friend, and I think he is now."

"It certainly seems so. You've made a big impression on him," I smiled, still in disbelief. Of course, time would tell, but I could barely believe that the insistence from a seven-year-old girl to play some games was the key to

Alabaster's mood. Yet it made perfect sense. A child's heart and happiness were why we worked so hard to provide Christmas after all.

Pip's innocence and persistence may have saved the future of Christmas and it had happened in the nick of time, with them leaving tomorrow.

36

Mrs C greeted us when we were back at the house. "Look at you all. You're all filthy," she shook her head at our colourful smeared clothing.

"We had another slime fight," Pip declared.

"Shinny and David cheated," I muttered, grinning.

"Is that right?" she laughed, patting me on the bum as I walked past her.

Suddenly everything that had happened overwhelmed me with happiness, and I couldn't resist turning round, grabbing her and planting a whiskery kiss on her lips.

"What's that for?" she asked, brushing down her dress, which was now smeared with slime.

"I'm just happy, because the elves are happy," I beamed with delight.

"Oh?" she asked, frowning, then her smile widened as she understood. "Oh, really?" she grinned. She gazed down affectionately at Pip, before she bent down and wrapped her arms around her, swooping her into a big hug.

Pip grinned back with a level of understanding about what she had done for Alabaster. She breathed in and clung to Mrs C tightly, and when she pulled away Pip smiled at Mrs C. "You smell of cinnamon. I like it."

Mrs C patted the top of Pip's head. "Thank you, sweetheart," she said, and those words were full of multiple meanings. "Now, all of you, go clean yourselves up. Dinner will be ready any moment."

That evening we sat down to eat one of Mrs C's finest thickly filled, rich meat pies in a beautiful golden crust, which gave an iconic crunch as Mrs C sliced into it.

Conversation around the table was excitable, as Pip gave Mrs C a detailed retelling of everything that had happened in the workshop. She also attempted to include a re-enactment of the incident when Sugarplum slid across the floor, which didn't quite go to plan when she got a slide burn on her elbow. It wasn't long before the effects of Pip's sleepover caught up with her and David whisked her away to put her in bed.

When David returned, he joined me and Mrs C in the sitting room to drink cocoa and watch David's favourite Christmas movie, Die Hard. His choice quite disappointed me, as I wasn't even in it! Instead, it focused on an action hero crawling around air vents, which I was all too familiar with.

Mrs C remained strangely quiet throughout, which was unusual as she normally couldn't help but throw a comment in about the actor's vest completely changing colour. Instead, her eyes were barely on the screen and she stared at the wall, deep in thought. I couldn't blame her. I think we were all feeling the previous delight and happiness slowly mutate into sombreness as the countdown to David and Pip's departure ramped up. By the time the credits rolled, I felt a weight in my stomach.

"David," Mrs C began, placing her empty cocoa mug onto the side table, making him glance across at her. "I've been thinking. How would you like me to be a silent partner in your business?"

David looked surprised. "What do you mean?" he asked

"I've had such a good time working with you on it I want to continue helping where I can. I'm not looking for any payment or anything. It's just that I feel invested in it now and I want to see you succeed."

I chuckled. "So not so much a silent partner, but a very vocal, free of charge consultant."

Mrs C smiled. "Something like that."

David grinned widely, and his eyes were alight with excitement. "I would love that."

"Excellent! We can communicate by email and have face-time calls."

"Sounds perfect." David then stifled a yawn, and his smile slipped. "Well, I guess I best go to bed."

He slowly stood up and hesitated as if he didn't want to leave, before he nodded and walked out of the room, looking sad it was his last night.

Mrs C jumped from her seat. "I just want to do something for David's business before bedtime," and she hurried over to her computer.

"Go ahead," I muttered, glancing across at my drink's cabinet. "I'll wait here with a little sherry."

I settled myself back in my seat and sipped my nightcap, whilst I listened to the distant sound of the keyboard bashing. I wondered if this was a sign of things to come; her being too busy and occupied for bed. I didn't mind though, as I could see how excited she was.

Eventually I sighed, having grown bored, my glass drained. I stood up and poked my head around the door. "I'm going to get ready for bed."

She didn't look up from the computer as she nodded. "Sure, I'll be two minutes."

I changed into my pyjamas, and then went to brush my teeth, comb my beard and rub some night serum into it to keep it soft and smelling fragrant of Christmas spices. When I returned to our bedroom, I found Mrs C rummaging around in my closet. "What are you doing?" I asked.

"I was in the middle of creating a list of new contacts for David to reach out to about his business; investors, marketeers, etc, when I had a thought," she muttered, her head buried in the cupboard as she moved coats and jackets from side to side on the railing. "Do you remember that man from London? The one who gave you his card."

I raised my eyebrows as I adjusted the elastic of my trousers around my waist. "The tornado?"

Mrs C paused and smiled at me. "Yes, that's the one. I know he was a bit eccentric and arrogant, but I could also tell he was very good at his job. I want to give David all options and then he can make his own judgement."

I chuckled. "I guess there's no harm in trying. At least it won't be us listening to his thunderous over the top personality."

"Precisely, if only I can just find your jacket," she muttered, distracted as she continued to rummage around. She then spotted my red velvet jacket on the floor, which had slipped off the coat-hanger.

She picked it up and shoved her hand into the inside pocket and began pulling things out of it. A pair of tweezers, a pack of playing cards, chewing gum, a map of London, an old hotel key card, different foreign coins, beer mats, several receipts, reindeer treats, a few tin foil cases from mince pies, and some sweet wrappers, which she gave me a condescending look about.

"Ah, here we are." She extracted the business card. "Seamus Conway," she read. "*Investor at Conway Business Holdings. Self-made, winner, extraordinaire and one hell of a great businessman. No venture too big or too small.*"

I raised my eyebrow. "Are you sure about him?"

Mrs C frowned at the card as she studied the picture on the front. A grinning, twinkling, white teethed photo of the man we met. "It can't hurt, can it?" she asked, suddenly looking slightly hesitant.

I shrugged. "No. It's only another person to add to your list."

She nodded, as she placed it on her bedside table, before she got ready for bed, climbed in and instantly placed her ice-cold feet on me. I pulled her in for a cuddle and kissed her forehead.

37

The following morning, we all sat around the kitchen table waiting for Mrs C to serve breakfast. David was particularly quiet, and Pip looked pale and close to tears. We ate breakfast in silence. I'd lost some of my appetite, and it seemed the others felt the same as they picked at their food.

David pushed his plate away and looked at Pip. "We best finish packing, hadn't we, Pip?"

Pip nodded miserably in return.

When they went upstairs, I noticed Mrs C looking close to tears. She quickly busied herself with washing the dishes and tidying things away.

Moments later, the heavy thump, thump on the stairs signalled David was lugging both suitcases down the stairs and a lump rose in my throat.

Mrs C stood at the side, a handkerchief in hand as she dabbed at her eyes. "It's been wonderful to have you both."

David looked like he was struggling not to cry as he roughly cleared his throat. "We've had a great time." Pip nodded sadly whilst squeezing Mr Stuffy to her chest.

"I'm so pleased you have, and I've got some things for you." Mrs C clutched her handkerchief tightly as she spun round and picked up a couple of folders from the hallway table. "The top folder is a business plan and information for your company. The second folder is full of our homemade recipes, which I hope you enjoy as much as we do."

David accepted them and stared at the folders for a moment, looking like he was struggling for words. He then straightened himself back up. "I feel so honoured to have these and I can't thank you enough." He cleared his throat. "You have both been wonderful hosts, full of warmth and kindness, and I can't put into words how grateful I am for not just an adventure of a lifetime, but for helping me become a different person. A better cook, businessman, and a better dad." He pulled Pip towards him and stroked her head affectionately. He then looked up at Mrs C and me. "I'm a lot more excited for the future now, and I truly hope that we are not only taking memories back home but also friends."

Tears were now spilling down Mrs C's cheeks. "Oh absolutely, I wouldn't dream of it any other way. I'm just so pleased we could help, and you have both definitely left your mark here as well." She then threw her arms around David and then to Pip. "Have a safe journey back."

Pip looked down at her feet. "Can I say goodbye to the reindeer and elves before we go?"

"Of course you can," I replied.

I took the suitcases off David and we stepped out into the snow, as Mrs C turned away and busied herself again in the kitchen. I dropped the suitcases off at the hangar, shoving them into the back of the plane, before we headed to the reindeer shed. The reindeer were still in their tinsel necklaces, but now they had bits of reindeer feed on them, and some of the tinsel, gems and baubles had come off and were sticking in various places on the reindeer coats.

Pip walked over to Dancer and held her hand out to her. "I'll miss you."

Dancer wasn't normally one for showing affection, so it surprised me when she started frantically licking Pip's hand. I couldn't be sure if it wasn't because Pip still had food on her hand, or if she was going to miss her, but I opted for the latter. "Bye Prancer," Pip sulked, moving on to pet him after he shimmied over to her. "I'm so glad I finally got to meet you."

"And I'll miss you too, Cupid," David said, as Cupid head-butted him and thrust his head underneath David's hand to be stroked.

I could see the melancholy in all the reindeer's behaviour as they took it in turns to nuzzle both Pip and David. It was a testament to how much it meant to them to see someone else around for a change; a testament to how much energy Pip and David had brought to the North Pole.

Once everyone had said goodbye and I made a mental note to come back as soon as possible to remove the ghastly necklaces from them, once and for all, we left the shed with Pip snivelling loudly and made our way to the workshop.

As soon as I opened the door, the elves immediately stopped what they were doing and raced over. Bushy appeared to have been crying, and the others looked pale and sad.

"Are you leaving now?" Shinny asked, his voice quivering.

Pip nodded as she clutched David's hand tightly.

"We wanted to thank you for coming here." Alabaster gave Pip a smile that softened his features.

Pip snorted loudly, sucking up air through her nose, as tears began falling down her cheeks. "I... I've had an amazing time."

"We all have," Bushy sniffled, reciprocating her tears, her nose red and blotchy.

"Don't cry, Pipshine," Wunorse said, smiling softly at her and handing her a questionable tissue he retrieved from his pocket, but it only made Pip wail even louder.

Sugarplum then raced to Bushy's workbench and picked up a large box from behind it, which was neatly gift wrapped with a large green bow. "We have something for you," she snivelled.

Pip opened her eyes wide as Sugarplum handed it to her. "Wow. Can I open it now?" she asked, looking from David to me.

I smiled and nodded. "Go ahead." I wasn't sure what the elves had given her.

She bent over the box and ripped it open, and as she peered inside, she gasped and then cheered. "This is amazing," she gushed, and started pulling dolls out.

They were exact replicas of me, Mrs C, all six elves, and all nine reindeer with a sleigh.

"The elves have our names on," Shinny declared proudly.

"These look so much like you all, I can tell who each one is," she shrieked. She held up one doll. "This is definitely Alabaster," she announced, before reading the name embroidered onto the doll's green jacket. "This one is Wunorse, this one is Sugarplum, this one is Bushy, this one is Pepper, and this, of course, is Shinny." She scooped them all into her body to hug them tightly. "They are perfect and now I don't need to play with my long gangly elves that look nothing like you."

Shinny grinned. "I hope you have fun playing with me."

"I will. I'm going to play with them all the time and never forget any of you." The tears were now streaming down her cheeks again.

"We'll miss you so much," Bushy cried. Then each of the elves jumped up at David and Pip to hug them. Pip around her waist, and David around his leg.

I watched the elves for a moment but particularly Pepper, who stood on the sidelines, her eyes watery, and a firm line formed across her lips as she pressed them together. "I guess congratulations are in order," I whispered, making Pepper tear her eyes away and look at me. "It looks like your meddling has worked very well."

Pepper's lips tweaked into a little smile. "Elf guidance magic is very powerful, but I never knew exactly what was going to happen. I just knew the end goal," she whispered, watching the scene in amazement.

I nodded. "Well, thank you for making this happen. I also don't think I'm the only one who should be thanking you. You seem to have brightened everyone up. The elves, Alabaster, me, Mrs C, David and Pip, but I guess that was part of your plan all along. The last few days have given everyone something they personally needed."

Pepper nodded humbly. "You're welcome, sir." She then rushed forward to be the last to hug David and Pip.

When Pepper pulled away, I stepped forward. "I think it's time to go now." We trudged away from the elves and everyone waved their last goodbyes.

"Bye Pipshine," Sugarplum called, as I closed the door to the workshop with a sense of finality.

I led David and Pip to the plane, and we climbed in. "Are you ready?" I asked, to the sound of silence, as Pip and David shrugged and stared out the window. It was a complete contrast to the screams of excitement I heard on our way here. I drove the plane out of the hangar and we took off into the air, and into the green dancing lights of the aurora borealis, which looked like it was waving us goodbye.

We hit the tip of the North Pole and we shot off through the vortex and landed back in Lapland.

"I'm sorry I can't take you back all the way, but border control will wonder where you are."

Pip shook her head. "I'll miss you!"

"I'll miss you too, but I'll be coming to visit you in a few months, so I hope you leave out a tasty treat for me," I said, smiling.

David nodded. "You can count on it."

I turned to get back into the plane, when I locked eyes on Him. He was on his way to the Santa Office, and he paused to give me a curt nod. I returned the nod with equal curtness, before I climbed into the plane, and drove off to the waves of goodbye from Pip and David.

38

Within seconds of leaving Lapland, I landed and tucked my plane up in the hangar before I went into the house.

Mrs C was cleaning an already spotless house to keep herself busy. "It feels even quieter than when we returned from London," she muttered, her eyes red from crying.

I smiled sympathetically. There was certainly an eerie silence in the house, not only from the quiet of Pip and David speaking, laughing, and shuffling around, but also from the drop of energy. It was as if the air had become stifled from their departure. "It just takes some adjusting to." I had a lump in my throat and a heaviness in my stomach that hadn't been there before.

Mrs C nodded, before she grabbed a cushion and began plumping it up, hitting it and moulding it into the shape it was already in. It hurt to see her so emotional, but there was now a gaping size hole in our house that came in the shape of Pip and David, which nothing else would fill.

Over the next few days, Mrs C's mood barely improved. She moved silently about the house and her eyes would fill with tears when she poured herself a glass of milk, reminding her of Pip, or she cast her eyes on the dining room table which held so many special memories. I even caught her a few times, standing in the guestroom's doorway, staring at it, looking pensive.

She then cried when it was time to demolish the house she had built from gingerbread and no matter how hard I tried, I could barely get her to laugh at my jokes. Her sense of humour had evaporated.

It was as if she was in mourning. She'd messaged David a few times to check his journey back had gone well, which fortunately it had, and she had helped him with a few bits and pieces for his business, but it was not even close to filling the void.

Despite my best efforts to cheer her up, her mood didn't lift, so I started giving her some space to watch films and wallow, whilst I spent most of my days in the workshop. It had taken a day or two for the elves to get over their sadness, but when they did, they bounced back stronger, right back to their full spritely selves that I hadn't seen in a few years. For how little energy there was in the house, there were now gallons of it in the workshop. The elves would dance and sing as they worked. They would chat and giggle constantly, and their communication had skyrocketed.

Alabaster's change in mood had lifted everyone, and he would now join in with the laughter and his constant praise of the other elves' work, made them double their output. Not to mention his problem-solving skills for any issues were back on top form. Instead of remaking defective stock which he used to insist on, he would now work out an efficient way to fix them instead.

One day, after Mrs C started vacuuming again, I went over to the workshop and watched the elves at work. Alabaster was throwing boxes across to Wunorse, for him to grab and package his fifth edition toy robot into them in a seamless routine. Pepper was teaching Shinny how to make some new craft items, with felt and furry pipe cleaners. Whilst Sugarplum and Bushy were giggling as Sugarplum held up a questionable orange stuffed toy she had made. It had two large googly eyes, a protruding nose, a tongue sticking out, and it was wearing a blue bowler hat.

I had no idea what it represented, nor did I bother asking as I sat in my armchair by the Christmas tree.

Sugarplum spotted me, lowered her toy, and hurried over. "Is everything okay, Santa?"

I sighed and ran a hand through my hair. "I'm just worried about Mrs C. It's been ages now and she's still struggling with Pip and David's departure. She's either frantically cleaning the place, or looking miserable. I wish I could cheer her up and help her move on."

"Poor Mrs C," she said, as her eyes darted to the sides rapidly, as if she was thinking just as quickly, then her eyes lit up. "I think it's time I showed you both something."

I frowned in confusion. "What, me and Mrs C?"

Sugarplum nodded. "Yes. Will you fetch her?"

I agreed and went back to the house.

"What could Sugarplum need to show us both?" Mrs C muttered, whilst scrubbing the oven.

"It's a mystery at the moment."

Mrs C sighed, and dropped her sponge into the sink, took her apron off and hung it by the door, before walking beside me to the workshop.

When we entered, Sugarplum was pacing back and forth, wiping her palms down her coat, looking anxious.

Wunorse's eyes lit up at the sight of Mrs C and he raced over to her. "Mrs C," he beamed, giving her a little bow. "It's wonderful to see you."

Mrs C forced a smile, which caused his cheeks to turn rosier. "Nice to see you too, Wunorse."

Wunorse grinned and ran back to his workbench.

"What did you want to show us, Sugarplum?" Mrs C asked kindly.

Sugarplum cleared her throat. "Follow me." She led us out of the workshop and down the corridor with the twinkling, shimmering elf lights that glowed red and green. She stopped in the middle of the corridor and placed her hand on the wall. I frowned, as I focused through the twinkling lights which flickered shadows on the wall and made out the faint outline of a door.

"What the… Is that another room?" I asked, confused, as I spotted a slight shimmer around it to signify a span-warp field behind the door, which had been masked by the elf lights.

Sugarplum nodded. "It's an old storage cupboard everyone has forgotten about."

I exchanged a bewildered look with Mrs C.

Sugarplum swallowed. "I've been working on something for you both inside, so I hope you like it," she said, and pushed the door open.

I stepped across the span-warp barrier and pulled Mrs C in with me, and as we entered the room, my mouth dropped in surprise and Mrs C gasped. There in front of us was a wonderland of our history. The room was a large dark winding tunnel, which was lit with more elf lights hung from the ceiling and wrapped around pillars. The enticing light display guided a path past displays from all our adventures, which were lit up under a warm golden spotlight.

It started with an exhibit of photos of Pip and David, including ones where the reindeer surrounded them in their necklaces; and some action shots of us all playing with the slime that I hadn't even realised she had taken.

Next there was the postbox we had collected from London. Its beautiful, eye-catching red colour was lit up against the black backdrop, and it had been decorated in photos that Mrs C had taken from our London trip. Beside it was a large painting, which was a replica of the fridge magnet we had given to Sugarplum, showcasing the London Eye, Tower Bridge, and Westminster Abbey.

Next there was another photo of Mrs C holding up her Christmas gift from me, with an amused yet outraged expression. It was a broom with a carved-out duck's head on the end of the handle. It was purely ridiculous and had made her laugh.

Following was the full-sized yellow taxi we had taken from New York, which made me chuckle as I remembered how crazy we had been trying to take one at Sugarplum's insistence. Beside it was another large painting of the fridge magnet we had given her from that trip showing the Empire State building, with the Statue of Liberty in front of it, directly in the centre of Times Square.

The sparkling trail continued, displaying more of our history, including pictures of us looking happy, and shining a spotlight on all the items Sugarplum had challenged us to take from each holiday Mrs C and I had taken together, including the lamppost from Paris.

Mrs C nudged me in the belly and sniggered when she spotted the large chicken ornament that we had taken from above a famous chicken restaurant in Portugal. We had to climb onto the roof at night for that one.

"We've had some great times, although we look like criminal masterminds," Mrs C confessed as we wandered through a century's worth of haulage.

"It's a good job the Christmas Laws don't cover a bit of holiday pilferage," I remarked.

Mrs C giggled, and it was music to my ears to hear that laugh again.

We continued along the display, which even included film posters of my favourite Christmas films from when they were released, storylines about me, and a whole host of other memories. There was even a display of all the reindeer's very first sleigh harnesses, which I had upgraded several times since.

"Oh my. This is a blast from the past." Mrs C stopped at a range of pictures I had taken nearly a century ago. I'd done my first public photo shoot for a company who wanted me to hold a coca cola bottle. I'd tried several poses to get the perfect photo, holding the bottle to my lips, by my side, in front of my stomach, looking at the bottle, looking at the camera, all whilst wearing different red outfits that they gave me in order to get the best effect. It was clear in the last picture how flushed I looked in my cheeks from the exertion and all the posing.

"I'm definitely glad they finally settled on the photo they did. I think the outfit with the holly leaf pattern on it just wasn't ever going to work."

"Well, you certainly fell in love with that final red outfit they loaned you. It made you sacrifice your green uniform, and you never looked back."

I chuckled and nodded. "I can barely believe nearly a whole century has gone by since then."

Mrs C grinned. "It's funny though. You don't look a day older."

"I'll take that as a compliment," I said.

Finally, we arrived at a glass case, and I smiled. "And there it is," I exclaimed, as Mrs C came to stand next to me. "I wondered where my first suit had ended up." We admired the green outfit for a moment. "It really does feel like a lifetime ago," I reminisced.

"Things have certainly changed a lot since then," Mrs C whispered as she placed her hand around my back.

Sugarplum, who had been slowly following us, watching our reactions from a few paces behind, appeared by our sides. "Do you like it?" she asked, wringing her hands together.

"This is fabulous," Mrs C beamed, her eyes glinting with happiness.

Sugarplum suddenly looked relieved. "I wanted to remind you of how much fun you two had before Pip and David came to visit. Your lives are so full with each other and everything you give to the world; I didn't want you to forget that."

Mrs C nodded. "You're right, and I guess I have been dwelling on missing Pip and David instead of focusing on all the wonderful things I have in my life."

"Like me," I joked and pulled Mrs C into my belly and kissed her cheek.

"Yes, you," she said, patting my belly. "I guess I haven't been following the same advice I gave to David." A determined look came into her eye. "Right, enough moping now," she told herself, tucking her hair behind her ears and straightening herself up. "We have a busy few months ahead of us and so we had all better get organised."

"We certainly do," I agreed. I enjoyed seeing the familiar glint in her eyes.

Sugarplum grinned. "Welcome back, Mrs C." She looked like she was about to burst with delight.

39

Mrs C smiled as we left Sugarplum's wonderland and made our way back into the workshop. "So, how are you getting on with all your new product ideas for this year?" she asked me.

"I think we're nearly there," I said.

"Great. Why don't you and the elves take me through them now?"

Sugarplum gasped. "Is it that time already?"

"No time like the present. Pardon the pun," she smiled.

"Right," I chuckled, gazing at her for a moment adoringly, before I turned to the elves. "Everyone, finish up what you're doing and meet us at the planning board."

For a few silent minutes, Mrs C inspected the planning board as the elves waited nervously in silence. Shinny was clutching both Bushy's and Pepper's hands tightly. Today was make or break, depending on Mrs C's verdict, and it was always an anxious time every year. If the toy ideas passed her approval, they were okay to move ahead. If not, it was back to the drawing board, and they would have to work frantically to come up with something better.

"Right, let's go through this one by one," she said and took a pen from under the board. She dotted the first toy idea with the tip. "What's this?" she asked.

I explained what the toy was, a colourful caterpillar that crawled along the floor, twisting its body in and out as it moved.

She pressed the pen to her chin as she thought. "I can't see any harm in that," and gave it a tick, which caused the elves to let out the breath they were holding. She tapped the following ones, and I explained what each one did.

We made our way across the board to a range of reactions. Mrs C's eyes would widen, she would smile, she would nod, and she would also grimace, or look horrified. She matched each reaction with a decisive tick or cross. A couple had a question mark next to it, where she liked the idea, but it needed further development.

A while later, Mrs C snapped the cap back onto her pen. "There, I think that will do it. You definitely have some good toy ideas this year."

"Phew," Shinny said loudly, looking from Bushy to Pepper.

Alabaster cleared his throat. "I think we're missing something off the list. With everything that's happened recently, we forgot to add it."

"What's that?" Mrs C asked.

"I'll show you." He raced back to his bench and returned, carrying the dolls Pip had created. "We're missing 'Fashion Factor'."

Mrs C's spirit wavered. "Pip's creation?" An emotional smile formed across her lips. "I never got to meet them."

"Let me introduce you," Alabaster smiled. "This is Delilah Sunrise," as he held up Pip's doll.

Shinny then leapt over to him to grab a doll. "This is Shandy Smiles," he said, waving the doll in front of Mrs C.

"This is Ethel Wilde," Wunorse beamed affectionately, taking one of them.

"And this is Holly Berry," Bushy announced as she grabbed the other one.

"Together they are Fashion Factor, an eccentric, eclectic band, who is on their way to superstardom," Alabaster gushed.

Mrs C grinned. "I think it's perfect. That gets a tick from me."

The elves grinned and cheered, except Sugarplum, who frowned.

"What's wrong, Sugarplum?" I asked.

"I don't think it's perfect," she said, causing the other elves to stare at her in confusion. "I think the band isn't complete yet. It needs an extra person in it."

My lips twitched at her innocent expression. "How interesting, and who might that be?"

"One moment." She rushed over to Bushy's workstation, where she quickly built a new doll. She raced back over to us and held it up. "I think it needs Pip Shine."

The doll was in a pink dress, identical to Pip's; it had curly long blonde hair and her shoes were green and curled up at the toes, like all the elves, and she had a necklace hanging from her neck, which looked similar to tinsel.

Mrs C smiled, her eyes moistening with unshed tears. "That's perfect," she choked. "She's a great addition to 'Fashion Factor'."

"Wonderful. I love the shoes." I drew the five members of the group onto the planning board before Mrs C came in with her pen and put a large tick next to it.

"I guess we're ready to build and perfect the prototypes of everything, and once we have them, I'll schedule your appointment," she said.

I was delighted to have Mrs C back on track, and our toy ideas ready to move onto the next stage.

Over the next few days, Mrs C got to work on the computer making some preparations, which I was grateful for. I wasn't a fan of the organisation and formalities of this part of my job, so it was easier for me to roam the kitchen for food, or disappear into the workshop whilst she tapped away on the keyboard and made some phone calls for me.

Meanwhile, the elves completed their prototypes, creating two of each. One was to go on our Christmas display shelf, and the other I packed into my suitcase, ready. There was an incredible energy in the workshop as the elves' excitement grew. We were getting closer every day, and it showed on how quickly and enthusiastically they raced around the room. We hadn't had such an efficient process in a long time, and it was all because Alabaster was back on top form.

"This is our last toy," Pepper suddenly cried out, as she walked over to the display shelf, holding the veterinary doll's house that she and Shinny had worked on together.

There was a moment of silence as she placed it on the shelf, and I stood back to admire all the elves' work. "Well done everyone." I walked along the row, delicately trailing my fingers over each toy, hoping they would make the children happy when Alabaster stepped forward.

"Sir! I just wanted to check if you had any other thoughts about what to do with our old stock from last year."

I tore my eyes away from the toys and looked at Alabaster, confused. "Just do the same as we've been doing the last few years."

Alabaster nodded and gave a quick bow. "Of course, sir. We'll get onto it right away, and transform everything into unicorn products," he confirmed and ran off.

Before long, the old stock was ready to go, and I added some items into my bag. "There, I think we're ready." I picked up my little case, patted it, and gave it a stroke. "Wish me luck," I called.

Shinny took a deep breath, looking very nervous as all the elves gathered round and held their little hands up to display their little crossed fingers. "Good luck," they chorused.

Then, just as I turned around, Pepper blew some sparkling dust from her palm all over me.

"Thanks," I muttered, wiping my cheek. Pepper smiled, satisfied. It was her safe travel charm, and despite her still not mastering the art of blowing without including her spittle, I left the workshop feeling confident.

Mrs C was sitting at the computer, frantically tapping away.

"I've got all the prototypes," I called, waving the case at her back.

"Great," she said, not looking away from the screen. "I'll confirm your appointment for tomorrow."

I went up to her and stared at the computer. "What are you doing?"

"I'm just finishing an email to David."

"Ah, I was meaning to ask about how he's getting on." I bent down to peer at what she was doing.

Mrs C clicked on the mouse and the letter she had been writing disappeared from the screen. Then she turned to face me. "He's doing great!

Since we changed his strategy and sales pitch, he's managed to line up several business meetings across the next couple of weeks to present to them. I've just given him a list of questions he should ask to ensure that whoever he partners with is also suitable for him. And if they all want to invest in his product, he should be able to make an informed decision about what they can offer, and then decide who to work with."

"Well, it all sounds very promising," I said, feeling chuffed for him.

"Yes, I think he'll be well on his way to success soon," she declared, her eyes glowing. "Anyway, speaking of success." She grabbed a black file next to her. "I've finished putting together the overview folder."

She handed it to me, and I flicked through the pages. It had a photo of each toy, with a little blurb about how it works and a concept of how the child might play with it. "This looks great. What would I do without you?"

40

The following morning, I dressed in my red chequered suit and green chequered tie. I slicked my curly white hair back with some hair oil, doused my neck in Old Spice aftershave twice, and slipped my reading glasses on. I picked up my case, clutched the folder to my belly and looked at myself in the mirror, stood up straight, and nodded. "Perfect," I muttered.

I met Mrs C downstairs, who was holding her standard black handbag and dressed in her comfortable flat red shoes, red high cut top and a dark green pleated skirt. She pulled on a dark red basin hat, with a bow on the side, which she'd had for decades.

We made our way to the hangar, and both climbed into the plane, and we set off. "New York, here we come," I shouted, as we flew into the vortex, through the swirling colours of light and landed in a deserted car park on the outskirts of New York. I'd made sure no one spotted us coming to land, and I pulled a cover over the plane to hide it from view.

We walked down a couple of alleyways and reached a busy strip. Men and women walked past us in all directions, popping into shops, bars, and restaurants. It was a mixed crowd. Some wore suits on their way to work meetings, others were casually talking to someone on the phone. There were tourists carrying maps and shoppers holding a suitcase worth of shopping bags. Everyone jostled past us as we walked hand in hand together. At this time of year, the last Christmas was forgotten and the next Christmas wasn't in anyone's thoughts, so no one looked at us with any curiosity. Meanwhile, cars, motorbikes, and yellow cabs drove past us, creating a din of noise.

"Shall we?" Mrs C grinned as she gestured to a yellow cab with its bespoke taxi light on.

I chuckled, both of us remembering our antics with another yellow taxi, as Mrs C stuck her hand out, and a cab instantly pulled up by our feet.

"Oh, no you don't," a woman suddenly shouted and barged in between us. The woman looked frazzled. Her cheeks were flushed, and her expression was one which made both Mrs C and me take one step back. "I've been waiting for a cab, and you think you can push in," she snarled, yanking the door open, climbing in and slamming it shut behind her.

"Is that…?" Mrs C asked in disbelief.

"Yes, it is!" I said in equal disbelief. "It's that Carol from London. What on earth is she doing here?"

"I have no idea, but it looks like she's having another bad day," Mrs C said.

Carol glared out the window at us as the cab barely moved in the traffic. I wasn't sure if she recognised us, but she certainly looked like all she wanted was to shoot away in a cloud of exhaust fumes and tyre marks.

Mrs C then stuck her hand out and instantly another cab pulled up next to us, and we climbed in before anyone else could barge us out of the way.

"Where you off to?" the cab driver asked.

I handed him the address that Mrs C had printed off, and the driver looked me up and down as if surprised. "Gold Corps?" he questioned, frowning and looking perturbed.

"Yes. Is something wrong?" I asked.

The cab driver shrugged. "Nah, you're good," he said as he pulled up beside the other taxi.

"Well, this is awkward," I muttered as Carol's face suddenly turned to recognition and she pointed at us.

The lights instantly turned green, and we were on our way, overtaking Carol, who perhaps now had steam coming out of her ears, and again, leaving me with a strange feeling about her.

I gazed out the window as we drove past multiple attractions, reminding me of how much I loved New York. There was something about it that made it the pinnacle of Christmas time, from having the most famous Christmas tree, to having such wonderfully gigantic toy shops, and not to mention, that several of my favourite Christmas films were set here. It was like New York and I had an unspoken partnership and I was more than happy about it.

"Look," I called, pointing out the window, as we drove past the Plaza, where we had stayed many times since it had opened in 1907. "We really need another good ding-dang-dong night at the Plaza," I chuckled.

"We certainly do," Mrs C laughed. "Something fun always happens there, but I'm wondering if they are sick of us by now."

"Never. They tell me I'm their most special guest."

"I think they tell most people that, but maybe next year I'll book it again," Mrs C winked.

We continued on our journey and as we got closer; the nerves kicked in. Mrs C placed her hand over my knee and I realised I had been bouncing it up and down. "You're not usually this nervous."

I nodded. "Yeah, it's just that since Mr Richford Junior took over from his father, we haven't always seen eye to eye. I hope everything goes smoothly this time, and he likes everything we have prepared."

"I'm sure he will. He's not let you down yet," she said.

I noticed the cab driver studying us in his rear-view mirror and quickly glanced back at the road. Soon, he pulled up beside the sidewalk in front of a tall, eye-catching office block, with a large golden sign above it reading Gold Corps. The building itself had gold plated doors and windows, which reflected the shine of the sun in a way that made it glow mystically. There was no way to see inside, and the only movement was the twist of a gold revolving door, as men and women dressed in suits entered and exited the building, their lips sealed with secrets.

"Here we are," the cab driver said, switching the button to show our fare. I handed the dollars over to him, but as he looked at me, he said, "I gotta ask. What happens in that building? It's one of New York's mysteries."

"What do you think happens there?" I asked.

"No idea. Some conspiracy theorists believe it's where the Government is creating some mind control techniques on us Yankees, others believe it's where A-list celebrities sneak inside in disguises. Others believe it's another location for the FBI."

I smiled. "It's nothing quite so intriguing, but I'm afraid it is a secret."

The man's face dropped. "Very well," he was clearly disappointed and repositioned himself in the driving seat.

We stepped out of the cab, and I took a deep breath. Mrs C stood opposite me, straightened my tie and pulled some fluff out of my beard. "Right, break a leg," she smirked, dusting my suit down with her hand. "I'm going to wander around, pop to some museums, and do some browsing."

I nodded and kissed her on the cheek. "Keep safe." I then turned around, entered the building and approached the reception desk, where a lady sat behind it with a headset on.

"Hello sir," she lifted the microphone of her headset away from her mouth. "How can I help?"

"I'm here for Mr Richford."

"Ah, he's now on the sixth floor." She smiled and pointed towards the gold-plated elevator doors behind me.

"Thank you very much," I said, swinging my case as I walked across the lobby to wait for the elevator.

The elevator chimed when it hit the ground and I stepped inside, and as I rode up the six floors, some jingly Muzak, which reminded me of my all-time favourite Jingle Bells, accompanied me. The doors opened on floor six. Opposite was another receptionist, a young woman with a kind smile, whom I had met several times before.

"Hello Cynthia," I grinned, swinging my case as I approached her happily. The music had sent me into an even better mood.

"Hello Mr Claus," she said as she adjusted herself in her seat. Her smile at me was genuine, but it didn't reach her eyes. "It's lovely to see you again."

"It's good to see you, too. How's the old boyfriend going?" I asked, confused by her sad expression when she was usually so happy and light-hearted.

"Oh, it's going really well. In fact, we're engaged." She flashed her diamond ring at me.

"Congratulations, he's a lucky guy."

"I think I'm a lucky woman." She forced a smile before climbing to her feet. "I best escort you to Mr Richford. He's waiting for you."

She guided me to a set of double doors and knocked briefly before poking her head inside. "Mr Claus is here, sir," she announced.

"Yes, let him in," I heard Mr Richford say.

She held open the door for me, and I entered the room.

41

Mr Richford was alone, sitting at the end of a large boardroom table with his laptop in front of him. He was dressed in a navy suit with a gold tie, and a gold handkerchief was tucked out of his jacket pocket. His hair was greying around the sides, but was fashioned into place with no signs of oil.

He stood up and welcomed me towards a chair opposite him. "Mr Claus, wonderful to see you again so early in the year. It's a little abnormal, but I won't complain, as it gives us more time to work through everything."

I smiled as I took the seat. "Yes, we have been a bit more efficient this year."

Mr Richford closed his laptop and placed his hands on the desk. "Now, I must say, we had a lot of fun coming up with the advertisements for Moco, the galloping horse and Space Cadet Collins last year. Everyone seemed to love them. Even my nephew insisted on getting Moco for Christmas, which may or may not have been a good thing. He drove us all insane with it after a while, but Christmas is all about gritting your teeth for the children, isn't it?"

"I guess so," I shrugged.

"Well, I hope you have some fruity toy options this year for us to entertain and entice our viewers into."

"I think I do." I laid my case flat on the table and opened it. I extracted the two files Mrs C had put together for me and slid one across to Mr Richford. "If you turn to page one, we have our Sausage Eating World Championship game," I read. I then pulled out the corresponding toy box and slid the game across to him. "You have to avoid getting another player's sausage, from another country, in your mouth. You can only eat the sausages from your own country."

"Ah, fantastic! A game that's opposite to Hungry-Hippo. I got you; I got you." He lifted the lid and began sifting through the contents of the box. He picked the toy sausages up, inspected them, and then sprinkled his handful back into the box.

"I've already witnessed this game in action and it's a lot of fun, if not slightly chaotic," I stated.

Mr Richford nodded distractedly. He then sat back in his chair and placed his finger to his lips, looking deep in thought. "I love the concept. The problem here is that sausages are somewhat out of favour these days. Can we make them vegan sausages?"

I raised my eyebrows. "Vegan sausages?"

"Yes," Mr Richford said, standing and turning away from me as he continued to think. "A climate friendly game. The global vegan sausage eating competition," he ran his hand through the air as if he was visualising the title.

"Err. You can't actually eat the sausages. They are made of plastic," I said.

Mr Richford waved my comment away. "Yes, of course. But the young generation will love it, and we can certainly work it into the advert."

"Well, perhaps, but I don't want to preach to everyone," I was feeling a little concerned.

"Leave it to me. I'll make a cartoon vegan sausage as the judge," he laughed. "I might call it Victor Vegan Sausage. Right, next…"

I blinked, wondering if I should object, but I guess this was the difference with dealing with Mr Richford Junior rather than Mr Richford Senior. I had to get used to the new ways of thinking and keeping with the times, so I moved on. "This is a coconut cracking game." I pulled out another box and handed it over to him.

Mr Richford rummaged through the box to inspect the contents, whilst reading the instructions in the folder Mrs C had provided.

"You have to move around the board with your monkey character, shimmy up palm trees collecting coconuts, which you then have to crack open. Each coconut has a different method of opening, so you have to discover the best tool to use from around the board. This includes throwing them from the top of the tree, cracking them on a rock, finding a human with a machete, and getting a vehicle to drive over it."

Mr Richford nodded along. "A tropical island game. I got you," he said. He leant back in his chair and tilted his head up to the ceiling and closed his eyes. There was silence, and I wasn't sure whether to continue. Time passed, and then he opened his eyes and looked at me. "This one is about music, tropical, Hawaiian, which we can build on. I see bold surrounding colours, grass skirts, leis, and cocktails." He slapped his palm on the table. "Right, I got it. Next."

I continued to pull each prototype out of my bag, and we got through several more items, including the veterinary practice, a stretchy caterpillar family, a kangaroo popper, and a dancing robot, with Mr Richford coming up with creative ideas on the spot. I was about to reach for the next one when there was a knock on the door before it opened.

"Cynthia, come in," Mr Richford called, as she entered, pulling a trolley of food behind her. "Ah, fantastic," he said, rising to his feet.

The top tier of the trolley had a flask of coffee and a pot of tea on it, along with an ice bucket with a bottle of champagne leaning out. The second tier was full of exquisite looking sandwiches and pretzels, crab cakes, and a selection of cheeses. The third tier was full of neatly styled deserts, which looked like they belonged in an upmarket French patisserie.

"Great looking spread." I licked my lips as my eyes trailed over everything, and then I noticed Cynthia staring at the prototypes on the table.

She looked thoughtful for a moment, and then resigned, as she shook herself. "Can I get you anything else?" she mumbled.

Mr Richford shook his head. "No, that will be all."

Cynthia looked at me and made eye contact for a few seconds. The sadness reappearing, and some sort of underlying desire, before she left the room. I stared after her, wondering what was bothering her, but my thoughts were interrupted.

"Well, we may as well take a break for lunch, so please help yourself to anything you like," Mr Richford said, handing me a plate.

I eagerly piled my plate up high and sat back down at the table. "So, how is your father these days?" I asked, referring to Mr Richford Senior.

"Oh," he said, a subtle cloud passing over his face. "He's doing fine. He's enjoying retirement, and his golf handicap is now lower than ever before, but he still likes to have regular check-ins with me to see how the business is going in his absence and provide his own... insight."

"I don't blame him; he's been a part of this business for decades and his father was before that."

"It's all well and good that he wants to ensure it's well looked after, but when you hand over the reins to someone else, you need to trust their decision making and not interfere."

"What comments has he made?" I asked, whilst tucking into my food.

"He said recently that our adverts are looking a little recycled, and I'm trying too hard to please an audience that will never be entirely pleased, so I should just do what I think is fun and captivating. He also said that I need something fresh, which I don't believe is true."

I stood up to collect some dessert from the trolley, unsure how to respond. It wasn't as though Mr Richford Junior hadn't done well with getting the message across to the world about the toys we had created, but I couldn't help but think there was an element of truth in what his father was saying to him.

"Well, I can understand why he's protective. It's hard to let go of something you love. I also know that everything we've worked on together has been a big success, but I guess it wouldn't hurt to throw the odd curveball into the mix to see how it lands."

Mr Richford blinked as he straightened his tie. I could see he was affronted, and I concentrated on eating the delicate dessert with a fork. "The data and statistics reveal that viewing figures on my advertisements are at an all-time high," he said defensively.

I looked up at him, knowing that it was impossible to compare stats to five years ago, when his father was in charge, because of the multiple avenue's adverts could be posted these days. "Of course, like I said, everything we've worked on together has been successful. I was just making a comment."

He nodded, then sighed. "I guess… I mean, perhaps it won't hurt to take a risk now and then."

"Sounds like a good idea," I said, waving my fork back toward him.

His eyes flicked to my plate, and he frowned thoughtfully. "Anyway, how's the dessert? The salted caramel and pecan is my favourite."

"Very good," I nodded, whilst thinking they were more style than substance and not a patch on the flavours Mrs C could create.

"Marvellous," he said, dabbing the corners of his mouth with his napkin. "Now, shall we continue? What's next in that magical case of yours?"

We still had so much to get through, but I was more excited about the second half of the day because I had saved my favourites for the end. He flicked the page in his folder and stared intrigued at it, while I pulled the corresponding toy out of the bag.

At first, Mr Richford's enthusiasm had dropped slightly, having brought up his father's comments, but he soon got back into the swing of things. He would nod, think, and come up with an advertising idea or slogan.

"The mysterious eight-legged creature is watching you, your every move, and you can never be sure where it lurks," he chorused, fiddling with the spider transformer. "Seems like we need a sinister setting here, but leave it with me."

"Ah, then we have this." I handed him a unicorn with pink hair that trotted around, rotating its head from side to side to show off its mane.

"This is Tallulah, the unicorn," I said, as Mr Richford eyed it curiously.

"Is this…?" he frowned.

I nodded. "We had some Moco's left over from last year, so we did the usual and refashioned the base into this new toy."

"Perfect. As usual, you can't go wrong with unicorns. So do you have more stock that you've done this to?" he asked, familiar with our usual routine.

"Yes, as you can see on the next few pages, we've got various stuffed animals and toys, lunch boxes, pencil cases and pens, and even children's dressing gowns. We've stuck a unicorn horn on everything, re-coloured it and renamed it something quirkily related to unicorns, so we are good to go."

"Fantastic," he said, flipping through the pages in his file. "I'm loving Zebracorn and Bearcorn. In fact, all these unicorn themed items don't really need advertising. They just get automatically thrown into the present mix at Christmas, but Tallulah, I'll do a short piece on it."

We continued going through the toys until we turned onto the last page of the file and my stomach clenched with anticipation. I had saved the best till last. "Now, there are these," I pulled out the four dolls Pip had created, along with the doll the elves had based on Pip, and passed them to Mr Richford.

"Interesting. Very interesting." He inspected each doll. "Creative outfits, very quirky."

"They all have names, Delilah Sunrise, Shandy Smiles, Holly Berry, Ethel Wilde and Pip Shine," I said, pointing to each one.

"Excellent names." His eyes danced as he continued to twist them around in his hands to study them. He paused to pull some green slime out of Ethel Wilde's hair.

"Oh," I frowned. "Sorry about that. They had been pristine when I had put them into the case."

"These are absolutely fantastic. They are definitely an eclectic mix." He wiped his fingers on his napkin and looked unfazed by the slime.

"Together they are a band called Fashion Factor," I declared.

"Fashion Factor," he said, musing on the name. "I like it. No, I love it! Now, I see this as being the big one we plug this year."

"I'd like that," I said.

Mr Richford stood up and started clicking his fingers with both hands, one after the other. "Right, they need a stage, spotlights, microphones, dance moves, different voices, and outfit changes. Maybe even a backstory, or an interview." He then stopped clicking and turned to me. "Which one would you say is the lead singer, or the main spokesperson?"

I chuckled. "I'd say that's Pip Shine."

"Excellent," he picked up the doll. "I can play on that." He looked at the dolls, and a big smile came across his face. "I think the kids will love it. They'll be dreaming about owning a set of these toys, along with some additional props and different outfits. I actually think Fashion Factor will be the next big thing, bigger than Moco, the galloping horse," he claimed.

"I think so too," I said, feeling pleased.

"Well, I'll brief my team tomorrow to get to work. I'll ensure you have final sign off before we go live, but this definitely calls for a celebratory drink."

Mr Richford went back over to the trolley and grabbed the champagne bottle. He popped the cork and as it burst from the bottle, so did a flow of the liquid, which covered the floor, but Mr Richford barely seemed to care. "Oops, that's an excited bottle," he chuckled. He topped two glasses up and passed one to me. "Here's to another successful Christmas," and he raised his glass.

"Cheers," I toasted, as we clinked our glasses together.

Mr Richford and I then got to work placing all the prototypes into several large boxes for them to work through. It was a stark contrast to my small case and represented the mountainous task they had ahead of them.

Once I finished my champagne, I picked up my case and made my way to the door, but as I did, I felt something move inside it. "Send my regards to your father," I said, to which he nodded as his excitement faltered.

"I will, and I'll be in touch soon," he frowned and became thoughtful as he turned his attention back to the boxes.

42

I exited the room, swinging my case slightly as I shut the door, and again I felt something inside slide from one side to the other. I wondered what was going on, so I opened the case and peered inside. It was dark, so I put my hand in to search around for the contents and my fingers pressed into something gooey and squishy. I peered in again to find a bucket of slime which had spilt over.

"What on earth?" I then realised that Shinny must have added his slime game to my case without telling anyone. In fact, in all the rush, we had never discussed his game at all. "That cheeky rascal. He could have told me he had done this."

I was about to turn around to go back into the boardroom to brief Mr Richford when I spotted Cynthia sitting at her desk, her head in one hand as she twirled a pen around in the other, staring into space. "Cynthia," I called, making her jolt and look up at me as I wandered over to her. "Are you alright? You don't quite seem yourself."

"Oh," she said, straightening up and putting the pen down. "Sorry, I'm being unprofessional. It's nothing. How was your meeting?"

"It was good, thank you."

She smiled tightly. "That's good to hear." She glanced down at her ring and began playing with it.

"Is everything okay with your fiancé?" I asked.

She nodded as she stared at the ring. "Yes, he's wonderful. It's just that since we got engaged, I've been thinking more about me and who I am."

"In what way?" I asked.

"I just always thought by the time I was married, I'd have everything, the career, the apartment, the self-belief in who I am. But I keep being confined in this box, where I need to stay as this personal assistant, and no more."

"What is it you want?" I asked.

"I want to work directly with Mr Richford. I want to be involved in the creative art of making these advertisements, but he never lets me contribute anything above my station."

"Promotions are hard to get. It takes a lot of time, effort and going the extra mile," I said.

"But I do. I always go out of my way to give Mr Richford the best of everything. I even cover up and fix errors he makes, and he's listened to some of my ideas and he's used them without giving me any credit. It's not that I'm saying he's a bad person, but I'm just invisible to him," she sighed. "Maybe I should put it on my Christmas list this year, a chance and a promotion."

I scratched my head. "Well, I, err... I don't really get involved with careers and job opportunities as it goes against the Christmas Law."

She shook her head. "I know, I was just joking."

The phone started ringing, and she glanced at it, then back at me as if torn whether she should answer it. "I really should..."

"Go for it," I said, stepping backwards with my case.

She pulled the microphone of her headset down to her mouth and pressed a button on the telephone system. "Hello, Mr Richford's office. How can I help?" she said brightly.

I glanced at the boardroom doors, when another thought occurred to me. I hugged my case to my chest as an idea bloomed and took shape. I then reached into my pocket, extracted a scroll, and went over to a side table. I laid it out flat, then scrawled out a special contract before I went back over to her.

"Yes, he has availability on 1st of September, so I can slot you in then," she said. "Perfect. Have a lovely day." She hung up the phone and sighed, before she glanced up at me, surprised by my smug smile.

"Cynthia, I've been thinking about a way I can help you. There's a toy I didn't present to Mr Richford. It's a simple one, but an exciting one. How about I let you have it to come up with your own advertisement for it? I'll make sure you present it to Mr Richford, which will certainly get you noticed."

"That would be amazing," she beamed. "What is it?"

I placed the scroll of paper in front of her. "You will have to sign this first. It's an elevated Christmas non-disclosure agreement. You will only be able to discuss this with Mr Richford and you won't be able to take the toy I'm about to give you out of this building, or any notes or content."

"Of course. Where do I sign?" she asked.

I handed her my quill and pointed to the document. She quickly signed the scroll, and the writing glowed red, then green, solidifying the agreement.

"What now?" she asked.

I rolled the scroll up and put it in my inside coat pocket, then picked my case up and opened it wide on her desk. "It's called Restyling Slime." I scraped all the contents that were matted into the lining of my case back into the bucket.

She nodded as a determined, firm look came across her face. "Looks like fun," she commented.

"Oh, it's definitely that," I said, before I explained how we had played with it in the workshop.

Cynthia dipped her hand in the bucket and gave it a squeeze. "Well, I'll definitely make sure the world knows just how much fun this can offer," she said, her eyes bright and her grin broad. She jumped to her feet and held out her hand to me, which I shook. "Thank you so much for this opportunity, Mr Claus. I won't let you or Mr Richford down."

I closed my case. "Good luck," I called. I made my way to the elevator and as I waited for it to arrive, I turned back round to find Cynthia already making frantic notes on a piece of paper as she inspected the slime I had given her. I was sure I had done the right thing, and it was all thanks to Shinny. Then I frowned in contemplation, suddenly wondering if Pepper and that dust of hers could have once again influenced my decision making. I shrugged and left Cynthia to allow her creativity to flourish.

Moments later, I met up with Mrs C near Central Park. She gave me a sheepish smile as I found her carrying a small shopping bag.

"What have you been shopping for?" I asked.

"I found a yellow cab keyring," she said, digging it out of the bag and holding it up. "I saw it and just thought that I had to have it."

I chuckled. "I like it. What else have you been up to today?"

"Oh, I've been for a walk around Central Park, hopped on a ferry to the Statue of Liberty, walked around some museums, and had a sandwich at Katz Deli, which was wonderful."

"Sounds fun, but it also sounds like you need a rest."

We stopped off for some dinner, where I ordered a New York cheese burger, which I devoured despite its monstrous size, followed by New York cheesecake, whilst I filled Mrs C in on Mr Richford's visions and told her about what I had done for Cynthia.

Mrs C laughed. "You really are a softy, aren't you? I've always liked Cynthia, so I really hope she pulls this off."

"Me too."

"And it sounds like this could be good for both her and Mr Richford, if things are getting a little stagnant for him."

"Let's hope he doesn't take offence at me interfering," I said.

"I'm sure he will see that your heart is in the right place, and that's precisely why I love you so much." She squeezed my hand across the table. "Well, it sounds like your job here is done. Shall we head back?"

"Actually, I need to pick something up before we go, for a special lad on his birthday," I grinned.

"Oh, of course," she said, shaking her head. "You know, you really should get something for everyone, not just Rudolph."

I waved her comment away. "Let's go. I'm sure there are plenty of late-night shops we can look in. This City never sleeps."

We started wandering around gift shops, clothes shops, stationery shops and convenience stores.

Mrs C then started picking up any item she found which was bright coloured and putting it back, a studious look in her eye.

"What are you doing?" I asked, after she picked up a blue and turquoise notebook, which had 'Dreams can come true, if only we allow ourselves to dream' written on it, and put it back.

"I'm just getting some fresh inspiration this year," and she lifted a fluorescent orange golf ball.

"Is fluorescent orange the way to go?" I asked.

She gave me a wry smile. "It might be. You'll have to find out."

I raised an eyebrow. "It's a bit… loud, don't you think?"

Mrs C laughed. "When has that ever been a problem for you?"

I laughed. "True."

We traipsed into more shops where she picked more items up and held colours together, yellow and red, grey and blue, sea green and brown, purple and black before she smiled. "I'm looking forward to getting stuck in when we get back."

"Well, you do an excellent job every year…" then my eyes fell on the perfect birthday present. I ran over to the shelf and picked the item up. "This is it. He'll love this."

Mrs C sighed and shook her head. "Can't you find something else?"

I glanced down at what I was holding and I shook my head. "I'm afraid not. This is perfect."

Mrs C sighed. "Very well. Only because it's his birthday."

I gathered up as many of the items as I could hold and hurried over to the checkout, ignoring Mrs C's cries of, "Hey, I thought you were just getting him one," and I happily paid, whilst getting a peculiar look from the checkout assistant because of the smug and self-satisfied expression I was wearing.

We headed back to get a taxi, where Mrs C gave an ear-splitting whistle to attract a cab driver's attention. I looked at her in surprise as a taxi screeched to a halt in front of us.

Mrs C chuckled. "I've always wanted to try that."

"You should have done that when Sugarplum sent us on that mission. It would have made things much easier."

"Yes, that's why I've been practising," she said.

We climbed inside, then drove back through the busy New York streets where Mrs C stared out the window, lost in thought. I could tell something was brewing in her mind, so I let her thoughts swell and develop by remaining silent throughout the rest of the journey home.

43

The following morning, I woke up to find the other half of the bed empty, which was unusual. I figured Mrs C must have left me to continue sleeping after a busy day in New York, so I got up and headed downstairs, eager to find her cooking me breakfast. But when I entered the kitchen, she wasn't there. There were no signs of breakfast, and even the coffee pot was empty.

I quickly scoured the rest of downstairs to find it cold and silent. Then I noticed that her snow boots and coat weren't by the front door and it suddenly occurred to me where she had gone, so I put my own snow boots on and headed over to her studio next door to the reindeer hut.

I hadn't expected her to be working so soon, but clearly, our trip must have inspired her to make a start.

The studio door creaked open as I gently pushed it, careful not to disturb her. I poked my head inside to find Mrs C sat facing a canvas propped on an easel. I couldn't see the content she was creating as she swept her paintbrush across it.

Her glasses were hitched up onto her forehead, and she had a smear of yellow paint on her cheek and flecks of green in her hair, as she concentrated intently, not noticing my arrival. Beside her was a desk which had a scattering of paints, felt-tip pens, crayons, paper with various sketches on it, and a curious half eaten packet of biscuits.

She was so beautiful in her element that I didn't want to disturb her, so I watched her for a moment as she tilted her head from side to side, examining her artwork. Then my stomach gurgled loudly, making her spin her head round in my direction.

"Oh, is it that time already?" she frowned, as her eyes flicked back to her canvas and she touched up an area she had spotted.

"How long have you been here?" I asked.

"I'm not sure, perhaps about 5am. I couldn't sleep as inspiration just hit me when we were in New York and I had too many visions of what I wanted to do this year, so I was eager to start working on them."

I raised my eyebrows. "That's early. I never like to see 5am unless it's on Christmas Day."

Mrs C gave me a stern, piercing look. "Yes, I know. You always moan if you don't get your self-prescribed sleep. But so far, I've had a really productive morning."

"That's great. So, can I see what you've done?" I asked, trying to peer round to see the canvas.

Mrs C shooed me away with her paintbrush. "You know the rules. No viewing until I'm ready."

I took a step back before any paint went on my coat. "Erm, what's happening about breakfast?" I queried.

"Oh, well, I'm on a roll, so can you make your own?" She lowered her glasses onto her eyes, to look at something on the canvas in finer detail.

"I guess so," I sighed as all my hopes of a lovely breakfast of waffles or pancakes were instantly dashed.

I returned to the house, leaving Mrs C to continue, and rummaged around in the kitchen. I picked up a banana, screwed my face up, and put it back. Then I considered making my own eggs and bacon, or trying my hand at some pancakes, but I didn't know the recipe. Finally, my eyes fell on a stash of mince pies. I knew Mrs C would disapprove of me having them for breakfast, but she wasn't around to tell me off, so I piled my plate up and sat down to eat.

Later, after a quick visit to the reindeer hut to tell Rudolph about my trip, I made my way to the workshop where the elves were seamlessly working together.

Alabaster rushed over. "How did the presentation go?" he asked.

I glanced at Shinny, who was looking at me cautiously and full of hope, as if he was waiting for me to mention the slime he had added to my case. "They went well, thank you. I think we will have some very successful adverts going out, which will make the children eager to wish for them for Christmas."

"Oh my sugarcanes, this is so exciting," Sugarplum beamed. "It will be Christmas before we know it."

"Yes, and soon it will be the Sleigh Ride concert," Wunorse announced, causing Shinny to gulp and look extra anxious.

I frowned. "I know the Sleigh Ride concert means a lot to you all, but there is something even more important that we need to focus on before that. It's Rudolph's birthday soon and I want it to be extra special."

"Oh of course," Alabaster remarked. "How could we possibly forget?"

"Well, it would be hard to, when it's on our calendar in big bold letters, and you remind us about it constantly," Sugarplum said, batting her eyelashes innocently at me.

"And I'm sure it will be very special, just like it is every year." Bushy darted her eyes to Sugarplum, where I detected a slight eye roll.

"Good, so make sure you get a gift for him," I ordered. "Now, I just need to convince Mrs C to do what I want her to do."

Over the next few weeks, most of my attention was on planning Rudolph's birthday party. I picked out the decorations from the elves' selection, plus the birthday wrapping paper I wanted for his gift that I had purchased in New York, then I carefully drew the design I envisioned for Mrs C.

Meanwhile, Mrs C continued to work on her paintings and pictures every day, but after finding out about my daily ventures into the kitchen and the mountains of mince pies I was getting through, she banned me from entering unsupervised. Instead, she reverted to her usual routine of making me breakfast first, laying out lunch for me, and coming back to make dinner.

She would then squeeze in some communication with David to check in on his business, and how his interviews had gone, but after that she would sigh and claim she was too tired and exhausted to do anything else, particularly anything to do with Rudolph's birthday party.

It was a few days before Rudolph's big day, and I was getting desperate. I hovered around the entrance waiting for Mrs C to return from her studio and as soon as she did; I ambushed her. "So have you given it any more thought?" I asked.

"Huh?" she asked, distracted, as she took her snow boots off.

"You know, Rudolph's birthday. It won't be a birthday if you don't help me," I pleaded and followed her into the kitchen.

"I thought your New Year's resolution was to stop showing favouritism. Don't you think you spoil him too much?"

"No, not at all. There's nothing wrong with treating my special pal on his birthday."

"The other reindeer have birthdays too, you know. Perhaps you should put more effort into celebrating them."

"Yeah, yeah. I'll do that too," I agreed, wondering what I had to do to convince Mrs C to help. "So, will you do it? The big day is fast approaching."

"I really don't get why you're so bothered about this. Like I said before, he will barely notice if he doesn't have the cake of your dreams."

"Yes, he will. He'll be all doe-eyed and sad. Please, I need it to be perfect."

"Perfect. You do realise your doodle of what you want this cake to look like looks more like an acrobatic monkey."

"An acrobatic monkey? I spent ages designing that!"

"Really? Ages? It was a wobbly outline with an arrow pointing to it with a label."

I shook my head, aghast. "Well, either way, you know what I want, so will you do it?"

"I'm very busy. I have a lot of ideas for my paintings this year, so I'm not sure I'll have time to squeeze it in."

"You squeeze David in all the time." I slumped into the chair at the kitchen table, feeling deflated.

"Well, I'm his business advisor. Speaking of which, he got another offer today."

"Another one, that's impressive. That makes it five now, doesn't it?"

She nodded as she began wiping down the counters. "I'm so pleased for him after all the bad luck he had before."

"Well, it looks like your advice has seriously helped him. So, is he going to accept this one?" I asked.

"He's holding out. It seems the list of questions I gave him to ask has made him really evaluate what they can give back to him, and he doesn't want to jump at the first offer."

"What are his main concerns about them?" I asked.

Mrs C paused in her cleaning. "There are a few things, such as, they don't have the right contacts in the industry, they want too high a percentage in the business, or they want to make changes to the product that David doesn't think is right. Others, he just hasn't clicked with, and he found them too rude and difficult to work with."

"Well, that's what these investors and business people are like. Are you sure he should be that fussy?"

"Some of them sound like proper dragons, so I don't blame him for looking at all his options to make sure he is getting the right match. Vintique Scanner is a labour of love for David. It's a massive part of his life and he's sacrificed a lot to get to where he is, so, of course, he's going to be very careful about who he invites into his world to be a partner. He would want them to love it as much as he does and respect his visions."

"But it's a fine line between recognising a good business offer, that might be less than what you wanted, and holding out for something perfect which might never come."

"True, but like I said, he's not said no to anyone yet, and if they are serious about investing in him and confident with the offer they have proposed, they should wait."

Mrs C then opened the fridge and started pulling out some tomatoes, when a whole scattering of carrots tumbled to the floor, and they kept coming. "Drat," she cried, as she started scooping them up and shoving them back into the fridge.

My eyes lingered on them in surprise. "That's a lot of carrots," I detected, as an enormous grin crept across my face.

"Yes, well…" she looked flustered as she pulled out a cauliflower and slammed the door shut to stop more carrots from spilling onto the floor.

She whipped her hair from her face, and started chopping up the cauliflower without saying another word, and that was when I knew that my lovely reliable wife wouldn't let me down.

44

Finally, the day of Rudolph's birthday arrived, and I headed to the reindeer hut. "Morning everyone," I called, as the reindeer stirred, opening their eyes and lifting their chins from where they were resting on their hooves, or the ground. Rudolph was the first to roll onto his feet, stand up and come to see me. "I think you all need some good exercise today to stretch those legs." I waited for the last reindeer, Dasher, to stand up, and I opened the enclosure and led them all out into the snowy paddock beside the workshop. "Run along and have fun," I said, noticing an exchange between Vixen and Dancer. Seeing as I did this every year on Rudolph's birthday, they probably knew what was in store.

I hurried back to the reindeer hut and started decorating it. I hung Happy Birthday banners across the walls, tinsel and bunting in every place I could find, and I poured mounds of red, green, and gold confetti into the hay. I blew up an inflatable Rudolph to stick in the corner next to an inflatable version of myself and positioned them so it looked like I was giving Rudolph a hug. Next, I laid out a table with a bowl of crisps and some drinks, before I proudly placed my wrapped gift on it. I neatened up the bow, making sure it wasn't askew, before I headed back into the house. "Is it ready yet?" I called towards the kitchen.

"Yeah, I've just put the finishing touches on it, so you can come in now," Mrs C called.

I entered the kitchen and beamed in delight. There, sitting in the middle of the counter, was the most perfect cake I had ever seen.

"I would say it's just like you asked for, but I think I made some improvements to your doodle."

"It's incredible." I walked around to the opposite side to get another look at it. It was even better than I imagined. The cake was in the shape of Rudolph's head which sat on top of two tiers of cake, which were bright red and bright orange. Its flaked icing looked like fur. The large red nose glowed and glistened as if it was lighting the sky on Christmas Eve. While the antlers were impressively constructed, and somehow stood tall without collapsing.

"The nose is made of carrot syrup and the rest of the cake is carrot cake with candy flavoured frosting."

"Thank you so much." I pulled Mrs C into my body and kissed her cheek. "He will love it."

She nodded curtly. "Can you take it across to the reindeer hut so I can clean up?"

I carefully picked up the cake, but I misjudged the height of the antlers, and one partially lodged itself up my nose. I readjusted myself and then tentatively made my way across to the reindeer hut, luckily not dropping it, and placed it in the centre of the table.

Mrs C followed shortly behind me. "Wow," she exclaimed, glancing around at the way I had decorated the place. "It's like a sand dune in here." She waded through the confetti and straw. "I particularly like the affectionate display between you and Rudolph," she smirked, gesturing to the inflatable versions of us.

"Thank you," I said proudly.

Then there was a burst of commotion behind us. "Quick, hurry up," Alabaster was saying as he marched ahead of the other elves. "We're here, Santa!"

The other elves followed close behind. They piled inside and haphazardly climbed over the mounds of confetti, but they were so light-footed they barely left an indent. They had swapped their elf hats for party hats, and they had whistles that inflated into horns dangling from strings around their necks.

Wunorse was holding a wrapped gift, which he placed on the table, and he smiled and waved at Mrs C.

"Thanks all for coming. I think it's time I fetched the lucky lad." I hurried out of the shed and over to the paddock, where the reindeer were spread out sporadically, apart from Comet, whose nose was very close to Donner's backside. I vigorously jingled my large reindeer rattle. "Round up," I called, causing the reindeer to trot across to me. "That means you too, Prancer." He seemed too focused on trotting back and forth to perfect his shimmy.

Rudolph was the first one to reach me, and he instantly jerked his head under my hand so I would stroke him. "There you go, boy. It's a special day today. Do you know why?" Rudolph lifted his head, so I scratched under his chin. "Shall we go find out? Follow me everyone."

I then walked backwards out of the paddock, giving my rattle a few more jingles to keep them in line, and I beckoned them all the way back to the shed. When I entered, I gave a signal to Mrs C and the elves, so that they burst into singing, as Rudolph entered. "Happy… birthday… to… you…," everyone started, and I bellowed along with them.

Rudolph's eyes widened as he looked around at what I had done to his home. It was the same expression he'd originally had when Pip had wanted him to wear the tinsel necklace, a mix of mortification and horror. Then he sniffed the air, and his eyes fell on the cake, which was now decorated with lit candles, and he licked his lips.

I grinned as I beckoned Rudolph over to the cake. "Go on lad, blow your candles out." I let Rudolph get as close to the cake as possible, whilst holding him back from licking it, before I gave an almighty blow and blew the candles out for him. "Yay, well done," I called as the elves and Mrs C cheered and clapped, and the elves blasted on their whistle horns, causing the paper end to unravel and shoot glitter out.

Rudolph once again jerked himself towards the cake to lick it, but I pulled him back. "Not so fast, lad. It's time for presents first." A trail of drool had now formed around his mouth as he continued to take deep sniffs towards the cake, and even the other reindeer were now getting in on the act.

I glanced at Mrs C, who was standing back watching the scene with a suspiciously amused smile playing on her lips, and it made me wonder what was in the cake to make the reindeer so keen.

"Give him our gift," Sugarplum burst, looking excited.

I picked up the wrapped item, which was long and thin. "Oo, what could this be, lad? Let's open it together, shall we?" I stepped in between him and the cake, so he could focus on exactly what I was doing as I tore into the paper, and pulled out a long stick with a strange knobbly brush on the end.

"It's a massage brush, which we designed specifically for him," Bushy explained, looking delighted. "It will feel great on his nose."

I started to rub the brush against Rudolph's neck and head, and soon got his full attention as he pushed his head into it, looking as though he was really enjoying it.

"I think he likes it," Sugarplum declared, giggling.

"He certainly does. Right, next, it's my gift," I said, putting the massage stick to one side. "Let's open it and see what it is, shall we?" I slowly unwrapped the present, trying to build up the anticipation, and then I pulled out a bottle of stout. "Ta-dah! It's all the way from New York. Look, there's a picture of the Empire State building on it." I turned the bottle round for him to see. "I think you'll love it; it says it's a very dark stout which has been brewed with oats and hops, and has notes of smoked hay, with an underlying sweet, earthy flavour to it."

"Wow sir, that looks very exotic," Alabaster said, noticing that Rudolph barely made any sign he was interested in what I was showing him. Instead, he was frantically sniffing again and trying to get around me.

I placed the bottle on the table along with the other five and sighed. "Very well, I know what you really want," I said, feeling disappointed as I stepped to one side. "I guess it's cake time."

Rudolph licked his lips. The other reindeer stepped closer, and the elves also let out a stifled gasp of excitement.

"Look Rudolph," I gestured at the cake as if his eyes hadn't been on it the whole time. "It's you, and what a handsome reindeer you are. Shall we cut it together?" I took the knife Mrs C was handing to me and fed my arm in between Rudolph's antlers. "Ready?" I asked, before forcing the knife downwards, straight through the middle of the cake.

"Wait, watch out for the nose!" Mrs C reached out as if to stop me, but it was too late. The knife cut through it and a stream of orange goo squirted out all over Rudolph so that it covered his own bright red nose and matted in the fur on his snout. He didn't seem to mind though as he eagerly started licking it up, his tongue just about reaching to get the goo on his own nose.

Mrs C took the knife off me and scooped up some of the syrup to salvage. "Sorry, I should have warned you about that. Why don't you go give him a wash whilst I cut this up? The top tier is for the reindeer and the rest is for us." She winked at Wunorse, who was standing right next to her.

She started carving the cake, cutting sections away, and placing them onto a plate. It was like a massacre. First, he lost his antlers, then his ears, then his eyes, whilst more syrup oozed out of it.

Although it was a cake, I found it difficult to watch, so I turned away and hooked up the hose, but by the time I had turned back around, Rudolph was almost clean because Cupid and Prancer had jumped at the opportunity to lick away every morsel of the orange syrup. Rudolph closed his eyes as if he was enjoying the attention, so I waited until they had moved away from him before I gave him a quick blast with the hose, anyway. Meanwhile, Donner and Blitzen began stamping their hooves in excitement.

"Cake time," Mrs C finally announced as she dolloped nine slices of cake along the reindeer trough.

The reindeer could not hold back, and they instantly nuzzled their noses into the trough to gobble up the cake like it was a drug to them.

There were two remaining large tiers of red and orange cake, with a layer of pale red icing on the top. Mrs C then turned back to the rest of us. "Now, who wants a big slice?" she asked.

All the elves' hands shot upwards. "Me," they all chorused, with Shinny jumping high in the air.

"And me," I said firmly, making sure that Mrs C didn't forget me.

"Of course," she said, smiling, but there was something in her smile that made me frown slightly. She divided out several large portions and handed them out to me and the elves before we all tucked in.

"Galloping snowdrops, this is your best yet, Mrs C," Wunorse exclaimed, as the elves eagerly nodded in agreement.

"Well, I'm glad you are all enjoying it," Mrs C grinned a little too much. It was as if she was sharing a joke with herself.

"I love birthday parties," Bushy gushed, shovelling the last of her cake into her mouth and licking her fingers. "I wish every day was a party with lots of cake and sparkles."

"Me too," Sugarplum said. She then picked up some confetti and threw it in the air, so it landed over the blow-up Rudolph. "Happy birthday," she cried gleefully whilst spinning around.

Alabaster grinned. "Oh, I know," he said, racing over to the old radio that I sometimes use when mucking out the reindeer, and inserted a dusty cassette of Christmas classics. "You can't have a party without music."

"Yay, it's a song about Frosty!" Bushy shouted as the music started. "He really is a jolly, happy soul, isn't he?"

Pepper grinned widely. "Wunorse, you can do the robot dance, can't you?"

Wunorse nodded vigorously in agreement. "I can do the worm, the robot, the spider and the fairy dance," he boasted.

Sugarplum snorted. "Stupid fairies."

"Go on Wunorse," Alabaster sniggered. "Show us your moves."

As Wunorse started jerking his body around, I stepped closer to Mrs C. "Is it just me, or are they behaving a little odd?"

"Are they?" she asked innocently, as she smugly finished the last bite of her cake.

"Yes. How much sugar was in that cake?" I asked, as Shinny started trying to copy Wunorse's moves.

Mrs C shrugged. "I can't remember," but the look in her eye told me she did. "I'm just pleased they're having a good time, and so should you." She picked up a bottle of beer off the table, twisted the cap off, and handed it to me. She then grabbed one for herself, clinked it against mine, and took a sip.

I grinned back at her and swigged from my bottle as we watched the elves

"Oo, let's make confetti angels!" Bushy grabbed Shinny's and Pepper's hands and pulled them to the ground.

"Good idea," Pepper agreed and flopped backwards so she lay with her arms out wide in the hay and confetti mix. They all started waving their arms up and down, and moving their legs in and out. They giggled loudly and jumped up to look at the splodges they had left behind. "Look at mine," Pepper cried, doubling over with laughter.

Wunorse, who was trying to writhe around on the floor, suddenly spotted the blow-up Rudolph. He raced over to it, crying out, "We need a birthday hug, Rudy." He leapt onto it, bounced, and then ended up on the floor, laughing his head off. "Rudy, that was naughty, but I forgive you," he said, as he clutched the blow-up Rudolph in his arms.

Soon Alabaster raced over. "You can't leave Santa out," and did the same thing to the blow-up Santa, where he leapt on it for a cuddle and collapsed onto the floor next to Wunorse. They both laughed as if it was hilarious.

Rudolph and the other reindeer had finished licking up every morsel of cake and syrup, and had slunk off to lie down in the corner out of harm's way. They seemed to be content in watching the surrounding chaos and staying out of it, and I didn't blame them.

Mrs C laughed and shook her head, as the elves continued to giggle. "I think we should leave them to it," she said, placing her empty beer bottle on the table. "Shall we take a snowy night walk?"

She took my hand, and we left the shed, just as Wunorse shouted. "Shall we give Rudy his birthday bumps?"

I looked at her suspiciously. "Okay, you can tell me now. Did you lace that cake with something? I've never seen the elves behave like that, nor the reindeer get so obsessed."

She laughed. "Well, you know what the elves get like when they have my extra strong candy cane syrup. I might have added more than usual this time. And as for the reindeer, that was just a new carrot syrup recipe I've been working on for a while now."

I opened my mouth wide in shock, then laughed. "You little mischief maker. It was pretty funny, though."

"Well, they work hard, so I thought they deserved to have a break and let off some steam."

We strolled leisurely around the snowy ground and walked past Mr Frosty. "Nice scarf today," I said, admiring his new red scarf, with a white snowflake pattern knitted into it.

"Sugarplum told me he wanted to wear this one today," Mrs C chuckled.

We then spent several blissful moments. My arm wrapped around her shoulders, her body pressed to mine, watching the sky as it bounced with a beautiful display of green, blue, and purple light. It felt both electric and peaceful, like lapping seawater moving across the entire sky.

"This place really does contain magic," she whispered.

"It does with you here," I said, kissing her cheek.

"You silly sausage," she said, and then after a while, she yawned. "That beer has made me sleepy. Let's head back."

"Okay. I'm sure the elves will tire themselves out soon and leave the reindeer in peace."

45

The next morning, following Mrs C's orders, I grabbed some bin bags, a sweeping brush, and went to check on the reindeer. I opened the door to find the elves fast asleep with the reindeer. Wurnorse and Alabaster, who was still cuddling the inflatable Santa, were both leaning up against Cupid who was lying down behind them looking quite content. They were both snoring, or more like cooing away, completely oblivious to what time it was and where they were.

Sugarplum, Shinny and Pepper were nestled snugly in between the other reindeer and they were covered in glitter and hay. When I looked closer, Pepper had stuck some hay around her mouth, forming a beard and moustache and Shinny had stuck red confetti all over his nose, making me wonder if they had gone through a phase of pretending to be me and Rudolph. I scanned the area, trying to find the missing elf, and then spotted Bushy asleep in the food trough.

"Everybody up," I called, making Wunorse's cooing snores turn into a jolted snort.

The elves opened their eyes, bounced to their feet, and instantly looked around at everyone in confusion.

Sugarplum burst out laughing when she spotted Pepper and Shinny's new disguises. "Oh my gum drops, I remember you both doing that. It was so funny," she chuckled, then her eyes landed on me and her smile wiped from her face, and she cleared her throat. "Sorry, sir."

"Well, you all seemed to have fun last night."

"Yeah, we had a great time," Alabaster yawned, before his eyes landed on the blow-up Santa next to him and he scratched his head.

"Well, I have lots of mess to clear up, so why don't you all go back to your dorm until you feel up to doing more work in the workshop?" Inside I was laughing, but I tried not to show it, as I needed to keep some order about the place.

"Certainly, sir. We'll get refreshed in no time," Bushy looked at her little elf shoes and tights, which were covered in reindeer feed mush.

As they traipsed lethargically across the reindeer pen, rubbing their eyes, Cupid let out a disgruntled noise. He had looked so comfortable being their support.

"See you later, Cupid," Wunorse called, blowing him a kiss.

As the door to the hut closed, the blow-up Rudolph floated down from the rafters in the ceiling and landed in front of me. "What the…" I looked upwards and wondered how it had got up there. I shook my head and chuckled before I got to work, and started filling the bin bags with rubbish and sweeping up the confetti.

Once I had gotten bored with cleaning, I went over to Rudolph and gave him a stroke. "One year older, aye pal. Did you have a good celebration yesterday?" He knocked his antlers against the fence eagerly. "Ah, I'm so pleased. You deserve it," I said and scratched him harder. "I only want the best for my pal."

I stood up and grinned. "Hey lad, you never got to try my gift to you." I grabbed one of the stout bottles from New York and poured it into a bucket with some reindeer feed. Rudolph sniffed and then began guzzling it up. I grinned at his eagerness. At least Mrs C wasn't the only one to give him something he loved for his birthday. "There we go lad. I bet that's nicer than the usual kind you get, isn't it?" He pulled his head out of the bucket and licked his lips.

Dancer huffed out a blast of air as if to remind me the others were there as well, before I gave Rudolph another pat on the head, leant my broom on the wall and returned to the house.

I kicked off my boots and found Mrs C sitting at the computer, finishing eating a shortbread biscuit.

"You're back sooner than I thought you would be." She quickly dusted some crumbs away with her cardigan. "Have you done a thorough job of tidying up the reindeer shed, or am I going to find half a job over there?"

I hesitated and glanced back at the door. "Of course I have," I lied.

Mrs C narrowed her eyes in suspicion. She clearly didn't believe me. "I'll look at it later," she said firmly. "Those reindeer won't be happy if they have to sleep in a bed of confetti for another night."

I contemplated going back to finish the job before Mrs C could see it, but then I decided against it. I felt exhausted, and I knew she'd finish what I had left. "Is anything interesting happening on the line?" I asked, trying to redirect the conversation.

"Yes, actually," Mrs C said, as a smirk spread across her lips, which she then tried to force away and mask. "I got a message from David, and after careful deliberation, he's decided who he is going to go into business with. Apparently, as soon as he met this man, he had an instant connection, and everything he said played right into David's question playbook."

"Oh… Don't tell me. Is it who I think it is?" I said, somehow sensing what was coming.

"Yep," Mrs C said, chuckling. "Seamus Conway."

"You're joking. You're winding me up."

Mrs C laughed. "Nope. It's true. David is very excited about the contacts this man can offer, his vision for Vintique Scanner, and his enthusiasm for the business. It looks like they hit it off immensely."

I shook my head in disbelief. "But he was so unnervingly confident and arrogant. I can't see him being David's cup of tea at all."

"Well, it looks like he is. I guess one man's distaste for someone is another man's business partner," she laughed. "Anyway, I'm pleased for him. I do think Seamus must be good at what he does and David sounds delighted, so I guess we'll see what happens."

"Fair enough, each to their own. I wish him the best," I muttered, still frowning.

"Oh, there's another thing. I've had an email from Mr Richford. He said to tell you that his commercials and advertisement plans for the toys are going well. He will send them over for you to sign off soon."

"That's good. I just hope they're not recycled, like the last couple of years."

"He also asked if you want to see each country's relevant advert, or just the American version?"

"I want to see all of them. He should know that."

"I'll tell him to send everything for you to review." She pulled her reading glasses down, spun round on her chair, when she stopped. "Oh, he also said that it was an interesting task you set, Cynthia."

"Is that right?" I asked, trying to cover my smirk.

"He said he's happy to review her content and give her constructive feedback."

"That's good. It sounds like he's open to new ideas. Hopefully she can bring a touch of freshness to the mix of adverts he's producing." I crossed my fingers in hope.

"We'll soon find out when we get to see them," she murmured, focusing back on the screen.

"Speaking of which, when do I get to see what you have been working on?" I asked.

"Soon. I have one more piece I want to make, which I think will be my best yet. Then you can see them all," she said, but I could see her smile, reflecting on the computer screen, dancing with a private joke.

"Looking forward to it," I muttered, whilst staring suspiciously at her crafty expression.

46

After lunch the next day, Mrs C came back into the house from her studio covered in red and brown paint splotches. "I've finished," she announced.

I placed my mug of tea and honey on the kitchen table and jumped to my feet. "So, do I get to see them now?"

"Let me go freshen up, then I'll take them across to the workshop to show you and the elves."

"Alright, I'll meet you there," I said, already back stepping to the door.

I rushed over to the workshop and found the elves busy at work. "Everyone," I cried, looking behind me to check Mrs C hadn't miraculously followed me. "Gather round." I beckoned frantically to the elves.

They exchanged confused looks before carefully placing their half-finished toys onto their workbenches and walked over to me. "Mrs C is about to present this year's paintings, so we have to all look impressed, okay?" I glanced behind me again.

"Oo, yay, I love her paintings," Bushy cried, and Shinny nodded eagerly next to her.

"Yes, that's it. I like the enthusiasm and just make sure you compliment her," I pleaded.

"But we always compliment her work," Wunorse gushed.

"Yes, I know, but she's been working particularly hard on these paintings this year, so we need to exaggerate our appreciation, no matter what."

"Is that right?" Mrs C's voice came from behind, causing me to freeze, and I slowly turned round.

Mrs C glared at me. "Exaggerate appreciation, aye? No matter what?" she repeated, and waltzed past me with a large black portfolio. She then began setting up her display on an easel beside the Christmas tree.

I grimaced. "Thanks for the heads up, all of you," I hissed towards the elves, who seemed to find the situation somewhat amusing.

Mrs C cleared her throat, and we all gathered around the easel, which now held A3 cards facing the opposite direction. The elves sat on the floor, crossed their legs, and rested their elbows on their knees and their chins in their hands, looking eager to see what she was about to present, whilst I sat down in the armchair.

"So, what delightful pieces do you have for us this year, Mrs C?" Wunorse asked, who was right in the centre of everyone to get the best view, and smiling eagerly.

"Right, this is the first one." She turned the first painting round, which was scarlet red, covered in white snowflakes, just like Mr Frosty's scarf.

"It's fantastic. Very traditional," Wunorse beamed.

"Yes, I thought I would start out with some quite standard, simple ones to add to the collection."

Next, Mrs C flipped through some more, which were red and green patterned, others had holly wreaths painted on, mixed in with candy canes, and the words Merry Christmas. Some were of snowmen, and presents, and others had traditional depictions of me carrying a sack, which were all similar to ones we had seen before, just subtly different to freshen them up. Each time, Wunorse would gush about how amazing it was, which caused Mrs C to smile in satisfaction.

After she showed us one with Christmas trees, floating baubles and stars on it, she advised that the next section was freshly inspired for this year. She turned onto a lime green background, which had several faces of Rudolph on it. His face was a caricature of him, and his nose was bright red with a tinge of orange in it, which looked just like the Rudolph cake she had made.

"Wow, that brings back good memories," Sugarplum said, licking her lips.

Bushy nodded. They then exchanged looks and smothered a giggle.

"It's certainly different and will stand out amongst the crowd," I commented.

"It's very… interesting." Alabaster tilted his head to the side, looking unsure about it. "It's not your usual portrayal of Rudolph."

Mrs C smiled. "That's the point." She then turned over another painting. "I personally like this one."

The painting had beautiful shades of vibrant blue and turquoise on it, and there were white snowmen covering the page with a fluorescent orange carrot poking out for its nose. The colours worked so wonderfully together, and it instantly reminded me of an orange golf ball, and a 'Dreams can come true' notebook cover we saw in New York.

I chuckled, as Mrs C grinned, looking pleased with herself. "I like it a lot. It will certainly catch the children's eyes on Christmas morning."

"It's absolutely charming," Wunorse said. "It will almost be a shame for the children to tear it."

She flipped over a few more, which contained unusual mixes of colours which wouldn't normally be related to Christmas, all of which I had seen her placing together and analysing in New York. They all looked fantastic, and I felt pleased that Mrs C's inspiration had really paid off.

"Great job, Mrs C," Wunorse kept repeating, with the other elves nodding along.

"Thank you everyone. Now, this is the last one," she said finally, her eyes glinting with mischief, as she flipped over the last picture.

"Oh, ha, ha, ha," I rolled my eyes as I saw the painting.

It had several images of me and Rudolph on it, only they weren't us. They were replicas of the inflatable versions of us. They were in various positions, cuddling each other, me patting Rudolph's head, or me feeding him a carrot, all in front of a bright orange sunset on a crystal blue background.

Mrs C smiled at my reaction. "Do you like it?" she asked, feigning innocence.

I found it amusing, but I didn't want her to know that. "You've made me look really bloated."

"You are bloated, though. You're meant to be full of air."

"You look very happy, Santa, in the picture," Pepper sniggered.

Mrs C smiled. "He does, doesn't he?" she stepped back to analyse the picture, and the dreamy look she had drawn. "Like he's in love."

I stuck my tongue out at her, and Mrs C laughed.

"So, which of these has your sign off?" she asked, glancing around at everyone.

"All of them have my vote," Wunorse said.

"Mine too," each elf chorused after him.

They all looked at me, waiting. I rubbed my chin, for an exaggerated effect, as I pretended to think. Then I sighed. "Go on then, all of them it is."

Mrs C grinned. "Well then, my job here is done. You have your wrapping paper designs for this year."

"Perfect. I'll get them printed off into rolls," Alabaster said.

Mrs C grinned and packed the paintings back into the portfolio and handed it to Alabaster. "Be my guest."

He dragged the portfolio, which was twice the size of him, behind him to his workbench.

"I can't wait. We'll be soon wrapping all the children's presents for Christmas," Bushy said, clapping gleefully.

"Yes, Christmas will be here very soon, which also means so will you know what…" Shinny whispered, wringing his hands together.

Bushy grinned and twirled back to her workbench.

I stepped closer to Mrs C and wrapped my arm around her. "Excellent work. I love them all, even if you are being cheeky."

She gave me a serious look. "Now do you actually mean that, or are you exaggerating your appreciation of them, just like you told the elves to," she said, giving me a serious look.

"No, I really do like them."

"Really, because I've been meaning to ask, how often do you tell the elves to pretend to like something I make?"

"Err, this was a one off," I said, feeling uncomfortable. But then I saw her eyes brighten and her smile widen.

"I'm just joking with you. It's nice that you care."

47

Soon, the sign on the workshop door changed to '*Elves Festively Focused on Christmas,*' as the elves ramped up their toy making, and Pepper started wrapping the toys in Mrs C's newly designed wrapping paper, ready to be allocated and have a name stuck on it.

"Gosh, things are really taking shape." I inspected the mound of presents Pepper had wrapped whilst sucking on a candy cane. "Mrs C's wrapping paper looks amazing when it is all bundled together. I can imagine the children waking up and seeing all these wonderful colours and pictures hiding their gifts, nestled together under their tree."

Bushy bounced up and down. "Yes, it's so exciting. Christmas is getting closer every day."

Shinny gulped. "Yes, and so is…. So is the Sleigh Ride Concert." He stared around at everyone, wide eyed.

"Yes, that's right. How are the plans going for that?" I asked.

Alabaster exchanged a look with Wunorse. "We're working on it."

"Have you decided who will be the star of the show this year?" I asked.

Shinny paled. "It's me." He raised his hand, looking terrified, while Pepper gave him an encouraging smile.

I nodded. "I see. Well, I'm sure you'll be great, and I'm looking forward to seeing what you all come up with this year."

When I returned to the house, Mrs C was facing the computer. "I'm glad you're back. I've had a file drop come through. Mr Richford has finished making all the commercials and advertisements for the toys, so we can watch them now if you like?"

"Excellent. I've been looking forward to this." I ran into the dining room to grab a chair, which I placed next to Mrs C.

Mrs C then thrust a notebook and pen at me. "Make sure you make notes, in case anything needs changing."

I settled into my seat, clutching my pen and notebook, and then Mrs C pressed the play button. The first advert came on and an overly loud, excited voice speedily began shouting about a bouncing kangaroo popper. There were faces of children laughing and smiling as they played with it, and the angles of the children and the toy darted back and forth rapidly, with an underlying message to the children telling them they needed it in order to have fun.

I laughed. "A typical toy advert there. Loud to capture everyone's attention and a speedy rhythm to evoke the feeling of fun."

"Not to mention the wink and the thumbs up from the child at the end," Mrs C laughed.

"Yes, it's perfect. I'll tick that one off the list."

We then continued to watch each commercial, one after the other. They all had a similar theme, loud, cheesy and fast-paced, which was fantastic at bringing the toys to life and inspiring children to play with them. As they continued, I remained impressed, despite making a few notes when I spotted a couple of issues with some translations, and also a few tweaks here and there.

On came the World Sausage eating competition game, which had a distinct style to the other typical commercials. Mr Richford had created sausage characters that humorously interacted with each other, as they claimed to be judges and contestants, before it merged into reality and they turned into plastic sausages and were the ones being eaten instead.

"Ah, so he went for Victor the vegan sausage in the end," I said.

We approached the end of the collection, and it moved onto another advert. The screen started off dark, before there was a crescendo of introductory music which caused my spine to tingle, and made me instantly look up from where I was making a note in my book.

There was then a burst of loud music as a spotlight beamed down on the Pip Shine doll, who was standing in front of a microphone on a stage. Behind her, the stage lit up with lights to reveal her name. Then another dramatic burst of music coincided with another spotlight shining onto Ethel Wilde, with her name lighting up the background, and the sequence repeated, one after the other, to light up Delilah Sunrise, Shandy Smiles and then Holly Berry.

The camera panned to Pip Shine, and a voiceover started speaking. "I'm Pip Shine. I formed the band a few years ago, and together we are Fashion Factor," she announced, as the lights at the back of the stage repositioned into the words Fashion Factor. "We love singing, we love fashion and we're on the hunt for global success." The voiceover said as it faded out.

I glanced at Mrs C, who was gazing at the screen with her mouth half open. The screen then went black again before the spotlights started dancing and flashing different colours over the dolls as they began miming along to a catchy chorus that Mr Richford's team must have come up with.

Pip Shine was lit up with pink and purple, Ethel Wilde, blue and red, Shandy Smiles, blue and purple, Holly Berry, green and red, and Delilah Sunrise, orange and yellow. The light display, the music, the way the dolls were moving was completely mesmerising, and then suddenly the lights went out and a rapid voice said. "Dolls and accessories packaged separately, and the advert ended."

"Wow," Mrs C blinked. "I have goosebumps. That music was incredible."

"That was the best advert I've ever seen," I said, feeling numb with shock. "I think the children will be banging down the doors for them. In fact, I actually want a Fashion Factor collection now."

"So, I assume that you're happy with it?" Mrs C asked.

"Yes, I'm definitely ticking that one off. Mr Richford has done a great job this year. Some of them were a little stifled and repetitive, but I think he's tried to be a lot more creative with some of the bigger toy pushes."

I started to get up, when Mrs C stopped me. "Hang on, there's one more video to show you. It's the one from Cynthia."

"Ah, I nearly forgot about that. I wonder how she's got on."

"Let's find out, shall we?" Mrs C pressed the play button.

There was suddenly a burst of colourful activity as slime blobs popped up on the screen. "Restyling Slime, the colour changing slime when it lands," a voiceover announced. The screen melted away, to a normal day of children playing with some generic dolls and building blocks, before one child turned to the other and shouted. "Let's have some fun," before there was suddenly a mad chaotic segment of children running around, throwing slime in all directions, which was broken up with slow motion action as children darted out the way, bursts of music, crazy camera angles, and manically laughing children and parents, as they became covered in slime.

The commercial seemed elevated to a higher level of intensity than I'd ever seen before, and it made my body tense as I watched it. Once the advert had finished, I turned to Mrs C, who slowly twisted her head towards me.

"Well, what do you think?" she asked, her lips twitching to fight off a smile.

"I think it was, err, different. It seemed to capture the storytelling that Mr Richford had in his better adverts, along with the crazy energy from a typical toy advert, plus something that was more unique and captivating. It certainly caught my attention, which is just what we want adverts to do."

"I thought so too. It's left me wanting to play with Restyling Slime, but I also think it might terrify every parent out there. So, does it have your approval?"

I paused to think about how it might be received, particularly with parents, but I quickly made my mind up. "Absolutely. I thought it was fantastic and fresh."

Mrs C grinned. "Perfect, I'll send Mr Richford our comments right now."

She rolled her chair up to the keyboard and began typing out our notes, whilst I heaved out of my seat.

Moments later, Mrs C spoke up. "Gosh, that was fast. Mr Richford has already replied. He must be working as we speak."

Mrs C read the email aloud.

"Dear Mr and Mrs Claus. It's great to hear your positive feedback

about our adverts this year, and I will certainly take action on all the comments you have given me. I will also pass on your feedback to Cynthia, about which I wanted to thank you for encouraging her involvement. Over the last few weeks, we have been working closely together to collaborate on some adverts and I believe we have delivered some fantastic content. We will now drip feed these campaigns and adverts over the next few months, and let's hope they all bring great inspiration to the children in time to add them to their Christmas wish list and make it a magical time. Regards, Mr Richford Junior. Chief Executive Officer at Gold Corporation International."

"That's interesting," Mrs C commented. "I can't help but think Cynthia has been more involved in these new adverts than we would have thought."

I grinned. "It looks like I might have solved both Mr Richford's and Cynthia's problems at the same time."

48

I looked at my calendar, and my stomach gave an excitable twist. Today I decided it was time for 'Operation Transcendence'.

"Honey, where's my special cleaning products?" I called, marching into the kitchen.

"They will be where you left them last year. No doubt thrown into a cupboard in the hangar," Mrs C replied, turning around from where she was peeling some potatoes.

"I checked my usual spot for them in the cupboard, but they weren't there!"

"Did you actually rummage around in there, or just gaze in, not see them and assume they were elsewhere?"

"Err, I'll go have another look," I pulled on a pair of Mrs C's marigolds. "If you need me, you know where I'll be."

I returned to the hangar and this time, after moving my engine oil for the plane, and an old jumper I wore, which was full of holes and engine grease to one side, I found my collection of special tonics.

I pulled them out and arranged them on the floor, along with some microfiber, streak-free cloths, sponges, my rubber squeegee, and a bucket.

I turned and faced her, my stomach twisting with glee. "Now, let's take a good look at you, my beauty." I grabbed hold of the protective cover and peeled it away, slowly revealing her shiny red body with gold trim. "There you are." I stroked my hand along her surface and felt the surprising warmth radiating back from her. "It's nearly time for our big day out, so we need to get you ready."

I stepped back and admired her entire stature, the curves of her body, the radiance of her colours, and her underlying energy. "Oh my lovely, what have those reindeer done to you?" I muttered as I spotted several scuffs all over her. "You look like you've been in a fight. Don't worry, my beauty. I'll transcend you into looking brand spanking new in no time. There won't be a scratch or scuff in sight."

I filled my bucket with water from the hose and poured in a dash of my sleigh tonic. It was a special tonic that not only left her looking great, but gave her a protective coating against the range of conditions we were about to face together. I took a sponge and started lathering her up, causing foamy bubbles which shimmered gold to cling to the sides of her body, whilst I whistled one of my favourite Christmas melodies to her.

I went round inspecting her, and using a fresh cloth, I dabbed a little extra of the concentrated tonic straight onto any of her noticeable blemishes, before massaging it into her body. "There, I bet that feels better," I whispered, already seeing her imperfections fading and a layer of shine forming over the top.

Her exterior was certainly under control. I just needed the tonic to work its magic, so I turned my attention to her interior and it was then that I spotted a tear in my cushioned seat. "Oh dear, we best get that fixed before it gets any bigger!"

I was extremely protective over the seat in my sleigh. I had gone through numerous trial-and-error scenarios to get the perfect compression in my chair, swinging from too hard that my bum would go numb, to too soft that getting out of it repeatedly on Christmas Eve would cause my thighs to burn.

Now, I had finally mastered it, having used careful calculations to get just the right cushion density, which meant I had to protect it at all costs.

I rummaged through my medicines and tonics, and found my little bottle of 'Stitchem', which Mrs C had made for me. Using a pipette, I dropped a few drops of the 'Stitchem' along the tear and watched as the fibres slowly knitted themselves back together. "It's such a shame we can't market this little bottle of magic," I said, admiring the bottle and feeling satisfied it had done the job I had wanted it to. "Silly Christmas laws. Those people down below don't know what they're missing out on."

By now, enough time had passed for the sleigh tonic to have done its job, so I sprayed her down with the hose. The suds slid to the floor, leaving her sparkling and looking dazzlingly clean. "Now for my favourite bit," I muttered, grabbing my squeegee and holding it up at the ready. "We can't have you going out there on your big day with any streaks, can we?" I stroked my squeegee over her, removing all the excess water and letting it splash to the ground.

Once I finished, I stepped back to admire her bodywork. She was now glistening and in pristine condition. "Now, you're ready," I said, giving the two curves at the front of the sleigh runners an extra buff with my rag. "Not long to go before the Sleigh Ride concert, and then we're off for our adventure. See you soon," I said, grinning, as I left her waiting for my return. I went back to the house, peeled off the marigolds, and handed them to Mrs C, unable to remove the grin on my face.

"Is it all sorted?" she asked, pulling a face at her yellow gloves, which were now shining unnaturally.

"Yes, she's ready to go."

"Well, now the sleigh is ready. Are the reindeer up to fitness?" she asked.

"I guess I do need to start getting them warmed up. I'll do that soon." I flopped into my throne and lifted the remote control.

"No time like the present." Mrs C yanked the control from my hand. "You have time to do it now, so chop-chop."

49

I sighed and pulled on my snow boots again and headed outside. I opened the door to the reindeer hut and found them dozing as usual. They all looked so peaceful. Vixen was making a loud snoring noise, and Rudolph was making a cute snorting noise. Donner and Blitzen were snuggled up together, with Comet just behind them. Cupid was sprawled out with his head tilted so far back that it looked almost unnatural. Dancer was in the corner by herself, looking pristine, whilst Prancer was sleeping in a strange position, so his hind legs were tucked under him and his front legs were sprawled out flat, causing his backside to be raised in the air and Dasher was lying on his side, but kept kicking his legs out as if he was dreaming about running. It was a shame that he rarely put his dream into practice.

I grabbed my special sleigh bell rattle and shook it vigorously, without warning. "It's that time, everyone up," I said, shaking it continuously as I walked down the pen.

The reindeer jumped, Cupid jerked his head around so fast, he probably caused himself whiplash, and I heard a little squeak of gas come out of Donner. They scurried to their feet and stood to attention in front of me, blinking rapidly to wake themselves up.

The sound of my sleigh bells only meant one thing, and that was business. "We need to get to work. Is everyone ready?" I yanked at the pen gate and swung it wide open. "Out you go into the paddock."

The reindeer trotted outside across the snow, into the wide-open paddock, where I guided them with my sleigh bells and made them line up in front of me. They were all evenly spread out apart from Cupid, who naturally invaded Dancer's space.

"Right, you all did well last year." I marched up and down the line. "But we weren't without fault, were we?" Rudolph straightened his shoulders and stared back at me resolutely as the other reindeer glanced down at the floor in a moment of shame. "There were definitely a few stumbles, a couple of slow take offs, some near misses and some actual hits. In fact, I've just been inspecting our sleigh and found several scuffs on her," I announced. "This isn't new. I know accidents happen, but over the last few years I can recall several similar events, which not only damages our sleigh but also impacts our Christmas style and flair. We should be proud of how we fly, so that means we need to make improvements." I smashed the sleigh bell into my palm. "We need to be fitter and stronger, with sharper turns, and working in closer harmony than ever before."

"Now, first, let's inspect you all." I walked along the row, examining each of them. "Prancer, I can see quite a bit of a belly, so that means extra cardio for you." The other reindeer glanced over and scrutinised him, whilst Prancer looked affronted and twisted his head round in an attempt to look at himself.

"Dasher, if you continue to be slow and lazy, we'll need to oil up your joints. You need to do some additional stretches to make yourself nimbler and stop yourself from pulling a muscle! Comet, you need to lift your head up rather than constantly bending down, sniffing the other reindeer's backsides! Cupid, you need to respect everyone's personal space! Step away from Dancer." Cupid gave Dancer a lick on her neck and shuffled to the side. "Vixen, you're looking a little droopy around the shoulders, so you need to strengthen up!"

I continued down the line and noted Rudolph was also carrying a bit of a belly, even larger than Prancer's. "And you lad…. no, you are absolutely perfect," I said, giving him a wink. The other reindeer stared at me in disbelief, their mouths open, but I ignored them.

I slapped the rattle against my shoulder. "Let's get to it. I want everyone to do some laps around the paddock to get warmed up."

I swung the rattle across to hit my other shoulder, so it gave a sharp blast, and with that the reindeer shot off, galloping across the snowy plain in their usual formation. Rudolph was at the front, followed by Cupid and Blitzen, then Comet and Dasher, then Prancer and Dancer, with Vixen and Donner, who were the largest of the herd, bringing up the rear.

"Heed," I cried, shaking my rattle, and the reindeer all galloped around the paddock in an almost seamless U-turn, with Cupid inching a little too close to Blitzen. "Cupid, fall to the side," I called, swishing my sleigh bells to the right as a signal, and Cupid scurried his feet to the side. "Good. Let's get those limbs and muscles working again."

I then swept my sleigh bells in a range of different motions, signalling which directions I wanted them to run. Rudolph was fantastic, as always, directing them exactly where I wanted them to go, but there was something niggling me as I watched them.

"Onward," I called, as I swept the sleigh bells upwards, and Rudolph instantly lifted into the sky with the others following him. They all left the ground with an elegance and grace that I always expected to see from them, although today it wasn't as light as it could be.

Rudolph guided them through the air on my command. They had been working together for centuries, so they knew how to work as one, even without the reins connecting them. They were beautiful as they shot over my head, and I willed them on from the ground. "Guide them with the glow of a fire like Rudolph. Pierce the air like Cupid's arrow, or like lightning from Blitzen. Be eager and urgent like Dasher and Comet. Be smooth and elegant, like Dancer and Prancer, and carry the weight of our heavy load like Vixen and Donner."

They swooped through the air, responding perfectly to my navigation, but again something was niggling me as I watched them working together. "Heel," I called, slapping the rattle, and the reindeer landed with precision.

I could see Rudolph's chest inflating and deflating much faster than usual. He must have become quite unfit over the last few months, but I refused to acknowledge it. "Excellent work, lad," I said, giving him a large grin. Rudolph stood straighter and slightly bowed his head at me. "That's enough for today. We'll continue to work on everything tomorrow, so rest up overnight."

After the reindeer settled, and I fed them a more nutritious reindeer feed that Mrs C had created, I returned to the house, my mind spinning with thoughts.

"Hey love, how are the reindeer faring up?" Mrs C asked, coming into the sitting room. "I saw from the kitchen window they looked a bit ragged. Do you think it's going to be a lot of work this year to get them to peak fitness?"

I barely heard her, as I poured myself a sherry, and took a steadying breath.

"Love, are you alright? You look like you're… err… thinking."

I sipped my drink. "You're right. I was thinking. It's just that the reindeer keep making silly mistakes on Christmas Eve. A collision here, a scrape there, a hesitation, or a bump somewhere else."

Mrs C nodded. "Yes, that's all part and parcel of frantically getting around the world in one night."

"Perhaps, but maybe we can do better."

"Sweetheart, it would be almost impossible not to have a few hiccoughs along the way. Don't put too much pressure on yourself and please don't overthink things."

"But how do we know it's not possible to have the perfect Christmas Eve, with no problems, when we've been doing the same thing year after year?" I downed my drink and slammed the glass down on the sideboard as I made my mind up. "I think I'm going to do something radical."

Mrs C sighed. "You don't need to, love. Things are fine as they are and it could be a disaster this close to Christmas."

I shook my head decisively. "No, I've been thinking and I can't shake it off. I want to change the reindeer's formation. I think a fresh line up could work wonders and I know just what I want to do."

Mrs C looked at me with an expression full of concern. "Well, you're a grown man, so it's up to you what you do. But if it doesn't work, then promise me you'll go back to the original formation and forget about it."

"Don't worry. I have this all in hand," I reassured her, feeling excited.

50

The following day, I jumped out of bed and went back across to the reindeer hut. The reindeer were dozing, but this time they jumped up with a new vigour, as if the exercise the day before had rejuvenated them. "Come on," I rattled my sleigh-bells again. "Everybody out. We've got a big day ahead of us." The reindeer trotted off into the paddock and lined up in front of me.

"I have big news for you all. It's time that we freshened things up a bit, so this year I want to change the formation."

Vixen and Dancer exchanged fearful looks. Comet's eyes opened wide, and Donner ran a tongue across her lips, looking nervous. "Now, I know change is scary, but I think we can be better and stop returning home with a scuffed-up sleigh."

Rudolph suddenly looked upset. "This isn't a reflection on you, lad." I patted his head. "You will remain at the front, guiding the way like usual." Rudolph nodded and looked satisfied.

"Now, behind Rudolph, I want Vixen and Dasher." I directed the two reindeer to go stand in position. "I can see you fiercely fighting your way through the sky with determination and urgency. Behind them, I want Prancer and Cupid to make up the joy and heart of the formation. You will both spur us on with your lightness and love for our mission. Next, I want Donner and Blitzen for that powerful electric burst to keep pushing us forward." They wandered over to find their places. "And finally, I want Dancer and Comet to leave a glowing trail of grace and beauty in our wake. Between you, you will light up the sky and mesmerise the children below who are looking out for us."

I took a step back to admire the new line-up. They were my army, and they looked like they fitted together perfectly. "You all look great. Let's give this a whirl, shall we?"

I waved the sleigh bell and swept it to the left, and with that Rudolph started running and lifted from the ground, followed by the others. He knew what sequence I wanted him to take and as he sped through the sky, my hopes rose, my smile widened, when suddenly... disaster!

Dancer kept racing too fast and pulling too close to Blitzen. Moments later, she head-butted him with her antlers, which caused Blitzen to have a burst of energy and veer to the side. Vixen was lower down in the air than everyone else. Comet began trailing behind everyone. Prancer kept looking left, then right, then glanced behind him, which caused Cupid to get distracted and he ended up kicking Donner in the face. Then, somewhere along the way, Rudolph ended up in the middle of the formation, which caused everyone to no longer know what they were doing. They then began twisting in different directions, course correcting and colliding with each other. I had never seen such a mess.

"Oh... Fudgesicles!" I glanced back towards the house, hoping Mrs C wasn't witnessing any of this, but there she was, staring horrified at me from the kitchen window. "It's fine. It's all fine..." I grinned forcefully to look casual before I turned away and frantically shook the sleigh bell to get the reindeer to land.

"Well, that was terrible!" I felt like throwing the towel in, accepting defeat and returning to the original formation, but I also felt like it was still right and that I should persist. I was facing nine angry reindeer, but I would not let it deter me, and I was certainly determined not to let Mrs C tell me she told me so. We just had to go back to basics. "It looks like we need to keep practising. Come on, let's keep going. Rudolph, Vixen and Dasher, do some laps together, so you can become familiar with each other, then Prancer and Cupid can join in when I signal."

That day I stayed out for hours until the reindeer could work in their new formation without colliding into each other. It was a knuckle biting journey, as there were several moments where I thought the reindeer might take each other out and get injured, but we got through it.

"So, is that your idea of improvement?" Mrs C asked, as she handed me a cup of cocoa to warm me up when I came inside.

I stared back at her. "Miracles don't happen overnight."

"Oh, is that what you are waiting for? A miracle?"

I rolled my eyes as I sipped my drink. "Just you wait."

"Okay. How long should I wait? Do you think this miracle will happen in time for this Christmas Eve or the following Christmas Eve?" She sat down opposite me, her expression a mix of amusement and concern.

"This Christmas Eve!" I looked at her and she raised a questioning eyebrow. "Trust me. I know what I'm doing."

Over the next few days, I rose early, and was so keen to prove Mrs C wrong that I even grabbed a banana for breakfast to take with me so I could get to work sooner. I worked with the reindeer from breakfast to dinner, coordinating them and testing them. We practised twisting and turning and getting them to move as one.

Prancer ran laps around the paddock during our breaks, whilst Dancer stretched out her front trunk and legs, and then her hind legs, where she rocked back and forth to ease into the stretch further. Dasher copied. He was stiff and inflexible at first, but over time, his flexibility improved, and his stretches deepened and lengthened. Vixen's shoulder muscles expanded and toned up, and Comet finally kept his head raised so he could become more in tune to his surroundings. Meanwhile, Rudolph's belly shrank back to normal, as I knew it would, and his breathing became less ragged. He was becoming primed for a great Christmas Eve.

One day, after I'd been letting the reindeer have a break and roam the paddock, Mrs C traipsed across the snow to change Mr Frosty's scarf, hat, and mittens to a freshly knitted set. These were blue, purple and orange striped, and they looked quite fetching on him. She patted him on the head, then continued en route to meet me beside the paddock. "How are the reindeer doing?" she asked, tugging her coat tighter around her and studying my blank expression. "You know, I won't think any less of you if you need to revert to your usual formation, because at least you can say you tried."

"Well, why don't you see for yourself?" I turned away from her to rattle my sleigh-bells.

The reindeer instantly stopped what they were doing and trotted over to me. Rudolph's eyes flitted to Mrs C and back to me, where I gave him a firm look which he understood. Today, we needed a good show. "Right, everyone, why don't you all show Mrs C what we have been working on?"

Rudolph nodded, and trotted across to his usual spot, whilst the other reindeer lined up behind him in evenly spread positions. I swept my sleigh bells to the side and Rudolph galloped across the paddock with each reindeer matching his stride and pace perfectly. When Rudolph lifted into the sky, there was a seamless movement like a ribbon smoothly flowing after him as the other reindeer soared into the sky as well.

Rudolph led the way, sweeping the air in circular motions, then weaving up and down, left and right, and all the while, the reindeer kept pace. Their movements were so fluid it was like a wave in an ocean, connected as one mind and one body. It was beautiful to watch as they took ownership of the sky and it was as if Comet was leaving a trail of dust and stars behind them as they soared through the air like a shooting star.

They worked wonderfully together before, but my new formation had created something extra special. There was heart and beauty in the way they moved. There was power and electricity, and there was a ferocity that left me watching in silent awe. They eventually came to land, with the elegance and lightness that I was used to seeing from my reindeer, but now there was joy, determination and an additional confidence in the way they landed and stood facing me.

A lump formed in my throat, through pride and emotion, as I turned to Mrs C, whose mouth was hanging open as she stared at them.

She then slowly turned to me and nodded. "I take it back. Whatever you've done has worked, and you've created something exceptional and magical. There's no going back now."

51

A few days later, Mrs C shoved a cup of cocoa into my hand as I watched the television after lunch. "Busy training the reindeer, I see."

I shrugged. "Rudolph has it in hand without me. He's a good lad, isn't he?" I was confident that even without me and my sleigh-bells, they were competent enough to keep practising their routines by following Rudolph's guide.

"Well, I'm glad you have everything under control because our trip to Chicago is coming up in a couple of days."

"Gosh, is it that time already?"

"Yes, it is. It's nice to see you're counting down the days for it."

"Well, you know how it is. It's always nice to catch up with the regulars again, but it's a challenge to find good ones."

"It will be fine. We always find some fresh talent amongst the crowd."

I gave her a dead stare. "We also find absolute dross."

"Well, that keeps it entertaining. Plus, it makes you appreciate who we do find. Anyway, on the plus side, guess who will be in Chicago when we are?" she smiled.

"Is it some kind of celebrity?" I asked, my eyes lighting up. "Oo, is it that man who plays that elf?"

Mrs C rolled her eyes. "No! It's David. He and Seamus are going to the Tech Forward AI and Apps Trade Show, where they are exhibiting Vintique Scanner. And guess what, they'll be right next door to us. Can you believe it?"

My mind flashed to Pepper and her meddling, and I could believe it.

"Wow. Right next door? That's a coincidence! It will be nice to see how he's getting on."

Mrs C nodded. "I'm looking forward to it. It sounds like he's really excited about the trade show, and it will be lovely to see him face to face, rather than constantly communicating over email and video calls."

A few days later, after giving instructions to Alabaster about the reindeer and their exercise schedule, Mrs C and I prepared for our trip. Our case was packed, of course, by me, and I pulled on my red coat and trousers, black belt, black boots, and I shoved my hat into my pocket. Whilst Mrs C wore her matching red dress, with a large black belt, golden buckle, and white faux fur adorned the hem, wrists and collar.

Together, we looked impressive, but our outfits weren't just about how great we appeared. We had a representation to uphold.

Mrs C and I then headed to the plane and shot off to Chicago. We flew amongst the skyscraper buildings, and I could see the reflection of our plane in the glistening turquoise blue Chicago River, as we soared over it. After a few twists and turns, we came to land in the middle of a large parking lot where I then drove into a basement carpark, which was reserved for me.

Once we emerged onto the street, I breathed in the air. "Good old Chicago. The land of conferences and forcing people to mingle and network." I stared up at the impressive convention and hotel centre, which was so gigantic it surrounded us.

Mrs C put on her reading glasses and studied a fold-up map of the hotel and convention centre. "Oh, this year we're in a building around the corner. Follow me." She folded the map back up and we set off.

We made our way round the concourse and spotted a makeshift sleigh out of cardboard, which had one fake reindeer with a dull red nose strapped to it.

"This must be it." I pulled a face at the shoddy representation of Rudolph.

I opened the door of the building, and inside, a woman with a clipboard and a headset greeted us. "Welcome. All applicants can go straight through to the North Suite. First, may I just take your name, and see some ID," her pen hovering above her clipboard.

Mrs C smiled at her. "You must be new to this. Let me introduce ourselves. I'm Mrs Claus, and this is Santa."

The lady's smile remained on her face, but tightened. "Yes, of course. We don't get many double acts and it's great that you're both already committing to character, but as I said, I need your real names and ID first."

Then, as she spoke, a man in a black suit, who had been frantically conversing with a young spotty lad, who was holding two coffee flasks, rushed towards us. "Steph, these aren't applicants." He then turned to us, adjusted his tie, and held out his hand. "Santa, Mrs Claus, it's good to see you both again," he greeted, shaking both of our hands.

"Good to see you again, Alex," Mrs C replied. "Thank you for all your efforts in organising this again."

Alex lowered himself into a bow. "It's been a pleasure, as always."

Steph hugged her clipboard to her chest. "Please forgive me. I'm new here, and you all look similar."

I waved her apology away. "It's an easy mistake to make."

Alex placed his hand on my back to guide me away, along the corridor which had a feeble hint of tinsel along it. "We already have our first group of applicants waiting. Are you happy to make a start, or did you want to freshen up in your hotel room first?"

"I'm happy to make a start. It's not exactly a long, treacherous journey for us from the North Pole."

"Of course," Alex said. "Well, the sooner we start, the sooner we'll be on our road to victory." He led us to the North Suite and placed a hand on the door. "Ready?" he asked.

I exchanged a look with Mrs C and we both nodded, before he pushed the door open to reveal a sea of red. There were men of different shapes and sizes, all wearing varying qualities of red coats and trousers. Some looked like they were thick and well made, others appeared to be made from cheap thin felt. Some men were wearing hats and fake beards made from cotton wool, whilst a few had natural white hair and real bristles, and others had red and white fluffy fabric sticking out of their pockets, ready to complete their looks later.

The men were all mingling around the large room, waiting for the day's events to begin. Some were forcing conversation with each other, with a few louder voices in the mix, which carried above everyone. One large man was shouting to anyone who would listen, a story about him hitchhiking across America, with a stuffy, self-righteous companion. Another loud voice was claiming he had been incredibly rich but lost all his money doing a dodgy investment in frozen concentrated orange juice. Others were crowded around the plates of pastries and coffee, which had been laid out on the tables at the side of the room.

Alex glanced at me and gave me a meek smile of embarrassment. "This is it, the first lot of this year's applicants all in one room."

"Great. I'm sure that once we get through the process, we will find some fantastic talent," Mrs C said, overly brightly. "Have they all completed their forms?"

Alex nodded. "They have all signed the special Christmas non-disclosure agreements that you sent to me, and they have filled out the form regarding their work experience and skill set."

"Perfect," Mrs C replied. "We're ready to begin."

"Follow me." Alex led the way through the crowd and onto the stage at the far end of the room. In the centre of the stage was a red velvet armchair, with a tall back, and gold trim around the sides. On the wall behind the stage were fairy lights hanging across it, and more measly bits of tinsel.

Alex stood at the microphone. "Can I have everyone's attention, please?" The men stopped talking and turned their attention to him. "I want to welcome you all to the Santa Claus Acquisition Meeting, or SCAM for short. It's great to see so many returning faces, but I wanted to thank all of you for travelling here from all over the world to be a part of this amazing event. Today will be a long day, jam-packed with interviews and activities where we find those lucky enough to make children's dreams and wishes come true. Those chosen will then have the honour of representing Santa across the country, and the world, in shopping malls, pop up grottos and winter wonderlands." Alex cleared his throat. "That said, I would like to introduce you to the man himself. The man who you will all be working for, the one, the only, Mr… Santa… Claus," he started clapping enthusiastically by himself, as he stepped to one side.

There was a pause before half the Santas joined in with the clapping, whilst the other half stared at me rather gormlessly, as I exchanged places with Alex and took hold of the microphone.

"Thank you all for coming. I'm sure you are all familiar with me, but I have been doing what I do for centuries now, and as you know, I have a reputation to uphold. My purpose is to bring children joy and happiness through the channel of gift giving and spreading magical cheer over the Christmas season. It is a great honour knowing that I have put a smile on children's faces and made their wishes come true." A few men were nodding along with me. "You are here today to become an extension of that. Those chosen will work directly for me and become the face of me. This is why I want each of you to approach this job with the respect and pride it deserves. When children visit you to share and explain their wishes, I want them to walk away feeling a lightness in their step, a smile on their faces, a happiness in their core and faith that Santa listened and will deliver on Christmas Eve to make their wishes come true.

"That is why the first step in this process is about authenticity. I need my Santas to have a convincing appearance. Now I know a lot of you don't bear any physical similarities to me, but to be Santa, it's more important to possess a certain aura, which is why I want you to take a few moments to get fully dressed up and get into the right zone. Hone your inner Santa. Then I want you to line up and do your best to emulate me."

I stepped away from the microphone as the group of fake Santas sprang into action to get themselves ready. They attached their beards and wigs, pulled their hats over their heads, tightened their belts, and gave their boots a quick scrub on the back of their trouser legs.

Alex and Steph then helped get everyone to line up in rows, with the new Santas at the front and the returning Santas at the back. They stood inflating their bellies as far as they would go in order to look like me.

Mrs C and I then walked along each row, inspecting the candidates. It was an interesting mix. There were some who looked quite decent, who stood tall and proud and gave us a beaming smile and a jolly tap on their bellies as we walked past. But others looked like they were in terrible fancy dress. Their fake beards were already peeling away, or dangling on one side from their chin. Some white beards were failing to cover the ginger and dark ones beneath it, and there were hats that barely covered a range of different hairstyles. There were jackets which were too tight, men who were too tall and gangly, whose trousers barely scraped their shoes, and there were plenty of felt outfits which hung like bin liners around them.

I didn't mind the bad outfits, but it was the ones with the auras and attitudes that matched their terrible appearances that troubled me. Some of them appeared like they couldn't be bothered to be there. They avoided eye contact with me, or slouched as Mrs C and I assessed them.

I didn't have to say anything to Mrs C. We'd been doing this long enough for her to know exactly what we were looking for, so I left it for her to mark each man off on a clipboard with our scoring system, which determined whether they could move ahead in the process and where they would be placed.

As we continued to amble down the rows, Mrs C suddenly jolted to a stop. "Oh, my…" she exclaimed, when she spotted one of the Santas in the line. She turned back to me with wide, horrified eyes.

"What is it?" I muttered, hurrying to her side.

She then nodded towards one man. "I feel like I've stepped into a horror film," she whispered.

I followed her gaze and recoiled. Within the line-up was a man with a longer beard than others and his suit was of good quality, but he had painted his face white, and his nose red. He had also used lipstick to draw a large, red, smiling mouth around his lips. He looked more like a sinister clown than me.

"Is this the Santa look you are going for?" I asked.

The man cackled and looked at me through hooded eyes, before his smile contorted to spread as wide as possible across his face. "Of course! I'm Santa!" he said, cocking his head to the side.

"You see, this look doesn't really say, happy, jolly Santa. More… I'm going to creep around your house and steal all your toys."

The man bellowed out another cackle. I wasn't sure if he found me funny, or if he was being creepy on purpose. "I'm Santa," he said, cocking his head in the opposite direction. "I'm here to make children's dreams come true."

I frowned at the strange man and then gave a signal to Alex. "It was nice meeting you, but I'm afraid you won't be able to go forward in this process."

The man's mouth dropped open wide in such a caricature way, I thought his tongue might unravel out of his mouth. "But I'm Santa, here to delight and mesmerise the children."

Alex then placed a hand on his shoulder. "It's time to leave now," he said.

The man bowed to us and when he straightened back up; he waved his fingers back and forth. "I'm sure we'll meet again," he said. Then, guided by Alex, he walked backwards, not taking his eyes off me the whole time, until the door closed behind him.

Steph looked almost sick with horror. "I'm so sorry. That man did not look like that when I let him in."

"It's fine. There's always someone interesting that turns up. It keeps us on our toes," I said.

We continued along the rows, until I eventually halted, when my eyes fell on a good quality fabric. The suit hung well on the man and the extra padding he had used to buff himself up looked natural and not an obvious pillow stuffed down his top. "Great suit," I said, as a spark of excitement came over me.

I then looked up at the face of the owner and noticed that his features behind his fake beard and moustache were strikingly youthful. "What's your name?" I asked.

"Arthur," he squeaked.

"Arthur, may I ask how old you are?"

The young lad cleared his throat and shot a panicked look at us. "Fifty-five," he said, in as deep a voice as he could muster.

"Great. Would you mind just quickly lifting your beard away?"

He took a deep breath and slowly pulled his beard down from his face. As he did, it was clear he looked about seventeen.

"Wow, Arthur, you look great for fifty-five. What on earth is your secret for looking so young?" Mrs C asked.

Arthur glanced around. "Hydration and a good face cream," he replied, in his fake deep voice again.

"I think I need some of that face cream," Mrs C said, glancing at Alex and Steph and winking at them.

"Me too," they agreed together, while Steph looked extremely embarrassed that someone so young had got through her checks.

"Well, I'm afraid we can't go any further, but you should definitely take it as a compliment that you look far too young to pass as me," I said.

"Come on mate," Alex said. "Nice try."

"Very well," Arthur sighed. "I just wanted to see what all this was about. Err, before I go, can I get your autograph?"

"How about I mail it to you?" I suggested.

"But you don't know where I live."

I raised an eyebrow. "Don't I?"

Arthur slowly realised who he was speaking to. "Oh yeah… Yeah, cool. I can't wait to show my mates."

I smiled, wondering if I should break the news to him that the non-disclosure agreement he signed meant that he couldn't discuss anything about SCAM and meeting me. Or whether I should leave him to find out for himself when his head becomes fuzzy, and he is forced into changing the subject. I opted for the latter and waved him off as Alex escorted him out before we continued.

We eliminated some more obvious horror stories, a man who kept screaming, to an ear-splitting degree, Ho, Ho, Ho when we went past, a man who kept winking at Steph and a man who looked like he was still drunk from the night before. Luckily, we also spotted a few excellent new candidates which caught my attention and left me excited to get to know them more.

We then made our way along the regular returning Santas. I nodded at them, and muttered 'Welcome back' on a continuous loop as we made sure they were still up to standard. Some had altered their appearance. One Santa now had an anchor earring hanging from his ear, and another now had a tattoo of a star under his eye, which we noted down. Some had lost weight, which meant their suit would need to be altered with padding, and others had clearly gained several kilograms, which gave them a more natural Santa look.

I stopped at one man and smiled. "Tim, isn't it? Great to see you again. That's a marvellous beard you have now."

"Thank you," he replied proudly. "I've been growing it all year. Those fake ones get itchy after a while."

Once Mrs C and I had done our rounds and updated our notes, I looked around at all the Santas, feeling a mix of hope and despair. "Is it usually like this?" I whispered to Mrs C, unsure if we had more bad than good this year.

Mrs C checked her clipboard. "Yes, the statistics look pretty normal. Plus, we always have tomorrow for the next group, which might fare better."

"Perhaps. I guess we now need to move onto stage two to see what's behind the appearance."

52

I straightened up my red coat and stepped back onto the stage. I clapped my hands together, which caused the men to twist their attention back to me. "Well, what an excellent turnout we have this year. You have all made a great effort with your costumes and I really think this will be another magical year for the children because of you. Now, our next step is to understand some more about you, your reasons for being here, and what skills you can offer. We will now hold our individual interviews, so feel free to enjoy the pastries while you wait. The cinnamon swirl looks rather delicious."

The men then all moved like a herd to the tables, where the conversation started again. Now they had a common ground; to discuss the people we had evicted from the room, and I instantly noticed a louder volume in the room as they did impressions and speculatively gossiped about their characters.

Alex then stepped over to me. "We've laid out a meeting room behind the curtain in the corner. Here is your call up list, along with all of their forms."

We made our way across the room to a red velvet curtain which cordoned off the corner. Behind it there was a table, with two chairs on one side and one on the other.

"Right, so first we have Billy," Mrs C said, consulting her clipboard.

A man then entered as he readjusted his beard so the elastic stretched and sprung back to fit around his slim face. He came to sit in front of us and slouched a bit more than to my liking.

"Hello Billy, tell me, why are you here? What made you come to this

Santa Claus Acquisition Meeting?" I asked.

He stared at me for a moment, confused by the question. "Err, I saw it advertised when I was scrolling online, and I thought, why not give it a bash? People told me it might be a cult or some kind of con, but I ain't listening to them."

"Yes, but why do you want to be Santa?" I asked.

Billy shrugged. "It's a job, innit."

"Well, yes, but is that the only reason?"

Billy hesitated. "Yeah, well, like you said earlier, it's about giving innit."

"Anything else?" I asked, almost surprised he had been listening to my speech.

Billy looked at me like he was searching me for the correct answer. "To make the children happy?" he said, as if it were a question.

"Ah, yes. Great," I said, exchanging a look with Mrs C. He had done just about enough to pass, but we would put him in a role where most interaction would be for him to turn up, wave, and leave.

"Is that everything?" he asked, already shuffling in his chair to stand up.

"Yes, thank you."

Billy jumped to his feet and exited through the curtain without a backward glance.

The next person who entered, to my relief, gave a much more encouraging answer to my question and from there on we got into the flow of interviewing. Mrs C and I worked in perfect synchronicity, alternating who asked each question to keep us entertained. Sometimes she would challenge them further on their answers, sometimes I would. Most interviewees were engaging enough, but others were stiff and some were clearly nervous. On those occasions, Mrs C would often throw in a curveball question about what their favourite present was that they ever received from me, so they would relax and connect more with the job they were interviewing for. It seemed to work as their eyes would light up and they would become a lot more thoughtful and outspoken with their answers. It also made me remember each time I visited them, and what gift I left them many years ago.

After a while, we took a short break, and Mrs C poured us a coffee.

"This is going well. I think we can place the majority somewhere," I muttered as I stood up to stretch my legs.

We were just finishing up our coffee when the next Santa entered, right on time. The man had caught my eye earlier. He had natural white hair and beard, and his stature was similar to mine. He wore a perfectly tailored suit, and he held himself with a confidence that was both friendly, and commanded leadership. Mrs C slowly lowered her coffee mug when she saw him and broke into a large smile.

"Sorry, I hope I'm not interrupting," he said, smiling, which made his eyes light up.

"No, no. We were just stretching our legs," Mrs C said. She glanced down at her clipboard and then smiled at the man. "And you must be Richard. Please sit down."

I glanced at her, noticing how her eyes were lingering on him as she sat back down at the table. "Now, tell…" I said, stopping as Mrs C had said the same thing at the same time. I frowned, as it was my turn to start the questioning.

She giggled. "Sorry. Why don't you tell us what excites you about being Santa and why you would like to do this?" She placed her elbow on the table and propped her head in her hand to listen to him.

Richard smiled at her. He looked warm and friendly, and I knew instantly the children would feel comfortable around him. "Well, what can I say? Being able to represent a man that I have idolised my whole life, for his compassion, generosity, and good heart, would be an honour. If I could even contribute a fragment of what Santa does and gives to the world, it would be a privilege."

I glanced across at Mrs C, expecting us to exchange our usual impressed expressions, but she couldn't take her eyes off him. She was completely enraptured, with a permanent enamoured smile on her lips.

"Also, I have dreamed of seeing those adorable smiles from the children as they ask for their wishes to be granted. If I can contribute to bringing out those smiles and creating that joy, then that is something that will make me a better man."

Mrs C sighed dreamily. "That's such a wonderful answer."

Richard smiled back at her. "Well, it's certainly how I feel, and I must say, what you both do every year is wonderful and whether I have the authority to, I wanted to thank you on behalf of everyone I know."

"Oh…" Mrs C said, wafting away the compliment, with a delighted look on her face. "It's what we live for."

Richard gave a slight shrug. "Either way, it would be amazing to be a part of something so incredibly special."

Mrs C stroked the length of her neck. "That really is great." I noticed her eyes were dancing as she kept her attention on him.

I cleared my throat, reminding her of my presence, but it didn't seem to work. "So, do you have any other language skills?" I asked.

Richard sat upright. "I do, actually. I speak French, German, Spanish, and of course…" He leant forward and cupped his hand around his mouth as if he was sharing a secret. "Sign language."

"Wow," Mrs C exclaimed. "That's very impressive."

I cleared my throat even louder this time. "Well, I guess that will be everything!" I watched the looks Mrs C and Richard were giving each other, but I couldn't deny he was perfect for the top position.

I then took it upon myself to test him, so I signed using my hands. "Congratulations. You are hired."

Richard grinned. "Excellent. Thank you so much. I'm looking forward to starting," he replied, using his hands. He then stood up. "Passe une bonne journée," he said, throwing his French skill on top.

"You have a good day, too," Mrs C grinned, as he exited through the curtain. She then blew out a trail of air. "He was amazing," she gushed, briefly wafting her rosy face with her clipboard.

"Yes, he was, but don't think I didn't notice the way you were looking at him and fawning over him."

"Me?" she asked, in exaggerated shock.

"Yes, you! You were flirting with him."

"Well, what can I say? He reminded me of you," she said, placing her hand on my knee. "You can hardly blame me for that."

I shook my head. "As long as you don't get confused as to who your real husband is."

"It's been centuries, and I haven't yet," she said.

"There better be many more centuries to come," I warned.

Mrs C laughed. "Without doubt. Now who's next?" she muttered, as the flush on her face faded.

Mrs C and I then continued to interview the rest of the candidates, instantly falling back into our rhythm. During that time, we only had to turn away another handful of men whom we found unsuitable, due to them saying something inappropriate, which on the whole was an excellent result.

Once we interviewed the last candidate, I had gained a good idea about who I wanted to work for me and where in their geographical area I wanted to place them, but it wasn't over yet.

"All sorted?" Alex asked, poking his head through the curtain.

"Yes, it's been an interesting morning," I said, stifling a yawn.

"Well, I'm impressed you got through everyone," Alex said. "We'll have a break for lunch and then crack on with the training, shall we?"

53

After lunch, I took to the stage again. "Thank you, everyone, for your time this morning. Now, we move onto the second part of the day where we go through some scenario training and role play. Can I ask for a volunteer from one of our regulars to play Santa?" Some hands raised in the air. "Tim, please come up on stage," I requested, still impressed with his new beard.

Tim climbed up onto the stage and sat down in the huge armchair. I then arranged for a selection of the new Santas to sit on his knee and pretend to be a child, asking for presents. Tim's eyes widened in fear when a particularly large man, called Kurt, headed his way. He clambered onto his lap and clung onto him so that he didn't fall off. It was an amusing sight and some of the Santas sniggered as he kicked his legs up and down to balance himself and practically lay horizontally across Tim.

"What would you like for Christmas?" Tim asked as his face turned red and he looked like he couldn't breathe.

"Now it's important to greet the child with a wide-open gesture, making them feel welcome, just like Tim did. Next, the tone of your voice needs to be jovial, intrigued, and as though that child is the most important person in the room at that moment."

The Santas nodded, listening and enraptured, before we alternated around the Santas so that they could practise a script of how to greet the children. We offered feedback and encouragement. Some needed to smile more, others needed to speak more clearly, and others had to sit up straighter so that the child could actually fit onto their lap. The Santas analysed and commented on each other, and I was thrilled they were embracing the learning.

Next, we moved onto some different scenarios, where I challenged the Santas about how they would handle a ludicrous request, a child having a tantrum or was absolutely terrified, an overbearing parent, or someone on the naughty list.

The returning Santas were able to help provide insights into situations they had faced, and how they handled it. They all impressed me, particularly Richard, who was extremely soft and gentle, with such a warm smile that even Eric, with the tattoo under his eye, sat on his knee and giggled like a toddler as he made his request.

It gave me time to reflect and realise that I had misjudged some of the Santas. Some of them really came into their own when they got into character, whereas others were more wooden than I had hoped, but overall, by the end, I was optimistic.

As the afternoon drew to a close, the Santas finished off by practising some trusty Christmas jokes, which they could use to break a difficult atmosphere. I could attest to how important it was to keep a few funny ones in your back pocket. I did, however, have to step in when Kurt decided his favourite joke was not appropriate for children, but by the time Alex approached me and Mrs C to wrap everything up, everyone was in a good mood.

"Is everything going well?" he asked.

I nodded. "Yes. Very well. Now we just need to make everything official."

Alex nodded, and he and Steph moved a table into the centre of the stage. I placed my case onto the table, opened it, and pulled out a stack of scrolls and the Santa manuals. Alex then coordinated the Santas to come up onto the stage one by one.

I unrolled a scroll in front of the first Santa. "Please sign your name," I said, handing the man my quill. The man smiled and signed his name on the contract. The name glowed red, then green, which sealed the deal. "Congratulations on being a successful Santa. Here is your manual which contains information on everything we have gone through today. It has a script, questions and answers, all the scenarios we covered and a list of jokes. There is also a recording of my laugh, for you to practise, and there is also a letter of sentiment, which summarises the importance of being Santa and the impact you now have. Please read it before you are called up." I refrained from telling him that once he read the letter, he would be bound to act in the best interests of the child.

"Thank you. I shall look forward to working with you," the Santa said.

I smiled back. "We will be in touch shortly to advise you of your post, and then every time a child tells you what they want for Christmas, we will get an alert and a notification at the North Pole."

"Fantastic," the man said, before he headed back to his life for another month.

The line of Santas went down as I witnessed signature after signature glow red, then green.

At the end, I leant back in my chair. "Well, that was an interesting day. Funny how meeting one right person can make an average day turn into a successful day," I said, thinking about Richard. I looked at the pile of scrolls and took a moment to recognise just how much we had done that day. It was almost as exhausting as Christmas Eve night and we had to do it all over again the next day, with a fresh batch of candidates.

"Yes, it has been a good day," Mrs C said. "The children will love them. Perhaps some more than others, but the children, all over the world, will still get to enjoy meeting Santa this year."

I frowned. "Though I wish we didn't have to employ fake Santas to send out across the world. I just wish I could be all of them, so I can meet the children myself. Plus, I sometimes feel quite guilty about it all. It's like we're conning the children into thinking they are meeting me, when they are just average men."

Mrs C smiled. "I know, love, but whilst you can do many miraculous things, travelling around the world in one night, fiddling with the space-time continuum, and packing a suitcase or a sack, I'm afraid being omnipresent isn't one of them. But with each Santa you employ, you send them out there with your love and good will, and the children feel that."

Alex came over. "It's a wrap for today. I've just escorted the last Santa out the door." He flopped into the chair next to us and handed us both a can of coke each.

"You did a great job today," Mrs C said. "Let's hope tomorrow goes as smoothly,"

"You know, I always get so excited when we have our Santa Claus Acquisition Meeting, because it means that Christmas is round the corner and the holidays are coming," Alex said.

I glanced down at the can I was holding and gave myself an indulgent smile before the three of us cracked open our cans, to the nostalgic and soothing hiss of fizz.

"Here's to the fast-approaching Christmas period," Alex said, raising his can of coke.

Mrs C and I tapped our cans against his before I took a long gulp of that sweet nectar.

When I looked up, whilst smacking my lips together and exhaling a satisfying blast of air, I found Alex chuckling at me. "That was a very picture-perfect moment."

I laughed and held back a belch.

54

Once Mrs C and I left the North Suite, we made a quick stop to go up in the lift to our hotel room, where we quickly changed out of our official Santa uniforms and dropped off my case. We then made our way across the courtyard of the conference centre to another building, where a swarm of people was exiting.

"This is good timing. It looks like the Tech exhibition has just finished," Mrs C said.

We squeezed amongst the crowd of people, and fought against the direction everyone was moving when suddenly someone bumped into me. I turned to see who it was, only to find it was none other than Carol, the angry woman from London, storming away and looking stressed.

I tugged on Mrs C's arm. "You won't believe this! Look who it is," I hissed, pointing at her.

Mrs C turned to stare in shock. "Not again! I really don't understand why we keep bumping into her. There's definitely something strange going on."

I frowned in agreement. "Very strange indeed," I mumbled thoughtfully, as Carol disappeared from view.

We eventually emerged into a vast hall, where stands with marketing banners and displays, advertising products, were evenly spaced out. It was clearly the aftermath of a long day, and there were leaflets and litter all over the floor. We began weaving around the pathway until we came to a six-foot rolling banner stand with the words 'Vintique Scanner' written on them in a jazzy font.

David was tidying up a pile of leaflets and Seamus Conway was a few steps away, talking on his mobile. I could see instantly that David's demeanour was different. He looked more relaxed and there was a glow on his face that hadn't been there before.

"David," Mrs C called as we approached him.

He looked up. "You made it," he grinned.

Her eyes trailed over the roller banner and smiled. "This looks even better in real life than on the designs you sent over."

David smiled. "Yeah, they do. Thank you for your design suggestions, and for making the final decision. I've had lots of positive comments."

"I'm happy to help. So, how was the exhibition today?"

"Excellent. Very busy. I've been talking to people non-stop and handed out piles of leaflets and swapped loads of business cards. I've barely had a second to stop and think."

"That sounds very positive," Mrs C said.

"I think so. There's a lot of interest, and people are impressed with the amount of detail that Vintique Scanner produces. One man I met knows an auction house that wants to market it, which I'll follow up when I'm back in Scotland."

Seamus snapped his flip phone shut and slid it into his inner pocket. He marched over. "Davey boy, I've just got off the phone to a big advertising company, Zultan House. I've managed to negotiate a discounted cost to create an advert for Vintique Scanner to be broadcast on television and I have prime air time."

David froze. "Like on the real television? Vintique Scanner?"

Seamus nodded. "Yeah, and on a real channel, not like one of those random shopping channels."

"That's incredible," David exclaimed, looking almost shell-shocked.

"Yeah, well, what can I say? When you know how to pitch, people will jump to be a part of it." Seamus pulled the cuffs down on his blue chequered jacket. "In fact, it was the head of the company, Mr Richford, who authorised the deal. It seems like he has a good eye for an excellent product."

My eyes strayed to Mrs C, who kept a fantastic poker face. "Mr

Richford?" I mouthed at her.

Her lips curled into a small smile, then she shrugged.

David shook his head. "I still can't believe it. Only a few months ago, no one knew anything about Vintique Scanner and now it will be on television."

"Yeah, and following on from that, we can also set up a regular advert on the radio. I have some contacts there. Also, I was thinking we could find a sports team to sponsor. I've always liked a bit of ice hockey, and we could get the Vintique Scanner logo and website address on their shirts. Although, it might be better to get a sports event with television coverage." He tapped his chin, thinking, when his eyes fell on me and Mrs C. "You both look familiar. Do I know you?"

Mrs C nodded. "We have met before, yes."

Seamus then clicked his fingers. "The Voydon restaurant, that's it, and then that ridiculous pantomime I was dragged to. Hang on, have you just come from that SCAM convention from the North Suite?"

I stared back at him, unsure how to respond.

"Don't tell me you've actually gone ahead with doing some part time work as a Santa. You should have called me. I would have wrangled a better hourly rate for you," he boasted. "I've got contacts."

"I'm not actually going to be a part time Santa, but you certainly seem to know a lot of people. I'm curious. Who is it you know, in charge of all the Santas?" I enquired.

David coughed, as if he was choking. "Actually Seamus, this is Mrs C, who I told you about. She's my business advisor."

"Ah yes. I remember you saying. A woman with a head on her shoulders. Davey boy told me that if it wasn't for you, he wouldn't have smashed his product and business pitch the way he did."

"Well, the product sells itself. David just needed a bit of guidance," Mrs C replied.

"Well, whatever influence you had, I'm pleased he presented his stats, marketing vision and target audience to me, as I was hooked. You know, I'm just waiting for the day someone uncovers a load of stolen artwork in someone's attic, from one of those infamous art heists, which could be worth millions. I'm telling ya, it will be Vintique Scanner that tracks them down," he said, slapping his hands together and rubbing them.

I clamped my mouth shut. I couldn't possibly tell him I knew exactly where there was stolen artwork hanging in people's living rooms around the world. I couldn't tell anyone, as it was part of the Christmas Law, but it made me wonder if it was possible they would now get caught, with a nosy friend or neighbour scanning the item with their app.

"Anyway, let me think," Seamus continued. "Ah yes. The guidance counsellor and the logistics and supply chain specialist. That's the great thing about technology, we don't need to hire someone in your position. We don't have a product that needs to be heaved around the world or have stock that needs to be stored. So, how's the job going?"

I forced a smile as he reminded me of a tornado again. "Well, we're approaching a busy period."

"Ah yes, Christmas is round the corner and consumer decisions are all over the place. Either sales rocket or they go down. Nothing ever seems to stay the same at this time of year. Am I right or am I right?"

I was about to reply when his phone started ringing. He grabbed his phone, flipped it open, and stepped to one side, whilst holding a finger up at me, to silently tell me he'd be a minute. I took a deep breath, relieved to have a moment's break from him. "What's it like working with Seamus?" I asked David, who still looked like he was coming to terms with having a proper commercial made for his product.

"Oh, it's fantastic. I never thought I would meet someone who is as passionate about Vintique Scanner as I am. As soon as we met, we shared the same vision about what was possible from it. Not only that, but we just clicked straight away. He would finish my sentences, he would understand things before I had to explain them, and we ended up laughing so much it was like I'd been reunited with a long-lost best friend."

"Really?" I blurted in disbelief. The two of them were so different, David with his humble, conscientious personality, quiet, and down to earth; and Seamus with his loud, overly confident, self-assured persona.

David laughed. "I know he can be intense sometimes, but that's what I needed, someone to give me confidence, and help drive this," he said, unhooking the roller banner and rolling it up so it went into a case. "Like even with this trade show, I felt incredibly anxious before I got here. I'm not great talking to people, but Seamus makes it look so easy. He'll approach anyone and they'll listen to him whether they want to or not. He encourages me to be assertive and deep down, I'm enjoying it."

"That's great to hear," Mrs C said, beaming with pride. "And you look happier and healthier for it."

I nodded in agreement, pleased that I had been wrong and that Mrs C had seen past Seamus's bravado and introduced them, because as unlikely as it was, they were a perfect match.

David chuckled as he looked at Mrs C. "I think between the two of you and Seamus, I'm a completely different person. I now have an investment and business partner, so I'm no longer panicking. The business is moving in a positive direction and I have much more security, and money coming in, which means I can keep to my promise to Pip. To give her one hundred percent of my attention when I'm with her," he said, smiling, his eyes lighting up with affection.

"That's wonderful," Mrs C gushed. "How is Pip?"

David laughed. "She's great. She's with her grandmother whilst I'm here. I felt guilty for leaving her, but she sent me off with her blessing. In fact, she practically helped me pack and kicked me out the door." He turned to break up the frame for the roller banner. "She knows that I have to do this, and when I'm back, we'll spend some quality time together."

"It certainly sounds like things are better between the two of you," I said.

"They are. We've been baking together, going for walks, chatting about Holly, and I even went to see her in a school play the other day, hopefully making up for the Nativity incident."

Mrs C smiled and leant over to touch his arm. "You shouldn't feel guilty about missing a play. Being a single parent is hard, but I'm so pleased for you."

David smiled, his expression suddenly becoming emotional. "I want her to know that even though Vintique Scanner is important to me, she is the priority in my life."

"She knows that," Mrs C said.

David took a deep breath. "I hope she continues to know it and doesn't forget because I'm going to be away a lot with this business over the next few months."

Seamus snapped his phone shut and marched back over to us. "Are you talking about all the conferences and talks we have lined up? Very exciting stuff. I'm going to turn this man into a confident business mogul, like me. He just needs some gumption to step out of his technical mindset, and embrace the idea of selling not just his product but himself, don't you, Davey boy?"

David nodded. "That's what Mrs C said as well. Actually, if you don't mind, Mrs C, I'd love to send across some of my new presentations for you to look at."

"Absolutely. I'm happy to help, and I'm so pleased everything is going well for you."

Suddenly, someone behind us cleared their throat and made us look over to find a cleaner trying to get past us to pick up some used paper cups.

"Right, we best get going," Mrs C said. "We've got another long day tomorrow."

As we walked away, David rushed after us. "I almost forgot. I'm sure you're going to get a letter about it anyway, but Pip has seen the Fashion Factor advert, and she's thrilled she's a member of the group. She's been watching the advert on a loop on my phone. Needless to say, she'll be requesting a set for Christmas, so I thought I'd just mention it."

I chuckled. "I wouldn't have it any other way."

That night, Mrs C and I settled into our hotel room and the following day we continued whittling down the Santas that pretended to be me across the world. The event was just as successful as it ever had been, and after a couple of long days, Mrs C and I headed home.

55

Once we arrived home, I eagerly wanted to check on the reindeer. "Aren't you going to unpack first?" Mrs C asked, a challenge in her voice, as I instantly made for the door.

I looked at her in surprised horror. "I thought the rules were that I pack, you unpack," I said as my hand inched around the door handle.

Mrs C chuckled. "I know, I'm kidding. Go do what you need to do. I'll put the washing on, do the ironing, and then sit here thinking about Richard." She winked at me, finding it hilarious.

I knew full well she was joking, but I gave her the satisfaction of playing along as the jealous husband. "You better not be!"

I trotted along to locate the reindeer in the paddock where they were performing their usual routine of twisting and turning, practising their take-offs and landings, and perfecting their seamless synchronisation. Alabaster had clearly done an excellent job of letting them out in the morning and putting them back at night, as they looked well fed and rested. They'd had plenty of practice, as now I couldn't fault them if I tried. It was magical to watch. Perhaps we really had a chance to make this the most efficient and sublime Christmas Eve ever.

After a while of watching them with a satisfied smile on my face, I left them to it, despite wanting to greet Rudolph and give him a head scratch. Instead, I headed over to the workshop to check on the elves.

Bushy screeched when she saw me. "You're back!"

"How was SCAM this year?" Alabaster asked.

"The usual mixed bag," I huffed.

"Did you see David?" Pepper asked, looking intrigued.

I nodded. "Yes, I definitely think your little elf magic trick has worked. He seems incredibly happy and I hear Pip is as well."

Pepper beamed with delight and clasped her hands together. "That's wonderful," she said, looking giddy.

"How are things going around here? Are you all ready for the Sleigh Ride concert?"

Shinny let out an impulsive, fearful shriek, and rushed off to the store cupboard to collect a pile of gifts for Pepper to wrap, whilst Pepper and Bushy exchanged concerned looks.

"We're getting there," Alabaster said. "We've all been practising, and Shinny is the star of the show, so he's a bit nervous."

"I'm sure this year's routines will be as fantastic as ever, and I'm certainly looking forward to it," I remarked.

Suddenly there was a loud trumpet sound, which I momentarily considered had come from one of the elves' bottoms, and then the Christmas looking glass dome glowed bright green. "Oh my goodness," Sugarplum jumped, dropping her doll's head with half a head of red hair on it, and raced over to the dome. "It's happening."

"Already?" I glanced at the countdown clock on the ceiling. "It's a bit early still, isn't it?" I said as all the elves darted over to the dome whilst I lumbered across, intrigued.

"I can't believe it's starting," Bushy cried.

The elves peered wide eyed into the dome. Pepper covered her mouth as she read the handwriting highlighted in the dome.

"What does it say?" I asked, as the swirls and squiggles looked a little blurry from where I was standing. All I could see was an attempt at drawing some presents and a Christmas tree at the bottom of the page.

"It's a letter from a girl called Ella in Germany." Alabaster read it in a firm voice. "Dear Santa, I've tried so hard to be good this year, and for Christmas, please can I have a unicorn, a kangaroo popper and for mein Bruder to stop picking on me, because he's really mean. Love from Ella."

"Oh dear. Is her brother on the naughty list?" I asked.

Alabaster peered into the dome. "No, it's just usual sibling rivalry."

"She must really want our help though to write to us this early," Shinny said, wide eyed.

"He probably just did something recently to upset her," Wunorse said.

"As typical brothers do. Either way, it's so exciting." Sugarplum hugged herself and smiled airily. "Our first Christmas letter! And Santa was here to see it."

Wunorse tapped away on a little scroll-like device he was holding. "I'll start cataloguing everything into the list and make the preparations." His job was to organise and cross reference the list with the correct distribution of presents when the right time came.

"Thank you Wunorse. It looks like we're on course and there will be a trickle of requests coming in now before the Christmas rush. I hope we're all ready to go."

Bushy let out a squeal of excitement, and she shook her little body as if she couldn't contain it within her. "We are sir. We're ready to go."

I grinned as bubbles of excitement tickled my belly, and sure enough, over the following weeks, I could feel the Christmas spirit ramping up.

Christmas adverts had started popping up on television. Supermarkets were spotlighting their luxurious, glimmering festive foods. There were dancing carrots and sprouts, packets of turbo-charged party food, which had taken a standard food item and sprinkled it with additional ingredients, like alcohol or nuts, to make it extra special and enticing. There were sparkling adverts for Christmas puddings and mince pies, making my mouth water as I watched them, and festive chocolates in Christmas coloured wrappers. There were adverts with caricatures of me, others which had a completely irrelevant character that they could market as a Christmas gimmick, and plenty which were peppered with snow, Christmas decorations, and fairy lights…much to the elves' irritation.

Some were funny and light-hearted, and others were sentimental and emotional, containing messages of giving, love, kindness, and hope. I enjoyed every single one, and in and amongst them were the adverts Mr Richford and his team had created for all our toys.

I loved how the world changed and how many people conformed to taking part in the period I had created and crafted. If it wasn't for millions upon millions of people accepting what this time of year meant, and buying into it, it wouldn't have the same glistening festive magic that I had only originally dreamed of.

Meanwhile, Mrs C and I went through all the Santas and finalised the locations where we would place them. Mrs C then sent them their official start dates, confirmed their assigned addresses and organised formal introductions with the relevant store owners or event organisers. We also helped source more appropriate uniforms depending which tier they were in. Those in the upper tier had tailored suits to fit, and anyone in the lower tier had a cheaper upgrade.

The Santas were soon prepped and ready to take up their podiums and begin listening to a stream of children's Christmas wishes. Following the contract they signed in Chicago, any request a child made to them would be instantly highlighted in the dome and would be prioritised and granted. That is, as long as it fitted within the realms of the Christmas Law.

By mid-November, some of the Santas undertook their roles, with more being called up by the day, so that by the time December arrived, nearly all the Santas would be in position for children to visit them.

"Things are getting crazy over there." I stomped my snow boots off after having returned to the house from the workshop. We were approaching the last week of November. The sign on the workshop door once more read *'Busy, Hectic Elves at Work, Enter at Own Festive Risk,'* and the elves had now started to race around the workshop, reacting to Christmas requests from children posting letters to the North Pole, and telling our early Santas their wishes. "It's exhausting just watching them, and it's only going to get more frantic."

Mrs C darted out of the kitchen, carrying a plate piled high with cookies. "Here you go. These are cranberry and nutmeg," she said, keeping to her busy timetable of baking in order to keep my and the elves' energy levels up.

"Thanks," I said, taking the plate off her. "I don't know what we'd do without you."

Mrs C smiled and brushed some hair away from her face. "Your next batch will be ready in two hours."

I hurried back over to the workshop where Pepper and Shinny were now swamped with wrapped Christmas presents, ready to go. "Cookies have arrived." I placed the plate onto a spare workbench.

"Wonderful," Wunorse said, inhaling dreamily as he darted over to grab one. "Mrs C's finest."

"How's the list going?" I asked, as the other elves grabbed cookies and raced back to their benches. "Are our new toys going down well so far?"

Wunorse consulted his scroll-device. "Oh yes. We have lots of requests for Fashion Factor dolls, the kangaroo popper, the sausage game, and as usual all our unicorn stock is popular. It's still early days, though."

I nodded, feeling excited to find out about how our toys were being received. I then glanced upwards at the large countdown calendar on the ceiling. "Not long now before the concert."

Shinny let out a gulp of a shriek, and the piece of sticky tape in his fingers folded over onto itself. He quickly fumbled to pull another bit of tape off, but his cheeks were now a darker shade of pink.

On the last day of November, I took a break from overseeing the workshop and Mrs C and I settled down in front of the television. It was the last moment of semi-calm I would have before the impending whirlwind.

We flicked onto the channel which was entirely dedicated to showing low budget Christmas films containing the same sentiment of finding love at Christmas. The films were cheesy and often about a single father, a workaholic woman, and a lonely child.

The one we watched was no different, and whilst I gnawed on my thumb, feeling anxious, Mrs C was rapt. "Wouldn't it be wonderful if David met a nice lady?" Mrs C gushed as the credits of the film rolled.

I turned to her and smiled. "He did! He met the nicest lady there ever is. He met you, and he's happier than ever."

Mrs C's lips curled into a smile. "He does seem happy." She then hopped out of her seat and switched the television off. "It's time for bed, and it's a big day tomorrow."

The following morning, the sound of bells chiming all around the house woke me up. I sat up, leant across to Mrs C and gave her a kiss on the cheek. "Happy Advent of Christmas."

She smiled at me with hazy eyes. "Happy first of December," she said, and kissed me back.

After breakfast, I popped across to the workshop to check on the elves. The workshop was already being transformed for the Sleigh Ride Concert. Some workbenches were now pushed together to create a stage at the far end of the room in front of the planning board. There were now two silver, glittery curtains which flowed from the ceiling and hung at the sides of the stage.

There was a nervous but excited energy in the room as the elves continued to work. Sugarplum kept doing a shimmy on her tiptoes as she moved from place to place. Pepper and Bushy kept tossing presents back and forth between them, and Wunorse kept muttering words under his breath, to rehearse his lines. Whilst Shinny kept taking long, deep breaths to calm himself down.

"Happy Christmas advent," I called. "Are you all ready for tonight?"

"Nearly," Alabaster said as he fiddled with a large spotlight on his workbench.

"Great, Mrs C and I will arrive at 6pm. We're looking forward to it," and I turned around to head back to the house.

That evening, after I showered and changed and Mrs C had dressed up in her favourite red tartan dress, we walked arm in arm over to the workshop as if we were going out for a date.

56

When we entered the workshop, there was a noticeable difference. The place was silent, and the elves were nowhere to be seen. There was also now a huge empty central space, which was usually cluttered with workbenches, scraps of toys, finished products and off cuts of wrapping paper. The elves had done such a pristine job of cleaning up; they had created a hollow, bare environment which was itching to be filled with chaos, joy and heart.

At the far end of the workshop, the silver glittery curtains were closed, blocking our view of the stage, and two chairs had been positioned to face it. On one chair, there was a bag of Christmas pudding flavoured chocolates, which I hurried across to. "I love these!" I cried, peeling the bag open as we both sat down. I shoved the bag towards Mrs C and we both dug in whilst we waited, listening to the sound of rustling and gargling noises coming from behind the curtain.

Bushy poked her little face out from around the curtain, then disappeared again. "Shh, they're here," we could hear her say. "Spit it out, quick."

"Okay, is everyone ready? Maybe pull them up a bit higher," Alabaster was saying. "No. Higher!"

"They are already as high as I can get them," Wunorse muttered.

Mrs C exchanged an amused look with me. "I have a feeling this will be good."

The lights suddenly went out, leaving us in pitch black, which lasted much longer than it should have. "Well, it might be good, if we can see," I whispered, trying to shove my hand into the chocolate bag and missing.

Then a white spotlight shone down on the stage, along with a warm glow which lit up around the edges of the stage. Sugarplum burst through the curtains, wearing her usual elf uniform and hat. "Welcome to the Sleigh Ride concert and ceremony." She waved at us with a big grin on her face.

Mrs C waved back at her, which delighted Sugarplum even more.

"Today is the first day of the official countdown to Christmas, so to celebrate, we have an entertaining show for you tonight. A feast of sparkle, merriment and mystery." Sugarplum waved her hands around at each word. "So, to start the show, we have Wunorse, who will do a Christmas rap."

She disappeared behind the curtain and seconds later; the curtain parted to an empty stage, with a black backdrop. Wunorse then ran onto the stage with his tights pulled up as high as he could over his shirt. His shirt was unbuttoned at the top to showcase a gold chain around his neck, made from chocolate coins tied together, and his hat was inside out and hanging halfway off his head.

"Yo," he cried, before he stood there and posed with his hands wrapped around his folded arms. Then some upbeat bouncy music started, and he began.

"*So, this is a story I'm telling you now. About children getting presents at Christmas, somehow*," he chanted as he strutted back and forth across the stage. "*There once was a man, let's call him Santa; who was a jolly fellow, full of laugh-ta. He woke up one morning with an interesting thought; along with an evolving plan of sorts. He wanted to use his gigantic heart; as well as some elves to each play a part. The idea was to give out millions of gifts; using the power of a great time shift. So children would wake on the same Christmas morning; with a pile of presents to tear through and laud in. Unfortunately for Santa, it wasn't enough; getting presents to all was a concept too tough. So that's when we created our incredible sleigh; to carry all the presents and get around in one day.*"

Then Alabaster stormed onto the stage, causing him to falter and look confused.

Mrs C glanced at me in surprise, wondering what was happening, but I wasn't sure.

"No, no, no," Alabaster exclaimed. "This is all wrong. We're elves. We don't Rap, we Wrap!" He then suddenly pulled out a long roll of wrapping paper from under his hat.

Mrs C gasped in surprise and glanced at me with her mouth open and her eyes wide. Both of us were wondering how the roll had fitted under his hat.

Wunorse scowled at Alabaster and continued to rap even louder. "*And here we are with twenty-four days to go; to welcome her onwards with this wonderful show*," he cried, as he tried to ignore Alabaster, who was now wrapping paper around his body.

Alabaster was circling and racing around him, faster than you could even blink, and he was extracting more rolls of wrapping paper from out of his sleeves and from behind his back, which was completely astonishing.

"*So, take up your seats, eat and be merry; for we have lots to get through with acts of the many*." Wunorse shouted, as he was now covered from head to toe, and Alabaster stood to one side grinning at us, which nearly made me and Mrs C rise from our seats to cheer. "*Now just one thing, before you start clapping; I have a few more words through Alabaster's Christmas wrapping*," Wunorse continued, now sounding muffled and standing still like a scarecrow. "*There's someone else I wanted to call out; it's Santa's wife who I need to shout about. Lest we forget her magnificent smile; a woman who paints wrapping paper into style*." Mrs C was now grinning in delight. "*She brought the best cookies into my life; so, here's a massive thank you to Santa's remarkable wi…*" he said, as Alabaster shoved a sticky bow right over his mouth.

"Stop," Alabaster cried. "No more rapping, just wrapping." He then threw a smoke bomb to the floor. The smoke instantly swirled through the air, filling the stage for a few seconds and distorting our view. When it cleared, the wrapping paper that had been around Wunorse dropped to the floor in a pile and Wunorse had disappeared.

My mouth dropped open as Mrs C and I clapped enthusiastically. Alabaster smiled and bowed before the curtain closed in front of him.

"How did they do that?" Mrs C whispered.

"I have no idea." I was in complete amazement at what I had seen.

We heard some scuffling at the sides of the stage. The curtain opened again and Pepper and Bushy ran on, both of them holding a large candy cane, about half their height, in each hand.

"Can we get you to clap along?" Bushy shouted, grinning enthusiastically, whilst Pepper stood next to her, wearing a much more forced smile of enthusiasm. It was clear she wasn't so keen on the attention.

Music started and Mrs C and I clapped along to the beat, as Pepper and Bushy poised for their routine.

Then, on the right note, they both twirled their candy canes in perfect unison. They picked up pace, spinning the canes so fast that the red and white stripes blurred into a vibrant pink colour. They threw them in the air; twirled them behind their backs; marched up and down the stage, and all the while, their little dexterous hands and fingers kept those canes spinning.

The speed and unison at which they worked, along with the timing with the perfect soundtrack, left me completely amazed as I happily clapped along. I leaped to my feet to applaud when they both threw their candy canes into the air, so they spun high towards the ceiling. They then cartwheeled sideways to catch each other's canes before they hit the ground and continued to twirl them so fast I was certain any faster, smoke would start coming off them.

Mrs C whooped and cheered as well, both of us loving the upbeat, fun atmosphere. When the music stopped, Pepper and Bushy took a deep bow, and we clapped even louder for them. "That was fantastic," Mrs C gushed, giving them both a thumbs up, which made them beam.

Pepper then turned the wrong way as she eagerly tried to run off the stage and collided straight into Bushy, who started rushing in the opposite direction. Both of them fell to the floor, causing Mrs C to gasp, but they instantly got to their feet. "It's fine," Bushy cried, yanking Pepper away with her, and they raced off to the side of the stage.

The curtains closed, and I sat back down in my seat. When the curtain opened again, Sugarplum was standing in the centre of the stage in front of a white backdrop, now wearing a pastel pink tutu and fairy wings. Her face was painted in a glittery white, and her ears had somehow been pinned back against her hairline to make her head appear even smaller.

"Oh, she looks lovely," Mrs C gushed, placing a hand on her chest.

I stared at Sugarplum in shock. "Yes, she does, but, err, does she know what she's dressed up as...?" I whispered to Mrs C, which caused her to snigger.

Sugarplum clasped her hands together. "I've been working on a dance. So, I hope you enjoy it." Sugarplum raised her arms above her head in an elegant pose and she pointed her toe out in front of her, causing the bell on the end of her elf shoe to tinkle.

The backdrop of the stage showcased snow slowly falling to the ground, in a calm, relaxing way, as music filled the room, which was '*The Dance of the Sugar Plum Fairy*' from the Nutcracker suite.

Sugarplum started dancing. She moved gracefully around the stage, floating her arms to the sides in a controlled manner, throwing her legs upwards and pirouetting faultlessly. With every move, it appeared that snowflakes flew out around her and swirled into the air, and the bells on her shoes tinkled and jangled, overlaying the music to form a beautiful composition in its own right.

"Oh, my goodness," Mrs C gushed as Sugarplum continued to create her enchanting dance in front of such a soothing backdrop.

I noticed her eyes were glassy, and that she was welling up with emotion. I reached out and took her hand to give it a gentle squeeze. She squeezed it back tighter, not taking her eyes off Sugarplum.

Then, as her performance progressed, Sugarplum's energy and rhythm increased, causing her bells to tinkle faster. The projected snow on the backdrop fell heavier, streaming down behind her and then magically, real snow started to fall over the stage, scattering on her hair and her outfit. It looked so beautiful that I couldn't even tear my eyes away to check on Mrs C anymore.

Finally, Sugarplum jumped up high, tapping her feet together as she lifted to create a fitting jingle, before she landed with an elf-like lightness that even stopped her bells from tinkling. She then followed the move through with a smooth curtsy.

Mrs C stood up and clapped profusely. "That was wonderful," she raved, dabbing at her eyes.

Sugarplum walked to the front of the stage as the curtains shut behind her, and she waited for us to sit back down in our chairs. "Now, I want to introduce you to our main act. To the star of our show. It is the one, the only... Shinny," she announced, holding out her arms wide as she walked backwards and disappeared through the curtain.

When the curtain parted, Shinny was standing on the stage encased in a gold star costume. His hands and legs stuck out the sides to form points of the star, and his little face stared out at us from the centre.

He grinned nervously and licked his lips, before he wobbled like a penguin as he turned in a circle to showcase his outfit, which simultaneously revealed the wire attached to him. "Christmas wouldn't be Christmas without the Christmas star," he called, trying to sound confident.

Suddenly, he was lifted from the ground at the same time an enchanting piece of music started playing. He swung across the stage, travelling the width of it somewhat haphazardly, and then swung back. He twirled around and took another journey, swinging back and forth through the air. Shinny beamed with happiness, despite looking a little out of control and unable to do anything except be tossed around on the wire he was dangling from. Shinny's smile then faltered. "I'm starting to feel sick," he said towards offstage, his mouth puckering into a grimace.

"Oh, sorry," Bushy cried from behind the curtain, and then Shinny crashed to the floor with a bump.

Mrs C gasped. "Was that meant to happen?" she whispered to me and I shrugged in response.

Shinny glared at Bushy off stage as he rocked himself to stand up again.

"Sorry," Bushy squeaked, and then Shinny plastered his smile back on his face. As he did, the projection on the backdrop started forming the base of a Christmas tree, and as he rose, the outline of the tree took shape. From the bottom spruces, weaving its way inwards, layer by layer, until Shinny reached the uppermost point and looked like a star had been placed on the top of the tree. He then switched a button on his outfit and it lit up with hundreds of bright little lights, causing Mrs C and me to clap enthusiastically.

Shinny took a deep breath and held it as the enchanting music turned to a drumbeat, which completely changed the mood and set us on edge. "It is now the time you have all been waiting for." He projected his voice as much as he could, but I could hear the nerves behind it. "The monumental arrival of our glorious sleigh," and he attempted to hold out his hand towards the opposite side of the room, but it didn't get far in his costume.

The drumming continued, and a thrill of excitement went through me, as the whole side of the workshop wall parted in half, revealing the sleigh in her full beautiful glory, sitting in the snow outside.

She was just as polished as she was when I had left her. Alabaster and Wunorse then walked ceremoniously along to the beat of the drum, pulling her behind them by the reins, which were attached to her body.

Mrs C and I stood up, completely transfixed at watching her arrival. I choked back the emotion that had risen inside of me as I recalled every year we had been on our journey together and all the adventures we had experienced with each other; and here she was, another year, just as loyal and as sturdy as ever. When the sleigh reached its destination in the centre of the workshop, the walls closed behind it, and that bare space the elves had created was instantly filled with heart and joy.

Shinny cleared his throat. "We welcome our sleigh, ready to be filled with billions of presents to transport all over the world on one starry night. We wish it a safe and successful journey as it soars across the sky like a shooting star, and we wish it protects the gifts that we place inside its walls with the fortitude and honour of a superstar," he said, whilst trying to wave his hands, which were sticking out of his star costume, around majestically as if he was sending it a special blessing.

Bushy then lowered Shinny to the ground, and he looked a mixture of elation, exhaustion and relief. "Did I do well?" Shinny asked, as Bushy raced over to unhook him from the wire.

"You did great, come on," Bushy said, grabbing his hand and dragging him towards the sleigh.

I took Mrs C's hand and joined the elves in a circle around the sleigh. "Who is going first?" I asked, looking around at the elves.

"I will!" Sugarplum reached into a bag and pulled out a handful of elf dust, which she threw into the air above the sleigh. When it settled on top of the sleigh, she gave out a brief pulse and a shimmer.

Sugarplum handed the bag to Wunorse, who also threw elf dust above the sleigh. Bushy followed, then Shinny, and Alabaster, all doing the same routine, and each time the sleigh's glimmer shone even brighter.

Finally, Pepper stepped forward. When she took out the dust from the bag, instead of throwing it into the air, she opened her palm and softly blew the dust over the sleigh. It made me wonder why she couldn't be as delicate when she blew dust at me. Once the dust landed, the sleigh then shone brightly and a shimmer of what looked like water appeared on the surface, showing the span-warp field was now in place.

"Excellent work," I said, knowing she was now ready to be filled.

Sugarplum picked up a neatly wrapped gift and presented it to me. "This is for Ella in Germany. Please do the honours."

"Ah, our first request. May she get many moments of enjoyment from her present," I said, before I lowered it into the sleigh. "There we go. Does that feel good?" I whispered to her, and the sleigh glowed and shimmered in response.

There followed a moment of silence as Mrs C placed a hand across my back and we stood and stared at the sleigh, absorbing her magnificence.

"I guess that concludes our ceremony," Alabaster whispered, breaking the silence.

Mrs C blinked. "Yes, that was a lovely concert." She then turned to Shinny. "And you were a brilliant star."

Shinny blushed. "Thank you. It was quite scary, but I'm really glad I did it."

57

Over the next few days, the elves became incredibly busy as children's requests came into the looking dome, thick and fast. Wunorse ordered out instructions, like a military leader, to get the other elves to wrap up the gifts and place them in the right section in the sleigh.

It was a much smoother operation than it had been in previous years. Alabaster vigorously quality checked all the products, whilst the elves seamlessly moved around each other, throwing gifts across the room, and darting around the place with a speed I could only ever muster on Christmas Eve night.

They certainly had it under control and whilst it was a serious operation, the atmosphere remained fun and exciting. Christmas music blasted into the workshop, the elves had added tinsel to their hats, the fragrance of the workshop was now full of Christmas spices, and Mrs C's timetable of cooking was keeping the elves happily energised, as well as a trail of crumbs on workbenches.

Everything was going well, and I would often make my authority known by pacing up and down the workshop, and peering into the sleigh to watch it become fuller and fuller.

We had arrived at the midpoint of December, and I was feeling a glow of excitement, when one morning after breakfast, Mrs C approached me just as I settled into my throne to watch a low budget Christmas film.

"I've had a message from the department store in New York. The tier one Santa we placed there has come down with food poisoning and they don't have a Santa today, on one of their busiest Saturdays. The store owner said they have someone willing to stand in, but we haven't approved him. What do you think?"

I shook my head. "We can't allow the children to have any doubt that they are meeting the real Santa. Tell them I'll stand in for him."

Mrs C's lips curled into a knowing smile, as if she had predicted my reaction. "Right. As long as you're sure."

I nodded. "Yes. I'll leave now."

"Great. I'll tell them to expect you shortly."

As I left to get changed, I couldn't help but feel excited. I rarely got to actually play the role of me to children, and it used to be one of my fondest experiences. I pulled on my replica Santa uniform and rushed back down the stairs.

Mrs C was waiting in the hallway. "One more thing, I thought you might need this," and she pressed the Santa manual into my hands.

I frowned and guffawed. "I don't think I need that. I wrote it."

"Oh, well, if you're sure. I just thought you might want a refresh before you get thrown into the department store chaos."

I rolled my eyes. "I can handle myself."

"Of course you can, love," Mrs C said, as she turned to dust the house. "Have a great time."

I flew to New York and landed the plane in a concealed location, and raced to the department store. Outside was a gigantic blow-up version of myself sitting above the entrance, which I likened to the one we had used at Rudolph's party. For a moment, it saddened me that I was on display like that without my best pal, and I contemplated having a word with the store manager.

It was midmorning now, and as expected, the shopping centre was brimming with people. The 'Greet Santa' section was at the back of the toy department, so I fought my way through, past men and women carrying enormous shopping bags that doubled each person's width, meaning it was even more difficult to squeeze through.

I reached the toy department to find a sea of chaos. It looked like a war of children versus toys. There were people running around, children playing, parents shouting and adults shopping. I made my way across the battlefield, ducking under foam bullets, shot from guns, and flinched when someone flicked a flashing boomerang at my head. Several children pointed at me, jumped up and down excitedly and cried out 'Santa', but I kept moving, whilst smiling and waving at people as I made my way.

"There you are," a man suddenly cried, pouncing on me.

The man looked worse for wear. His tie was hanging away from his neck with the knot having been pulled taut, as if he had been frantically yanking it away from him. His hair was sticking out at different angles, as if he had been jabbing his fingers through it, and there was a paleness in his face that was pasted on from stress. "I'm so glad you're here," he said, looking relieved. "I'm Grant, the store manager."

"Nice to meet you," I instantly decided not to make a comment about the external display, due to it possibly tipping him over the edge.

"Thank you so much for coming. It's such an honour that you would act as a stand in for us at such short notice."

"I'm happy to help. I would hate to let the children down."

Grant smiled tightly. "I'll lead you to your post. We've moved the 'Greet Santa' to a different location, away from the chaos." We forced ourselves through the crowds. "You know," he said, twisting to check I was still behind him. "It surprised me you agreed to this. I would have thought you would be far too busy at the North Pole at this time of year."

"My elves have it all under control," I said.

He guided me in the direction that several signs were pointing and labelled the North Pole. We reached the fake North Pole set, where a large throne-like chair was positioned in the centre of a stage. Fake snow covered the stage, apart from the red carpet that led up to the chair. Around the edges was a gloriously decorated scene with multi-coloured lights, lamppost sized candy canes, and bauble drenched thin Christmas trees. Just like in Lapland, there were normal sized adults dressed up in elf costumes with green hats and uniforms. It was always the most jarring of experiences seeing humans behaving like elves, as they looked so different.

"Here we are," Grant said in a rather jovial, high-pitched tone to cover up his stress. There was already a queue which was wrapped around nearly the entire 'Greet Santa' section and went out the door, full of itchy children and exasperated parents. "Good luck," he said, and he scampered off before anyone could attack or challenge him.

The human elves wore plastered smiles as they tried to calm the crowd down. "Please. Just stand in line and Santa will see you soon," one female elf was saying.

"The store said that nine a.m. is the time you can visit Santa. We've been waiting here for well over an hour now," a woman in the crowd screeched, whilst tapping at her watch aggressively. "What the hell is going on?"

I swallowed, stood up straight and marched over to my chair whilst smiling and waving at the children.

"Ah, here's Santa," a male elf said, his smile tight. He looked like he had been inches away from either legging it or using the candy cane lamppost as a weapon to ward off the increasingly disgruntled crowd.

"Sorry everyone," I called. "I just had a slight problem with the reindeer this morning. But don't worry, the elves and I solved the issue and they will be fit as a fiddle for Christmas Eve, ready to deliver all of your wonderful presents."

The children gasped and grinned, whilst staring at me in awe. It made me feel alive when children did that. I went to sit down on the throne and gave a subtle nod to the elf by the rope barrier. The elf unhooked the rope and bent over the little boy. "You can go through now," she said, smiling and letting him and his mother enter.

The little boy ran forward to me, and I pulled him onto my lap. "Now, Tom, err, I mean, what's your name?" I asked, glancing at his mother, who had momentarily stopped to say a few cursory words to an unfortunate elf, and had luckily been out of earshot.

"Tom," he grinned as his mother walked over to stand next to us.

"Now, Tom, what would you like for Christmas?" I asked.

"I want a gigantic tank to drive over my school," he said.

His mum glared at him. "Tom," she warned.

I chuckled. "Well Tom, do you have a tank driver's licence?"

324

The boy fiddled with his snowman jumper. "No. But I can learn."

"Ah, well, I'm afraid that present might need to wait until you're older. Is there anything else you want?"

Tom shrugged. "A remote-control tank?" he said as if it were a question. Then his eyes lit up. "Oh, and Restyling Slime."

I nodded. "Very well. I will see what I can do."

One of the human elves standing next to me then handed me a small wrapped present. I took it from her, frowning at the rushed quality of the wrapping. "For the kids," she whispered.

"Ah, Merry Christmas, Tom," and handed him the gift. "This should tide you over until then. No child visits Santa and leaves without a little something."

"Thanks Santa," he jumped off my lap, and an elf guided him away.

"We can put that under the tree," his mother said, but she was too late to take it off him, as he was already tearing into the paper.

His grin then faltered as the paper opened around the gift. "What is it?" Tom asked as he stared at some sort of cheap Christmas ornament.

It looked like it was supposed to be a plaster-of-paris cartoon version of me, next to a speech bubble with the words ho, ho, ho, handwritten on it. However, instead the words looked more like no, no, no, which was rather apt considering my face looked like it was drooping downwards, and red paint had trickled from my lips, which made me look more like a deranged vampire. No, no, no, was right, I thought, as I instantly had flashbacks of the quality issues we'd had with Space Cadet Collins.

The elf guarding the queue, then ushered the next child forward. It was a little girl with freckles across her nose and her hair in bunches. "Welcome, La…" I stopped myself from using her name. "What's your name?" I asked, pulling her onto my knee.

"Lauren," she said, as she snuggled against my belly and gazed at me with round brown eyes.

"Well, Lauren, it's absolutely lovely to meet you. What would you like for Christmas?"

"Fashion Factor dolls," she announced so loudly that the human elves all spun round to look at her.

Her mum stood next to us and shook her head. "I'm sorry. She's been absolutely obsessed since she saw the advert for them."

I smiled, and a thrill of delight went through me. "So, you like the Fashion Factor dolls, do you?"

Lauren nodded enthusiastically. "I want to have hair like Ethel Wilde," she said, as her mum's expression changed to horror.

"Well Lauren, I think your hair is beautiful as it is, but I will make sure you receive the Fashion Factor dolls at Christmas." I then felt a nudge from the elf next to me as she tried to impose another excuse for a present on the child. I grimaced as I took it from her, then plastered a tight smile on my face and handed it to her. "Merry Christmas," I said, hoping she wouldn't think this gift actually came from me.

"Thanks Santa," Lauren beamed, as she grabbed the gift and leapt from my lap. She then turned back to me. "Oh, can I also have some Restyling Slime? All my friends have said they are asking for some."

I smiled and then noticed her mother's eyes widen in further horror. "Of course," I said.

Her mother sighed, took Lauren's hand, popped the gift into her bag, and guided her away to browse around the rest of the store.

The elf then escorted the next child, and the process continued. The line of children moved along in a never-ending stream as more people arrived to join the queue throughout the day.

Seeing each child smile and make their request filled me with so much joy, and as the day progressed, I made so many promises to deliver an array of toys. I'd had several requests for Fashion Factor and a surprising number for Restyling Slime, along with other dolls, teddies, games, plenty of unicorn related products, and so much more. I was enjoying myself immensely, and was smiling reminiscently as a child walked away from me, when I felt a slight change in the atmosphere.

58

I drew my eyes back to the queue when a boy I infamously recognised with short spiky hair and a glint in his eye poked his head out from the line and gave me a malicious smile. His name was Kevin, and when he narrowed his eyes at me, I saw the glint in them I knew was associated with the naughty list. As he got closer, he folded his arms, as if he was getting ready for a challenge.

A few more children stood between us, but as I continued to greet them with a smile, I couldn't help but keep one eye on Kevin, and felt slightly distracted by the impending inevitability of having to greet him, too. When he was next, I shifted in my seat as I saw his lips curl into a determined, cunning smile.

"Hello," I said, my smile wavering as I welcomed Kevin towards me. My eyes flickered around the perimeter, wondering if he was with a guardian, but I couldn't see anyone who appeared to be with him. Although there was a woman in a long brown expensive coat, with earrings that sparkled in a way that only genuine diamonds did. She was standing at the side of the North Pole set, with her back to us whilst talking to someone on her mobile, so I couldn't be sure.

Kevin then grinned before he jumped onto my lap and plopped himself down on me as hard as he could. He briefly winded me, and I momentarily pursed my lips together to stop myself from reacting. It was only a second before I had recovered and I forced a smile. "Comfortable?" I asked through gritted teeth. Kevin nodded, looking pleased with himself. "Good. Now, what's your name?" I asked, more curtly than usual.

"Kevin," he replied. "What's yours?"

"I'm Santa Claus."

"No, your real name, dummy," he said.

I cast my mind back to the Santa manual, trying to think of the standard response for a child who questioned my identity, and a fuzzy memory of instructions formed. Remain polite, and good humoured. A child can be curious, but don't allow them to dwell for too long.

I forced a laugh. "My real name is Santa Claus. Now, Kevin, what can I get you for Christmas?"

Kevin's smile contorted into a malicious grin. "You know, I know you're just an old man in a fat suit," and he shoved his elbow sharply into my belly.

I jerked further back into my seat and let out a noise that sounded like a wince and a grunt at the same time. "Nope," I said, trying to ignore the pain he had caused me. "That belly belongs to me."

Kevin then turned around and, before he said anything else, he grabbed hold of my beard and yanked it. The pain caused my eyes to tear up, and I swung my head away from him. "Is that stuck on with glue?" Kevin asked, narrowing his eyes.

"No," I exclaimed, feeling more irritated by him. "It's all real, just like my belly." I glanced at the woman I speculated could be his mother, who was still chatting on her phone with her back to us.

"Now Kevin, pulling on people's facial hair and elbowing people in the stomach isn't nice behaviour." I tried to remain calm and in good humour; despite wanting to chuck the boy off my lap and tell him I only speak to children on the nice list.

"Can't you hack an innocent kid like me trying to seek the truth?" he asked, his malicious smile spreading over his face.

"Well, I told you the truth. Now, what do you want for Christmas?" I asked, my humour waning quickly.

Kevin's eyes strayed to the woman on the phone, and his face hardened slightly. "If you are who you say you are, then I want firecrackers, a tarantula, and a BB gun," he said, with a glint in his eye.

I took a deep breath. "I see," I said, as I contemplated what a weird concoction of presents it was. "Well, you will just have to see what you get at Christmas."

I was certain the real elf's back at the North Pole would already be detecting the flashing red sign on Kevin's name in the looking dome, and deciding exactly what presents he should be aptly receiving.

The human elf next to me then handed me another wrapped gift to give out. I pursed my lips together, knowing Kevin didn't deserve to be rewarded for his behaviour even with something as tacky as what was buried in that wrapping paper. "Merry Christmas, Kevin." I reluctantly presented it to him.

Kevin wriggled off my lap and jumped down, kicking the back of his foot into my shin as he did. He tore open the gift and looked disgusted at the ornament inside. "This is crap," he cried, as an elf ushered him away. The woman in the brown coat noticed and began walking ahead of him, but remained glued to her phone. "This place sucks," he cried, and as he trailed behind the woman, he launched the ornament at the head of a teddy bear on display, causing the teddy to fall to one side, and for its button-eyes to fixate on me.

It made me even more hopeful that the elves were going to give him a gift he truly deserved, one that might teach him a lesson or two. I frowned in disgust and shook my head. I then opened my arm out to the little girl at the front of the queue, who was clutching her brother's hand tightly.

"Go on," her mother coaxed behind them, but the girl stayed where she was clinging to her brother's hand. "Sorry, she only goes where he goes," she said, looking at a loss.

I smiled at the closeness between the two siblings. "That's fine. I have two laps."

The boy grinned, then carefully guided his sister across to me, encouraging her and smiling at her in such a way that I knew his name would be glowing in neon green.

I pulled them both onto my lap, one on each side. "So, who do we have here? What's your name?" I said to the girl, knowing full well what both their names were.

"Her name is Allie," the boy said. "And I'm Max."

"Wonderful names, and it's lovely to meet you both! Now, Allie, what would you like for Christmas?" I asked, smiling at the girl. She bit her lip and looked down at her lap.

"Go on Allie," Max said, giving her a reassuring smile. "It's Santa. Tell him what you want for Christmas."

Then Allie, whilst still looking down, muttered something nearly incomprehensible. "A kitchen set?" I asked. She nodded towards her own lap as she fiddled with the hem of her skirt and muttered something else. "With a washing machine?" I asked.

She nodded. "With saucepans," she whispered, glancing at Max for reassurance. He nodded back with a big, warm smile of encouragement. "And a sink." Her voice sounded more confident. "And cupboards, and a bin, and an oven, and a microwave," she said, getting increasingly enthusiastic and comfortable. I chuckled as she transformed into a different child, and her excitement caused her to nearly burst. "And a fridge," she declared.

"Wow. You've definitely given this a lot of thought. And I'm sure I can rustle up a lovely kitchen set for you for Christmas," I said, unable to suppress my smile.

Allie settled down and glanced at her brother, who grinned back at her. "Well done," he whispered, causing Allie to beam in delight. Her brother's praise clearly meant a lot to her.

I then turned to Max. "What would you like for Christmas?"

Max glanced at the ceiling as if he was momentarily contemplating. "I want a science kit… and Restyling Slime."

"That's great. I'm sure I can arrange that." I made a mental note to throw in a couple of special surprises for him for being such a lovely brother to his sister.

The elf nudged me and handed me two of the gifts, which I then presented to them. "Merry Christmas."

"Thank you very much, Santa," Max said, looking delighted at the gift.

"Thank you very much, Santa," Allie said, copying her brother.

Max then held out his hand to Allie, who took it without question and they both walked over to their mother. As they walked away hand in hand, Allie turned back to look at me and smiled.

My spirits felt lifted as I continued to make my way through the rest of the queue, and even the grumblings and frustrated sighs from parents who had been waiting for a long time couldn't deflate my good mood.

Eventually, we reached the closing time of the store. The customers cleared and the store manager, Grant, approached me, finally daring to come out of hiding. His hair was flatter now, and he had repositioned his tie neatly against his neck. "You did an excellent job. Before you arrived, I was predicting some kind of riot. These parents can go crazy at this time of year, so I can't tell you how grateful I am that you showed up."

I stood up from the chair and stretched my back. It cracked in several places, and I could feel my behind was aching from where I had been sitting for so long. The chair's cushion density and lumbar support certainly hadn't been perfected, like my sleigh. "It was my pleasure. I had a great time. It's always fun getting back in the field sometimes to remind me of why I do what I do."

Grant's expression flickered with concern. "Well, I hope you haven't been considering packing the whole thing in."

"That could never happen," I said.

Grant smiled in relief. "The good news is that the old Santa thinks he should be able to return to work tomorrow. So, we should be fine moving forward."

"Then my job here is done. Good luck with the rest of the festive countdown, and I'll visit you and your kids in a couple of weeks' time," I said, hitching my trousers up.

I wasn't ready to head straight back to the North Pole, so I went for a stroll to digest everything and to capture and absorb the beautiful Christmas lights of New York.

The night time darkness was aglow with beautiful twinkling lights of different colours. There was an abundance of warm orange and crystal white lights everywhere, with blues, greens and reds mixed in, dazzling the City. Hanging from lampposts were shapes of stars and winged angels. Lights on strings cascaded across the tops of streets, going from one side to the other. Projections of snowflakes danced on walls. And there were window displays everywhere of snowy scenes, presents wrapped in beautiful paper, and models of me, the reindeer and the elves, appearing to be in mid-action to make one night perfect.

My impact on the world had turned an already bright, active city into a magical wonderland, and I couldn't help but love it. It always made me feel equally humble that so many people made the effort to celebrate what I was doing every year. Not just down to the individual, but entire cities and countries played along.

The streets were blissfully atmospheric and busy with people still in the flow of festive celebrations and activities. There were large boisterous groups going out for parties, others sipping mulled wine and on dates with loved ones, and many were partaking in outdoor ice-skating and strolls in the frosty air.

I stopped when I arrived at one of my favourite places in the entire world, and that was a great testament to the number of places I had visited. It was Rockefeller Center, home to one of the world's most iconic Christmas trees.

The tree towered above the central square, making itself known to the many people surrounding it and snapping photos. It was adorned with multi-coloured Christmas lights, which looked like it was covered in jewels, and it was as regal as it was worthy of them. At the top of its crown was a huge glistening star that glowed and shone so brightly that it was like a beacon to the crowds below.

It was a magnificent spectacle and to me it was like staring up at the aurora borealis on an active night; it evoked so many emotions, many of hope and inspiration.

After a while, I gave a bow towards the tree, as if we had a mutual understanding of each other, and I turned away. I made my way back to the plane feeling calm and satisfied. It had been a glorious trip, and I was ready to return to the last couple of weeks of chaos.

59

The following morning, I headed over to the workshop, where the elves were in full swing that they barely noticed I had arrived. They were racing back and forth from the sleigh to the span-warp cupboard, where they extracted presents, labelled them and placed them in their rightful place in the sleigh.

The looking dome was lighting up frantically with green names, along with snapshots of their letters which floated through the swirls of white smoke that looked like cotton candy. However, the odd red name and letter, which was accompanied by a vicious swirl of the white smoke around it, sometimes interrupted the flow of green. It was impossible to read everything coming through, as the letters were streaming in from all over the world in substantial, inordinate numbers.

Wunorse read out the incoming orders from the scroll device in his hand, which correlated with what was fleetingly displayed in the looking dome. He read them so quickly that to me; he sounded like a constant hum, but the elves understood him, and would, just as quickly, fetch the corresponding present to the child to keep up with the streams of requests.

"I can't believe how many orders of Restyling Slime we're getting," Bushy declared, as she skipped to the sleigh.

Alabaster frowned as he wrapped up a pile of presents at his workstation. "Yes, we didn't forecast this much demand. It's as if it's a craze exploding before us. We might need to make more."

"Yes, we are definitely running low on stock by the looks of it," Wunorse said, breaking his constant hum.

Alabaster then grinned, happily. "Why are you so happy?" I asked.

"Well, it's not a complex toy to make, and it's taking the pressure off us having to keep up with demand for more complicated toys."

"It's true," Pepper said, looking happy. "Shinny will produce plenty in no time."

"Yes, and it lets me monitor the quality control of all the other toys. It's perfect," Alabaster confirmed.

"So, no Space Cadet Collins incidents this year, then?" I asked.

Alabaster looked like he was floating on air as he shook his head. "No. Everything is running perfectly because of Restyling Slime."

"It's just what we hoped for," Pepper said, and I noticed the same self-triumphant smile she had worn when Pip had softened Alabaster.

"Well, it looks like we need a lot more. Probably another million to begin with," Wunorse suggested.

Shinny peered over his station and grinned, looking rather pleased with himself. "One order of one million Restyling Slimes coming right up," he confirmed.

"Also, we need four hundred thousand Fashion Factor dolls," Wurnorse ordered.

"On it," Bushy said joyfully.

"Oh, I just love that we have lots of requests for Fashion Factor as well," Sugarplum said, as she spun around in a pirouette before she dropped a present she was hugging into the sleigh. "Now, everyone can feel the joy of playing with Pip's invention."

"Yep, that is wonderful too," Alabaster beamed satisfactorily to himself.

Mrs C arrived, sticking her head through the door. "Cooey," she called, as she came inside carrying a tray with a plate heaped with mini stollen pieces, a jug of her eggnog, and eight cups. "I hope I'm not interrupting anything, but it's time for snacks."

The elves paused in what they were doing, their mouths opening in delight. Wunorse's hum stopped immediately. "My favourite part of the day," he cried, racing over to her and giving her a quick bow and a beaming smile.

Mrs C smiled and lowered the tray down to him as he reached for a piece of stollen. The other elves then quickly joined him, crowding around Mrs C eagerly.

"You all look so fresh and happy. I don't even know if you need a pick-me-up," Mrs C said, handing them around.

"Oh, we definitely do," Wunorse gushed, spraying crumbs from his mouth, having shoved a second piece of stollen into it.

She then poured out the eggnog and handed the glasses out to everyone.

"Yum," Shinny said, taking a big gulp and getting a white coating across his upper lip. Bushy giggled, then took a big gulp and looked just like Shinny. Shinny then stepped closer to me. "Santa, is it true that you were pretending to be a fake you yesterday?" he asked.

I chuckled. "Yes, that's true."

Shinny's frown deepened. "So, you were pretending to be someone else who was pretending to be you, when you are actually you," Shinny asked again, as if it was hurting his mind.

"Yes, he was, Shinny," Alabaster confirmed. "How did it go?"

"Tiring but joyful," I said, a little smile playing on my lips.

"The looking dome was going crazy whilst you were there. We received a lot of green messages, except one, which was very red indeed," Wunorse said.

"Yes, Kevin. He was very naughty. He certainly needs a lesson or two in being nice. Have you worked out a suitable present for him?"

Wunorse looked at Pepper, who nodded. "Yes. We have sorted out some more appropriate gifts for him, along with a concoction of karma and calmness."

Sugarplum nodded. "Yes, karma will definitely teach him it's not nice to be mean and if you are, it will come back and bite you in the…"

"The thing is," Pepper said, cutting across her. "Deep down, that boy is just craving attention from his parents. It's all he wants."

"Yes, his mother did appear to be rather aloof," I said, thoughtfully.

"That's why I think we should send a little something extra too," she said.

"I agree with you, but either way, whatever happens, I refuse to give him what he asked for."

"What was that?" Mrs C asked.

"Firecrackers, a tarantula and a BB gun."

Mrs C blinked in shock. "Goodness. What a strange request."

"That's what I thought. Who knows what he's plotting?"

Alabaster then placed his cup onto the surface. "I think it's time we returned to work."

"Once again, exquisite stollen and eggnog, Mrs C," Wunorse declared, as he raced back over to his station to check on his scroll device. He gulped when he looked at it and his eyes bulged as he saw the flurry of orders which had come in during the break. He glanced at Shinny, then back at the list. "Err, Shinny, change that order of Restyling Slime. Let's make it five million instead."

Shinny's eyes bulged wider than Wunorse's. "Wow. I'm on it," he confirmed.

Alabaster looked delighted. "Everything is going so wonderfully this year," he said happily.

"Five million," Mrs C whispered to me. "That's insane. I guess sometimes you really can't predict what will take the world by storm."

"I know." I glanced suspiciously at Pepper, who wore a constant smile as she worked. "Although it looks like it is thanks to Cynthia's crazy advert for Restyling Slime that we are seeing such a demand for it." I wondered how much the dust Pepper had blown on me, before I met Mr Richford, had influenced my decision to hand over the reins of the Restyling Slime advert to Cynthia. Either way, I was pleased I had taken a chance on her.

"It certainly seems that way," Mrs C agreed. "I just hope Mr Richford will take that onboard and do the right thing by her."

"I'm sure Mr Richford will. I think they need each other," I said.

Over the following days, the elves made their way through the torrent of requests coming in. The incoming stream slowed down in the last days before Christmas, as it always does, which gave Wunorse plenty of time to check his list and ensure we allocated each child with what they had asked for.

I was particularly relieved that whenever I visited the workshop, the elves continuously reassured me we were on track and things were going exceptionally well this year. It was wonderful compared to the previous year, where Alabaster had been snapping because he'd been trying to build and fix too many complicated toys. That mad rush was gone and everything was so much more under control this year. It was particularly clear that Alabaster was continuing to revel in the fact that our two most popular requests this year didn't sit under his workstation, and that they could be so easily produced by Sugarplum, Bushy and Shinny.

The atmosphere was magical, and I knew as a result the children would feel the joy coming from out of our workshop, and it was all thanks to Pepper's crafty strategy with Pip, Alabaster, Fashion Factor and Restyling Slime.

Soon it was the day before Christmas Eve. My stomach twisted with excitement as I walked over to the reindeer hut carrying a bucket containing bottles of Mrs C's special tonics and lotions. I opened the shed door to find the reindeer tucked up on the floor, snoozing. Cupid was making cooing noises, but as soon as they heard me, they all scuffled to their feet and stood to attention. They knew that time for lazing around was now after their job on Christmas Eve.

"Morning everyone. Not long to go now. Are you all ready for the big day?" I asked Rudolph, who stood taller than usual. Rudolph exhaled a blast of determined air, which looked like a silver cloud coming out of his nose. "Good. Now, we best get you all clean for your big trip."

All the reindeer suddenly took a step forward, with Vixen banging into Prancer, making him sidestep from the impact, and Comet walked into Donner's behind, which made her give out a huff of irritation.

"Calm down, everyone, not so fast. I'll get to you all. Gosh, I hope you aren't all this clumsy later." I noticed Dancer had stepped into a pile of reindeer droppings in her haste to be washed. Dancer looked down, repulsed at her hooves, and Blitzen snorted as if he found it funny.

I picked up the hose and filled up the bucket I had brought with me, and poured in some of Mrs C's orange and cinnamon bubble solution. Sure enough, bubbles started rising out of the water.

"Here we are. Rudolph, you're first." I wanted him to have the freshest of the bath water. "There we go, lad. We've got to make you as fresh as possible," I said, as he walked out the pen gate to meet me by the bucket. I started by hosing him down before I dipped my scrubber into the water and started lathering him up. Rudolph closed his eyes as the suds covered him, and the fragrant smells wafted up.

Afterwards, I hosed him down again to get rid of the suds, and then grabbed a large fluffy towel and patted him dry. Next, I used my special cloth with orange essential oils to give his nose a buff, so it shone even brighter and gleamed redder than before. "We've got to take care of this bad boy, don't we?" and I polished a spot I had missed.

I stepped back to inspect him and grinned. "Yes. You look absolutely perfect. Now, lad, how about we use that stick the elves got you for your birthday, and give you a good old massage?" I grabbed the peculiar nobbly massage stick and rubbed it deep into his shoulder blades. "Does that feel good?" I asked.

Rudolph drooped his tongue out of the side of his mouth in answer. It was so good; he couldn't even nod his head. He was enjoying it that much.

"Right, lad. That's you all sorted and ready for our big day. Now who's next?" I called as I turned round to the eager reindeer. "Dancer, you're up next," I said, as she made a conscious effort to be the closest to me.

Rudolph trotted off back into the pen and allowed the other reindeer to sniff him. While I got to work on Dancer, I noticed Rudolph ease himself out of the herd and stand to the side, where he stood upright as if he was refraining from plonking himself onto the floor to ensure he kept his coat clean.

I made my way through each reindeer. The aroma of Christmas fragrances grew stronger, which I always found reminiscent of this time of year. The soapy water grew murkier with the muck coming off each reindeer, but by the end I had nine clean, intoxicating, and supple reindeer ready to go. They looked fabulous together with their fur coats spruced up and new, and it then reminded me of my own. It was time!

60

I headed back to the house as quickly as possible with my walk turning into an excited jiggle as I picked up the pace. "Love," I called out as I stomped my boots.

"Yes, honey-kins," Mrs C replied from the kitchen, as if she was playing with me.

"Is my outfit ready?"

"What outfit?" Mrs C said, looking confused.

I tilted my head to one side and stared at her, unamused.

She then grinned. "Oh, '*the*' outfit. Well, I've washed it, ironed it and steamed the cuffs and hem, to spruce them up. I've fixed the ambient temperature setting on it as you mentioned it was on the blink last year. I've polished your boots and belt buckle; and it's all hanging up for you, upstairs in the guest room, ready to go."

I grinned at her. "You're an absolute star."

Mrs C chuckled. "Any issues, let me know. I'm just finishing your tool kit," and she placed several items into a bag for me.

I went up to the guest room, and sure enough, my thick red coat was hanging up waiting for me, with its buttons sparkling. The belt hung over the shoulder. The boots were on the floor, pressed together. The trousers were draped over the back of a chair, and my stocking hat was resting on the table. Mrs C had done a wonderful job making it look brand new, with its rich colour, its plush, thick fabric and snow-white fur trim.

"It's time for our journey together," I whispered, before I stripped off my clothes and pulled on the trousers and coat. I fastened the buttons up, feeling pleased that it once again fitted perfectly around my belly. I tightened the belt around my waist, pulled on my boots, positioned my hat on my head and slipped on my soft silky gloves, before I inspected my appearance in the full-length mirror.

The coat was comfortable, and wrapped around me like a cocoon, but it also made me feel powerful and important. This outfit, although it looked similar to my other Santa uniform, which I pulled out for events like SCAM, and giving 'Him' in Lapland a show, was by far different. This made me who I am. This made me Santa, and tonight I had something exceptional and serious to do.

This mission was between me, my uniform, the sleigh, the elves' magic, and my nine fabulous reindeer. I could already feel the energy mounting, and it sent a tingling thrill through me.

I made my way downstairs to where Mrs C was waiting for me in the hallway and watching me with a proud, emotional smile on her face.

"You look perfect," she said as I came towards her. She ran her hands across my shoulders as if she was removing any remaining fluff or dust mites from my pristine coat and gave my upper arms a tight, comforting squeeze.

"Here's your kit." She handed me the bag she had been preparing earlier. It clunked with the wide range of tools I needed for my mission.

"Excellent." I took a peek inside and appreciated the internal organisation. There were labels and instructions on everything, and I knew Mrs C wouldn't leave me without something I might need. I popped the tool bag into my pocket with it shrinking as I did.

"Are you going to keep to your word this year about the mince pies? We agreed you would collect the mince pies instead of eating them, so that we can give them out to some food banks and charities after Christmas."

"Oh, sure…, now I best go check on the sleigh," I said, my stomach somersaulting.

I entered the workshop to find the elves racing around. "Quick, last three presents. Restyling Slime, Fashion Factor and a Pandacorn," Wunorse cried. Shinny and Pepper, who were standing at their workstations, threw them across to Sugarplum and Bushy, who were standing by the sleigh, to drop them into the appropriate section.

As soon as they landed, Bushy jumped up and down in glee. "We did it!" She clapped her hands, and her hat slipped down to cover her eyes.

Wunorse nodded. "All present and correct, and checked twice." He snapped his scroll shut, walked over to me, bowed his head, and held out both his palms to present me with the scroll device. "It's over to you now," he said, and the other elves went silent with bated breath as they watched me accept the scroll from him.

"It's an honour. I promise I will make sure that everything you have all worked so hard on over the year gets delivered."

The silence continued as we all turned to take in the sleigh's marvel. It was piled high with presents which barely accounted for the number of presents inside, all squeezed in with the span-warp field.

"How many presents this year?" I muttered, unable to take my eyes off the sleigh.

"Billions," Shinny whispered.

"It's all on the report," Wunorse said, gesturing to the scroll I was clenching in my hand.

I glanced at the number and nodded. "Slightly more than last year, however I have a better feeling about this year though."

"Me too," Pepper whispered. Her eyes met mine, and she gave me a small smile, and in that smile, she was telling me I was right. She stepped closer to me and handed me her special bag of dust. "It's all assigned correctly, and there's one more gift I'd like you to give to someone," she whispered, handing me a wrapped gift with a name on it.

I raised my eyebrow in surprise when Pepper told me what was inside. "Very well, if you're sure?" I said, confused by the request.

Pepper nodded firmly.

Alabaster gave the sleigh one last wipe with the cloth he was holding and stepped back. "I think it's time to finish it off," he said.

The elves grinned at each other before they reached under their hats to each pull out an elf made party popper and aim it at the sleigh. "To

Christmas," they cried, as they all pulled the string.

Several almighty blasts burst from them, along with long streams of glittery string, reaching from one side of the sleigh to the other and settling on top to create the elf-shield. The streamers then appeared to melt away and left the top of the sleigh to sparkle and twinkle as if it was covered in stars to match the night sky. It formed a protective barrier to prevent the presents from falling out mid-flight.

"Now, the sleigh is officially ready," Alabaster announced.

"Excellent work. We best get her hooked up then."

Alabaster nodded, and he and Wunorse raced to the side of the workshop and drew back the large sliding shutter to make way for the sleigh's exit.

The reindeer were now roaming around in the paddock, having a gentle warm up and ensuring they didn't exert too much energy or ruin their clean coats. I picked up my sleigh-bell rattle and called the reindeer to approach. Instantly, the nine reindeer stopped what they were doing and stood up straight before they approached with confident strides and a look of serious determination on their faces. As they approached, they intuitively fell into their formation, with Rudolph taking up the rear, following his group behind at a slight distance.

"Comet, Dancer. In you go," I said, as they both paced round in a circle, and then backed up towards the sleigh, and shuffled their behinds into the correct place. "Well done you two, that's it." I pulled their harnesses, which were covered in bells, around their necks and bodies. "Donner, Blitzen, come on," I said, as they moved in perfect synchronisation to back into their positions carefully, and I attached their bell encrusted harnesses.

Next were Cupid and Prancer, then Vixen and Dasher, and finally, it was Rudolph's turn. "Come on, lad." I stepped aside for him to take his place, front and centre. "Are you excited, boy?" I asked, as I stared at him proudly. Rudolph met my eye with the usual grit and steel he possessed at this time of year, and his nose shone so brightly it was clear he was also full of excitement and adrenaline. "Yes, me too," and I pulled his harness over him.

The elves picked up the straps from the sleigh and secured them around the reindeer, attaching each one to it. They were ready.

"Aww," Sugarplum grinned at all the reindeer. "They look splendid. A force to be reckoned with."

Mrs C appeared in the open doorway. "Are you all set?" she asked.

I nodded and smoothed down my coat. "The sleigh is packed and full. I have my list, my bag of tools, the elves' lucky charms, the reindeer are strapped in, and we'll soon get our full quota of time-warp power. We're ready."

I glanced at the gigantic clock on the ceiling, which was counting down the minutes and seconds. "It's time for us to get going."

Mrs C nodded and stood on her tiptoes to kiss me on the lips. "I'll see you in thirty-two hours, then."

I climbed up into the sleigh and sat down. The cushioned seat contoured around me in the perfect way, giving me the correct support, and was just soft enough. I picked up the thick reins that reached round to Rudolph, and connected to each of the reindeer. "Here's to a successful Christmas," I said, as the elves stared up at the clock.

"Five, four, three, two, ONE," they bellowed as the clock suddenly rang out a loud chime.

I lifted my reins up high and brought them down, nudging Rudolph and the others to make their move.

"Good luck," the elves cried.

"Be careful," Mrs C called as Rudolph led the way, and the reindeer followed, pulling the sleigh out of the workshop doors.

61

With each step, the reindeer picked up pace. Their hooves churned the crisp snow, and the sleigh sliced through it. Faster they ran, with the combination of their feet sounding like a distant roar of thunder. I gave the reins a guided pull, and Rudolph tilted his head back, and his front feet parted from the ground, followed by his rear legs. The other reindeer followed in suit, and the sleigh seamlessly lifted from the ground behind them. As we swept into the sky, the jingle jangle of bells rang through the air like music. I took one last look behind me to see Mrs C and the elves waving us away before we reached the tip of the North Pole.

The pole was vibrating with its strongest energy on Christmas Eve night, and I could see it sending out pulse waves around it, which made the air shimmer. I braced myself, and when we arrived at the tip, we were hit with a surge of power, and the force caused us to shoot off down a twirling, light spiralling vortex to our first destination.

Within seconds, we arrived in the tropical climate of the South Pacific. The heat hit my face, and it was a huge contrast to the icy conditions of the North Pole, but fortunately my ambient temperature setting worked instantly, thanks to Mrs C.

I expanded my hands out, using the energy from the North Pole to create a time-warp. It meant that everyone would go about their normal routine and interact with me, but they wouldn't remember it in the morning. It would be a distant dream, a sense of déjà vu, or nothing at all, and it was a lot of fun.

"Well done, boy," I shouted, as Rudolph guided the way, his nose like a beacon, to the first shack on the list. He led the other reindeer to land silently on top of its thatched roof, their feet light.

I put my reading glasses on and opened up the scroll Wunorse had handed me. I took a quick glance at the names on it, which gave a chart next to it listing how nice the child was, which presents were assigned to them and their locations. Throughout the year I was as forgetful as any man, but on Christmas Eve I could memorise lists and children's names better than anyone in the world.

"Here we go," I muttered as I climbed out of the sleigh and pulled with me the small sack which was dedicated to the minute population of the Republic of Kiribati, the first country to reach the correct time.

The shack didn't have a chimney, but the small island didn't seem to be too conscious of making their homes impenetrable, like those in big cities. I could drop the rope ladder from off the sleigh, climb down and enter easily through the front door where I left humble, but valued, gifts for each child.

On Christmas Eve, I always found a spritely bounce in my step and I hopped along the street with my sack. Sometimes I was airlifted by the reindeer on the ladder to take me to different destinations. It wasn't long before I was delivering my last gift on the island, and we flew off to the next location.

Rudolph and the other reindeer glided across the ocean and they swerved and weaved around each of the Pacific Islands, allowing me to duck in and out of people's shacks or houses to deliver their gifts. The reindeer worked well in their new formation, and it already felt like there was something special about the way they moved.

In no time, we completed all the South Pacific islands and made our way to New Zealand and then Australia. Rudolph once again navigated us to the first house, which was conveniently large enough for all nine reindeer to land on and take a rest. I scouted the roof for a chimney but, like most houses in Australia; they didn't have one.

"Not to worry." I closed my scroll, having studied it to memorise the children in the country. "Like every year, we find a way, don't we, lad?"

I loved a chimney; it made my life so much easier. They were usually a comfortable size for me, and much easier to access from the roof than having to go down to the ground and enter through the front door. If I could avoid doing it that way, I would, as it was a lot more time consuming.

Fortunately, a lot of houses in Australia have handy air vents leading up to the roof, which I can change to act as a chimney. I grabbed the sack allocated to Australia and located the air vent. I sprinkled some elf dust down to ensure it worked the way I wanted it to. The air vent glowed gold and as I crawled down the gap, it moulded and expanded around me until I landed in the downstairs sitting room.

"Ta-dah!" I exclaimed, standing up and brushing the dust and cobwebs off me, which evaporated into the air rather than gathering on the carpet as evidence of my arrival. Plus, I always aimed to be polite in people's homes and not leave a mess.

I checked myself to ensure that no spiders were crawling on me, which fortunately they weren't, then took a deep breath, feeling oddly warm from my activity. My neck was moistening with sweat, which was unusual, and my throat was dry from the dust and the heat.

I frowned, before I recognised that the ambient temperature setting in my suit was acting up again. "I thought Mrs C had fixed this," I grumbled as I looked around the room. My eyes fell onto a glass on a table which contained an amber liquid under a frothy white head. "Beer!" I exclaimed in delight. Condensation dripped down the side of it, and collected onto the table.

I raced over to the glass to pick it up, marvelling at how ice cold it was and how many effervescence bubbles were still rising to the surface. The residents of the house must have recently poured it and gone to bed, and I was incredibly grateful. I lifted the beer to my lips and gulped it down quickly, enjoying the cold, refreshing taste. I let out an embellished sigh of satisfaction, but my delight wasn't over. Next to the glass was a plate of cookies, and I grinned as I munched my way through them, ensuring to keep the crumbs on the plate. There was also a carrot that I placed into my pocket. "Thank you very much," I said to no one in particular.

I darted over to the Christmas tree and pulled out the designated presents for the house, and placed them under the tree. The presents reformed to their correct size to fill out the space. One gift was larger than the rest, a surfboard, which I rested up against the wall, hoping it would lead to some fun the following day. I stood back and checked my arrangement before I returned to the air vent opening. I extracted my claw-grip launcher and shot it up into the air vent. Then I pressed the button, and I flew up the vent.

Rudolph and the other reindeer were patiently waiting for me. "Here you go, lad." I presented him with the carrot. "This will keep you going." Rudolph gobbled it up and followed it with a lick of my hand. "You enjoyed that, didn't you? Now, come on." I then hopped across to the next house with my sack. I wiped my forehead and the back of my neck with my hand, and continued to dive into their air vent.

Several houses later, it was clear my ambient temperature setting was completely broken, and I was uncomfortably hot. My forehead and neck were now dripping with sweat, and I couldn't understand why my suit wasn't working after Mrs C had fixed it.

"Well lad," I muttered to Rudolph, unable to cope anymore. "I guess this calls for some serious action." I pulled off my coat and shirt, leaving on my red vest and then looked down at my thick trousers. I shrugged. "When down under, I best get down to my undies." I chuckled at myself as I pulled off my trousers to reveal my red and green striped shorts.

I kept my hat and boots on to maintain a partial Santa look and placed the rest of my outfit in the sleigh. I grabbed the sack, threw the elf dust down the air vent and started my descent, fighting, once more, through the cobwebs and dust, before I landed in the sitting room.

"Excellent," I muttered, spotting another ice-cold glass of beer; more cookies and another carrot. I pocketed the carrot, munched through the cookies and necked the drink, before I found the tree and placed the presents under it. The place looked great and as I stood back to check my work; I felt it, something crawling across my thigh. I reacted by slapping my thigh, but it just made me feel it crawl even further up my leg. I launched over myself, knocking into a lamp, in a frantic effort to hitch my shorts up and inspect myself, and there it was, a small spider.

My blood turned to ice, but I tried to remain calm. "Here Spidey, Spidey,

Spidey," I called and spotted a box of tissues in the room. I edged towards it and pulled a tissue out, which I used to grab the spider and tear it from my leg. I breathed a sigh of relief as I continued to check my leg for bites. "I think elf dust needs to contain an anti-spider formula," I grumbled.

I picked up the fallen lamp and raced to the air vent where I shot back up it, eager to put my clothes back on. I released the spider at the far end of the roof before I returned to the sleigh. "That was a bit of a hairy moment," I told Rudolph as he guzzled down his new carrot.

I gazed into the sleigh at my outfit, debating the risks of continuing in my current attire or sweltering in my suit. There must be something I can do. I pulled out the tool bag Mrs C had given me and delved inside, searching for a fan, or an ice pack or something to assist me, when I found a note Mrs C had left me.

"Enjoy yourself on your journey. Be safe and I'm thinking of you. P.S. If you still have any issues with the ambient temperature on your suit, dab some of the liquid in the red bottle around the collar and cuffs. P.P.S. I meant it about the mince pies!"

I smiled as I folded the paper back up. Mrs C always looked after me. I pulled out the red bottle labelled Thermo-lotion and dabbed some with a cloth along the cuffs and collar, which caused a faint hissing sound. It looked like some kind of reaction had taken place, so I pulled my coat and trousers back on and felt perfectly neutral in temperature again. "That woman is a dime." I smiled as we set off to continue on our journey.

Once we finished up in Australia, we stuck to our usual tradition of soaring past one of Australia's most significant landmarks, the Sydney Opera House. As we flew past, I gave the reins a few good thrashes to ring out the bells on the reindeer's harnesses. "Ho, ho, ho," I cried as loud as I could to the whole of Australia. "Merry Christmas!" Then we shot off through a vortex.

62

By the time I completed Asia and Africa, including Japan, where I had spotted lots of Kentucky Fried Chicken buckets in everyone's dustbins, I was still on track and in full swing of my routine. I had ticked off several names on my list and delivered a variety of interesting gifts, many including anime characters and toys about a cat with a bow in its hair.

In each country, I had stuck to our tradition of wishing each one a heartfelt, euphoric, 'Merry Christmas' as I flew past their most famous landmarks, including Tokyo Tower, the Great Wall of China, the Taj Mahal, and many more. The reindeer enjoyed it just as much as I did, even if it meant zig-zagging back on themselves before we left.

"Come on everyone, time for Europe," I cried, feeling excited as a vortex appeared in front of us and we shot across to it.

The reindeer soared around, and landed on or hovered beside each building and I instantly got to work, hopping from house to house, finding my way inside and leaving presents behind. I always had so much fun on Christmas Eve and, in particular, I always found Europe delightful with its wide range of houses, cultures, and tasty treats.

Each country had its own culture of what to leave for me, and I loved both the variety and the thoughtful acts. I collected and ate cookies and biscuits, rice pudding with cinnamon, porridge, panettone, sponge cake with rum, and dried fruit and nuts. I drank glasses of milk, coffee, beer, cider, and tumblers of whisky, brandy and sherry. My belly was growing, and my list was getting blurrier the more I drank.

I accumulated hay, carrots, oats, and water to share out between the reindeer. I collected thank-you letters from countries whose culture it was to leave them, and some from houses depending on the thoughtfulness of the child. They all made me smile as I took a moment to sip my drink, attempt to decipher their handwriting, and devour each one, even though they often reiterated the same sentiment.

'*Dear Santa. Thank you for all the presents and sweets you bring us at Christmas, and for making me happy every year.*'

I would fold each one back up and place them in my pocket to show the elves and Mrs C on my return.

On my travels, I came up against a range of issues, from stubborn doors that took some jangling with my Santa key, to not being able to find a way in and having to use emergency elf dust to get me inside. I often found children who weren't in bed yet, unable to sleep from excitement and keen to spot me in the act. I would wave at them as they peered round doorways, or burst in on me, as I placed their gifts under the tree, exclaiming, 'Santa, you're real'. A few times they made me jump and caused me to slosh my drink down my front, so I was glad Mrs C had included a bottle of instant stain remover in her handy bag of tools.

I would speak with several adults, who were still partying and welcoming Christmas Day in with alcohol. Others had so much family staying that the house was bursting at the seams and they were forcing people to sleep downstairs on floors and sofas. Plenty of them were excited and happy, wanting to meet me. Others were grumpy from family conflicts, or were stressed that their children weren't staying in bed. Some of them fired a tirade of questions at me, asking me to explain how I do what I do; whilst others moaned about their recent family problems.

If I had time, I listened to their questions and stories, as I munched on my food, drank my drink and laid out their presents. Other times, I would have to politely decline their interactions, as I had to be on my way. Deep down I'd have loved to have stopped and talked to each one, but even if I did, I knew they wouldn't remember meeting me in the morning.

Throughout my journey I abided by the Christmas Law, and didn't snoop around people's homes, but it was not to say I didn't see some interesting sights, such as strange objects, ornaments, or intriguing artwork. It also didn't stop me from admiring their Christmas decorations, which ranged from the traditional trees, baubles, lights and tinsel to the less traditional, including Christmas trees hanging upside down from ceilings and fake spiders and cobwebs as decorations. At one point, I wondered if one country had mistaken Christmas for Halloween and it made me snigger in delight.

As my journey progressed and the alcohol took an effect, my antics grew wilder and my enthusiasm increased. "Hippety hop, ho, ho, hooray. Look out, children, presents are on their way," I would call as I danced over rooftops and slam dunked presents down chimneys, air vents, or threw them in through windows, before I would jump in after them. It always added to the fun, and despite being slightly more flamboyant, I didn't miss a single name off my list, even as the names blurred ever so slightly.

When I left each country, I kept up with tradition, to soar past wonderful landmarks, such as the Colosseum in Italy, the River Danube in Budapest, the La Sagrada Família in Spain, the Parthenon in Greece and the Eiffel Tower in France, where I would thrash out a 'Merry Christmas' to all.

We would certainly cause a stir roaming around each country, and several times on my journey, defence planes would fly past me, ensuring they protected their land from unauthorised flying objects entering their airspace. The planes would fly close and despite them not being able to keep up with my reindeer, it always comforted me to know the agreement I had with all the Governments of the world to ensure they didn't see me as a threat and target me. In fact, most of their pilots would wave and tilt their planes sideways as a communal welcome to me entering their airspace. I would wave back before shooting off to our next destination.

"Right, my rascally reindeer, next stop is England. Home to the mince pie." We shot off through the vortex and flew over the twinkling lights of England. We landed on the roof of our first house, and for a moment, I sat in my sleigh admiring the chimney. "Now that is a work of art." I studied the masonry of multi coloured bricks neatly cemented together in the perfect chimney formation. "Far too many places do not even have a glorious chimney, let alone craftsmanship like that," I practically drooled.

I hopped out of my sleigh and brought with me the sack for England. I comfortably descended the chimney, breathing in the faint sooty smells and feeling transported to decades before, when chimneys were used more often and were full of soot and acrid fumes. It was intoxicating for me, and I really missed those days.

I stepped out from where a fireplace should be with wood fires, but was now, unfortunately, superseded with an electric fire. It left a lingering disappointment that my arrival these days where I could step majestically out of a fireplace, had become much sparser.

Fortunately, my disappointment was short-lived, as there, sitting on top of the mantelpiece, like a glorious ray of sunshine, was my first mince pie, next to a glass of sherry. "Now that's what I'm talking about," I muttered as I lifted the mince pie upwards like a trophy.

I peeled the silver foil away from it and as I brought it to my lips before I paused as Mrs C's words filtered through the fog in my mind. I lowered the mince pie and took a good look at it, inspecting its crimped pastry around the edge and smelling the faint smells of woody fruit notes and cinnamon.

"I'm meant to collect you and not eat you," I muttered, remembering how Mrs C wanted me to take them to a food bank. My conscience suddenly felt like a swinging pendulum. My desire to eat it mounted. I then sighed. "I know this whole food bank thing is just a ploy to stop me from eating too many in one night, and I'm sure Mrs C can make plenty more for me to take to them."

I took a deep breath as I caved in and smashed the mince pie into my mouth. "I'll deal with Mrs C later." The crumbs sprayed onto the floor in my excitement, which I never normally do. "It will be worth it," I mumbled, as I turned around to search for the Christmas tree.

I wandered around, peering into the hallway and then into a study. "Where have they put the darn thing?" I muttered, getting increasingly frustrated. Finally, I peered behind a long curtain in the dining room, only to find it led to a conservatory. And there it was, the tree with tinsel wrapped around it and the glitter on the baubles glistening under the starlight.

"I think people should leave directions for me," I huffed. I opened the door and went inside. I pulled out the presents and laid them out under the tree. I made to leave when a black shadow shot through the door and made a beeline for the presents and the tree, miaowing as it did. "Oh fiddlesticks," I cried as I raced after the black cat. "Please, I need to put you back just as I found you," but it darted behind the tree and pawed at one of my nicely wrapped presents with its claws.

I tried to waft it out, chanting the word shoo, when I realised it was not going to budge easily. "Fine, I know what this calls for." I pulled out my tool kit, found a bag of special catnip and waved it around in front of the cat. "Come on," I called, as its eyes and head followed the motion I was making. I chucked a couple of pellets onto the dining room floor and the cat sprinted after it, its claws clattering over the floor as if it couldn't get to it fast enough. I slammed the conservatory door, pulled the curtain back in place, and shot back up the chimney.

"On to the next one," I called to Rudolph, and I raced across the roof and leaped over the gap onto the adjacent roof, shouting "Yee-haw." I jumped down another exquisite chimney and continued my venture, leaving presents and mentally ticking names off my scroll.

Along my travels, I gloried in the mountains of mince pies and sherry. So much so that I created my personal entertainment, the ultimate taste test. I collected a range of mince pies and then lined them up on my sleigh when I had a quick break.

I inspected each one, looking at the pattern on top, the paleness of the pastry, the size, and how much icing sugar was dusted on top. I leant back, placed my booted feet onto the edge of the sleigh, and slowly chewed on the mouth-watering flavours and textures. Some had a buttery pastry, others large chunks of fruit, some had a tangier or alcoholic flavour, and some were flaky and crumpled apart in my fingers. My aim was to pick the ultimate mince pie, but I just couldn't. None were a match for Mrs C's and yet I couldn't fault any, even the bad ones.

"If only every day was as fun and indulgent as this, aye lad," I said, as Rudolph devoured his umpteenth carrot. "Right! Time to continue," I called, unfurling from my relaxed position. We then made our way to

Birmingham and pulled up on top of a house that I had been anticipating since I had left the North Pole.

63

"Do you know whose house this is, lad?" I said to Rudolph's blank expression. "It's Carol, that angry woman Mrs C and I saw in London, then in New York and again in Chicago." I frowned, recalling the intriguing exchange I'd had with Pepper before I left. "Well, wish me luck." I hitched my trousers up and made my way down the chimney. When I climbed out of the fireplace, I came face to face with Carol, who was pacing back and forth.

"What the…" she cried, jumping back from the fireplace in alarm.

"Don't worry, it's just me." I stood up and dropped the sack by my feet. I looked up to find her glaring at me. "It's Santa," I confirmed, signalling to my floppy red hat, and wondering if she was confused.

Carol continued to glare. "I know who you are, but why are you here, trespassing?"

"Err, because I've got some presents that your two boys have asked for, along with something for yourself."

"No, no, that can't be right. I specifically forbade my boys to write to you."

I dug into my pocket for my scroll, which I consulted, the writing slightly blurry. "Yes, it's correct. I have two children listed here, Clive and Glen, and they asked for some Restyling Slime, warship toys, and a pogo stick each. Now, I'll just drop them off and get out of your way." I glanced around the room. "Err, where is the tree?" I asked.

"We don't have one. Why would I want a gaudy, tacky plastic tree in my house?"

"Ah, very well. I'll just leave them…err…here." I dropped my sack next to an old charming writing table.

I started to unload the gifts when she suddenly screeched at me, making me freeze. "Stop it! Just take everything away. I don't want anything in this house that reminds me of Christmas. Now just go." Her eyes welled up and tears trickled down her cheeks.

I sighed, unsure how to proceed, when I spotted a decanter and two crystal glasses on the desk. "Carol, come on, let's have a brandy. It might help you relax." I poured us both a drink and sprinkled a pinch of elf dust into one. I didn't have the benefit of the hypnotic aurora borealis to help me this time, but I was determined to get to the bottom of why this woman seemed to be constantly angry.

She grabbed the glass and took a rather impressive swig before she returned her watery, but angry, eyes to me.

"Now, what's going on? What did Christmas do to offend you so much?"

She slammed her empty glass onto the counter and inhaled, the elf dust working its way through her system. "When I was ten, my dad stormed out of the house and asked my mum for a divorce on Christmas day, just as dinner was being served."

I grimaced as I sipped my drink. "That must have been painful."

"It was awful. But then two years ago my husband did exactly the same thing. He asked me for a divorce on Christmas Day." She now sobbed uncontrollably.

"Wow, I'm sorry your husband left you. But surely, it's not Christmas causing this?"

"Well, it's certainly coincidental, isn't it? So forgive me if I think Christmas is cursed. I mean, to top it off, I even got conned out of a lot of money last Christmas."

Something fluttered inside me. It was the same feeling I had when I suggested to Mrs C we deliver the post from the postbox. Something that was guiding me on a particular course I couldn't control. "What happened?" I asked.

She swallowed hard and poured herself another drink. "Well, it's to do with something I'm incredibly passionate about. You see, I have an idea for an app which centres around original manuscripts of classics, and the history of them. Last Christmas I trusted a man to create it for me, only he sold me a pack of lies and left me out of pocket. When I was in London in January, I was doing everything I could to get my money back, but to no avail." Then tears rolled down her cheeks. "It's so hard to trust anyone anymore."

"Yikes, no wonder you were in a terrible mood when we met you in London."

"You met me?" She frowned, then suddenly it seemed to click. "Was that you in the spa?"

I nodded.

"I'm sorry about that. I was in a mess, and I guess you reminded me of…well… Christmas, and it just riled me up even more."

"There's no harm done. But it's funny, because I have a friend who owns and created Vintique Scanner, which is a very clever and intricate app."

Carol looked at me, surprised. "Vintique Scanner! I saw them at the tech conference earlier this year. They are doing incredible things."

"Perhaps I can introduce you to David in the New Year as he might be able to help you," I said, the words bursting from my lips. I then smiled, as it suddenly dawned on me what Pepper had been up to all this time.

"That would be great," Carol said, looking astonished.

"Great. So, now we have that sorted, are you going to give Christmas another go?"

Carol stared at me; her face was full of horror. "No. I can't."

I took a deep breath and placed my glass down. "I am sorry that Christmas hasn't been great for you, but it should be a time that is full of joy, love, and family spirit. You should be creating a happy time with your family, not creating a negative atmosphere and telling your children it is cursed. Can you honestly say that is fair to them?" I marvelled at how similar my advice was to that I had given David earlier in the year.

Carol shook her head and looked down at the floor. "No, it's not fair to them, but how can I celebrate love and joy when I feel rejected and lonely?"

"I know it must be hard feeling lonely. But you'll never get over that unless you take a leap to open your heart again. Perhaps you need to make peace with your past and start again, even if it's just for the sake of your children."

Carol swallowed. "Perhaps."

I smiled, and then Pepper's strange gift to this woman all suddenly made sense. "Anyway, I best be on my way, but I think now might be a good time for you to open the present I brought you."

Carol frowned as I handed her the slim parcel. "For me?"

"There was a request on your children's Christmas list. They wanted you to have something to lighten you up around Christmas, and even though it's a bit unorthodox, my elves sent you this."

She stared at it, her hands trembling slightly, before she tore into the paper, opened the box and blinked into the twinkling lights.

"They are elf lights. We aren't supposed to give them out to people, as the world is fairy territory, but my elves have made an exception."

She pulled them out of the box, and they caused the whole room to sparkle and shine. "They are beautiful," she whispered, her face transforming under the elf-light glow. Her features appeared to soften and her eyes danced, making her look younger and alive. "Why would they make an exception?" she asked, her voice softer.

I smiled fondly at Pepper's meddling. "I guess because Christmas is about making people happier, and my elves wanted to do that for you." I took them off her and draped them over the fireplace, when she sighed and looked at me.

"Fine. I'll give it a go. I'll make sure we celebrate Christmas tomorrow. I have a ham in the freezer, and hopefully we can get through it without it being cursed." She gave a half smile, which made me see the real woman behind her angry mask.

"That's the spirit. And I'm sure we'll meet again in the New Year." I stepped into the fireplace, thinking that introducing her to David could be the beginning of a new friendship, maybe more, but I was certain it would be great for her.

"Santa," she whispered, making me pause. "Merry Christmas."

"Merry Christmas," I replied, just before I shot back up the chimney knowing that in the morning, she wouldn't remember me, but there would be gifts for the children, a ham thawing away, and I knew her heart would be doing the same.

I had a strange feeling after leaving Carol's house, with many thoughts filling my mind, but we still had more deliveries to make, so I climbed back into the sleigh. "Right, lads. Let's carry on, it's onwards to London."

We began our course around London, where I visited accommodation that ranged from the hugely wealthy, living in mansions, to the poor who were living in squalor. It was a huge range on the spectrum, but I didn't leave anyone behind, even those in apartment blocks with no access via an air vent or chimney.

The alcohol was really starting to go through me now, and I shimmied into one apartment and did a jig, dancing on my tiptoes in a vain effort to dispel the feeling of how full my bladder was. I glanced at my list to find that three children, glowing in green, were assigned to the small apartment, which meant that the place was very cramped. The mother was lying on a camp bed with one of her children in the sitting room, and I assumed the other two children were in the bedroom.

I squeezed inside the sitting area, making sure not to knock into anything in the tiny space, and spotted a glass of water they had left out for me. "Perfect." I was happy to receive the kind gesture. It was wonderful timing, as my mouth and tongue were feeling dry from all the alcohol. I quickly downed the water and ate the cookie next to it.

"That's a really cute tree," I muttered, admiring the attempt to add some Christmas spirit to the home. The tree was no bigger than my foot, but it was decorated from tip to base in tinsel and paper drawings from the children.

I pulled out the relevant gifts and laid them around the tiny tree, feeling sad that I couldn't provide the family who needed material possessions so much more. I so wanted to give them the world, to take away any sufferings they experienced, but the Christmas Law meant I could only give in line with their means, which wasn't much and meant I couldn't deliver the games console one of the boys had requested.

I popped my head into the small bedroom where the two boys were sleeping in a bunk bed and spotted two socks decorated in Christmas stickers hanging from the bedframe. I filled them with basic presents like sweets and plastic toy cars, topping them up as far as possible, which might have gone above their designated allowance. "Merry Christmas," I whispered, tiptoeing back out and swaying ever so slightly.

I left the apartment block and climbed back into the sleigh. "Let's go, lad," I said. Rudolph and the reindeer took off again into the sky, and before long, we had finished the last house in London. "Let's say goodbye to England," I called, tugging the reins slightly to the left. Rudolph grunted, and we weaved past Big Ben, creating another iconic picture-perfect moment. "Ho, ho, ho," I cried, as I thrashed my reins to invigorate them as we zig-zagged around it. "Merry Christmas," I bellowed, wondering if anyone was watching me out of their window before we shot into a vortex.

Then, once we completed Wales and picked up some Welsh taffy, and some thank-you notes addressed to Sion Corn, it was time to move on again. "You know where we're going don't you, lad," I said, as we entered another vortex and swirls of colour whipped around us. "We're off to Scotland, home of David and Pip."

64

We began our journey, and I soon got into the flow of tasting a whole range of different Scotch whiskies. The Scottish knew how to treat me well, and I was soon enjoying the different malts and fragrances. A whisky was always an excellent accompaniment to the mince pies.

Within time, my eyes became even blurrier, as I bustled down chimneys and nearly fell over a couple of tripwires that some rascally children had set up to catch me. I clattered into more items and had to use Mrs C's super-super glue to piece back together a vase I had accidentally knocked. Fortunately, the glue was so good that it left no signs of my clumsy breakage.

I was halfway through my journey when I clambered into a house as stealthily as I could. "Tree, where is the tree?" I muttered, twisting around and squinting at the now blurry tree next to the sofa, where a young teenager that I knew was called Gary was sleeping.

I hopped towards it, squeezing my thighs together as I really needed the loo, whilst already struggling to walk in a straight line from the increasing amount of alcohol. I turned the sack upside down, so the relevant presents tumbled out, and I spread them around the tree with my usual flair, creating haphazard piles. "Voila," I said, chuffed, but when I spun round, I knocked a bauble off the tree which rolled towards the sofa. "Drat," I whispered as I scrambled after it.

Gary shuffled, with what looked like a struggle, and he rolled over. He briefly opened his eyes, only to find me a hair width away from him, as I grabbed the bauble. Our eyes met, and then suddenly Gary let out a scream.

"Ahhhh," he cried, as he scrambled with difficulty on the springy sofa bed to sit up.

"It's okay, it's just me." I held my hands up to show I was harmless.

Gary's eyes were wild, his breathing heavy and he then suddenly yanked the covers up around him, but not before I spotted he was wearing some fascinating dinosaur pyjamas. My eyes fell on them, impressed, and Gary gave out a little awkward laugh. "These are a present from my nan. My mum forced me to wear them while she visits."

"That's good of you. Been kicked out of your room for her as well, have you?"

"Yes, as per usual. I'm young and apparently bad backs don't exist for us youth," he moaned, shifting in his seat and making the springs in the sofa ping. "Funny though, because my back is killing me on this thing."

"Ah, yes, it happens to the best of you. But it must be nice having your nan stay." I reattached the bauble to the tree.

"Yeah, it's nice to see her, despite the fact I have to keep repeating myself all Christmas, constantly fetch her sherries, and then be quiet when she has a sleep during some black and white film she wants to watch."

I chuckled and then pressed my thighs together even tighter. The irritation of a full bladder had now progressed to painful cramps. "Gary, can I use your loo?"

"Err, sure." He lowered his protective blanket, about to guide me to the toilet.

"It's fine. I can find it." Unable to wait any longer, I darted towards a door and burst into the hall. I grabbed the first door handle I came to and yanked it open, only for a mop to crash on me. "Nope, not that one." I shoved it back inside and noticed Gary watching me.

I yanked open the next door and found the bathroom. I fumbled for the light switch, then stood against the toilet and felt the sweet relief as I emptied the millions of drinks I had so far consumed. It was like a never-ending stream, and was taking forever, so I placed my head against the wall, feeling its soothing cold temperature, and I closed my eyes. I then heard a knock, and I jolted my head up.

"Excuse me, Santa. Are you still in there?" Gary asked, sounding awkward.

I blinked in shock as I looked down at the now overflowing toilet. "Yikes," I exclaimed, wondering how long I'd had my eyes closed for. I finished relieving myself and zipped up. "Err, yes, I'm still here." I watched the bowl slowly go down, then looked around to inspect the mess I'd made whilst cringing about the situation. I pulled the chain, which emitted a groaning sound, and then another knock came.

"Erm, Santa, I think my parents are going to wake up. Are you alright in there?"

I panicked, wondering what to do, when I realised I knew where there was a mop. I uncomfortably opened the door to find Gary in his dinosaur pyjamas, and it surprised me to see just how short they were on him around the ankle. Gary stared past me at the flooded floor, and I felt my cheeks turn bright red. "Sorry, I had an accident, but I'll quickly clean it up and be out of your way." I rushed past him, grabbed the mop from the cupboard, and cleaned everything up.

Gary watched in silence, and then I clumsily shoved the mop back into the cupboard. "Anyway, I better be going now." My face, now crimson. "Merry Christmas, and make sure you enjoy every moment with your nan. They aren't around forever." Gary nodded, watching me, as I hurried past him, doing my best to walk in a straight line and failing.

As I shot up the chimney, it then occurred to me I should have used the mop in my tool bag and avoided the humiliation, but I shook my head, and tried to clear my thoughts. Fortunately, Gary wouldn't remember anything once the time-warp sprang back into place and my reputation would remain intact.

I arrived on the roof to find Rudolph in a huff with me, with how long I'd been inside the house for. "Don't look at me like that," I retorted as I climbed into the sleigh. "There was an … incident, and I'd rather not talk about it."

Rudolph snorted in irritation, but I ignored him. "Now, we best get a move on. We've got some catching up to do." Rudolph kicked off from the roof and we continued to weave in and around Scotland, whilst I left gifts for the children, ate more mince pies and drank more whisky.

Along my way, I found some of the lanky dolls that are meant to be elves. Some had been set up to look like they were up to mischief, holding a marker pen, climbing up a wall, looking like they had spilled something. They often amused me and as the alcohol levels inside of me grew, I sometimes would join in the game and move one or two around.

I positioned one in the tree, wrapped around a bauble as if it was swinging on a wrecking ball. On another occasion, I left behind the tin foil from my mince pie and placed one of their heads inside it to look like they had eaten it and not me. One place had a very dusty chimney, so I wiped my soot on an elf to make it look like it had been climbing up the chimney.

Then one time, when I was haphazardly throwing presents around, I caught my finger in some wrapping paper, and ripped it. Usually, I would use Mrs C's special mending tape, but this time I positioned an elf right next to the rip, so it could take the blame instead. I wasn't sure if I was supposed to play along, or leave it to the parents to concoct inventive ideas, but I didn't really care either way. I was having a great time.

It wasn't long before we stopped at a familiar house. There was a little crooked picket gate at the end of the cobbled front path, and there was a backdrop of hills and a lake, which glowed in the frosty night under the full moon.

"Do you know who this is, lad?" Rudolph gave a snort, and then Dancer snorted too. "Yeah, I knew you would." I grabbed my Scotland bag, stepped off the sleigh, and nearly tripped over my own boots. Fortunately, I caught myself in time, then glared at Vixen as if he had tripped me, even though he wasn't anywhere near me.

I cleared my throat, threw some elf dust into their chimney, and started my descent. When I emerged in the living room, I spotted the toy reindeer with the sleigh positioned on the table next to the toy Santa, who was now carrying a sack which Pip must have made from an old sock. The toy elves and Mrs C were positioned in a cardboard shoebox made to look like a house on the other side of the table. I grinned at them, pleased that Pip had clearly been playing with her gifts in the run up to Christmas.

I glanced around and spotted a plate of mince pies next to a glass of sherry with a candy cane sticking out of it. "Ah, a Mrs C special." I felt delighted, as I grabbed the drink, and sucked the end of my sherry-covered candy cane, before I swallowed the drink.

I picked up a mince pie and examined it. The pastry looked rich and buttery. I bit into it, and my eyes opened wide. "Ummm. Now that's what I'm talking about," I said, rather loudly, before I clamped my mouth shut, hoping not to disturb them, whilst also shoving the crumbs back into my mouth. They were almost as good as Mrs C's, which meant she had trained him very well. I then spotted a letter, leaning against the wall, which I took and read, whilst reaching for another mince pie.

It was from Pip:

Dear Santa,

Thank u for having us come vizit u this year. I can't stop thinking about u, Mrs C, the elvs and the raindear, becus I luv u all so much.

Since we vizited my Daddy has spent lots of time with me and he tells me storys about my mummy all the time.

I really like them becus I miss her so much. They make me laugh, and sometimz I feel sad, but I don't mind that.

My Daddy is so much happyer now and he makes yummy dinners. His cooking is so much better.

I am so happy and I luv playing with my Santa dolls. Thank u.

Also, I'm so excited to see I am in Fashion Facter. I sent you a letter askin for them so I hope I do.

Luv Pip.

I placed the letter in my pocket and quickly dabbed at my eyes before I reached for another mince pie, but my hand grasped only air. I then realised there were none left, and I had mindlessly eaten all of them. "Darn," I said.

I made my way to the tree, and carefully extracted the gifts from my sack and placed them in as nice an arrangement as I could. The Fashion Factor dolls for Pip, along with some other lovely presents and some retro cars for

David.

I reached into my sack again and pulled out another item for David. I held my breath slightly, contemplating whether I would break the Christmas Law if I gave it to him. I sighed. "What the hell," and placed the wrapped bottle of whisky next to the other gifts, along with a brief note which read, *'I recommend you use your Vintique Scanner app on this before you crack it open. Very best wishes S.'*

It was a bottle I'd had for a few decades, which I didn't imagine would be life changing, but would no doubt fetch a decent price, if sold. "A little extra to help the business won't do any harm. Plus, I see this as a personal gift from one friend to another." I glanced around, as if the walls could hear me.

I shook myself and then went to find Pip's stocking to fill up. I entered Pip's bedroom to find her fast asleep with a painted red nose and cheeks, and a little green elf night-cap she'd made from a scarf. It looked like she had been pretending to be elf Pipshine before bedtime.

I filled her stocking up with sweets and presents and then I blew her a kiss, passing it on from the elves. I turned to sneak away when Pip mumbled, "Goodnight Santa." Her eyes were still closed, and she simply hugged her pillow tighter to her head.

"Good night, Pip," I whispered before I snuck back out of the room and out of the house.

65

"Right rascals," I called, as I clambered into my sleigh, whilst rubbing away the essence of a tear in my eye. "Let's carry on." The reindeer set off and before long we soared over Loch Ness, and I shouted 'Merry Christmas' to Scotland and to the monster that may or may not exist.

"Bye Nessy," I called to my old friend, as we shot through the vortex to Ireland, where I topped off my alcohol intake with more whisky and a heck of a lot of Guinness. I reasoned with myself that it was good for me, having such a large intake of iron, and it re-energized me just before we said goodbye and shot off through the vortex to Canada. We began travelling around the country dropping off presents but I was a lot more intoxicated after all the whisky, sherry and Guinness I had drunk in the UK.

Soon after arrival, I accidentally steered Rudolph and the reindeer over the top of a skyscraper so that the sleigh scraped along the top. "Whoops-a-daisy," I cried, but within nanoseconds I had steered Rudolph and the sleigh into another building, where it bounced off.

"Oops!" I leaned over the edge to see if I could see any damage. I slipped the reins to the right and instantly I heard the grind and scrape of the other side of the sleigh slicing next to another building. "Rudolph, what are you playing at? That's definitely going to leave a mark now," I yelled, as I flopped back onto the seat and squinted ahead of me, trying to focus on the direction we were going. "I'll definitely remember this one tomorrow," I muttered, feeling disappointed that all my efforts in training them up had become undone. Rudolph shook his head at me, as if he was blaming me, whilst he continued to gallop and fly through the sky.

Once we finally got into the rhythm of house hopping, I noticed how much the alcohol was affecting me. I jumped head first down chimneys; I crept across carpets and in rooms, accidentally knocking things over and swaying whenever I stood still. I accidentally dozed off at one point and Comet had to snort loudly and back kick the sleigh to wake me up.

One time we landed on a roof which was decked out with a tremendous display of nine reindeer and a sleigh. The fake reindeer and sleigh were such a good resemblance that when I returned from delivering my gifts, I got back into the wrong sleigh. I started thrashing the reins, getting increasingly frustrated that my reindeer weren't moving. "You can't be tired yet. We've still got plenty to do. Come on. Don't tell me it's time I need to put you all out to pasture."

It wasn't until I turned to face my own reindeer and found them all staring at me as if I was bonkers that I realised what had happened. I turned back to look at the fake sleigh, not even having realised I was sitting on a wooden plank rather than my cushioned seat, and then I burst out laughing. "I thought you were them," I cried, pointing at the model reindeer. Rudolph huffed out a blast of indignant air as I staggered back into the sleigh and we set off again.

Fortunately, Canada's tradition was more focused on giving me milk and cookies, so by the time I completed the country, I felt more sober. We then flew past the CN Tower, and I wished Canada a Merry Christmas. "Come on, lad, we're off to America now," I said, as we shot through a vortex again. We arrived in America, and this time, I could steer the sleigh smoothly around all the houses without bumping into anything.

Christmas Eve never became a chore for me, but it had certainly lost its initial giddy excitement now that the alcohol buzz had worn off. Now I was much more aware of my footing, and this was an absolute necessity in America, because it seemed to be the land of entrapment. There were many times I would enter a house, only to find a tripwire in front of the fireplace with a camera pointing at it, or flour dusted on the floor to catch my footprints. In one house, I even found a series of laser lights surrounding the tree waiting for me to walk into them and set an alarm off.

My senses would tingle whenever there was any form of a trap. I would hop over the tripwires, and Mrs C's bag of tools came in handy. It contained a remote control that worked with all electronic devices, so I would point it at the cameras and wipe all traces of my arrival. Not that they could detect me. My arrival, at best, would appear as a nanosecond on their screen, which would be impossible to see; but I could never be too careful of technology these days and what they could decipher. I would also use the bag of flour Mrs C had provided to cover up my own footprints before I left. I had everything covered, and their amateur attempts at capturing me at least kept me on my toes.

I eventually stopped at a house that I instantly knew who it belonged to and I didn't need my scroll to tell me how naughty the child was. It was Kevin, and I found myself rubbing the area on my belly that he had elbowed. I braced myself before descending the chimney of the lovely large house in a quiet suburb, because he was certainly the type to lay traps. Not necessarily to catch me in the act as proof that I exist, like many others attempted, but more so to stop me from continuing my journey of giving presents to other children.

I arrived in the living room, which was tastefully decorated, with green foliage around the fireplace, and a sparkling red and gold adorned tree. I scanned the room. There was no flour on the floor, no cameras pointing at me, and no tripwires, so I cautiously approached the tree. We had not given him a BB gun, firecrackers and a tarantula, but the elves had given him a toy spider, a plastic gun, some toy soldiers and a dressing gown, as we always aimed to please.

Once I was satisfied with the aesthetic layout of the presents, I cautiously crept upstairs to Kevin's room. I glanced around and spotted some strange, congealed substances in jam jars on a shelf, a suspicious-looking plan on a piece of paper on his desk, as well as some melted, reshaped bits of plastic. It appeared that he was up to something, but fortunately, it looked like I wasn't the target of his plan.

It was clear, however, just how much he needed Pepper's special gift. I reached into my pocket and took a pinch of the elf dust Pepper had given me. I rubbed it together before I lifted my hand to my lips and blew it over him. "Perhaps this might help you learn how to behave better, have empathy, control and self-restraint."

I stared at Kevin for a moment, knowing that deep down, his inappropriate behaviour didn't come directly from him. I then wrinkled my nose at what was suspiciously in the jam jars and left his room to take a visit to his parents.

His parents were asleep in a luxurious king-size bed, and I stood beside them and took another pinch of elf dust. "Perhaps the two of you can give Kevin the attention, affection and love he needs to grow and develop into a mature young man," I said, before blowing the dust on them. I waited for the dust to settle on the parents, which shimmered like glitter on top of them, before I left the house and made my way back to the reindeer.

We flew onwards, and now that I had a clearer head, I took a moment, once more, to admire the way the reindeer were flying together as we swooped over houses. It was seamless, and the new formation was such a joy to witness. "Are you all having fun?" I called, jingling the bells as I brought the reins down on them.

The reindeer responded by instantly weaving downwards, then upwards to create a wave. It was their way of nodding at me, and it made me chuckle. "Me too," I called, and I thrashed the reins again with delight as we soared through the air, and Comet and the rest of the reindeer left a trail behind them, glittering across the sky.

It wasn't long before I was delivering my last gift in America. We zigzagged back to the Empire State Building. "Ho, ho, ho," I shouted as loud as I could. "Merry Christmas, America," I cried, before we shot off through a vortex.

"Not long to go now, lad," I shouted, as we got to work in Mexico. I picked up the pace, wanting to focus on rounding off the night in a professional style. In one house, I entered to the barking and snarling of an aggressive dog. Normally dogs didn't bother me, but this one was particularly vicious and it made my heart pound as it came charging towards me.

I searched in my tool bag and found a special squeaky toy that looked like a steak, which I threw into its path. The dog immediately course-corrected and sank its teeth into the toy instead. The toy gave out a loud squeak, which surprised the dog before it sunk its teeth in again. As the dog kept biting the toy, it became drowsier, until shortly, the dog was snoring away, giving me the time to sneak back inside and arrange the presents around the tree.

Once I finished with my present arranging, I hopped back over to the dog, took the toy back and kept giving it the odd squeak to keep the dog pleasantly relaxed before I scarpered as fast as possible. Soon I was delivering my last present in Mexico, and we flew onward to South America.

As the number of presents diminished and I crossed more names off the list, a melancholy feeling set in. The night was coming to an end and then, sure enough, we finally pulled up to the last house. It was very modest, and the presents I had for the two children were meagre in value. I left the presents under a small tree and stepped back to look. I hoped the children wouldn't feel that because their presents were basic, or that they were last to be delivered after a long day, that they were any less special.

I left the house and headed back to the roof. With each step, I forced a smile of jubilation, pushing aside my melancholy. "We did it," I cried to the reindeer.

The sleigh was empty, and we had some extra minutes left of the night. I pulled the sleigh out towards the sea, where the ripples of water lapped beneath us, and the modest sun was rising and casting an orange glow around us. Rudolph's nose was dimming in brightness, and the sleigh bells on the harnesses around the reindeer glinted and sparkled as they hovered in midair.

As I felt a new day coming, I sat back in my sleigh and stared inward, as far as I could see, to the land we had just covered. "We did good!" I felt both relieved and humbled as I watched the world.

Even as I sat there, I knew millions of children were opening their presents at that moment and beginning to play with them. I could feel their joy seeping into me, and a smile formed across my lips. I breathed in deep, enjoying the silence and the peace, before I faced towards my reindeer and my heart swelled even further. "You were wonderful." I swallowed hard. "All of you," I muttered, as I looked at each and every one of them.

After a few glorious minutes, I picked up my reins again. "Time to go home, everyone." I gave them a thrash, and the reindeer shot off again. "Merry Christmas," I called, much more quietly than previous times, before we travelled through the vortex and headed back to the North Pole.

66

When we emerged out of the end, a bright dazzling light, like a bolt of lightning, flashed around us as we hit the top of the North Pole. My job was done, and the powers I'd had that night were now stripped from me. Well, almost all of them.

The reindeer gracefully landed on the snowy ground. I unhooked them from the sleigh and led them back into their hut. Mrs C had cleaned up everywhere, changed their hay beds, filled up their food troughs, and placed some bottles of stout on a workbench as a way for me to thank them.

I instantly obliged and cracked the bottles open and poured them into the food trough, so that the stout mixed with their feed. "You all definitely deserve this," I said, as they started lapping it up. Within moments, they had cleaned the trough, and their eyes were drooping with tiredness. "I know. It's been a long day," I sympathised.

I walked up the pen, giving each one a thank you and a good scratch on top of their head and under their chin, and I meant each one with all my heart. "Now get some rest, all of you." The reindeer paced towards a comfortable bed each and flopped down heavily and closed their eyes.

"How did it go?" Mrs C's voice whispered from behind me.

I spun around. "It was incredible. The reindeer flew perfectly. There weren't any hiccoughs, and we ticked every child off the list with no issues."

"So, another typical Christmas," she said, smiling lightly. "It's also nice to see you treating all the reindeer so evenly."

"Well, they were all crucial to the mission."

"Yes, they are. Sometimes I wonder if you forget that."

I chose not to respond. "Thank you for sorting everything out for them, though. I've never seen it so fresh and cosy looking."

"You said the same thing last year. Come on, let's leave them to sleep. Plus, I'm sure the elves are dying to hear the gossip."

I followed Mrs C out of the hut and stifled a yawn, but as we walked past the sleigh, I spotted a meteor sized scuff. I immediately rushed over to be by her side. "Oh no, how did that happen?" I cried as I ran my hand along the side of her bodywork.

Mrs C came over to peer at the scuff. "You must have hit something."

"I don't remember anything that would have caused this." I shook my head, completely thrown to see her so tarnished.

"And that couldn't have anything to do with the gallons of alcohol you've consumed."

I stared at her, appalled. "I can handle my liquor."

Mrs C sighed as I bent over to have a look underneath the hood of the sleigh to check for more injuries, but I didn't get far as I struggled with the strain of my coat. Mrs C noticed, so I quickly stood up straight. "Let's go, I guess it will all get fixed later in the year," I said, trying to redivert the attention.

She glanced purposefully into the sleigh, then looked me up and down. "So, where are they?" she asked.

I knew what she was asking for, and so I pivoted away from her, keen to head to the workshop. "Where are what?" I muttered.

"You know full well what I'm talking about. All those mince pies you said you wouldn't eat?"

"Did I say that?" I frowned and scratched my head in exaggerated confusion.

"Yes, you did. So where are they?" She folded her arms and blocked my path of escape.

"Well…. They may have accidentally fallen into my belly."

"Oh right. I get it. Those pesky mince pies. So, what, were they all positioned from a great height, teetering on the edge of a ledge, and they accidentally fell into your mouth? Or…were they all set up to catapult across the room into your mouth? Or… perhaps they grew little mince pie arms and legs, and they crawled into your mouth?"

I scratched my chin through my beard. "Erm, I quite like the idea of the last one. Oo maybe that's a good toy idea; Crawling Mince Pies."

Mrs C sighed and shook her head. "Come on you, we can discuss this later. Let's head to the workshop. I'm sure the elves are ready to burst right now."

I opened the door to the workshop and found Bushy and Pepper pacing around the room, looking lost in thought. Alabaster had returned to work, and was mindlessly making a pile of bouncing balls, while Wunorse was leaning up against a workbench, bouncing one of the balls against the wall and catching it. Sugarplum was sitting on the floor opposite Shinny, both in some sort of meditation pose with their eyes closed, holding each other's hands.

"I'm back," I called, making them all stop what they were doing and race towards me. "It all went great, and I delivered all the presents."

"Oh, I'm so excited," Sugarplum beamed. "I hope the children love their toys. All over the world, children are touching the presents we created." She looked at her two little hands in wonderment.

Bushy jumped up and down. "I can feel it now. I can visualise their smiles and excitement."

I smiled at the dreamy looks in the elf's eyes. It meant so much to them, and it was what kept them churning out the same routine every year. I dug my hand into my pocket. "I thought you might want to read these." I pulled out a stack of thank-you letters.

"Oh, I love reading these," Shinny gushed, reaching his hand out and stepping towards me.

I handed him a stack and then passed more piles out to the others, with Pepper smiling gratefully as she took her share. I watched as each elf rapidly raced through them and passed them around. There were thousands, but they didn't miss a single one.

"This one mentions us," Shinny cried, putting the letter to one side. "And this one." He pulled out another and created his own unique pile of any that mentioned the elves. Within seconds the elves finished reading the letters and Shinny picked his special pile back up and devoured them intently with a huge grin on his face.

"Did you visit Pip and David?" Pepper asked, looking at the stack of letters like she was missing something.

"Of course." I then turned to Mrs C, who looked more emotional at the mention of them. "And I must say, you did an excellent job training David to make mince pies. They were, to use Pip's term, scrumdiddlyumptious."

Mrs C laughed. "I'm so pleased. He was a talented student."

"Oh, and I almost forgot," I said, turning back to the elves. "I have one more letter to show you, and it's from Pip."

Pepper smiled and appeared to let out a breath, as if she was relieved.

"Oh my gum drops," Sugarplum screeched. "How is she?"

I turned to Mrs C. "Why don't you read it first?"

Mrs C smiled and took the letter and started to read it. She was much slower than the elves could read, and so they stared at her, trying their best to remain patient. Mrs C then made a noise like a sob as she covered her mouth. Her eyes were shining with unshed tears. "That's so lovely. I'm glad she is happy." She then passed the note to Pepper, who grabbed it eagerly, scanned it and passed it to Shinny. By the time the elves had finished, there was definitely a heightened emotion in the room.

"I'm so pleased she hasn't forgotten us," Bushy said.

"She most certainly hasn't," I said. "She also looked like she'd been having lots of fun playing with her Santa set as they were all laid out in the living room. And when I visited her, I found her dressed up as Pipshine, with her rosy cheeks and elf nightcap."

The elves beamed at each other, and Sugarplum clasped her hands to her heart. Tears were rolling down her cheeks. "I'm so pleased," she gushed. "She will always be an honorary elf to us." The elves nodded enthusiastically as they agreed wholeheartedly with her.

As the elves devoured their letters again, Pepper creeped towards me. "Er, so did you manage to give Carol her elf lights?" she asked.

"Oh yes, but I think you knew that would happen." I stared down at her, as she looked anxious. I then chuckled. "Gosh, Pepper, you and that guidance dust have been very busy. You know, I was wondering why we kept running into that woman and why you gave me elf lights to give her. I guess you wanted me to pay attention to her, and now I know why."

"You do?" Pepper asked.

"You want me to introduce her to David, don't you?"

Pepper shrugged, and she held her breath.

"Hang on," Mrs C exclaimed. "Are you setting David up with that, Carol?" she asked in disbelief.

"Yes, I believe I am in the New Year."

Mrs C frowned. "The grumpy woman and David? Surely not."

I chuckled. "I'm as surprised as you, but let's just say I saw Carol in a new light when I spoke to her, and I think a bit of matchmaking might be what they both need."

Mrs C glanced in amazement at Pepper, who had a little smile of satisfaction playing on her lips.

I then had another suspicious thought. "Pepper, did you have anything to do with Seamus as well?"

Pepper shrugged. But now she had the biggest grin on her face as she turned around and hurried back to the others.

"What on earth has she been up to all this time?" Mrs C asked.

I smiled as I watched Pepper happily jumping up and down with Sugarplum. "Well, it seems like Pepper has listened to Holly's wishes and taken it upon herself to act as David's guardian angel. And I, for one, am delighted for him."

Then, as the adrenaline faded from my body, I couldn't hold it in anymore and I broke out into a loud yawn. My eyes were stinging now, and my body was starting to tremble and become shivery from tiredness, which was now hitting me like a tidal wave.

"Right, you," Mrs C said. "We best get you to bed. It's been a long night for you."

"The longest of the year," I muttered.

"Sleep well, Santa," Shinny called timidly.

"Don't worry about the reindeer, and we'll catch up in the New Year," Alabaster confirmed as Mrs C took my hand and led me away.

She guided me to our room and with every step; the tiredness felt more intense, and when I saw the bed, I couldn't imagine a more alluring sight. I fumbled with the buttons on my coat to pop my belly out, which was a relief, and shook it off me.

"Don't leave your suit on the floor," Mrs C tutted.

I didn't care about my suit at that moment. It took all the energy I could to unbuckle my belt, pull off my trousers, and crawl into the bed. There was no time to fold it or hang it anywhere.

Mrs C hung my coat on a hanger and wiped it with her hand. "It's absolutely filthy," she muttered, as she inspected her soot covered hand. "I guess my dirt repellent wore off." It was the last thing I heard and saw, as I fell fast asleep.

67

"Come on, time to wake up. You've had long enough." Mrs C's voice filtered through to me as I rolled back and forth. I forced my eyes into a squint to find myself in bed, with Mrs C shoving me. "If you don't wake up now, you'll struggle to get back into your routine."

I slapped my mouth together. It was dry and my head hurt. "I need a drink."

Mrs C instantly handed me a glass with a bright red liquid in it. "Here. Drink up and you'll feel better."

I quickly downed the concoction which Mrs C gave me every year to make me feel better. I asked her once what was in it, but the list was too long for me to remember. It was full of caffeine, lemons, sugar, protein powders, electrolytes, and some of Mrs C's special ingredients.

"Come down for breakfast," she ordered and disappeared out of the door.

I pulled on my dressing gown and snug Rudolph slippers, and inspected my face in the mirror. My cheeks were chubbier than usual, and my beard whiskers were sticking out all over the place, but there was a healthy glow in my face, which was from a job well done.

I headed down the stairs to find Mrs C had laid out some bagels, cream cheese, smoked salmon and some other breakfast items, as well as a freshly brewed pot of coffee. I grinned as I sat down and began methodically constructing my bagel.

"Well, merry belated Christmas." Mrs C came to sit down opposite me and poured out the coffee.

"Merry Christmas," I mumbled through a mouthful of food, even though it was now Boxing Day.

"The turkey is in the oven," she said.

"And that makes Christmas Eve's antics even more worth it," I grinned.

That afternoon, Mrs C and I celebrated Christmas in our own way. We exchanged gifts and, seeing as she loved our spa trip in London so much, I got her a foot spa, so she could sit in her armchair with warm water bubbling around her feet.

She got me a pair of fluffy socks. On them were the words, 'My perfect partner and the love of my life', and beneath it was a picture of me hugging my pal, Rudolph. But on the flat of the foot were the words, 'I do mean your awesome wife, you know'. I instantly slipped them on, feeling delighted.

We then drank sparkling wine, pulled crackers and ate turkey with all the trimmings, whilst I told her all the stories from Christmas Eve night. She listened, enthralled in my tales, and laughed at my anecdotes.

"Eww," she frowned and wrinkled her nose. "What do you think was in the jars?" she asked, after I filled her in on my visit to Kevin.

I laughed. "I honestly have no idea."

After dinner, we shared a moment of quiet reflection as we watched a film, and drank our night caps. It gave me a chance to imagine how everyone else's Christmas Day had panned out.

Over the next few days, I still felt exhausted from Christmas Eve night, so I happily used it as an excuse to do very little. I watched plenty of films and in between I took some rather satisfying naps. I also made good use of Mrs C's foot spa, and we both continued to indulge in rich Christmas food, mulled wine, hot chocolate and tipples of sherry.

By the time New Year's Eve came round, I was feeling much more like my usual self.

"So, are you making any New Year's resolutions this year?" Mrs C asked me, as she peered over her mug of coffee during breakfast.

"Huh, what's that?" I asked.

Mrs C sighed. "New Year's resolutions. You know, things you want to improve on for the following year and make a fresh start on."

"No point. I never keep to any resolutions you set for me."

"That's because you don't seem to understand the importance of them and want to do them yourself. Last year, I challenged you to treat all the reindeer equally, as well as go on a healthier diet, and you didn't do either."

I glanced at her and frowned. "I do treat the reindeer equally. I treat them all exactly how they deserve to be treated."

Mrs C scoffed loudly. "You absolutely don't treat them equally. You treat Rudolph with so much favouritism."

"It's not my fault if Rudolph does things that the others don't and gets additional praise."

Mrs C sighed. "It seems like I'm not getting through to you, but perhaps you actually are turning a corner, because the most I've seen you treat them fairly was when you returned from your mission on Christmas Eve. You were stroking them all and telling them all how important they were. It was lovely to see."

"See, I think you're making a big deal out of something tiny."

"Perhaps. So why don't you make another resolution and keep it this time? To ensure that you treat all the reindeer to the same standard as Rudolph and form deeper bonds with all of them."

"Fine," I huffed, shoving a large chunk of bagel into my mouth.

"And as for the healthier eating," she said, her eyes lowering to my stomach, which was squashed up against the table. "I think you will feel better for it, and you will fit into your favourite trousers sooner."

I glanced down and patted my enormous belly. "I don't think I need to eat healthier. This is just full of love and it will go down soon." Mrs C gave me a disapproving look and so I sighed. "Fine. I'll make more of an effort with the other reindeer, and I'll squeeze two salads in this year."

Mrs C stared at me. "At least that's a start."

"And what are your resolutions going to be?" I asked.

"I'm going to lay off the biscuits," she promised with a decisive nod.

"Didn't you say you were going to do that last year?"

"Well," she said, standing up and clearing the table. "Yes, but it's my resolution for this year as well."

"Excellent plan. That's us sorted for next year then," I muttered, but I was feeling distracted as more pressing thoughts were coming to my mind.

"Yes, we will start them tomorrow," she pledged.

Once Mrs C cleared up, I jumped up, unable to cope with the anticipation anymore. "Can you put me on the line now?" I asked, wondering if enough time had passed for me to get a flavour of my impact.

Mrs C finished wiping the table and gave me a knowing look. "Okay, I'll get you set up." She then went to the computer, booted it up, and tapped away on the keyboard before she stood up and I jumped in her seat.

68

I stretched out my hands, so my fingers and knuckles cracked, before I carefully searched for the right letters and thumped them accordingly to spell out each toy we had created that year. "Fingers crossed, there are no Space Cadet Collins incidents," I hoped, as I navigated my way to the review sections. There were already plenty to read through.

'Loved playing this family game of Sausage Eating competition. We had a great time throwing sausages around. Except it left us all craving a fry up the following day.'

I chuckled at the reviews. Hundreds of people loved it, even if some of them claimed things had become a little competitive as the game had progressed. "Success," I muttered. I then continued onto several other toys and grinned as the positive reviews continued.

'My daughter was so happy to add a trotting Unicorn named Tallulah to her vast collection of unicorn toys. She spent the last few days in her unicorn dress, with her unicorn teddies and unicorn wand, making Tallulah walk around after her. She's been in unicorn-topia all Christmas.'

"You go Moco," I smiled. It had been a great idea to transform the leftover stock of Moco into a unicorn toy. I then braced myself, before I typed in Fashion Factor. It was the toy I had the highest anticipation for, and I wanted it to do well. The name popped up on the screen, and under it were thousands of five-star reviews. Instant relief washed over me.

'My daughter absolutely loved playing with these dolls and they managed to distract her for a long time. We were loving the peace and quiet until she kept wanting to showcase their arena tour to us and we had to listen to our

daughter's tuneless vocals all day.'

'This was a present for my son, who has taken a keen interest in fashion recently. He loves these dolls and making them strut around the stage with him. It's great to see him so happy.'

I only found one negative review which simply stated. *'Now my child wants red and green hair. Great.'*

I laughed and felt a warmth of delight go through me. Everything was perfect, and the more I trawled through everything, I found no quality control related issues to any of the toys, which I knew was because Alabaster had been back on form.

I stood up from my desk, feeling satisfied, and ready to search for a snack, when I realised there was a toy I hadn't checked. "R", I muttered. "Where is R?" I searched the keyboard before I spotted it. I then thumped out the letters for Restyling Slime, and instantly thousands of reviews from the parents popped up. It was a mixed bag, and I grimaced as I read them.

'No. Never again. It causes carnage.'

'I told my kids they could play with it outside, but it's too cold and so instead they tore up our kitchen. The kitchen now looks like a brightly coloured cesspit. Fantastic...'

'Who would have thought giving kids such a simple toy would come with so much regret?'

'Kids love it. We hate it. If only we could stop the mad craze because every child seems to have this evil substance in the palm of their hands.'

"Oh dear," I muttered as I saw how much the parents hated it. "Maybe Restyling Slime wasn't the best idea." I bit my lip as I continued reading. Then one review caught my eye.

'Yes, it's messy, yes it causes chaos, but playing it with my children was like... magic. It's just a shame I had to spend Boxing Day cleaning it off my ceiling. Carol.'

I reread the review several times, and then a sly smile crept across my lips as I powered down the computer.

"How was it?" Mrs C asked as I went into the sitting room.

"Great! The toys went down a storm and there weren't any issues like last year."

"That's fantastic. Let's hope next year is just as good."

That evening, I brought out my New Year's Eve jumper, which was a sparkling explosion of glitter and colour to represent fireworks. Mrs C and I had some lovely food, shared a bottle of wine and watched the London fireworks bring in the New Year.

We spent the evening reminiscing about the year we'd had, the wonderful holiday, the joy of having visitors, and the incredible transformation of the elves. Mrs C was delighted to have been a part of an incredible new start up business with David, and we were both overjoyed that we had played a hand in bringing father and daughter closer. But the best thing of all was that when the clock hit midnight, I could share a kiss with the woman I loved more than anything in the world, and we started another journey into a new year, one full of hope, expectation and intention.

The following morning, I woke up with a thrill in my belly. Mrs C was already downstairs making breakfast, so I headed to the kitchen. She had made crumpets and a selection of breakfast items, whilst she sat at the table drinking a steaming cup of coffee.

"Morning," she said. "Happy New Year."

I kissed her head. "Happy New Year." I sat down and tucked in. I smothered my crumpets in lashings of butter, and happily devoured them, before reaching for a mince pie that Mrs C had made.

"You're hungry?" Mrs C stared at me, but she said nothing more. She then grabbed a ginger biscuit and dunked it into her coffee. I frowned but didn't comment. It was like we were having a standoff, both of us not wanting to mention the resolutions we had set the day before.

"Well, I can't resist your cooking," I smiled.

After breakfast, I dusted off my hands and stood up, the thrill inside of me swelling even more. "I'm going to make sure the reindeer are alright." I hadn't seen them since we had returned from our Christmas Eve mission.

"Are you now?" Mrs C watched me leave, her eyes narrowing slightly in suspicion.

I pulled on my boots, traipsed across the snow, pulled back the door, and grinned widely. There he was, his nose red and bright. "How's my lad doing?" I gushed.

Jokes

- **Who's Santa's favourite singer?** ~ Elfish Presley (of course).
- **Why does Santa go down the chimney?** ~ Because it soots him. (I do love a chimney!)
- **What's big and jolly and says "Oh, Oh, Oh"?** ~ Santa Claus walking backwards. (I guess I could give it a go.)
- **What was wrong with the ~~Grinch~~ on Christmas?** ~ He was feeling claus-trophobic. (I told Shinny not to cross this out!)
- **What breakfast do Santa and his wife like to eat together?** ~ Mistle-toast. (I tend to prefer pancakes though.)
- **How did the bauble know that she was addicted to Christmas?** ~ She'd been hooked on Christmas trees all her life. (Better that than being hooked on all that witchcraft and wizardry malarkey.)
- **What does Santa say on the night of Christmas?** ~ Time to hit the sack. (It truly is the best feeling when I finally get to go to bed on Christmas Day.)
- **Why does Mrs Claus love the Christmas season?** ~ It makes her feel so Santa-mental. (She loves Christmas and she loves me, so this is true.)
- **Why was the snowman embarrassed when he was spotted rummaging through a bag of carrots?** ~ He was caught picking his nose. (This never happened. It was Sugarplum who told me which carrot he wanted.)
- **What did the snowman say to the aggressive carrot?** ~ "Get out of my face." (Hmm, I hope Sugarplum didn't choose the wrong carrot.)

- **I have this incredible ability to predict what's inside a wrapped present.** ~ It's a gift. (Well my gift is the ability to pack all those wrapped presents into a tiny sack or case!)
- **Why did Santa have to go to the hospital?** ~ Because of his poor elf. (Normally Mrs C can fix any of our ailments with her trusty collection of tonics. That woman really is a dime.)
- **I got a universal remote control for Christmas.** ~ This changes everything. (As long as it points towards the TV I'm happy.)
- **What do you call a blind reindeer?** ~ No-eye deer. (Can you imagine? The poor thing. Hopefully nothing like that will happen to Rudolph.)
- **What does Santa do when his elves misbehave?** ~ He gives them the sack. (I would never do that, although, admittedly, I did consider it with Alabaster.)
- **What did Mr Frosty's girlfriend give him when she was mad at him?** ~ The cold shoulder. (I didn't know Mr Frosty had a girlfriend, but according to Bushy, this is true.)
- **Why did the red-nosed reindeer help the old lady cross the road?** ~ It would have been Rudolph him not to. (He's a good lad, isn't he?)
- **Why did the turkey join the rock band?** ~ Because it had drumsticks. (Speaking of turkey… I wonder what Mrs C is doing for dinner tonight.)
- **Where does Santa Claus go swimming?** ~ The North Pool (Well, this year it was in London. It's far too cold to do it here in the North Pole)
- **Who tells the best Christmas jokes?** ~ Reindeer. They sleigh every time. (I bet Rudolph has some cracking jokes to share if only he could speak.)
- **What do gingerbread men use when they break their legs?** ~ Candy-canes. (Well, we have plenty to spare if they need some.)

- **Why is everyone thirsty at the North Pole?** ~ No well. (To be honest I do get quite thirsty from all the alcohol on Christmas Eve. So this is true)
- **What is every parent's favourite Christmas song?** ~ Silent Night! (I bet it is, but I bet my little antics on Christmas Eve stop that from happening.)
- **What do you call Santa when he stops moving?** ~ Santa Pause (Normally it's when I'm thinking deeply.)
- **What's every elf's favourite type of music?** ~ Wrap! (Well, it's definitely Wunorse's, but Alabaster isn't a fan.)
- **What do they sing at a snowman's birthday party?** ~ Freeze a jolly good fellow! (We don't tend to celebrate Mr Frosty's birthday, but Rudolph on the other hand…)
- **Who is never hungry at Christmas?** ~ The turkey - he's always stuffed. (Speaking of turkey again, I'm going to go find Mrs C - Merry Christmas everyone!)

Thank you for reading Santa's Christmas Year. I had a lot of fun writing it and I hope you enjoyed reading it. If you want to learn more about what's coming up from me, please follow me on the following platforms:

X - @MichelleGrenv1
Instagram – michelle.grenville
TikTok – michelle.grenville

Made in the USA
Middletown, DE
15 December 2024

67056588R00231